"WAIT." HIS VOICE AS SOFT AS HIS HAND ON HER LEG...

She looked down to see it sitting there, just above her knee, gentle and strong, warm on her skin. Already, her nerves were on high alert, and a ripple of pleasure was stirring between her thighs.

"Yes?" Damn, her voice was weak. She was barely controlling the strain of her body and the easy way it gave in to the slightest graze of his touch.

"Your car." He cocked an eyebrow, and in the shadows of the darkness, his deep-set eyes looked devilish and inviting, like he was suggesting she do something she knew she shouldn't.

"My car." She nodded, but all she could think about was that hand on her leg and how badly she wanted him to shift his thumb a little higher.

"Why don't I take a look at it tomorrow?" He pulled his hand back, and leaned onto the armrest.

Ivy frowned, trying to understand what he was saying. But one thing was glaringly clear. He was suggesting they see each other tomorrow. And as much as her body wanted to scream, *Yes, yes, yes,* her mind was saying, *No, no, no.*

"Tomorrow's my day off—"

"Perfect."

Also by Olivia Miles:

LOVE BLOOMS ON MAIN STREET

Book 4
in the Briar Creek Series

OLIVIA MILES

FOREVER

NEW YORK   BOSTON

Copyright © 2016 by Megan Leavell
Excerpt from *Christmas Comes to Main Street* © 2016 by Megan Leavell

Cover images © Shutterstock
Cover design by Elizabeth Turner
Cover copyright © 2016 by Hachette Book Group, Inc.

Forever
Hachette Book Group
1290 Avenue of the Americas
New York, NY 10104
forever-romance.com
twitter.com/foreverromance

First Edition: July 2016

Forever is an imprint of Grand Central Publishing.
The Forever name and logo are trademarks of Hachette Book Group, Inc.

The publisher is not responsible for websites (or their content) that are not owned by the publisher.

The Hachette Speakers Bureau provides a wide range of authors for speaking events. To find out more, go to www.hachettespeakersbureau.com or call (866) 376-6591.

ISBNs: 978-1-4555-6717-1 (mass market), 978-1-4555-6716-4 (ebook)

Printed in the United States of America

OPM

10 9 8 7 6 5 4 3 2 1

For Avery

Acknowledgments

None of this would have been possible without the two great women I have in my professional corner. I would like to thank my editor, Michele Bidelspach, for her sharp insight and intuitive guidance in the fine-tuning of this book. I'd also like to thank my agent, Paige Wheeler, for her hard work and unwavering support.

Thank you as well to Lori Paximadis, Carolyn Kurek, Marissa Sangiacomo, and everyone at Grand Central Publishing who had a hand in the publication of this book.

Thank you to my friends and family, who continue to cheer on my writing endeavors.

And of course, thank you to my readers, for welcoming my characters and their stories into your homes and hearts.

LOVE
BLOOMS ON
MAIN STREET

CHAPTER 1

If Ivy Birch closed her eyes, she could still feel the sweet taste of Brett Hastings's lips on her mouth. Still feel the flutter of anticipation as he leaned into her and she realized that finally, *finally*, after years of waiting and hoping, her lifelong crush was actually going to kiss her. Her pulse still skittered as she replayed their first touch, so tender, so wished for, but her heart began to positively pound when she remembered the way he brought his arms tightly around her waist, pulling her against that hard chest, the heat of his breath and body so all-consuming she still got dizzy just thinking about it! And oh, did she think about it. More than a little. More than she probably should.

The bell hanging over her shop door jangled, and reluctantly Ivy pulled herself from her dream world, opening her eyes and blinking rapidly at the long-stemmed roses she still clutched in her hands, in a vain effort to unite with reality and not cling to that one, wonderful moment that had come and gone so quickly. So quickly, in fact, that she sometimes wondered, a little disconcertedly, if it had ever really happened at all. Seven months had passed since that bliss-filled night of her best friend Grace's wedding to Brett's cousin, Luke. Seven months with nothing to hold on to but a memory.

Seven months that should have been spent reminding herself of the phone call that never followed, the roses that were never sent, and the plans that were never made...

"Ahem!"

Ivy jumped, turned quickly, and nicked her hip on the corner of one of her wooden display tables, sending a glass vase askew. She caught it before it shattered to the floor, ignoring the water that had sloshed, and adjusted the irises. Grimacing against the pain, she smiled cheerfully, hoping the same would be offered from her impatient customer.

Mrs. Griffin, Briar Creek's resident innkeeper, just stared her down and pinched her lips a little tighter. "I was beginning to think you'd fallen asleep," she huffed.

Ivy laughed easily and shook her head. Mrs. Griffin was a regular at Petals on Main—in here at least twice a week—and such loyalty was never overlooked. "That would be quite an accomplishment, now, wouldn't it? I had an early morning," she said. Long before the doors of Petals on Main opened, she was hard at work trimming stems, going over orders that had come in overnight, and making sure each plant presented was in the best condition possible.

"At the inn, I start my day at four sharp," Mrs. Griffin remarked. "Sunday through Saturday, and I've never slept through the alarm once in all these years. My guests expect a hot breakfast and a newspaper set outside their doors when they awake, and I wouldn't want to let them down, after all." She gave Ivy a pointed look.

Ivy stifled a sigh and grinned a little wider instead, even though she was clenching her teeth. She and Mrs. Griffin had one thing in common, and that was customer service, no matter how inconvenient. She'd put too much time and energy into the flower shop to let things slip through the cracks now, and between forgetting where she'd set the scissors for thirty-five minutes this morning (in the storage room's mini-fridge: troublesome) and failing to place the order for vases before close of business yesterday, she was in danger of just that. All because she couldn't stop thinking of Brett. It was juvenile, she knew. After all, the man had only kissed her. It wasn't like he'd proposed marriage or anything.

Marriage. Ivy's heart skipped a beat. Imagine that.

Her eyes roamed to a beautiful bouquet of peonies, in creamy shades of pale pink and apricot, and she could almost feel the stems in her hand, brushing the ivory satin skirt of her dress. Or would she go with lace? Once there had been a time when she imagined Brett waiting at the end of the aisle for her, but with heavy disappointment, she'd finally erased that image from her mind. For the most part.

"Ahem!"

Snapping to attention, Ivy felt her cheeks grow hot as she guiltily met the innkeeper's gaze once more. "Sorry," she muttered. Okay, this was officially ridiculous. She couldn't exactly carry on like this indefinitely, not unless she wanted to be alone *and* broke.

Mrs. Griffin folded her arms in front of her calmly as amusement glinted in her steady gaze. "If I didn't know better, I might think the love bug had finally caught up with you, Ivy Birch."

Ivy snorted at the use of the term *love bug*. "Just lost in thought. There's a lot to do today," she added. She checked her watch with a start. My, how time flew when you were having fun, or thinking about Brett Hastings. Dr. Brett Hastings. Dr. and Mrs. Brett Hastings.

This had to stop. Next thing she'd be doodling his name on scrap paper. She was thirty—who *did* that?

She blew a strand of hair from her forehead and made a few quick calculations. Mrs. Griffin liked to take her time with her selections, hemming and hawing over seasonal varieties and color schemes, careful to ensure the bouquet in her lobby was both elegant and understated and, above all, welcoming.

"Were you thinking of roses this week?" Ivy asked.

"No, I thought I'd peruse *all* of my options today." Mrs. Griffin bent to smell some blue delphiniums. "Not quite what I had in mind. Welcoming and understated, but certainly not—"

"Elegant." Ivy knew. She crossed the room and gestured to a personal favorite. "Sweet peas are certainly special and, in my opinion, unexpected."

Sometimes she wondered where she came up with this stuff. She loved her job, loved the simple pleasure of being surrounded by beautiful, colorful flowers every day, loved the creative freedom she had in putting together a mixed bouquet, but what she didn't like so much were the indecisive clients. God knew she had enough of those with her brides, and there were more and more of them popping up in Briar Creek these days. It seemed like everyone was getting married. Everyone but her.

"Hmm, those certainly are pretty and different from my usual arrangements." Mrs. Griffin hesitated and tapped her pointer finger to her lower lip. "Let me think about this..."

The door chimed again, and right on cue, Jane Madison walked in, carrying a blast of warm June air. It was already muggy and it wasn't even noon, but Ivy didn't mind. It just meant hydrangeas and delphiniums and calla lilies were bursting into bloom, and who couldn't be happy about that?

Ivy grinned at her future sister-in-law, and began untying

the strings on the apron she always wore in the shop. She'd hoped to freshen up before Jane relieved her, but she'd been too busy daydreaming and now there was no time, unless she wanted to be late. Still, she'd grab a quick snack for the road, just so she didn't have a sugar crash.

"I actually have an appointment, Mrs. Griffin, but Jane will be able to assist you. She's quite the expert with arrangements these days."

Jane could barely suppress her smile. "I have to admit I'm having more fun planning this wedding than I did my first."

"Probably because you have that cute little girl to share your excitement," Mrs. Griffin said. The whole town knew how much Jane's now six-year-old daughter, Sophie, was looking forward to being a flower girl again.

"That, and Henry." Jane glanced down at the ring that Ivy had helped her twin brother select this past winter. The wedding was scheduled for September, and with any luck, that meant in only a few short months, she might be spending another wedding reception flirting with Brett. Not that she'd be letting him kiss her again...not unless he explained where he'd been for the past seven months. Though he lived in Baltimore and rarely visited, phone or email would have been better than nothing.

"Right, well, I'd better be off," Ivy said quickly. She left the women to mull over the bright spring blooms and ducked into the storage room, where she hung her apron on the hook and grabbed a few crackers from the box she always kept on hand. If traffic—and her car—cooperated, she'd get to the appointment with room to spare. Then she'd have every excuse to sit and relax and think about exactly what she'd be wearing the next time she saw Brett Hastings...She'd show him what he'd been missing.

And he wouldn't know what hit him.

• • •

Half an hour later, Ivy darted through the automatic doors of Forest Ridge Hospital, cursing under her breath. Thanks to her car's less-than-reliable temperament, she was now five minutes late to her appointment. That and sweating like she'd just run a marathon, when really, she probably couldn't run to the end of her block if she tried. She plucked the front of her sleeveless white cotton blouse in an effort to air it out, and then dropped into a chair to cool down. Soon she'd have to get a new car, or at least do something about the current one, but repairs cost money—money that could be spent on more important things, like a new sign for her shop or additional help.

Her blood glucose monitor was in the inside pocket of her tote, where she always kept it now, and one prick confirmed what she already knew. Sprinting through a parking garage and taking the steps instead of waiting for the elevator had dropped her blood sugar level, and now she'd need to eat to bring it back up. She fumbled in her bag for some pretzels and quickly tore open the packaging.

She knew that regular exercise was part of her doctor's plan, but honestly, who had the time?

Make time. Henry's voice echoed in her head. But that was easy for him to say. He didn't spend hours on his feet, and he didn't have to work long into the night to make sure the books were balanced and orders were placed on time. He didn't worry that his creation could make or break a wedding day or would mark an occasion that only came around once in a lifetime. Too often customers consumed her shop hours, not that she minded their company, but that meant her work-day extended long after she'd turned the sign on the door.

Still, she made a mental note to get in shape before Jane and Henry's wedding. She'd try that Pilates class her friend

Kara was always raving about. She'd get highlights, too, and have her legs waxed—just in case. She'd be toned and smooth, with an air of *je ne sais quoi*, as the French said, and, of course, impossible to resist. And Brett would have to kiss her again, right then and there, with a newfound eagerness and a promise never to go back to Baltimore again.

Ivy shook away the fantasy. Time to face reality.

She tossed the plastic wrapper in the trash and pressed the button for the elevator. She tapped her foot with growing impatience as the metal doors slowly unfolded, eager to get inside and up to her appointment, but as the doors opened fully, all anxiety of running late disappeared and a newfound dread landed squarely in its place.

Brett Hastings, object of her childhood and, of late, adult fantasies stood before her, tousled brown hair and all. Ivy blinked at him, wondering if her imagination had finally gotten the better of her, and resisted the urge to reach out a finger and poke him, just to put herself in check.

But no, he was real. Real and, as luck would have it, oh so much cuter than she'd even remembered. His chin was tipped slightly, accentuating the shadow of its cleft, his hands were casually tucked into gray slacks, his nut-brown hair glistening under the fluorescent lighting, and those perfectly arched brows furrowed with thought as his eyes bored steadily through her.

She could have stared at him all day, until she felt the slow, cold drop of sweat that had collected just over her top lip in her mad dash through the parking garage begin to trickle…

She licked her lips quickly and smiled as if nothing was amiss, as if her heart wasn't thumping against her rib cage, or that she hadn't dreamed of this moment night and day for months until she'd come to accept the fact that like plenty before him, the man simply wasn't interested.

"Brett!" She tried to casually toss her hair over her shoulders, but the damp locks clung firmly to her neck.

Brett's brow pinched slightly. "Well, this is a surprise." *To say the least.* "What brings you here?"

Given that Brett Hastings rarely surfaced in the state of Vermont since he'd first left for college a dozen years ago, Ivy thought she should really be the one asking that question, but right now her tongue was tied, her brain had gone mushy, and she was blinking as quickly as her eyes would let her as her gaze raked over his broad shoulders to the hard wall of his chest to the black leather belt on his pants.

She snapped her eyes upward. So he was hot. Plenty of men were good-looking. Not that she'd had the pleasure of kissing them all…

"Just an appointment," she said casually, hoping he wouldn't press further. She'd kept her diagnosis to herself ever since she was a kid, and even as an adult, she preferred it that way. Briar Creek was small, and people in town had held enough opinions on how she had grown up. Why give them any more ammunition? Besides, now was hardly the time to bore him with tedious details like her battle with diabetes. Now was the time to rekindle the romance they'd shared that brisk autumn night. Or at least bring it to the forefront of his mind…

The man *was* busy, she reminded herself. And he did live several hours away. And he did look damn good in that dress shirt. Maybe she could find it in her heart to cut him a little slack…

Brett jutted his lower lip and rolled back on his heels, his gaze roaming over her quickly before shifting away. She let her eyes linger on those lips, and felt her own part slightly, wondering if he might catch her subtle reminder.

· Instead, he folded his arms and cocked his head. "Have one of those myself, actually," he said with a lazy grin, and Ivy felt a warm tingle spread over her skin. That grin was her undoing every time, ever since the seventh grade, when she'd beat him in a math bee and he'd congratulated her after class. He checked his watch. "In fact, I hate to run, but I don't want to be late."

Ivy tensed. "No, of course. Are you—" Kicking herself for even posing the question, she finished, "Are you…in town for long?"

"Not sure." He frowned slightly. "I just drove up yesterday."

She fought back the twinge of hurt that he had been back in town for a day and hadn't called. Just as quickly, she reminded herself that he was probably busy with his mother and brother, especially since he hadn't seen them in a while. He'd probably planned on coming into town today, stopping in to say hello, ask her when she closed for the day…

Or maybe…just maybe he hadn't planned on doing any of those things. Maybe the fact was the man was just a jerk, someone who'd kissed her, had a little fun with her, run his hands up and down her skin, and then never given her a second thought.

Her stomach knotted at the thought. Silence stretched. She waited for him to say something more, maybe suggest dinner, or even drinks. Instead, he said nothing at all. He just stared at her with those dark, determined eyes. Stared at the beads of sweat that she uneasily suspected had collected along her hairline.

"Well, I guess I'll see you again while you're in town," she said carefully. Just the right amount of insinuation. Just the right amount of suggestion.

"Yeah, probably. But I should really get going. It was good seeing you, Ivy!" Brett grinned, but before she could respond, he thumped her on the upper arm and went on his merry way. No mention of the kiss. No suggestion of a get-together. Not even an invitation for a lukewarm cup of coffee from the hospital cafeteria.

Ivy stood in stunned silence, her mouth still slack from her unspoken response, and stared at the metal elevator doors, catching her blurred reflection. She didn't look happy. In fact, she looked downright crestfallen.

For the second time in a matter of months, Brett had managed to turn her world upside down. Only this time, not in the way she had hoped.

CHAPTER 2

Ivy narrowed her eyes at the silver-framed medical chart that hung on the otherwise bare white wall of the examination room. To think of the time she'd wasted on that man! To think of the energy, the emotion, the hope! For what? Some cad in a white coat? He'd been such a *nice* boy growing up—quiet and studious, so different than the other guys she knew—but now...

Now he was no different than the others she'd dated throughout her twenties. No different than the fleeting series of dates she'd had on and off over the years with men who seemed so promising at first and ended up being a complete disappointment. Each time she'd told herself, good riddance, no matter, he wasn't the one, and each time, in the back of her mind, she thought of Brett. Sweet, brown-eyed Brett who was so easy to talk to, so easy on the eyes, so serious, smart, funny, and...perfect. And she'd thought, if only he'd just move back to town, then maybe...

A tear began to fall and she brushed it away before her doctor came into the room and started jumping to false conclusions. It had been a night of fun, as weddings usually were. She'd built it up to be more than it was. And that hurt. A lot. And as soon as she got out of this damn appointment, she was going to go home and erase every reminder of that evening from her life, starting with the crimson bridesmaid's dress.

Always a bridesmaid, she thought, thinking of the upcoming weddings with newfound dread. It would be difficult enough to sit through Henry's, but at least she'd be busy, sister of the groom and all, but Anna and Mark's would pose a new challenge, as Brett would certainly be there as brother of the groom. They hadn't set a date yet—too busy running their restaurant to find the time. Selfishly, this had tried her patience. Until today. With any luck, they'd just elope.

Two knocks gave her ample warning to swipe her fingers under her eyes before her doctor opened the door, his balding head bent over a clipboard. He flipped a page and settled himself onto a stool before looking up at where she sat on the edge of the examination table. "The bloodwork looks good," he said. His eyes roamed over her through his wire-framed glasses. "How have you been feeling?"

"Fine. Great." *Never worse.*

"Any dizziness?" He stood and removed his stethoscope from his neck.

She decided not to mention her little jog through the parking lot and the hit she'd immediately taken. If she tried to explain, it would just lead to a line of questioning she didn't want to deal with and a lecture about her daily routine. She'd pushed herself a little too hard; it was hardly the same as the mistakes she'd made in her past. "Nope, not really. I've been following the diet plan you gave me."

"Good." He pressed the stethoscope to her back. "Big breath in."

Ivy did as she was told, wondering if the metal object could decipher a broken heart. But the doctor pulled back, seemingly satisfied, and made a note on the chart.

"You're taking your insulin every day?" He gave her a long, pointed look.

Ivy swallowed hard. "Haven't missed a dose." *Not in seven months* was the unspoken understanding. Not since the last time she'd been chauffeured to the emergency room by an ambulance back in the fall.

She wouldn't be making that mistake again.

"Good. Monitoring your blood glucose throughout the day?"

Ivy nodded again and forced herself not to sigh as the questioning continued. She deserved it, after all. In time she'd hopefully convince her doctor that she was behaving responsibly. And her brother, she thought, thinking of the stern talking-to that Henry had given her when he'd come back to town to clean up her mess last year.

"I'm taking my meds now," she said. When the doctor cocked an eyebrow, she confirmed, "All my meds. Not skipping doses." It had been risky, she knew, but years ago when she was feeling okay, it was sometimes easy to pretend everything was fine, that she wasn't sick, that she didn't have to worry about pesky things like insulin shots and blood glucose levels. That she could just be normal.

When had she ever been normal, though? *Never*, she thought, shuddering when she recalled the gossip that used to fly around town about their mother.

"I'm writing you a prescription that will take you through our next appointment."

"I'll be there," Ivy said, taking the slip of paper. When the doctor held her gaze, she swallowed a sigh. "I promise."

And she would be there, because she didn't want another

trip to the ER. And because if her condition didn't kill her that time, then Henry sure as hell would.

Well, that rut was behind her now. In time, she'd find a way to pay back her brother, even if he neither wanted it nor expected it.

"The pharmacy downstairs is open today." The doctor's hint was more of an order and another deflating reminder of how irresponsible she'd been.

The thought of lingering in this building, where Brett was roaming the halls, was enough to make her break into a cold sweat, but allowing that to happen would only ring the alarm bells and lead to another sugar reading, so Ivy hopped off the table, willed herself to ignore all emotions, and said, like the coolheaded adult that she was, "I'll do that right now."

She grazed her back teeth together as she slowly walked to the elevator and pressed the button, bracing herself for the sight of those long legs, broad shoulders, and silky brown hair she'd tangled through her fingers. What was he doing here anyway? She supposed just as he said—a meeting. A professional reason to be back in the area. Certainly not a personal one, she thought bitterly.

She held her breath as the doors slid open seconds later, and let a long sigh roll through her shoulders when she locked eyes with an elderly man proudly clutching a bouquet of pink roses. "New great-grandbaby," he boasted, and Ivy gave a weak smile in return. She didn't have the heart to tell him he was taking the elevator in the wrong direction. Besides, if she missed this ride, there was no telling what— or who—would be behind the next set of doors.

"Congratulations." She stepped inside, pressed the button for the lobby level, and waited for the doors to close. The elevator moved slowly, its descent noted on the illuminated numbers near the ceiling. Chances were he'd be gone, she reminded himself. He'd had an appointment. Unless that was just an excuse. She was no stranger to those—empty promises to "do it again sometime," or loose suggestions of a phone call that never came. Just once she'd like a man to tell her straight up that he wasn't interested. No more bull. No more dancing around the obvious. No more trying to spare her feelings in the wake of saving face.

She was a big girl. She could take it.

Still, as the elevator settled itself and the doors once again spread open, revealing an ever-broadening view of the wide-open atrium, with its glass ceilings and not so much as a potted plant to hide behind, Ivy felt her heart began to pound. She swept her eyes quickly over the room, hurried to the pharmacy, and snatched a random magazine on her way to the counter.

She slid the prescription to the pharmacist and darted her gaze to the right and then the left, careful not to move her neck. "I'm in a bit of a hurry," she explained. "Maybe I should come back—"

"This should only take ten minutes." The woman gave a pleasant smile.

Ivy glanced out to the atrium. Every second that ticked by was another chance to run into Brett. And she didn't want to. Once, she would have loved nothing more. But she'd clearly been a fool then.

Ivy slid into a chair at the far end of the row against the back wall and opened the car racing magazine in front of her face.

So maybe she was overreacting. The chances of Brett stopping into the pharmacy were slim; she doubted he'd be picking up a prescription or stopping in to browse the periodicals, and there were vending machines for snacks all over the building. She'd carefully touched up her makeup with the few cosmetics she carried in her handbag while she was waiting for her doctor to get the test results, and so while she certainly looked better than she had during their little run-in, she didn't want to repeat the event. Ever. In fact, she'd be quite happy never seeing Brett again in her life. Never being reminded of the dream he had shattered. Never being reminded of the tingle of her lips long after they'd been pulled back into the reception to wave off Grace and Luke...

He'd probably been drunk. Either way, one thing was clear, and that was that Brett Hastings hadn't enjoyed that kiss as much as she had.

"Ivy?"

At the sound of her name, Ivy startled, dropped the magazine onto the floor and turned, white-faced, to the woman standing above her. "Dr. Kessler!"

"You sound relieved," Suzanne Kessler remarked with an amused smile. "Were you expecting someone else?"

"You surprised me," Ivy said, waiting for her pulse to resume a normal speed. "How's your daughter?" It had been nearly a year since Ivy had overseen the flowers for the Kesslers' youngest daughter's wedding: white French tulips mixed with Queen Anne's lace. Simple, slightly old-fashioned, but intrinsically elegant.

"Never better," Suzanne said. "I've been meaning to come by the store and give you some photos from the wedding. People still stop me to comment on the centerpieces."

Ivy couldn't deny the pride she felt hearing this.

"In fact, I'm happy I ran into you today. I don't know if you're aware, but the Forest Ridge Hospital puts on a fundraising event each year. It's a big to-do; all the donors come out, there's a silent auction, and the proceeds go exclusively to the hospital."

"I'd be happy to donate something for the auction," Ivy ventured, thinking of what kind of exposure that would give her. Business was steady in Briar Creek, but a few more big weddings and events a year would go a long way.

"Actually, I had something else in mind. We don't hire an event planner—we'd rather put the money toward the hospital—so in the past, I've helped oversee things. Could we hire you to do the flowers? It's a big event, so if you don't have the time I understand."

Have the time? She would *make* the time. "When is the event?"

"Not until August," Suzanne said. "Do I take that as a yes?"

Ivy thought of Brett, roaming the halls, stepping off that elevator as if he owned the place, and then dismissed her concerns. "Yes!" Ivy stood to shake the woman's hand. "Yes, absolutely. And thank you."

"You have a real artistic eye," Suzanne said warmly. "So consider the thanks all mine." At that moment, the doctor's pager beeped. She glanced down with a tired sigh and glanced back at Ivy. "I'll be in touch soon."

Ivy nodded and walked over to the pharmacy counter to check on her medication. She hadn't done a big event in a while, and this was just the kind of project that would help take her mind off that kiss...and today's disappointment.

Ten minutes later, as promised, she was paying an outrageous amount of money for three months' worth of her medication and then speed-walking through the lobby with a darting eye and as much feigned nonchalance as she could muster.

For once her car decided to cooperate, starting after only

a few good whacks on the hood, but her heart felt heavy as she wound her way out of the garage and back onto the main road that led to Briar Creek.

She'd spent enough time thinking about Brett Hastings, living in a dream world and drifting off from reality. Now was the time to think about herself again. Her business. Her health. And the gig that could finally bring her out of the red and give her a chance to repay her brother once and for all. She'd go back to the shop and come up with some sketches, work out a color theme to present to Suzanne when she called. She'd stay focused, busy herself with what she loved, and eventually that kiss would be as forgotten as it was to Brett. And so would he.

Brett Hastings never stuck around Briar Creek for long. With any luck, he'd been gone again by tomorrow, not to return again for a long, long time.

Brett Hastings adjusted his position in the low-backed visitor's chair and willed himself not to fall asleep. The only thing keeping him from drifting off was the hard wooden seat digging into his middle vertebrae. He'd known the twenty-two-hour shift he'd pulled before getting behind the wheel for nine hours yesterday had been a mistake, but he'd assumed by the time he reached his mom's house, he'd collapse into his childhood bed and sleep like a baby. How easy it was to forget that the single bed frame was almost as uncomfortable as the break room in the ER, and between his calves hanging off the edge of the mattress and the cold grip of reality taking hold, he'd only managed a few fitful hours of sleep before the smell of percolating coffee roused him, reminding him, with sinking dread, that he wasn't in his sleek apartment in Baltimore anymore.

The director of the emergency department was staring at him over the length of his long nose and Brett had the unnerving suspicion he'd posed a question Brett hadn't quite caught.

Ignoring the twitch in his left eye, Brett shifted his weight on the chair again. "I'm sorry, could you clarify?"

Dr. Gardner frowned slightly before saying, "Forest Ridge is a relatively small hospital. The closest trauma center is in Burlington. It's hardly the pace you were used to in a city like Baltimore. So tell me, why us?"

Because he was out of options. Because he didn't know where else to look on such short notice. Because he didn't need an employment gap on his résumé while he looked for something long-term.

Because as much as he hated to admit it, maybe he could use a break from the fast pace of an inner-city hospital. And because maybe by coming back here, even for a little while, he could put the guilt at bay once and for all, focus on his family for a bit, even if deep down he knew it couldn't make up for lost time.

"I have a lot of connection to Forest Ridge Hospital," he said instead, feeling his stomach tighten on the words. He'd hated this place from the moment he first stepped foot in it, more than a dozen years ago, when he was still just a kid and his mother was first diagnosed with cancer. Hated the bare white walls, the sterile smell of disinfectant, the mysterious metal machinery that beeped and flashed. But it was the sense of hopelessness he'd hated the most. The fear that rested square in his chest every time he turned a corner, or looked up to see a stone-faced doctor enter the room. The fact that everything was unknown, and all of it was completely out of his control.

He'd vowed never to feel that way again. And he hadn't. Until recently.

"That you do." It was a small community, and when you'd been in and out of this place as often as Brett had over the years, people knew the reason. "So your decision to leave Baltimore is personal then?"

Brett slid his hand over his jaw, hoping his expression remained neutral. "Strictly personal."

He knew what his last boss had said. The words echoed in his ears the whole drive up to Vermont. *A change of speed will do you good.* More like it would take him out of the game, give him too much time to think about everything that had led to this, undermine every sacrifice he'd made for the sake of his career.

It happened to everyone at some point, he knew. Losing a patient was part of the job. Sometimes, no matter how hard you tried, the ambulance didn't get there in time, or the damage was just too deep. *Or someone messed up.*

Brett swallowed back the bitter taste that rose in his throat and reached for his paper cup of coffee, drinking it back even though it had grown cold. Now was the time to stay focused. He didn't have a choice. He hadn't given himself one.

Despite the caffeine, his eyelids felt heavy as he verbally walked through his résumé, tensing as the unease built, just like it always did when he thought back on his life. He knew he should be proud, that feeling guilty undercut the decision, but he couldn't help it; no matter how many times he looked at it, he felt one thing: selfish.

What was the alternative? he told himself. No one passed up a full undergraduate scholarship to Yale. Or a free ride to medical school at Johns Hopkins. He'd been top of his class four years in a row. Impressive, yes, but the way he saw it, he had no other choice.

He had to make the most of the opportunity. How else did you justify leaving behind a sick mother or not returning years later when she relapsed?

"Well, I don't see any reason to postpone the obvious." Dr. Gardner took off his reading glasses and smiled. "When can you start?"

The realization that he was back in Briar Creek, right back where he'd started, so far from where he wanted to be, hit him again. Briar Creek, with its winding back roads and town square festivals. With the people he'd known since he was too young to talk. There'd be questions. There'd be speculation. There'd be nowhere to hide. From what happened in Baltimore. From the bad memories that were already surfacing.

He gritted his teeth when he considered his run-in with Ivy, looking pretty as ever with those blue-green eyes and that glossy auburn hair that brought out the pink in her cheeks. Ivy was sweet, and he could tell she was fishing for an invitation—one he'd successfully danced around, careful not to mislead her. Girls like Ivy didn't kiss just for fun. He'd known it when he'd first leaned in to her, seen the curve of her smile, felt the race of her heart through the swell of her chest as he pulled her close to him. He knew he should have resisted, but she was a beautiful girl, always had been, and besides, he was just in town for the night.

Except now he was in town for a lot longer than one night. And from the way her smile had slipped when he'd dodged her suggestions for a date and excused himself, something told him that kissing Ivy Birch last November was a much bigger deal than he'd intended it to be.

Still, he couldn't help but smile when he thought of the way her ass had looked in those tight jeans, accentuating every curve in her crazy long legs. Better than that stuffy bridesmaid dress he'd been desperate to peel from her skin, that much was sure.

It's for the best, he told himself. He didn't need any more distractions from his job at the moment, and Ivy didn't need a guy like him. Ivy was the kind of girl who wanted a picket fence and a quiet life in Briar Creek. Someone who could make a promise and keep it. He couldn't.

"When do you need me?"

"Well, Dr. Leery starts her maternity leave on Friday, so I'll put you on the on-call schedule for this upcoming weekend. Saturday nights can get a little crazy around here."

Brett managed to nod politely. Compared to the stab wound he'd treated less than forty hours ago, he doubted a few overserved locals in need of an IV and a good long sleep could really constitute *crazy*, but who knew, maybe his old boss was right. Maybe taking a step back would do him good. He could clear his head and start trusting himself again.

"I should be wrapped up in Baltimore by Friday," he said, standing to shake the man's hand.

"Excellent. And, Dr. Hastings, this may be a temporary position, but if everything works out, we may be able to find a permanent place for you here."

I wouldn't bet on that, Brett thought to himself.

Tomorrow he'd drive back to Baltimore and grab a few things, but he wouldn't break his lease. Forest Ridge Hospital may be where he landed, but if he had anything to do with it, it wouldn't be where he stayed.

By Wednesday, Ivy had stopped frantically brushing her hair in between customers. She'd also stopped checking her compact mirror to make sure her lip gloss hadn't somehow made its way to her teeth. She'd also almost stopped jumping every time the bells over her door jingled. But she hadn't quite lost the feeling of disappointment every time she glanced up to see that the person standing in her shop wasn't Brett.

When would she finally give up the last thread of hope and realize that he was not sweet and special but, sadly, was just like all the rest? Men couldn't be trusted—hadn't her mother told her that a hundred and ten times?

"You don't look happy to see me," Kara Hastings remarked as she approached the well-worn farm table Ivy used as her workbench and counter. "Were you expecting someone special?"

Just your drop-dead gorgeous cousin, Ivy wanted to say. Instead, she forced back her shoulders and said brightly, "Last I checked you were pretty special."

Kara dropped her handbag onto the old rocking chair

near a rack of locally made candles and soaps and sighed. "Nice to know at least one person thinks so."

Ivy slid a sheaf of purple freesia into the vase and frowned. "Trouble at the restaurant?" She'd always been under the impression that Kara loved working at Briar Creek's newest restaurant, Rosemary and Thyme, but the hesitation in her friend's expression seemed to say otherwise.

Kara waved her hand through the air and shook her head. "Forget I said anything. It's just been a busy couple of weeks and I'm tired. Standing on your feet all day can get old."

"Tell me about it," Ivy agreed. She'd promised herself a decent lunch break today. She'd even made a chicken salad and tucked it into the mini-fridge so she wouldn't have to trek upstairs to her apartment. But instead of sitting down for ten minutes to enjoy it, she'd managed a few bites in between customers.

Kara picked up a Burgundy Iceberg rose and admired its lush purple color. "Do you ever get lonely, being here on your own all day?"

"No, but I wouldn't mind receiving the flowers for a change," Ivy joked.

"That makes two of us. Tell me, is chivalry all but dead?"

"Given the amount of orders I fill each day, I can firmly say it is not. I guess I'm still waiting for the right guy to come along. At least I love my job. That's something."

Ivy shucked the leaves from the few remaining assorted stems she'd chosen and finished her arrangement for the dance studio lobby. She knew Rosemary Hastings tended to like her flowers "pink, pink, and pink!" but she was fresh out of pink roses and peonies today. If she ever received an arrangement of her own, though, she hoped it would be peonies. She'd waited long enough—and a small part of her thought that the flowers, like the guy giving them to her, should be worth the wait.

"But to answer your question, I don't get very lonely, no. I'm so busy most of the time, and I have my customers to chat with." She tipped her head. "Why do you ask?"

Kara's cheeks pinked. "Just wondering," she said with a little shrug, shifting her eyes to the window.

Ivy transferred the vase to a sturdy open box and hoisted it into her arms. "I have to drop this off at the studio after I close. Want to join me?"

"I'll walk with you, but I'll wait outside. My mother's been on my case again. Wondering when I'm going to finally settle down, what I'm doing with my life. If I hear one more word about Sam Logan or Jackson Jones..."

Ivy pulled a sympathetic face. The town sheriff and mayor were the most eligible bachelors in town, and it didn't surprise her that Rosemary had targeted one of them for her oldest daughter. No doubt the other would default to Kara's younger sister, Molly, if she ever moved back to town.

"I've tried telling her, I've known these guys since they had missing teeth and skinned knees. There's no excitement in that." Kara picked up her bag and followed Ivy to the door. "Unless safe and boring is what you're looking for."

It had been exactly what Ivy had been looking for. Well, minus the boring part. There was nothing boring about Brett, with those steady dark eyes and that rich, warm laugh and the electric tease of those fingers. He'd made her feel... *special*, as Kara would say.

Well, he certainly hadn't made her feel special on Monday afternoon, had he?

"Are you okay?" Kara's voice was laced with amusement, and only then did Ivy realize she had been jamming the key in the lock with a little more vigor than usual. Embarrassed, she quickly turned it and put the keys in her pocket.

"It's old and tricky." She smiled. "I keep meaning to get it fixed." It was just another item on her ever-growing to-do list. There were many things she wanted to buy for the shop. She was forever thinking up new ways to improve it, new items she wanted to offer in addition to the artisan candles and soaps she sold alongside the flowers. For a while now she'd been planning to offer a flower-arranging class, but when she'd casually mentioned it to her brother, his complexion went all ruddy.

She'd stopped talking then and there, remembering her promise to him to slow down, to take on Jane's help, to cut back her own hours. But now that her diabetes was under control again, maybe she could start thinking about that class. If enrollment was high, the income would go toward that new sign she'd had on her wish list for over a year—after she'd paid back every dime she'd borrowed from her brother, of course.

Her eyes swept Main Street as they walked toward the town square and then waited at the light. She watched the cars pass by, trying to make out the faces in the windows, and then slid her focus over to the tall windows of Rosemary and Thyme at the corner of Second Avenue. It was entirely possible that Brett would have stopped by to spend time with his brother. Or maybe he was at Hastings, the diner up the street that was owned and run and by their mother, Sharon. She chewed her lower lip as they crossed the street, wondering if she should ask Kara directly.

"I ran into your cousin the other day." Damn. Her voice sounded tight and overly cheerful. She tried again. "He was over at Forest Ridge Hospital when I went for an appointment."

"Yeah, Mark took Sunday night off from the restaurant to have dinner with him and their mom."

"How's he doing?" Ivy pressed, wondering if she was really prepared for the details. Did she really need to hear that he'd moved on, found a girlfriend? That some other girl was enjoying the tingling pleasure of his hands grazing her hips? He could even be engaged for all she knew. That kiss had happened more than half a year ago. And from the looks of things, he'd already forgotten it.

"I didn't get to see him," Kara replied. "He went back to Baltimore yesterday morning."

Well, that cemented it. Ivy did her best to mask the disappointment that landed square in her chest, and quickened her pace up the hill to the dance studio, where small girls wearing pink tutus were spilling from the door. So he was gone. Come and gone without so much as a goodbye. She swallowed back the lump that had wedged tight in her throat, knowing she was being ridiculous, that she was holding on to a kiss, of all things.

It's just that it had been such a good kiss. Such a long, heavy, passionate kiss. Full of such...promise.

Somewhere deep inside her, in a tiny little corner she didn't want to acknowledge, a part of her had still held out a tiny morsel of hope that something wonderful would happen, that the door to her shop would open, and she'd look up, and there he'd be, with that dazzling wide smile and those twinkling eyes. It would be like a scene out of a movie...

Except real life was never like the movies, was it? She *had* seen Brett again. And it had been far from magical. And that was just the cold, hard truth.

Kara was hiding behind a large maple tree, completely shielded from any view of the studio, when Ivy reemerged a few minutes later. Rosemary hadn't been particularly thrilled to learn that her favorite pink roses wouldn't be in until next week, but after a few tight pinches of her heavily lipsticked mouth, she'd finally admitted that the current arrangement was a refreshing change and a cheerful burst of color for the otherwise pastel-hued room.

"Did she see me?" Kara asked, darting her eyes to the left, her back firmly to the trunk.

"No," Ivy replied, glancing back at the renovated red barn Rosemary had long ago transformed into a dance studio. "But you can't hide from her forever. She's your mother."

"My very smothering mother," Kara insisted. "Believe me, if she knew I was out here, she'd come running out, waving her lipstick, telling me I should never leave the house without it because...you never know who you might run into!" The last part was mimicked in Rosemary's larger-than-life trill, and Ivy had to laugh, until she was reminded of the bitter truth in the statement.

If she'd been wearing that cute dress she'd spotted rather than old jeans, looking freshfaced and calm instead of sporting a beaded sweat 'stache, would Brett have maybe reacted a little differently to her?

Guess she'd never know. Probably best not to think about it, either.

"Feel like grabbing a coffee?" Ivy asked. The thought of going home to her empty apartment was far from appealing.

Main Street Books was just around the corner and down Main, and Ivy was happy to spot her friend Grace through the big, lead-paned windows as they approached.

Brightening at the sight of them, Grace closed the cash register and handed over a brown paper bag of books to a customer. "Here to browse?"

"Here for coffee," Kara replied. "Can you join us?"

Grace looked around the empty shop and nodded. "I doubt we'll have any more customers before closing time, so why not?"

The girls walked into the equally subdued adjacent café, dubbed the Annex, which typically cleared out near the dinner hour. "Jane's teaching tonight, so I've been manning both sections on my own. I could use a break." She sighed as she sank into a wooden chair at a table near the window. "Help yourself to whatever you want. It's on the house."

Ivy walked over to the bakery counter and eyed the sugar-coated scones, oversized cookies, and gooey coffee cakes, longingly thinking of how comforting their sweetness would be after such a crummy week. Before she did anything she would live to regret, she plucked a mug from the shelf and filled it to within an inch of the rim from the half-full pot of coffee warming on the burner.

"Normally, I'd demur, but I made these cookies today, and I've been thinking about them ever since you stopped by the restaurant to pick them up." Kara happily added a large chocolate chip cookie to her plate and filled her own mug.

"I didn't know you made these," Grace remarked as Kara pulled out a chair. "I had three different customers comment on them."

"Really?" Kara flushed as a small smile parted her lips.

"Really." Grace motioned to the cookie as Kara and Ivy sat down. "Mind if I see what all the fuss is about?" She broke off a corner of the cookie and chewed it thoughtfully. "Wow."

Kara gave a modest shrug. "It's just a cookie."

Grace broke off another piece. "No, it's just about the best cookie I've had in years. Don't tell Anna," she added quickly. "Ivy, you have to try this."

Ivy felt her own cheeks warm. "Oh, I trust you."

But Grace wasn't backing down, and why should she? She had no clue about the condition Ivy had battled since first grade, even if she had been Ivy's best friend all that time. She'd be supportive, of course—probably too supportive. Ivy already had one person in her life who judged everything she put into her mouth, frowned with concern over the smallest perceived sign of distress, gave her endless lectures on kidney damage, and looked for symptoms of too much or too little blood sugar in pretty much everything she did. She didn't need Grace going there, too.

Grace broke off another piece and thrust it at Ivy. Ivy stared at the moist, gooey cookie with the large chunks of milk chocolate, and swallowed hard. It was just *one* bite.

A really big bite, she could hear Henry's voice stern in her ear.

With a grin, she took the piece of cookie and shoved it in her mouth, closing her eyes as she tasted the brown sugar, vanilla, and smooth, creamy chocolate. "Wow is right, Kara. You have a gift!"

"Oh, I'm happy to help at the restaurant," Kara said, sipping her coffee. "Your sister has taught me so much."

"Well, up until today I would have said no one could beat her when it came to baked goods. If she knew she had anything to do with this, I'm sure she'd be pleased. Has she tried these?" Grace broke off another piece.

Kara shrugged. "I'm not sure. We're so busy. Just all doing our part..."

Her smile slipped, ever so slightly, and unnoticed by Grace, but Ivy caught it and frowned. "Well, I call this more than your part. You should start offering this on the dessert menu there. Maybe with some of that homemade vanilla bean ice cream Mark makes." Not that Ivy had ever tried it.

"Maybe." Kara shrugged again.

"Look at me!" Grace laughed and pushed the plate away. "I'm going to end up eating this whole damn thing. Here, take it."

Ivy didn't move. She reached for her coffee mug with both hands and took a long sip instead.

"Ha, like you have to worry about your figure," said Kara.

"Because I'm married now?" Grace shook her head.

"Hey, you have it easier than we single girls do," Kara pointed out. "It's a miserable dating scene out there."

That it was. Ivy reached over and broke off another piece of the cookie. A smaller one this time. The damage was already done, after all. She'd have to sneak off to the bathroom soon to give herself an injection of the insulin she now religiously carried with her at all times.

"What about Sam Logan? Or Jackson Jones?"

At the look of wrath Kara flashed at Grace, Grace's expression turned to one of bewilderment, and Ivy laughed at her best friend's mishap. "That's who Rosemary is fixated on setting her up with," Ivy explained.

"Oh. Well, why not? I always thought they were both sort of cute..."

Kara groaned. "Not you, too!"

Grace held up her hands in mock surrender. "Okay, okay. So they're not your type. What about you, Ivy?" She waggled her eyebrows suggestively.

"Oh. No. I'm—" She considered her words. *I'm still hung up on Brett, nearly twenty years after he helped me pick up my books after I dropped my open backpack down the stairwell? Still thinking about that high school dance, where I sat on the sidelines, pretending to nurse a single glass of punch, and willed the other wallflower in the room to cross the gym floor and talk to me? Or how about, I'm still thinking about that passionate kiss I shared with Brett Hastings while you and Luke were feeding each other wedding cake?*

"I'm happy being single," she blurted.

Grace and Kara blinked at her, and Ivy had the uneasy feeling they could see right through to her heavy heart. Nausea began to stir, rearing another unfriendly reminder, and she reached behind her chair for her bag. "I'll be right back."

She hurried back into the bookstore, thinking of what she'd just done, what Henry would say. By the time she frantically locked the bathroom door behind her, her fingers were shaking as she unzipped her bag and retrieved the syringe. She lifted her shirt and expertly pushed the needle into her abdomen.

There. She had it all under control.

Kara and Grace were chatting about Rosemary when Ivy retook her seat. Her coffee had gone slightly cold, and her taste for it was long gone. The cookie, she noticed, was thankfully finished, and all that remained on the plate were a few delicious-looking crumbs.

"I was just telling Kara that Jane and Henry are having a cookout this Saturday night. Are you coming?"

Henry had left a message for her earlier that day, but she'd been too busy handling a rush order for a new baby to even listen to it yet. Her mind rattled with potential excuses. The thought of going to a party with a bunch of married and engaged people suddenly felt like too harsh a reminder of how far she was from that phase.

But then again, the thought of sitting at home, all by her lonesome, on Saturday night was even more unappealing.

She opened her mouth and then closed it again. There was no use trying to lie her way out of this. Grace and Kara both knew she had nothing planned for the weekend, and work was only an excuse for so long. Besides, a night out with her favorite people in the world might be just the thing she needed to take her mind off Brett once and for all.

CHAPTER 4

Brett pulled the last box from the trunk of his car with a grunt and carried it up the creaking stairs to the place that was now officially home. At least temporarily. The top step was a bit loose, and he made a mental note to fix it before he moved out.

"Are you sure you don't want to just take your old room? I kept it intact for you all these years." His mother stood in a dusty corner of what was technically the living room of the carriage house, wringing her hands and doing a poor job of disguising the worry that lined her face.

Brett thought of the too-small twin bed covered in a baseball-themed comforter, with matching flannel sheets, and the corkboard covered in science fair ribbons and, with confidence, said, "No."

"But it's so musty in here!"

"I'll open a window."

Sharon wrinkled her nose. "I guess I can't understand why you'd want to live in a garage when you have a whole house just a hundred feet away."

"It's not a garage; it's a carriage house. And I need my

own place, Mom. I'm thirty years old." He set down the box and gave her a wry smile, which she matched with reluctance.

"I just got so excited when you said you were moving home."

Brett tore open a box. He hated how much it meant to his mother that he was back, stirring up the mixed feelings he had over staying away for as long as he had, sometimes not even coming back for holidays. He told himself it was part of the job, that the hours came with the territory, that he had to be the best damn doctor he could be and this was part of it, but deep down he knew it was more than that. Being here brought too much back to the surface. And being away, being busy, made everything so much easier.

"There's no telling if the job at Forest Ridge Hospital will work out," he said, seizing a chance to plant that seed again. He didn't want to get her hopes up only to end up feeling like he'd let her down. Again. He was here, and he wanted to make the most of his time, but how could he justify moving back now when he'd stayed away when he was needed the most?

He couldn't. And with his experience, he was better suited to a trauma center, not a community hospital's emergency room. He needed to be where his skills were a match. Where he could help.

Once he got his head straight again.

"Nonsense! With your experience? They're lucky to have you!"

Brett wasn't so sure about that. Once he might have thought so, but now…He walked over to the window and turned the lock, suddenly in need of air. His mother was right, it was musty in here. It was once his father's test kitchen and office for the days he wasn't busy at his restaurant, and it was clear that no one had been up here since he'd hightailed it out of town when Brett and Mark were just kids.

Brett glanced at his mother, wondering if being here stirred up bad feelings for her, reminding her of their father. He had thought it would be easier to stay here, rather than in the house, but now he wasn't so sure. He'd lived for so long without a father that it always seemed impossible to believe he'd ever had one. But he had. He'd had a dad. A dad who'd left without another word. Who never gave him another thought.

"You don't mind that I'm taking this space over, do you?" He watched her carefully, knowing it'd been left empty all these years and wondering if there was a reason. He hoped that his mother didn't hold on to some hope that his dad would return. Even Brett had given up on that dream...eventually.

She looked at him with surprise. "What? No. No, definitely not. Your father's been out of my life for years, and I don't hold on to sentimentality anymore. He chose to leave us behind, never look back."

Brett nodded slowly. Wasn't that what he'd done in a way, when he'd chosen to go to college, leave his family in the lurch? Oh, sure they'd pushed and encouraged, told him he had to do this; his mother had all but insisted. But it never sat right. And now, what was done was done.

"I've missed you, Mom. I know I haven't visited as often as I—"

She dismissed his apology with a wave of her hand. "My son, the brilliant doctor, is off saving lives. What mother can complain about that?"

Brett ground his teeth. Saving lives, or losing them? He'd given up so much, and for what?

Sharon looked out the front window and onto the patch

of lawn that had once been a thriving vegetable garden but had years ago been reseeded with grass and sighed. "I guess you're right. You need your own space." She turned, grinning at him. "Maybe you'll take pity on your old mother once in a while and share a meal with me?"

"I figured you'd be cooking me breakfast every day," Brett said, deadpan. "I was counting on a hot dinner, too."

His mother's mouth fell open. "Oh. Oh, I can. I mean, I'd love to! I'm usually at the diner before seven but—"

"Mom," Brett said gently. "I'm joking." He kissed her on the cheek. "And this is another reason why I'm not moving back into the house. I don't want you thinking you have to take care of me." *It should be the other way around*, he thought.

Brett frowned as emotions brewed to the surface again. He forced them back by ripping the tape on another box and peering inside.

He'd unpack the essentials—summer clothes, bedding, some of his favorite books—but the rest he'd keep in the spare closet. No reason to pack up twice when he'd be on his way soon.

"Want me to stick around and help you set things up?" his mother asked. "The girls at the diner can hold the fort for a while."

"Nah, I don't think I'll bother with it today," Brett said. Unpacking, in any sense, still made things feel more permanent and real than he wished them to be. He'd been tempted to just pack a single suitcase, but that would have raised questions he didn't have the desire to answer. And as much as he hated to believe it, he was now officially employed at Forest Ridge Hospital, and though it was temporary, it wasn't going to change overnight.

He thought of the position in DC he'd seen on the job posting boards that morning and felt his spirits rise. It was the perfect fit for his skills, and he could keep his apartment and what little social life he maintained in Baltimore. He didn't mind the commute. Driving cleared his head. He'd get back on track, on the path he'd set in motion all those years ago. And all those sacrifices would be justified.

"What do you have planned for your first official night back in town?"

His first official night back in town. He hated the sound of it. "Mark said something about a cookout tonight at Jane Madison's house," Brett said. His brother had also told him that Jane was now engaged to his old buddy, Henry Birch, and so chances were Ivy would be there, too. He hated the thought of letting her down again, but as he'd learned along the way, it was better to nip these things in the bud than give women a false set of expectations. "But I don't want to leave you here alone."

She'd been looking a bit pale, run-down. He didn't like it. He should stay home. Cook her dinner. Even if that meant scrambled eggs—his specialty.

"Nonsense! We have all the time in the world to catch up now that you're home again! You go and have fun. Maybe you'll find a nice girl." His mother winked. "It can't be all work, you know."

Oh, but it could. And it would. Long ago he'd made the decision to put his career above his personal life. He certainly wasn't going to take that all back now.

Anna and Mark were both in the kitchen when Kara pushed through the swinging door ten minutes after her shift had officially ended. She didn't mind staying a few minutes late, and she didn't bother drawing attention to it or marking it on her time sheet either, but what she did mind was being stuck out at that hostess stand day after day, nearly a year after Rosemary and Thyme had opened.

She'd assumed at first that it was a temporary position. She'd just been happy to be a part of the team, one of the original three, from the ground up, standing front and center on opening day when a crowd had gathered down Main Street, eager to see the new establishment. Her skin still prickled at the memory, that feeling of expectation as she opened the door and welcomed everyone inside. Anna and Mark had looked so proud, so joyful, and why shouldn't they? This restaurant was their dream, something they'd finally created and were eager to share. Imagine being able to say the same?

Kara did imagine. She imagined that a lot. The only problem was... how did you break that kind of news to two of the closest people in your life? They assumed she was happy here. That nothing was amiss. She did her job with a smile on her face, but there was increasing heaviness in her heart. One that was filled with dissatisfaction and... guilt.

Back when she was still working just for Anna at the café that was once housed in this very space, Kara had felt excited about the prospect of her future for the first time in, well... forever. Anna was a friend, but beyond that, she was a mentor, and Kara looked forward every day to learning a few baking tips from someone she admired, being Anna's right-hand woman when business was busy—and it was always busy.

She'd thought when Anna and Mark joined forces and opened the full-service restaurant that her own responsibilities would increase, too, that maybe she'd be asked to handle the desserts even. Instead, they'd brought on a team of talented people—people with culinary backgrounds, sous chefs—and Kara was left standing on her aching feet for hours at a time, plastering a smile on her face, showing people to their tables, and sometimes, only sometimes, being asked to help in the kitchen when someone was thoughtful enough to take a sick day and give her a reason to step in.

It was soulless. Oh, she liked chatting with the locals who stopped in, and she was good at her job, always sure to note a repeat customer's favorite table and ensuring it was available for their reservation, but it was hardly what she'd set out to do, and honestly, she wasn't sure how much longer she could do it without feeling like her spirit had been completely crushed.

She was going to quit. Today. It was as good a day as any. She'd give two weeks' notice. Maybe even a month, considering Mark was her cousin and Anna, one of her best friends, would be a Hastings herself by the end of the summer. She'd just march over to them, ask if they had a moment, and say the words she rehearsed every morning in the shower: *It's not that I don't love working here; it's just that it's time I pursue my own passion.* Surely they'd understand that much!

The thought of letting them down had kept her quiet for too long. They loved her. Wanted the best for her. And the best thing for her was to leave.

She rolled her shoulders back and lifted her chin, her stride purposeful as she aimed her body directly at the longest workstation near the back of the brightly lit kitchen, where Anna was standing over a stainless steel range, her back to Kara. The energy of the kitchen was overwhelming at times and, really, downright intimidating at others. Whereas at Fireside Café, she'd loved nothing more than slipping into the cozy kitchen and mastering a perfect piecrust, she had come to have an almost physiological response to stepping into the hot, steaming, and clanking kitchen of Rosemary and Thyme, and it had nothing to do with the fact that its name was in honor of her mother, who had helped orchestrate Anna and Mark's reunion. No, it was the fact that when she walked in and saw all these crisp white coats and chefs expertly and almost casually wielding knives and whipping up delectable creations, she couldn't help but feel like she was an outsider. That she should just go back to her station near the front door. Front of house, where she belonged.

But not where she intended to stay.

"Anna." Her voice came out as a croak, and between that and the ball of anxiety lodged in her throat, Kara had the distinct impression she looked like a frog in that moment. "Do you have a minute?"

Anna blew a strand of hair off her forehead and set her hands on the hips of her apron. "Oh, no. Is there a problem with the reservations for tonight? Don't tell me we're overbooked. I suppose we can open up the bar tables for dinner, but not everyone wants to be seated in that corner." She shook her head in dismay.

By now the blood was positively rushing in Kara's ears, and she willed herself to stay strong, to blurt out the words she had memorized, finessed, and repeated for over a month. Once it was out, it was out. The worst would be behind her. Then she'd . . .

Well, she didn't know exactly what she'd do. All she knew was that she couldn't do it while she was standing at that hostess stand, fielding calls, and bearing long looks from impatient and hungry customers, as if she were somehow in control of the pace of everyone's meals, as if she could just go over to the nice young couple in the corner and tell them to hurry it along, because people were getting antsy.

"It's not the reservations," she said quietly. Her cheeks were warm, and the heat of the kitchen was almost suffocating. She darted her eyes to the left, noticing the heavy stare from Mark's sous chef, and pinched her lips together. "Could we maybe go to your office?"

Oh, boy. This was the closest she'd gotten to going through with her plan in weeks. How many times had she marched through that kitchen door, determined to seize control of her fate? And how many times had she cracked under the fear of the enormity of the possibility? Of quitting her job. Of taking a risk. Of letting down two of the people who meant the most to her in this world.

Anna looked helplessly at the stove where five pots were simultaneously simmering or boiling. "I have to get the soups finished if I stand any chance of making it to Jane's tonight. Do you mind if this waits until next week? Before your shift, grab me. I'm all yours. Promise."

Kara felt herself wilt. She'd been about to do it this time; she was sure of it. It had been Grace's comments about the cookies, the thought that customers had actually commented on them, that had pushed her into action. After she'd left the bookshop the other night, she'd thought of little else, and she'd happily offered her baking services up to Anna again the next day, only by then the pastry chef was back from her vacation, and that meant Kara wasn't needed...at least not in the kitchen. Nope, she was sent back through the doors, up to the front desk, with a list of messages to return and a heavy heart.

"Sure," she said now, swallowing back the disappointment that landed squarely in her chest. Her dreams had already waited this long. What was another couple of days?

"You're the best, Kara." Anna grinned. "Seriously, look at this place. I'd never keep it afloat without everyone's help."

Kara struggled to believe that. A chef was one thing, but a hostess could be easily replaced. She'd best remember that, lest she lose her nerve again.

"You're one of the only reasons I'm able to even consider setting a date for the wedding. It's hard to think of leaving this place behind for a day, much less a week or two."

Kara all but stuck her fingers in her ears as her pulse began to race. She didn't need to hear this! Not now. Not when she needed to stand firm.

"You deserve a nice wedding. And a honeymoon," she told her friend. The realization that she could be responsible for robbing this from Anna made her almost start to shake.

"I just hope you know how grateful I am. We have the best team, don't you think?" Anna grinned.

"We're all just doing our part," Kara said through a tight smile. And that's what she was doing, her small, yet necessary and very uninspiring, part.

CHAPTER
5

Ivy pulled up to Jane and Henry's house at seven sharp, noticing by the lack of cars on the street that she was probably the first to arrive. Holding the salad she'd brought as a side dish, she let herself in through the front screen door and called, "Hello!"

Henry came around the corner first, grinning and swiftly taking the serving bowl from her hands before giving her a peck on the cheek. She'd started having dinner with her brother and Jane on a regular basis, but she hadn't yet been able to let her guard down in the house, despite its cozy, lived-in feel. It was probably because of the ulterior motive she suspected her brother had for inviting her. Because of the way he and Jane eyed her over the table, watching every morsel she placed in her mouth. The way they never offered any dessert, no matter how much Sophie, Jane's six-year-old daughter, protested.

She reminded herself on each occasion that they only did this because they cared, but each time she left, each time she saw Grace or Kara, she was happy she'd continued to keep her secret. Once upon a time she'd kept it so that it didn't further separate her from the rest of the kids in town—thanks to their mother, she and Henry were already misfits, and she didn't need to fuel the fire. But now, as an adult in a town whose only population growth stemmed from the dozens of babies being born each year, for which she could recite every birth date, because she was the one making the celebratory floral arrangements, there were some things that she'd rather keep to herself. As it was, every person in Rosemary Hastings's book club probably knew who'd given her her first kiss. But did they know who gave her her last one?

Ivy pinched her lips. That was another thing she'd be keeping to herself. No one would know what happened between her and Brett. There was nothing to tell.

Jane was busy in the kitchen when they got to the back of the house. "Oh, a salad, great. Anna's bringing a dessert tray and Kara offered an appetizer. No clue about Grace."

Ivy exchanged a knowing glance with her best friend's youngest sister. Grace was good at many things. She was a best-selling author after all, and she'd turned her father's bookstore around and made it a thriving success. But cooking? Or even baking? Nope, not high on Grace's priority list.

"I'm thinking ice cream, or maybe something store-bought disguised on one of her best platters."

Jane laughed as she set some hamburger rolls in a basket. "I'm guessing cheese and crackers. But I think you're right about the plate. She does love putting her new registry items to use."

Ivy washed her hands and plucked a knife from the block near the fridge. She'd assumed it would be a small party— the Madisons, Hastingses, and Birches, probably with an appearance of a few other girls they knew and, of course, much to Kara's chagrin and Rosemary's delight, Jackson and Sam. But still, Ivy always hoped that eventually someone new would make an appearance at one of these events. Someone they hadn't known since they were still eating sand off the playground in the town square.

"So, how's the wedding planning coming along?" She began slicing a tomato for the burgers while Jane washed the lettuce.

"Sophie is especially excited about her dress."

"Pink and white. The sweetest color combination." Ivy smiled. Jane's flowers were going to be gorgeous. Simple, but soft, and elegant but in an accessible sort of way. Just like Jane herself.

"I guess it's the ballerina in me." Jane smiled. "Of course, I can't say Henry is as thrilled about it. He's worried it will all look like Pepto-Bismol."

Ivy clucked her tongue. "You leave my brother to me. He'll love it when he sees it. And really, does he have a better suggestion?"

"Are you talking about this pink wedding again?" Henry came into the room, Sophie clinging to his back.

"Hey, I like pink!" Sophie cried.

"I think brown would be better," Henry said, and Sophie's face crumpled in confusion, as if trying to process whether he was joking or not. From the skittish glance she threw her mother, it was clear the jury was still out. "Tell me, what's so pretty about pink?"

"Well..." Sophie put a finger to her lips in thought and then smiled triumphantly. "It's the color of cotton candy!"

"Okay. You sold me." Henry tossed Ivy a wink and jogged into the dining room, Sophie squealing in delight.

Ivy watched them wistfully, imagining what it might be like to have her own little family unit like this some-day. Growing up, she and Henry only had each other, and they'd done the best they could without a proper role model. Their father was gone before they'd been born, and even when their mother was home, she couldn't be counted on to be sober. They were usually happier when she stayed away, knowing she'd gladly keep her seat warm at the local pub until the owner stopped refilling her glass. It was the Madisons who had shown Ivy how a real home should be. Full of laughter, and even tears, of people who were happy to see you, and lively dinner conversations over hot, home-cooked meals.

She was happy that her brother had found his way into the Madison family, that after years of drifting, he'd finally found a real home, the one they hadn't been able to make for themselves despite their efforts. It gave her hope that in time, she might be able to do the same.

"Should I cut up another tomato?" she asked Jane.

"Better make it two. Mark was able to cut his shift early tonight and he's picking up Brett."

Ivy had the good sense to set down the knife. "Brett?" Her voice was so small, she wasn't even sure Jane caught the question.

But Jane just nodded and reached for a tomato. "Yeah, he moved back to town. Didn't you hear?"

Of course Ivy hadn't heard the news. And all she could hear now was the rushing of blood in her ears, and she had the sickening, horrifying realization that in a matter of minutes he would be walking through that door and that there was nowhere to hide. She couldn't even have a glass of wine to take the edge off. She eyed the patio doors greedily. The fence really wasn't so high... The walk back to town would do her good.

"Wait." She paused to think about what Jane had said. It

wasn't just tonight. It was... *Oh, no, no, no.* "You said he... moved back?"

"That's right." Jane gathered the tomato slices onto a plate and started peeling a red onion. "Sharon must be so excited."

The doorbell rang, and Ivy jumped. Her eyes darted for a place to run, anywhere she wasn't so... exposed. Anywhere she wouldn't be forced to make direct eye contact with the man who had kissed her and carried on, without so much as a glance back, much less a phone call in all these months to keep the spark alive.

That should have been your first clue, Ivy.

She watched helplessly as Jane walked to the front door, her ponytail swinging, and as her friend's hand reached for the handle, Ivy dashed around the counter and into the powder room, which she quickly locked with a firm click. She closed her eyes and leaned her head back against the door, straining her ear for the sound of his voice. That rich, smooth, sweet-talking voice.

Jane was laughing, and Sophie was talking incessantly, and Ivy held her breath, not wanting to miss a sound. But ah, there was Luke's voice—unmistakable—and Grace, who was already asking Jane about the wedding plans.

Ivy leaned into the mirror and gave herself a stern, silent scolding. Look at her. Hiding in the bathroom while her closest friends were out there enjoying themselves. Well, at least now that the house was filling up, her presence wouldn't be so obvious. She'd talk to Grace, help out a lot with Jane. She'd make an early departure. And tomorrow she would start an online dating profile. Or she'd ask Sam Logan out for coffee—wouldn't Kara be relieved! Yes, she'd do just that, because one thing was certain. She was not going to look like some gobsmacked schoolgirl who still had a crush on Brett and was still going to bed every night waiting for him to kiss her.

He *had* kissed her. So she could cross that dream off her bucket list.

And really, he hadn't been *that* good of a kisser.

She closed her eyes. Her body tingled. *Oh, stop it!*

Ivy smoothed her hair and checked her teeth for lipstick, and then, with forced confidence, opened the door, already smiling at the thought of seeing Grace. Only the face she was smiling at wasn't her best friend's. It was Brett's. And he wasn't smiling back.

He stepped back, his jaw squared. "Sorry, didn't know it was occupied."

Her cheeks flared. "I was just... brushing my hair."

She gave an internal eye roll. Couldn't she have thought of something a little more casual? A little less obvious than primping in the bathroom?

She scooted to the side with a tight-lipped smile, stiffening as their bodies skimmed each other, and she wondered if he could feel the pounding of her heart as he drew close. Every nerve ending went on high alert, and a rush of warmth pooled deep inside her.

The bathroom door closed, followed by an abrupt click of the lock, and Ivy gritted her teeth against the sinking of her heart as she walked over to Grace and started commenting on the food trays, certain that her friend would notice the wild look in her eyes, the way her voice was unnaturally high even to her own ears, or that she wasn't retaining anything Grace was saying to her.

Somehow she made it to the backyard, even opened a can of diet soda, and was soon fully immersed in a conversation with all three Madison sisters, who were poking fun at Grace's rather impressive cheese platter. She kept her back firmly to the house, refusing to give in to temptation, even to steal a look.

So Brett wanted to pretend they hadn't spent hours laughing and talking, that he hadn't slid his hand over her hip, and down, around, and under the hem of her dress and up her bare thigh, until she'd gasped from pleasure as his mouth nibbled her earlobe?

She could, too. And she would. Because it was time to put this crush to rest for good.

Brett eyed the bucket of ice cold beer and, begrudgingly, reached for a soda instead. If he was a gambling man, he'd pin every dime to his name that he wouldn't be getting a call from the hospital tonight, but he wasn't a betting man. Or a risk-taking one. He played it safe. Always had. With his head. And his heart.

"Not drinking tonight?" Mark chided.

"On call."

"Has that ever stopped you before?" Mark cracked the top on his own bottle.

"I never drink when I'm on call," Brett said, his temper rising.

The amusement vanished from his brother's dark eyes. "Whoa. I was just joking. Lighten up."

"Sorry." Brett shook his head. He was still tense. Still jumpy. Still mentally back in Baltimore, even if physically he was here in sleepy Briar Creek. "I have a lot on my mind."

"Care to talk about it?" Mark tipped his head.

Brett tried to push back the unease he felt, but knew he couldn't. "Do you think Mom's working too hard?"

Mark pulled the bottle from his mouth, his expression turning quizzical. "At the diner? She loves that place."

"Yes, but she's on her feet for all those hours..."

"So?" Mark shrugged, but a flicker of worry soon replaced his earlier attitude. He stared at Brett closely, looking for any hint of reaction. "Why? Do you think something is wrong?"

Brett felt like an ass for worrying his brother, who had no idea about their mother's health scare earlier in the year. He told himself to calm down, to stop looking for problems where none existed. The test results had come back negative. Why couldn't he focus on that, celebrate it even? "I just worry. That's all."

"It's probably because you haven't seen her in a while," Mark said.

Brett nodded away the guilt and sipped his soda. "Yeah, probably." He was back now. He'd make up the time, if such a thing were possible.

Mark grinned at him, then slapped him on the back. "Relax, Brett. She's fine. If she wasn't, I'd know. And I'd have told you."

It was true, all true, but the anxiety continued to gnaw at him. Normally, he had the high-stress pace of his job to distract his mind from traveling down these worried roads, but tonight, there was nothing to take his mind off his troubles. Not even a drink.

Brett glanced around the backyard, noticing he wasn't the only one taking it easy tonight. Ivy Birch sat at a picnic table near the edge of the deck, her back firmly to him, as it had been all evening, holding a half-empty bottle of water while her friends sipped white wine.

He remembered teasing her over dessert at the wedding,

when she passed up a slice of cake, slipping in a chance to compliment her figure, which had very nicely filled out that red bridesmaid dress. She'd blushed and set her hand on his wrist. That touch…It had been all he needed to crave more, and he'd fought the urge all night, telling himself that words were one thing, that a little flirtation at a wedding helped pass the time, that he deserved a little fun. Only he couldn't stop there. Not when her smile sent a fire to his groin and her quick wit kept him eager, wanting more, needing more.

He'd been reckless. Selfish, really.

But he wouldn't take it back. Still, he wouldn't repeat it, either.

From across the lawn he watched as Ivy tossed her head, laughing at something one of the other girls had said. His skin prickled with awareness at the sound and he suddenly had the urge to cross the lawn, to settle himself down at the knotty pine table at the edge of the deck, to immerse himself in that laughter, that banter, and forget about his troubles for a while.

Ivy glanced at him, for the second time that night, and Brett had the uneasy feeling that she was looking for something, no doubt more than he could give.

He excused himself from the guys, leaving them to hash out the latest baseball scores, and began the long, slow walk across the grass. If life had taught him one thing, it was that taking control of a situation was always best. And he was going to take control of this awkwardness right now, before it got worse.

As he approached, he watched as Sophie spilled her hot dog on the ground. Her face crumpled with tears, and Jane and Grace both sprung to their feet.

"I'll make you a new one, honey. There's plenty more." Jane bent to pick up the mess.

"But my dress!" the child said, wiping her eyes with her fists. "It's my favorite."

Grace took her hand. "Come inside with me. We'll get you a fresh one while your mommy gets you a new hot dog."

The little girl sniffled, as if considering the offerings. "Okay," she said hesitantly.

Brett smiled as he watched Grace lead Sophie into the house, but his shoulders immediately tensed when he noticed that Ivy now sat alone at the table, her auburn hair glistening with gold in the warmth of the setting sun.

No use dwelling on that, he told himself. Now was as good a time as any. Pulling in a breath, Brett circled the table and slid onto the bench. Her eyes slowly narrowed on him.

"Nice party," he tried, feeling her out. God, he could use a drink right about now. Something to take the edge off. Something to temper the inconvenient urge he had to lean across the table and wipe that surprise off her lips. He hadn't dared to properly look at her the other day in the hospital. Hadn't wanted to. He'd been so shocked to see her, and even more so to be reminded of how damn pretty she was, how his body still reacted all on its own to that face...that body. Now, sitting here, with the evening shadows softening her already delicate features and bringing out the green flecks in those clear blue eyes, he struggled to stay firm.

Then he thought of his father—a man who had promised more than he could give—and the three bystanders who had paid for it dearly. Ivy didn't deserve the same fate.

No one did.

"I heard you moved back to town," she said after a brief hesitation. Her tone was pleasant enough, but he detected a slightly defensive edge.

Damn, word traveled fast in this town. And from the steely glint in Ivy's eyes, she'd taken the news personally. "For now," he commented, and immediately wished he could take back the words. No doubt that would get around, too, and everyone would wonder what was meant by it, where he was going, why he would leave again.

He studied Ivy, relaxing a bit. Ivy kept things to herself. She clearly hadn't told anyone about their kiss. God knew he would have heard about it if she had. Mark would have never let that one pass without a comment or jab, especially now that he'd traded in his bachelor days for domestic comfort.

"I'm filling in at Forest Ridge. One of the emergency room doctors is on maternity leave, so I'm the replacement. I was late for my interview when I ran into you on Monday."

Her smile seemed a little easier. "No wonder you seemed a little harried."

Brett eyed her warily. He knew that look, the sweet way her plump lips curled at the corner, the way she tucked her hair ever so carefully behind her ear and then fiddled with the lobe. She probably didn't even know she was doing it, but the effect it had on him was as intense as it had been the first time. He gritted his teeth. He had to remember the plan. Stick to his rules. Keep focused. Get back on track.

"Yeah, I..." *Just say it, man. Let her down gently. You know what to do.* "I felt bad I had to run off."

"Oh?" She tipped her head, unimpressed.

Brett swept his eyes over the party, making sure they wouldn't be overheard, before leaning into his elbows on the table. This close he noticed the flecks of turquoise around her pupils. The faint dusting of freckles on her nose. And those lips...His groin stirred. Had they always been so pink, so...soft looking?

He inched back. He wasn't offering anything. Not to her. Not to anyone. "That kiss. I feel bad about it."

She narrowed her eyes. "Bad about it..." She seemed to mull over the words.

"My life is really complicated right now. I'm not looking for a relationship at this time."

She now hadn't blinked in an alarming amount of time. Finally, she said with a strange little smile, "Neither am I."

He frowned. He hadn't seen that coming. Normally when he got to a point of having to be direct with a girl, he had to sit through a half hour of listening to her list all her qualities, try to convince him she was flexible, that she didn't mind a doctor's hours, that really, they could make this work. He'd watch as her eyes become all watery, and he'd patiently hand her a napkin or tissue or, once, even his sleeve. He'd kindly tell her she'd find someone better suited, someone to give her the attention she deserved, that she was a great girl, that it was him, not her, and reluctantly agree that maybe someday he'd find a way to balance his life. He'd give her a hug, put her in a cab, and then shake off the guilt he felt, reminding himself it was a necessary evil, that he hadn't promised her a damn thing and that it was better for her that he hadn't. Just like he'd never promised Ivy anything. But from the curious tilt of her head, it seemed that this was one situation he may have read all wrong.

"Oh. I just assumed—"

"What? That one kiss had me planning our wedding flowers?" Ivy laughed. "Please, Brett. It was a wedding. Alcohol was involved. It was just a kiss."

Now here he disagreed. It wasn't just a kiss. It was a flurry of mouths and hands and heat. And no alcohol had been involved. She'd kissed him with a clear head. Not that he could say the same for himself. He'd been stupid, and it wasn't on account of a glass of wine. He'd wanted her.

"Besides, that was months ago," she pointed out. She gave him a pitying look as she cocked an eyebrow.

"It was. I just…" He frowned, at a loss. He wasn't used to the conversation going this way. Wasn't prepared for it. "I just wanted to make sure you weren't…let down."

"Let down?" A wrinkle of confusion appeared between her eyebrows.

He gave her a kind smile. "You know, that you didn't have any…expectations."

She laughed. "My goodness, someone's full of himself."

Brett felt his brow flinch. "I just wanted to make sure there wasn't any misunderstanding. I'm glad we cleared the air."

"Me too." Her tone was sharp, and she was already unraveling one long leg from the bench, using the surface to steady herself. "But it was good seeing you, Brett. And now that you're back in town, I'm sure this won't be the last time."

She smiled as she turned and walked away toward the Madison sisters, who were gathered at the edge of the lawn, and he watched her hips move and sway as she strode across the grass, her long auburn hair bouncing against her back. Brett frowned, wondering what exactly he had accomplished in that conversation. He and Ivy had never been close, but they saw each other a lot when he was in town—she was always at some party or event he was invited to—and he liked her. Liked her smile. Liked her laugh. Liked her face.

He liked her a lot, actually.

"Someone sitting here?" Shea O'Riley, who had been a couple of years behind him in school, hovered next to the table, holding a glass of white wine and smiling at him.

Brett hesitated, his mind still on Ivy, his head still spinning over the conversation they had just had. He waved a hand over the table, smiling politely. "It's all yours."

"Perfect," she said, and then startled him by scooting onto the seat next to him rather than across from him, where Ivy had sat.

He laughed under his breath, surprised, but not entirely, and started thinking of an exit plan. He was used to girls making moves on him. Maybe it was because he made so few of his own; they had no choice but to take the lead. In high school, it was out of shyness, but later…He didn't want to give the wrong impression. Sure, there were girls he was interested in, but he was always careful with that first move. He usually waited for a lead, however subtle. He wouldn't say he didn't enjoy it, especially when a girl was as attractive as Shea, with her long legs, jean shorts just barely skimming the space between her thighs, and a dimple in her left cheek that revealed itself when she smiled. If he'd been back in Baltimore tonight, he might have stuck around, had a few drinks, and enjoyed a pretty girl's company. But he wasn't in Baltimore right now. He was in Briar Creek. A town where everyone knew everyone and everyone talked, and if he got to talking to Shea for too long, all of Main Street would be talking about it tomorrow.

Already his cousin Luke had noticed the exchange and was giving him a discreet thumbs-up sign from across the deck. Brett muffled a sigh and thought fast. He didn't want to hurt the girl's feelings, but he didn't want to feed into her advances, either.

"Hey, I—"

In his pocket, his phone vibrated against his leg. Happy for the distraction, he pulled it out and glanced down at the screen. *Well, what do you know?* Looked like his services were needed after all.

He stood, readying himself to make an excuse that was, for the first time that night, the truth. And the flicker of his pulse when he watched Ivy turn and glance at him over her shoulder confirmed it.

CHAPTER 6

Be careful what you wish for. Ivy repeated this over and over to herself all night long as the humiliation of Brett's rejection burned strong. Hadn't she been the one who claimed to want a man to just come clean with her, tell her he wasn't interested, rather than make up some lame excuse for why he didn't want to date anymore or offer up another empty promise that would leave her waiting by the phone?

It had been bad enough that he'd sought her out, felt the need to put her in her place, but then to carry on with his fun as if the conversation had never happened! Flirting with Shea O'Riley from the stationery store! It was *shameless*! How could she have ever even thought he was cute? Okay, so yes, he was cute, technically speaking, but he was also a total ass. And really, that smile that had once made her all but swoon was, on closer look, more of a smirk. And those deep-set eyes she had found so penetrating and intense and soulful were, on reflection, simply laced with menace.

Oh, she was plenty mad at Shea, too, until she remembered that Shea, like everyone else in town, had no idea that Ivy had held a torch for him for—she cringed—eighteen *years*, or that she had kissed him a few months ago. Shea was simply doing what any other normal, confident, heterosexual woman under a certain age would do in this town, and that was make a play on the most eligible bachelor. Handsome. Smart. A doctor. A real catch. But of course, an uncommitted catch. At least to her.

Ivy picked up the stack of self-help books she'd bought four towns over that morning and bit into a carrot stick, wishing it was a bowl of raw cookie dough instead. She closed the shop on Sundays now, after much pressure from Henry to give herself a rest, and she had to admit—to herself only, of course—that she liked having the entire day off. Sometimes she caught up on orders, or did a bit of housework, or, in recent months, used the entire afternoon to fantasize about a certain undeserving someone, but today she was using it as a self-improvement day. And it started with the glossy cover on the top of her stack: *Say No to the Narcissist! Everyday Strategies to Help You Stop Loving Men Who Only Love Themselves.*

She snorted. It wasn't like she had loved him. Strongly liked, yes. She supposed she should be grateful it was just a kiss, that her entire fantasy hadn't come true and she hadn't ended up another notch on a bedpost.

With most of the men in her past, they hadn't revealed their true colors until after it was too late—after she'd already fallen in love and slept with them. Oh, she supposed there were warning signs, looking back. Like Craig, who saw her only once a week and never told her what he did with the other six nights. Or Lance, who was completely reluctant about quitting the co-ed volleyball team... or letting her join. And then of course there had been the last guy she'd "dated" nearly two years ago, who, after six months and what she thought was the start of something real, hadn't invited her to have dinner with his parents when they came to town.

She'd been hurt every time, but she was determined not to give up the hope that she would find one guy who was looking for the same thing: a nice, quiet life in Briar Creek and a family to come home to at the end of every day. She hadn't had that chance for the first half of her life. Was it so much to wish for it now?

And all along, in the back of her mind, whenever another date turned into a bust, whenever another guy gave her the "it's not you, it's me" speech, she thought of the one man she knew who seemed so different from the rest. The one man who just had to go and move to Baltimore.

The one man who had turned out to be no different than the others.

"They're all the same," her mother used to say bitterly, when Ivy confessed her latest dating woes. At the time, she'd tried to shut the words out, tell herself that she wouldn't end up like her mother, that she'd meet a nice, sweet man and have a cozy, comfortable life.

But now she began to wonder... Was it even possible?

The kettle whistled in the small kitchen at the back of her apartment, and Ivy crossed the cramped living room to the sun-filled galley space where her favorite hand-painted floral mug was already on the counter. She grazed her thumb over the chip as she turned the stove knob with the other hand. When their mother had passed away last summer, Ivy had kept few things from the house before they sold it: the photo albums from when she and Henry were babies up through age five, when their grandmother and keeper of the albums had died. A few of her favorite childhood books that kept her company on those nights when her mother had one too many glasses of Cab. And this dainty porcelain mug with the sweet little petunias painted on in a variety of colors—chipped, but not ruined, and too pretty to part with.

She'd loved flowers for as long as she could remember. She loved the symmetry of the petals, the way they could transform even the dreariest of rooms. And their house had been dreary. Damp and cold and uninviting. Flowers always made it better. She'd light up at the pastels, at the sunny yellows and vibrant reds. Every season brought something new, something to cheer up a room, something to evoke the spirit of a holiday, even if holidays were never celebrated much in their home growing up. Henry had stepped up, she realized as she grew older. Even though they were twins, he had always looked out for her in that way—tucking aside money and buying gifts for Christmas or their birthday in case their mother forgot, which she often did. She smiled sadly as she carefully filled her mug with the steaming water. She supposed he still was looking out for her.

Ivy let the tea steep and carried it back into the living room, which was so very different from the dark and gray house she'd grown up in. What money she had, she tended to put into the shop, but just as with Petals on Main, she made her small apartment her personal jewelry box, with long, brightly colored curtains to frame the tall windows that looked out onto Main Street, a crisp white slip-covered couch with patterned throw pillows, and soothing celery-green walls that made her think of springtime, even in the winter. She settled herself once more on the armchair that was tucked next to the big bay window and looked down onto Main Street, wondering, despite herself, if Brett was strolling the sidewalk at that very moment.

Well, who cared if he was? Certainly, she didn't.

She set her tea on the coffee table she'd salvaged from a secondhand shop and refinished herself with some elbow grease, sandpaper, and a can of white paint—she was quite proud of that piece, really—opened the book again, and forced herself through the first chapter, hoping for a nugget of inspiration. Something, anything, to end this crush once and for all, and to ensure it wouldn't happen again.

Next time she fell this hard for a guy, she had better be damn sure he was worth it.

She flicked to the next chapter and found herself skimming it. She'd read enough of these over the years to know what to do. At least two dozen were hidden under her bed, dog-eared and highlighted, some passages even memorized. Focus on herself. Live a happy life. In time, she'd attract the right person. She could spend all day trying to cheer herself or come to her senses, holed up in her apartment, or she could get out in the sunshine and truly move on.

She decided on the latter.

Ivy picked up her phone, scrolled through her contacts, and dialed Kara. Her friend answered on the third ring.

"I've been thinking," Ivy said. "It might be time for me to finally try out that new gym you've been talking about." The cost was dear, but the payout was big.

Plans made, Ivy set the phone on her coffee table and went into her bedroom to scrounge up some workout clothes, already imagining the promise of lean, long muscles.

So Brett may not be looking for anything. And so she might not even want him anymore. But that didn't mean she couldn't have a little fun making him live to regret it.

Kara was already on the treadmill when Ivy walked into the gym an hour later, her stomach full of the banana and peanut butter she'd eaten in advance to offset the exercise. She waved to her friend and wound her way through the machines, catching a few glimpses of people she knew from the shop and others she'd gone to school with since kinder- garten. She knew Henry hated this aspect of Briar Creek— that there was no getting away from everyone you knew, no escaping the dark side of their past, but Ivy saw it differently. She'd grown and evolved, and she was happy to have the chance to show everyone she wasn't the same sad scrawny kid with the drunk mom making a spectacle of herself at every town event. It was redemption, closure really, and it helped ease the bad feelings she had about her youth.

Speaking of redemption...

A group of girls Ivy went to high school with were fake stretching and staring shamelessly at the weight section of the room. For a minute, Ivy's pulse pricked with inter- est, until she caught Brett's image in the mirror and stopped dead in her tracks. Of course. It seemed Shea wasn't the only one in town who had gotten wind of Brett's arrival. It wasn't every day a handsome, single guy moved to town. Throw an MD in the mix, and they were probably lining up around the block. No doubt Rosemary would be pushing Kara to the front of the queue if they weren't already related.

Brett finished his set, his biceps straining at the effort through the tight material of his gray cotton T-shirt, and he lowered the weights when he spotted her—a signal that she couldn't turn and run, as she'd been hoping to do. Seeing no other choice, she waved and walked toward him, sparking a wave of whispers from the gaggling women on the mat. Stand- ing to give her his full attention, he raked a hand through his brown hair and picked up a towel he'd set on a nearby bench.

Ivy cursed under her breath. She'd love nothing more

than to turn on her heel and take the long path to the row of machines where Kara was hard at work, but that would just show Brett that she cared. And she didn't care. At least, he couldn't think she did.

She plastered a breezy smile on her face, hoping that would suffice, but oh God, no. He grinned back, wider than she expected—a smile that probably won him a lot of hearts over time. Well, not hers. She bristled, telling herself it was just a smile, and a cocky one at that, and continued on her path.

"We meet again," Brett commented as she neared the weight section.

"Briar Creek is small like that." Why hadn't she considered that Brett would have joined the gym? He hardly maintained those hard abs working in the emergency room or with mere sit-ups alone. She wondered if it was too late to revoke her shiny new membership, which was costing her more than she should be shelling out.

She gave a tight smile that she could only hope passed for polite and inched to her left in an effort to create some distance between them and that sweet smell of soap and musk and spice that had lingered on her bridesmaid dress long after their kiss was over, but Brett stopped her.

"I'm glad you're here, actually."

"Oh?" She felt the blood drain from her face as she stared up into those warm chocolate-brown eyes.

"I kind of had the impression you were mad at me last night after our talk."

She narrowed her gaze as the little bubble of hope burst inside her. The little bubble that whispered, *Maybe he's had a change of heart. Maybe he saw you walk into the gym in those yoga pants and tight tank top and thought, What a fool I've been.*

When would she stop hoping he would say what she wanted to hear? When he stopped looking like that, she decided, tearing her gaze from his perfectly sculpted chest. The very one she'd run her hands down, pressed her nails into...

"Why would I be mad at you?" she asked. "You established you weren't interested—"

His brow pinched together. "I didn't say I wasn't interested. I said I wasn't looking for a relationship right now."

She refused to allow herself to read into the first half of his statement any more than she should. He was letting her down—again—and stroking his sorry ego in the process.

She held up a hand and managed a smile. "Relax, Brett. It was just a kiss."

Only it wasn't just a kiss and they knew it. She could tell by the way he nodded slowly, as if digesting this information, reflecting on it. It had been an entire evening of laughter and flirting, small touches, and unbreakable eye contact. By the time their two bodies had finally fused, they could barely keep their hands off each other. The kiss was deep, and long, and if they hadn't been tucked in the old telephone vestibule of the Main Street B&B, they probably wouldn't have stopped.

She'd kissed enough frogs in her lifetime to know when a kiss was good. And when both people knew it.

She watched his Adam's apple roll on a swallow. "Just a kiss."

"I mean, it's not like we slept together or anything." She shuddered, thinking of how much that would have hurt. "Thank God for that!"

His gaze darkened and narrowed steadily on her. "Here I thought you were enjoying yourself that night." His voice was as smooth as melted chocolate, and just like the dessert, she stamped it out. Not allowed. Not in her world.

But his words still echoed in her head, followed quickly by red-hot anger. "Did you?" She tipped her head, hoping the flush of mortification would stay at bay. Had it been that obvious? She stiffened as she recalled the moan she'd released in his ear when his fingers had slid up her thigh . . . "Huh. Well, I don't really recall. It was so long ago." She shrugged.

He stared at her, his square jaw pulsing, and she fluttered her lashes, released a sigh that mercifully didn't shake and betray the jumping jacks that were going on inside her right now, and said a silent prayer that he couldn't possibly see through her painfully neutral expression to the sad fact that she not only recalled but had also replayed and could easily reenact every second of that kiss.

She glanced around the room, looking for an escape, for somewhere to let her eyes linger other than on that handsome face, that perfect body. She could do this. She'd pretend she didn't care. That she was cool with it. That that night was simply one distant event in what had since been a very exciting few months in her dating life.

The more she did it, the easier it would get. And considering Brett was now back in Briar Creek, she'd better hope it got easier and that next time, her heart wouldn't be racing like a Thoroughbred coming out of the gate.

"I should find Kara," she said, backing away. "I was supposed to meet her here ten minutes ago, and she's probably wondering where I am."

She took another step backward, feeling confident with her honest excuse, and felt the back of something hard hook her heel. Weightlessness hit her in slow motion as her feet came out from under her and her free fall began—until

Brett's hand was tight on her upper arm, and all at once he was yanking her up, the force so unexpected that she stumbled forward, right into his chest.

She allowed herself one long sniff of his shirt before pulling herself back from the hard wall of his torso. So much for staying cool. She'd almost smacked her head on a barbell in her hurry to get away from him.

"Are you okay?" Concern crinkled his brow, but his dark eyes positively danced.

His hand was still on her arm, and the touch spread tingles over her skin, chasing butterflies through her stomach and pulsating parts of her body that hadn't been touched in way too long, reminding her of the way he'd gripped her tight as he'd pushed her against the wall, his body so close to hers she had gasped for breath, and then lifted her leg as his hands reached under her dress...

She looked into his eyes, feeling what little willpower she was clinging to start to dissolve. On a nervous laugh, she nodded her head frantically. "Nice save, Doctor."

"It's what I do." He grinned again and dropped her arm.

She hated that the absence of his touch was so obvious, and that, based on how things were going, she'd probably never feel it again. But another girl might. Brett Hastings might not be looking for a relationship, but something told her that casual fun wasn't out of the question.

And she wasn't looking for casual fun.

It was time to get a grip. Time to start thinking with her head instead of her heart. Because from the looks of things, there was no room in Brett's heart for her. And therefore, there was no room in hers for him, either.

She turned and carefully traced a path over to Kara, who was still jogging steadily on the treadmill, watching the television propped in the corner, oblivious to everything that was taking place on the other side of the room, and climbed onto the machine next to her friend's. She punched firmly at the buttons, starting at a slow pace, and kept her gaze away from the mirror that lined the far wall.

No good would come from that. No good at all.

CHAPTER 7

Brett listened patiently to the octogenarian who had presented with chest pain as he went over everything he had eaten for lunch that day. He nodded and jotted notes on his chart and tried his damn best to avoid skirting his eyes over to the poor man's wife, who was watching her husband with barely suppressed rage as he rattled off his daily food intake.

"You're supposed to be watching your cholesterol!" she boomed when he came to the cheese fries and sloppy joe that had followed hot wings and a couple of beers. "You're going to kill yourself eating like that!"

The patient turned to her with a ferocious look. "The only thing that's going to kill me is your cookin'!" he growled.

The wife's hand flew to her heart. "My cooking!"

"Men weren't made to eat like rabbits, Ethel. I'm losing my will to live with that diet you have me on."

"That diet is supposed to save your hide!" Ethel's eyes blazed as they hooked on Brett's. "He had a quadruple bypass last summer! Do your charts mention that? This man loves nothing more than a good stick of butter, I tell you."

"I am aware of your husband's medical history, but I can

assure you, he is not having a heart attack." Not today, at least. Brett scribbled a note on his pad and tore off the sheet. "Here's the name of an over-the-counter antacid. And as much as you might not want to hear it, your wife is right. You can't eat that way anymore."

"What about my nachos?" the man grunted.

Brett handed the chart to the nurse, who was biting her lip as she unhooked the blood pressure cuff from the patient's arm, and told her to start the discharge papers. His shift was nearly halfway over and so far he'd treated a spider bite, a sprained ankle, a broken arm, and, of course, heartburn.

Oddly enough, he was more tired than ever. Without the surge of adrenaline kicking through his veins, the hours ticked by slowly, and he'd spent entirely too much time thinking of Ivy Birch and the way he'd felt when he'd caught her fall yesterday. It had taken everything in him to finally let her go, and that was only once he'd come to his senses and realized he was holding on to her well past the point of her being in danger of falling. What had started out as a knee-jerk response to help had resulted in lingering thoughts of the kiss they'd shared, the softness of her skin, the way she'd sighed into his ear, sending a surge of heat straight to his groin.

It was pointless to be thinking this way. Even if he wanted to—and maybe he did—he couldn't kiss Ivy again. Next time there wouldn't be a party to get back to, or friends just around the corner—there would be nothing holding him back from taking it further. And oh, had he wanted to take it further. He'd thought she had, too. Now…He frowned. He wasn't so sure.

Normally girls would be calling and leaving tearful voicemails after he'd given them "the talk," but Ivy had been strangely detached. She'd almost seemed confused by his need to explain. If he didn't know better, he'd almost say she was...uninterested.

It was better this way, he told himself. The last thing he needed was some girl getting all emotional on him, wanting more than he could give, and making things worse than they had to be. For both of them. It was for the best that she wasn't interested in him. One hundred percent for the best.

His jaw tensed, and he squinted at the clock, trying to clear his head.

Right. Time for another coffee.

The chief of staff met him at the vending machine as he was retrieving a stale-looking premade sandwich in a sad plastic container. "Dr. Hastings, do you have a moment?"

Brett felt his pulse skip, and he mentally tallied up everything he might have done wrong that day, coming up blank. Still, his mouth went dry as he nodded. "Sure."

"As you might be aware, each year Forest Ridge Hospital hosts a fundraiser. The proceeds go to one specific project of the board's choosing."

Brett inhaled. It was crazy, he knew, to assume the worst, to start replaying the morning, thinking of how he might have slipped, messed up. It had been happening ever since that night—even though he'd been more diligent than ever. He was shaky, off his game, and he didn't like it. Even when he was fresh on the floor, a first-year resident, he'd been confident and eager. But then, no one had died on his watch yet.

"Dr. Kessler, who usually helps oversee the planning of the event, fell over the weekend and broke her knee." The chief tutted under his breath. "Climbing a ladder to clean out her gutters. Don't get me started."

Brett popped the lid on the container and took out half of the sandwich. "I'm sorry to hear that."

"Yes, so am I. I depend on my staff to take care of themselves. Their patients do, too." He shook his head. "I was thinking you might want to stand in her place."

The stale bread lodged in his throat, and Brett pumped his fist to his chest to get it down. "Oversee the hospital fundraiser? I'm not really qualified for that sort of thing."

"Oh, you wouldn't need to do much. It's the same venue each year, and Dr. Kessler already had most of the details in order. We'd need your help spreading the word about the silent auction, and cohosting the event, with me. A few hours a week of your time at most."

Brett started to protest again, but the chief silenced him. "This year's proceeds go to the new oncology wing. With you being back in the area, you were the first person I thought of." The reason behind this didn't need to be explained, and it underscored all of Brett's trepidations about returning to Briar Creek. He didn't want to think about that time in his life, and here...he couldn't get away from it. "But if you're not interested, I understand."

Brett considered his options. There was no way he could turn down the request now, not when the only reason his mother was still alive was the very department the benefit was helping. And it wouldn't hurt his résumé, either, he thought, thinking of the position in DC he was planning on applying to this week.

"Happy to help," he said.

"Good! Excellent. One of the vendors is on her way in now to go over some plans. If you have a minute—"

A minute? Unless something that required more than a nurse's skills presented itself soon, he had all day. He had his phone and pager. And talking about a fundraiser was slightly less depressing than listening to Ethel reprimand her husband about his inhalation of fried mozzarella sticks.

"That new Dr. Hastings is so cute. When he smiles..." The nurse pushed out her lips and wiggled her hips.

"Hey, I saw him first," another woman in scrubs said as she approached the receptionist's desk. "But then, you'd have to be blind not to see a man like that."

"Oh, the sound of that voice would be music enough," the first nurse replied.

A third nurse appeared and set her files on the desk with a sense of purpose. "He doesn't have a girlfriend. Not yet anyway."

A round of giggles erupted. Ivy rolled her eyes. Honestly, to hear these women talk, you'd think Brett was Adonis or something!

She wondered what they would say if she told them that she had had the unique—well, maybe not so unique, she realized with a start—pleasure of having kissed Dr. Hastings. That his hand had grazed her breast, that his teeth had teased her earlobe. That she could tell them in vivid detail exactly what his hair smelled like (wood and spice), what his mouth tasted like (mint and scotch), and that it was probably even better than they dared to imagine.

They'd be riveted, she knew. Or more determined than ever.

And she didn't like the idea of one of them catching Brett's eye. The possibility of it depressed her.

She suddenly felt a stab of jealousy that these women had the pleasure of seeing Brett for hours on end, day after day, that they were innocent to his easy charm and loose laughter.

Then she remembered just how difficult it had been seeing Brett the past two days and told herself it was for the best. He might make good eye candy, but keeping her wits together around him was too exhausting. And deflating. It was better to keep her distance until this ridiculous crush had passed.

"Can I help you?" The receptionist, who had been happily joining in the love fest over Brett, finally noticed her standing there.

"I'm here for a meeting about the fundraiser. I'm Ivy Birch, the florist," she added.

"Oh. Certainly." The woman picked up the phone and made a quick call before setting back the receiver. "Room one twelve. Just down the hall and to your right." She smiled warmly and then quickly pivoted her chair to join in the gossip once again.

Ivy began walking in the direction she had been told. Her eyes darted to the sides, daring for a glance of Brett, but then she squared her shoulders and huffed out a breath. The emergency room was in the opposite direction—she knew from past experience—and Brett was probably hard at work saving a life at this very minute, not roaming the halls or standing around to chat with the ladies at the nursing station. If she wanted to make a good impression on Dr. Kessler, she'd have to stay focused. Too much was at stake here, given the amount of income and exposure an event like this could bring her. She was a strong, assertive businesswoman on a professional errand. Now wasn't the time to be getting all weak-kneed and starry-eyed over what was simply a good-looking man who wasn't available.

She thought of the designs she'd come up with and carried in her tote and felt her spirits lift. She could only hope

Dr. Kessler would be as happy with them as she was, but if past experience had taught her anything, it was that working with Dr. Kessler wasn't going to be any trouble at all.

She stopped outside room 112 and tapped her knuckles on the slightly open door. Poking her head in, she had opened her mouth to voice a greeting when her breath stalled in her lungs. His back was to her, but she would know that hair anywhere. She'd memorized it, staring at the back of his head in honors English both junior and senior year. The silky brown waves, the way they curled slightly at the nape of his neck. Those shoulders...

Quickly, she snatched her head back, checked the room number again, and began power-walking back to the receptionist desk. That darn girl had been so enraptured by Brett's beauty that she had clearly given Ivy the number to the exact room he was sitting in, not the room she should be going to.

"Excuse me?" a man's voice boomed down the hall, and Ivy stopped and turned.

She tipped her head at the older doctor in the business shirt, tie, and white coat who was standing with one foot outside the door she'd just fled. "Sorry. I had the wrong room. I didn't mean to interrupt."

"Are you the florist?"

She paused. "Well, yes, actually. I'm looking for Dr. Kessler."

He gave her a wan smile. "Dr. Kessler wasn't able to make it today."

"Oh." Ivy felt her shoulders slump. She'd had to ask Jane to come in an hour early so she could make this appointment. She had eight orders to fill and deliver before the end of the day, and with every minute that went by, she was falling that much further behind. "Well, thank you for letting me know."

"I'm afraid I haven't been clear. Dr. Kessler is on medical leave. She broke her knee over the weekend." He held up his hand when he heard her gasp. "She'll be fine but she needs surgery. Anyway, she won't be overseeing the fundraiser this year, but, please, come in. I'd like to go over everything."

Ivy didn't move from her place. She glanced at the open door. "Come in . . . there?"

The doctor nodded with impatience and Ivy hesitated. Finally, on a sigh, she began the short walk back to room 112, where Brett sat waiting. It was the first time she'd seen him in scrubs, looking casual and capable and irresistible all at once. Just another image she'd now have to work hard to banish.

"Ivy." Shock registered on his face, pulling his thick brows to a point over his hawklike eyes.

She gave him a casual smile. "Brett. I wondered if I'd see you here."

"You two know each other?" asked the older doctor, whose name badge read Dr. Feldman.

"Brett and I grew up together," Ivy explained before Brett had the chance to say anything that would further humiliate her. He'd already told her he didn't want to pursue things; she didn't need him reminding her of it on every occasion they happened to see each other.

"Great. Well, Dr. Hastings is taking over the fundraiser in Dr. Kessler's absence. Seeing as you're already acquainted, I'll leave you to it."

Ivy felt her mouth gape but no sound came out. She watched with a pounding heart as Dr. Feldman left the room, leaving her alone with the one person she was hoping to avoid for at least a week, or a month, or, if there was any chance of getting over this crush again, until she was happily married with a baby on the way.

She glanced at Brett. Nope. Not awkward. Not in the slightest.

"I hadn't realized you were overseeing this," she said, pulling out a chair across the table.

He ran a hand over his square jaw, and in the otherwise quiet room, she made out the crackle of stubble. "I hadn't either until five minutes ago."

Ivy unzipped her bag. The sooner she got to work, the sooner she could get out of here, away from him and this endless reminder of how foolish she'd been to think there was any hope of a future with this man.

"Well, I have a few examples for the centerpieces. I can change the scale for bar tables or—"

"I don't care what the flowers look like."

Ivy stilled. She thought of the hours she'd put into making her presentation just right. The consideration she'd put into the color scheme, careful to include the right touch of elegance, set the right tone for the audience. Some of the neighboring towns' most successful businesspeople and benefactors would be in attendance. It was her chance to shine.

"Still, you should give me your opinion." This wasn't going to be all on her if she got it wrong. Dr. Kessler would have had something to say about the options, and she would have been happy to hear it. Ignoring his protests, she reached into her bag and pulled out the folder full of designs and photographs from previous events.

She slid them across the table to Brett, who studied them with a bored expression and then shrugged.

"Whatever you think is best. Do you think we even need flowers?"

Ivy managed not to roll her eyes. "It's a black-tie affair. Yes."

"What about candles instead?"

Wait? Was he trying to push her out of the job? Or just cut costs? She stared at him, trying to judge his position. "We could do candles, too," she said carefully.

Brett made a face as he leaned back in his chair. "I don't really like flowers."

Ivy blinked. "I'm sorry; did I just hear you say that you don't like flowers? Who doesn't like flowers?"

Brett jutted his lower lip. "I don't."

Ivy's shoulders sagged as she continued to stare at him, incredulous. "I just... I mean... flowers. What's not to like?"

A shadow crossed his face. "You wouldn't understand."

She resented that assumption. She may look like someone who'd enjoyed the simple pleasures of small-town life, but she knew all about the dark underbelly, and something in Brett's tone told her that, like herself, he had a few demons. "Try me."

Brett dragged out a sigh and tented his fingers on the table as he leaned forward. "When you see flowers, you see something pretty. Something cheerful and uplifting. Am I right?"

She widened her eyes. As if that much wasn't obvious. "Yes."

"Well, when I see flowers, I see something else. They, well... I guess you could say they feel like a bad omen."

"You must see plenty of flowers around the hospital," Ivy considered. She personally delivered several bouquets here a week, never to the actual patients, but to the front desk.

"Exactly." Brett's tone was firm, and there was an edge of something she couldn't quite place. Sadness, she realized. Of course. She hadn't stopped to consider what he must see every day in his job.

Still... "So you're telling me you've never sent a girl flowers?"

A knowing smile played on his lips. "Well, I never said that..."

Ivy's eyes narrowed. She shouldn't have asked if she didn't want to hear the answer. And she shouldn't be feeling jealous over the thought of some woman she would never know receiving flowers from Brett. Would she really want flowers from a man who had no intention of investing in her?

She stole a glance at that square jaw and the perfect slope of his nose and realized, sadly, she just might.

But then she would be right back here again. Right back here without a hope or a prayer of him actually caring about her on a deeper level.

"Well, I'm not here to discuss your seduction tactics," she huffed, gathering her folder. "Do I have the job or not?"

He looked startled. "Excuse me?"

She stood, shoving the folder back into her bag. "Do you want me to do the flowers or not?" He liked to tell it straight, and she didn't have time to sit around, hinging on his whims anymore.

He was his feet now, too, towering a good six inches above her, and even from across the table she could see the laugh lines around his eyes, the squint of confusion as he stumbled on his words. At first glance, they looked like such kind eyes. Sincere and warm, with just the right amount of depth. Except Brett wasn't looking for anything deep, was he?

And she wasn't looking for anything surface level.

Brett had nothing to offer her in this moment. Except this job.

"If you think flowers are really needed—"

"I do." For the love of God! She opened her eyes wider, lest she roll them in front of him. The man might be able to charm a woman with a flash of that smile, but he had a lot to learn when it came to appealing to female sensibilities. What was he going to tell her next, that he didn't like chocolate?

"Then great. Thanks for the help. I know where to find you if I have any questions."

"Considering I live and work on Main Street, I'm easy to find." She stiffened, hoping he didn't take that as an invitation, which it most certainly was not.

"Good. Don't be surprised if I call on you then." His eyes roamed over her, as a slow grin curved his lips, and he held out his hand.

Ivy eyed it steadily, dreading the thought of his touch as much as she craved it, and set her fingers in his palm, fighting against the warm current that traveled straight to her stomach and rolled down deeper, lower and lower, until—

She snatched it back. "Excellent." Ivy forced one of the smiles she gave to her most tiresome customers and excused herself before her emotions got the better of her. Her heart pounded with each step she took back to the parking garage. It would have been so easy to hand the job over to someone else, let some other florist take over the party, let some other woman interact with the hospital's newest heartthrob.

But she had a loan to pay off and a business to think about, and if Brett was going to be living in Briar Creek again, she'd just have to learn to live with him. And without him.

CHAPTER 8

Kara took her time walking down Main Street on Tuesday afternoon, slowing her pace as Rosemary and Thyme grew closer. She knew there was nothing to be nervous about, really. After all, people gave their notice all the time, especially in the restaurant business. No one really expected you to stay in one place forever, did they?

Well, maybe they did, came the nagging thought. Especially when, by all accounts, she was working for a family business.

But no, no, there were many businesses in town connected to her family. The bookstore, for example, now that Grace was her sister-in-law, and of course the dance studio her mother ran. She pursed her lips at the thought. Luckily her mother had Jane Madison to help with that, otherwise she'd be on Kara's back about more than her nonexistent love life.

She wanted to say to her mother, *Who has time for a love life when their actual life is a complete mess?* In addition to there being pretty much no interesting prospects in the entire town, she had far too much else on her mind to worry about than landing a man. She needed to feel good about herself for once, do something just for herself, and see what would come of it.

And it started with giving her notice. Letting down the people she cared most about. Putting her own needs first. But was it selfish? She didn't think so. Not really.

Oh God. Rosemary and Thyme was only a block away now. She eyed a shady bench greedily, wondering if she could just drop onto it and bide her time for a bit, but obviously that wouldn't change anything. She was giving her notice today. Whether it was in five minutes or twenty, it was happening.

She hurried the last block while she still had her nerve and walked around to the back door, as the front door didn't open until she officially turned the lock at five sharp, just in time for happy hour. The front of house might be dark at this time of day, but the kitchen was loud and alive, with smells filling the warm air, music blaring, and pots banging.

Kara stared longingly at the pastry station, where Anna and her sous chef were rolling out dough. Not so long ago, that used to be her alongside Anna, making chocolate croissants and their famous scones for the café. Now the offerings were a little more refined: French tarts with a smooth pastry cream and fresh berries, rich chocolate pot de crème, and a flight of petit fours that were almost too pretty to eat. And too intricate for her limited experience.

A little pang reminded Kara of what she needed to do. There was no room for her. Not in this kitchen. Not with what she had to offer. She couldn't pipe a perfect rose. She was hardly able to spin sugar.

But she could bake cookies. She had suspected it, and Grace and Ivy had confirmed it.

Anna brightened when she noticed Kara across the room

and called her over. Shoulders sinking, Kara walked over to the pastry area. "Is now a good time?" *Please say yes*, she begged.

Anna wiped her hands on her apron and untied the strings. "Absolutely. Let's go into the office," she said, grinning.

Kara waited until the door was closed behind them to take a seat across from the desk covered with papers, recipes torn from magazines, and a stack of invoices marked with a yellow highlighter.

"This paperwork!" Anna frowned as she rifled through the top of the stack and set it to the side of the desk. "There are many things I love about having my own restaurant, but the business side of things has never been at the top of my list."

Kara managed a benign smile, but her heart was doing jumping jacks and she was already forgetting her well-rehearsed speech. *Just spit it out already!*

"Thanks for taking the time to meet with me," she began. She hesitated, knowing what part came next, and cleared her throat. "I know how busy things are around here."

"You know you never need to apologize to me! I'm the one who feels bad for not being able to break away the other day." Anna's smile turned mysterious as she wiggled her eyebrows. "I wanted to talk with you, too, actually."

"Oh?" Kara gritted her teeth together. Things were already getting derailed, and if she didn't say what she'd come to say soon, she wasn't sure she ever would.

"I've been thinking lately that you might be better doing something else. Don't get me wrong, you're a great hostess, but it might be time to grow here, since you're one of our most valued employees."

Kara stared at her friend with wide eyes, barely able to suppress the glee she felt bubble within her. So Anna had recognized it; she'd maybe tasted that cookie last week, come to her senses, realized that Kara should be helping in the kitchen, learning on the job instead of answering phones and walking people to their tables.

"I...couldn't agree more," she gushed. "I mean, I like interacting with the customers and everything, but—"

"But you're ready for more," Anna finished.

Kara felt her shoulders relax. "Exactly."

Anna grinned. "How does the position of office assistant sound to you?"

"Office assistant?" The words squeaked out of her.

Anna nodded eagerly. "Mark and I need someone we can trust to handle the paperwork and bills, someone we can lean on to take care of the business side of things. You were the first person I thought of for the job."

Kara stared at her friend in bewilderment. Anna could barely mask her excitement and Kara could hardly match it. Her friend thought she was doing something wonderful. What could Kara say to that?

Maybe Grace and Ivy had just been polite. Maybe she had overestimated her baking skills. Maybe she should face reality and take the new position. Even if it wasn't what she wanted for herself.

"So...what do you say?"

Anna was looking at her expectantly, and Kara's mind muddled with confusion, and all the confidence and energy she'd felt last week at the bookstore vanished. Who was she kidding? So she liked baking cookies and thought they tasted good. Lots of people could bake cookies. Cookies they provided for bake sales or tucked in their kids' lunchboxes.

It was one thing to be able to make a decent cookie. It was another to make one good enough to warrant commercial value.

It was bad enough that at her age, she'd flitted from one job to another. But turning a hobby into a glorified business… What had she been thinking?

Kara felt her heart begin to break a little. And because now her speech seemed moot—downright silly and immature, really—and the thought of announcing to Anna that she was instead going to start her own cookie company made her cheeks warm with embarrassment, she forced a smile she didn't feel and, with a pain in her chest, muttered, "Sounds wonderful."

Kara was standing at the hostess stand when Ivy opened the door to Rosemary and Thyme, balancing a bundle of sunflowers in her arms.

"Everything okay?" she asked, noticing the knit of Kara's brow. "Let me guess, your mother is playing matchmaker again?"

Kara's smile seemed a little forced. "I've managed to avoid her for a few days. She's probably scheming something, though, just when she thinks I'm not on to her."

"Well, I'm sorry I'm late with these. The shop was buried with orders today. I'll swap these out right away."

"Oh, I already emptied out the vases for you and added fresh water," Kara said.

Ivy looked at the two large vases anchoring each end of the bar. "So you did. No wonder Anna keeps you around."

Kara didn't laugh at the joke, and Ivy hesitated for a moment. "You sure everything is okay?"

"Of course. In fact, I got a promotion today." Kara's

tone was bright, but Ivy swore her eyes were glistening with something other than pure joy.

"Congratulations! What are you going to be doing?"

"Office assistant." Kara looked at her hands. "So, uh, once they find a new hostess you won't be seeing me as much around here. I'll be in the back office. Doing paperwork, that sort of thing."

It didn't seem like the kind of position Kara would be especially interested in, but then Kara had never been very focused on one exact thing. She'd worked at the stationery store, the old café, of course, the diner, and a handful of other shops that Ivy couldn't list offhand. "Well, an office assistant sounds like a big step up. A real...professional job." And it was. It was the most stable job Kara had ever taken, Ivy considered. If not possibly the most boring.

It was a reminder that they were all getting a little older. That it was time to buckle down, settle for the straight and narrow. So Kara wanted a nice stable job with decent pay. Good for her.

"It was nice of Anna to think of me for the position. She said I was the first person she thought of. She mentioned that now she might be able to finally nail down a wedding date, thanks to my help with the business." Kara frowned again, and her bottom lip seemed to wobble.

Okay, now something was definitely wrong. Ivy reached out and set her hand on Kara's wrist, but her friend jerked her head up at that moment, smiling at the customer who had just walked through the door.

Ivy turned, annoyed at the interruption, and locked eyes with none other than Brett. His brown eyes sharpened on her, but a hint of a smile slowly curved his lips. Butterflies that had finally quieted a few hours ago burst to life once again and danced wildly through her stomach.

Well, that sealed it. Tomorrow. An online profile. With her name on it.

"I should finish these arrangements before things get too busy," she said to Kara, and strolled over to the bar, hoping that her butt looked halfway decent in these jeans...just in case Brett was watching, which she was sure he was not. She could feel him behind her, hear the murmur of his deep voice as he said something to Kara that made her laugh, and somehow, just knowing he was in the room made her heart beat a little faster.

This was not good. As her self-help books so clearly explained, if a man was interested in you, he would find a way to have you, and Brett had done no such thing, which meant that she really needed to stop her body from going all crazy on her every time she saw him.

It's just lust, she reminded herself firmly. *Is That Your Body Talking, or Your Head? The Mindful Approach to Finding Lasting Love* had detailed the warning signs, and they were all there: rapid pulse, stomachaches, an inability to stop staring, all while knowing, deep down, that he was no good or at the very least all wrong for her. She was attracted to him, that was all. It was a human, primal reaction. She just needed to find someone else to lust after. Someone who could top those deep-set eyes, that strong, straight nose, that squared jaw that framed those perfect lips...

She might need to move to Hollywood.

Ivy jammed the stems into the large ceramic vase, letting them fall whichever way nature decided, and then, because unlike some, she genuinely liked flowers, fluffed them out a bit to make sure they were symmetrical from every view.

Gathering up the remaining half of her bundle, she turned to start on the next vase, when she slammed right into something rock hard. And warm. Sweet musk and spicy soap filled her senses, and she looked up into the twinkling eyes of Brett.

"Hey." His voice was hoarse and scratchy and oh so sinful, enough to conjure up images of fresh mornings and slow grins and—*Pipe dreams*!

"Hey." Cool on the outside but hot as fire on the inside, she flashed him a small smile and scooted past him to the other end of the bar, where she took her time filling the second vase, carefully placing one flower at a time. After she finished this arrangement, her hands would be empty; she'd have no more excuse to keep her back to him, and if he didn't turn and leave first, she'd probably have to say something to him again. And she didn't want to. She'd said all she needed to say to Brett. And he'd said more than enough to her, thank you very much.

"Hey, Ivy."

Oh God, he was talking to her.

She closed her eyes, reminded herself that he was, beneath that handsome façade, a pigheaded jerk, and turned to catch that lopsided grin from where he now sat at the bar. Damn. Yep, still cute all right.

"Yes?" She tipped her head, reminding herself of the calls that never came, the conversation at Jane's house, the cocky stride that made women swoon.

But his smile broadened, and her heart turned over when he said, "Have time for a drink?"

CHAPTER 9

What the hell was he doing? He'd told himself to stay away from her. To let her be. To stop noticing that little lift of her nose and the funny way she pinched her full, rosy lips when he was talking.

But then she had to be here…in his brother's restaurant. In jeans that showed off those smooth, long legs and that sleeveless shirt that dipped low enough in the front for him to make out a hint of cleavage and crave a better view. He didn't want to let her out of his sight. Not yet. And thanks to the fundraiser, he didn't have to.

"Come on," he said, tossing her a grin and pulling out the bar stool next to his. "First round's on me. I'm gonna owe you one by the end of tonight anyway."

Her gaze narrowed in suspicion. "Why's that?"

He gave the seat a pat. "Saddle up and I'll explain."

She hesitated, but only briefly, and then slid onto the chair next to his. God, she smelled as sweet as she looked. Honey and vanilla and something deeper, something fresher. The kind of perfume that didn't come in a bottle but no doubt came from the very air she breathed. He swore he hated the smell of flowers. The cold, visual reminder that things were dire, that people were helpless, and since there was nothing they could do, they did the one thing they could. Sent a bunch of brightly colored petals in place of a real solution.

He wanted to pull away, but something about her warmth, her nearness, and the little flick of her rich auburn hair over her shoulder made it impossible.

The bartender came over to them and cocked an eyebrow. Brett turned to Ivy. "What'll it be?"

"A club soda," she told the man behind the counter. She was doing her finest not to look his way, and the more she resisted, the more he was determined to get her attention.

"Aw, come on. I offered you a drink; don't be shy."

Her cheeks flushed, spreading a rash of pink down her neck. All at once Brett remembered and felt like the ass she clearly thought him to be. Of course. Her mother.

"A club soda for the lady, and I'll have whatever beer you have on tap." He waited until the bartender had moved away to turn to Ivy. "Sorry about that."

"It's okay. I don't like to drink much."

Brett nodded. He knew that Ivy's mother had passed away last summer—and that not long afterward Henry had returned to town. He could still remember the passing comments Ivy's twin made back in high school, how he couldn't wait to get out of Briar Creek, couldn't wait to put this life behind him. That made two of them, Brett thought. But then Henry had gone and moved back to town, settled down with Jane Madison, and was now living in that cute little house and hosting bar-beques for his friends. The American dream, Brett supposed.

And what was Brett doing? Saving lives, he'd once thought.

Or maybe losing them.

The bartender brought them their drinks, and Brett felt happy not to be on call. He needed something to take the edge off, something to banish the dark images that were fast encroaching. It would be another sleepless night—he'd learned to spot them. Another night plagued with guilt that bounced around, never leaving him. Guilt about his mother. His patient. The family who had lost a husband, father, brother . . . because of him.

He needed to distract himself. Have a few drinks. Have a few laughs.

He eyed Ivy, letting his gaze drift to the swell of her breasts and back up to the curves of her profile, his gut tightening.

Normally he'd say have a good time. There were plenty of women up for that sort of thing, happy to go out, enjoy a nice dinner, some light conversation, and spend the night. They knew where he stood, and even if they were disappointed that things didn't lead to more—and, admittedly, they usually were—he made no promises.

But Ivy wasn't one of those girls. And he didn't want her to be. He took a long slow sip of his beer, letting the foam roll back on his throat.

"That's a local draft, you know." Ivy was looking at him pointedly, that cute little pinch on her lips again.

He held up the glass, perplexed. "I'm surprised you know that since—"

"Since I don't drink?" She shrugged. "I learned more than I should about these things growing up."

Brett nodded. He'd always been closer to Henry grow-ing up—they were both on the quiet side, both spent more time in the library than some of the other guys their age. Both seemed to be hiding out, seeking something in the peace and solitude of their studies or a good book. It helped, even then, for Brett to fill his mind with science, innovations, new concepts, than to think about his dad leaving, or later, his mom getting sick. Everyone, it seemed, was leaving him. Nothing was certain. But proven theories, facts...those were things he could count on, things he could build his life on.

Unlike Ivy, her twin had been tight-lipped about their home life. Ashamed, perhaps. But Ivy didn't seem to share the same feelings.

"Small-town life can be difficult," he said.

"Is that why you stayed away for so long then?"

Brett rubbed a hand over his jaw. "I like city life. I like the more challenging cases you find in an urban environment and a major hospital." There were personal reasons, too, but he didn't need to get into that.

"Then why move back?" she inquired.

He reached for his glass as he thought of an excuse. "I thought I'd change up the pace for a bit. Don't want to burn out too young." He shrugged, realizing how much truth was in the statement, the fear he had that he'd done just that: burned out. He'd sworn he hadn't, insisted he was fine, that he just needed to work, stay working, work harder than ever. But what he really needed was a break. Even if he wasn't enjoying it, and even if he worried what it was costing him, the reality of what could happen if he didn't take a step back now was devastating.

His boss had been patient, let him stay on until he'd found something else, suggested he go home for a bit, to the sleepy town he'd grown up in. But he'd also put him on the easier cases or put another doctor in the room with him when it was something more severe, just in case his nerves caught up with him, just in case he slipped...

He cleared his throat, hoping to shift the conversation back to her. "Do you ever plan on getting out of town?"

"Nope." The swiftness of her answer surprised him and sent a pang of something he'd almost call jealousy straight to his chest. When was the last time he'd be so sure of something? "I love Briar Creek. It's my home."

Brett nodded slowly. "So...it doesn't bother you that you could probably name just about half the people in this town?"

"Half?" Her scoff was good-natured, and her eyes sparked. "Try three-quarters. I could probably tell you their birthdays, too." She swiveled in her chair, and her thigh brushed his, sending a surge of heat straight to his belly. He waited to see if she'd realize and pull back, but instead she stayed put, taunting him with her nearness, the reminder of her touch, the temptation of those thighs, so close, he could reach out and touch her. He shifted slightly, feeling her leg slide along his, and tensed against his growing arousal.

"Oh, right. Flowers." He reached for his drink.

"Is that what you wanted to talk about?" She looked at him expectantly, and Brett blinked, almost forgetting the reason he'd given her for joining him for a drink. It was too easy to get caught up in the gentle ring of her laugh, the slip of her smile, the way she kept tucking her hair behind the ear he'd had the pleasure of grazing between his teeth.

A steady need stirred deep in his groin and he shifted his gaze, getting back to the point of the conversation while he waited for Mark to finish up in the kitchen. "I was actually wondering if you could recommend a good caterer."

She looked at him like he was half crazy. God, it was a cute look. Her eyebrows pinched, her head tipped, her mouth quirked. He swallowed hard.

"Why not ask your brother? Isn't that why you're here?"

He laughed with her. It felt good. Easy, natural, and right. Too right. It was the history, he told himself, the comfort that comes from being with people you've known all your life, even if he'd never really noticed her most of that time. As a boy, he was already buried in a book. As a teenager, when most of the other guys were hitting on girls or pumping themselves up for the courage to ask one on a date, he was sitting in a sterile hospital. And as an adult, well, he noticed them, but that didn't mean he had time for them.

"Can you tell I'm used to treating patients and not planning parties?" He grinned and was relieved when she smiled back. So she didn't hate him. But that didn't mean she liked him, either. And he couldn't remember the last time a girl hadn't liked him. "I actually just stopped in to pay my brother a visit. I hadn't even considered that he'd offer to cater with how busy he is here."

"I'm sure Mark will help," she said. "Dr. Kessler told me this year's proceeds go toward the oncology department. That must mean a lot to your family."

Sobered, he turned sharply from her and took another sip of his drink. "It does. It also made it damn near impossible for me to turn down the request." He slanted her a glance, giving a sheepish smile that he hoped would keep things light.

"I wish my interest were as noble as yours," Ivy admitted on a sigh. "But I'm afraid it's a plain and simple business move for me."

"No ulterior motives?" He winked, but the way her eyes darkened and her face blanched made him realize he'd upset her somehow.

Her easy smile was all at once replaced by that prim pinch, and she began fumbling through her oversized bag, the contents of which seemed to include everything from fruit snacks to piles of receipts. "As I said, strictly business. And on that note, I really should be getting back to the shop." She slid off her bar stool, her jeans pulling tight at her long legs.

Okay, so he'd offended her. He seemed to be good at that. "Wait. Sit down. You haven't even finished your . . . water."

She locked his gaze for a split second, and he could see her waver, see her eyes soften and the set of her jaw loosen into something that could almost pass for a smile.

Her wallet was tight in her grip, and after a clear hesitation, she set it back in the bag. "It's club soda, actually, but I may as well finish it." She inched past him, using the bar to leverage herself onto the stool, a little farther from him this time.

"Okay, look, I can tell you're still mad at me about . . ." He lowered his head and whispered, "*You know.*"

Her eyes were sharp on his. Flat. And bored. And entirely unimpressed. "No, I don't, actually, because I can think of about ten different things to be mad at you about right now."

He sputtered on the sip of his drink. "*Ten?*"

"Yes, ten. Maybe eleven, but at least ten." She sniffed and hugged her handbag tighter in her lap as she stared at the mirrored backsplash behind the bar. He stared at her profile, the slight upturn of her nose, the purse of that mouth, his own jaw slack.

"Are you going to enlighten me?"

She slid him a glance from the corner of her eye. "Aren't doctors supposed to be smart?"

So now she was insulting his intelligence. But considering he had no clue what he'd done to so massively piss her off, other than the obvious disappointment, he supposed he deserved it.

"I shouldn't have said that," she added quickly. "You are smart. But for someone so smart, you are awfully stupid when it comes to women." She gave him a pitying look and shook her head on a little sigh.

Brett blinked, unable to even find words to match the emotions that were stirring within him. Confusion. Annoyance. Frustration. Maybe she was right. Maybe he didn't know much about women.

But one thing he did know was that Ivy Birch was like no other girl he'd met before. Usually one kiss was all it took for a woman to be sending him texts, suggesting drinks, or hanging around the break room or hospital lobby, hoping for a chance to talk. But Ivy was doing none of those things, and the few times he had seen her since letting her down, she'd seemed more annoyed than disappointed.

This was new territory. And one he couldn't resist exploring.

Ivy didn't know what had come over her. She took another sip of her soda, just to make sure the bartender hadn't accidentally given her something stronger, like, say, a tumbler of vodka on the rocks. But nope, tasted just like the same boring club soda she drank at every function, except this one was missing a much-needed wedge of lime.

Beside her, Brett ran his hand through his hair, tousling it in a mess of directions and succeeding in making himself look even more adorable than he had two minutes ago, if such a thing were even possible.

Her heart did that little dance it was hell-bent on doing every time she saw that face, but her head replayed his words, over and over. The insinuation that maybe she wasn't doing the fundraiser for a professional reason or even out of charity, but out of something so much worse.

The egomaniac thought she was doing it to get close to him.

And it didn't matter that his nut-brown hair conjured up all sorts of images of what he must look like when he rolled out of bed in the morning, or that his deep-set eyes were a notch wider than usual and more earnest looking, too, or that his mouth…*Oh, that mouth.* No, none of it mattered. Because a man could be handsome off good looks alone, but a man couldn't be attractive without personality to back it up.

"Forget I said anything," she said, wishing she'd never said anything at all. She knew the type. The inflated egos that came with good looks and female attention. Engaging would just stoke that fire.

"But now I'm curious," Brett insisted.

She drained her club soda, plucked a five-dollar bill from her wallet, and set it on the bar.

"I invited you for a drink." His voice was low and smooth, and she could listen to it all day long. And all night. And that was just the problem.

"And then I went and insulted you. Consider us even." She started to get off the bar stool again, but he reached out and grabbed her wrist. His hand was warm, his grip firm, and she knew she wasn't going anywhere. As much as she'd love to snap free of his hold on her, another part of her wanted him to never let go. Her stomach fluttered and tightened, and she fought against it, willing herself to fight the attraction, to stay focused on the facts.

Brett tipped his chin. His expression had turned serious, almost grave. "I think we've established that you aren't interested in me."

Actually, it was more like the other way around, but Ivy listened.

His thumb grazed her skin before he dropped her hand, just long enough to send a tingle down her spine and straight to her belly. His mouth quirked into a small smile as he tented his fingers. "But I'm hoping we can still work together on this fundraiser."

"Of course. I already told you I would do the flowers, and I appreciate the opportunity." And she needed the opportunity, too, she reminded herself, thinking of the stack of bills waiting to be paid, the money that had never come from the sale of her mother's house, the fact that in addition to helping her out, Henry had covered the cost of fixing up the old place, only to have it sell for far less than he alone had sunk into it. *Simmer down now, Ivy. The man may have rejected you on a personal level, but you don't need it messing with your professional life, too.*

Brett was still watching her, his entire body shifted on the chair now, his focus so intense that she had to shift her eyes away for a second to collect herself.

"We'll keep in touch then," Ivy said, eager to get away. Quickly she added, "About the event."

Brett's brow furrowed slightly. "Here. Let me give you my number." He held out a hand, and, blinking, Ivy reached into her bag and handed him her phone.

She watched as he tapped the screen with his thumbs and then handed it back to her.

She had Brett Hastings's number in her phone. *Now don't get all crazy, Ivy. It's just for the fundraiser. It's nothing personal.*

Except something about the way his hand lingered on hers and his eyes locked on hers with intensity made her wonder if it wasn't just a little personal.

Nonsense. He'd told her straight up where he stood. He

wasn't interested. And that was just something she'd have to live with.

"Great," she said, tucking the device in her handbag right next to her insulin shots. Just great.

Because just what she needed, in addition to having to see him around town and now suffer through this event, was the image of his name lighting up her screen, giving her hope where none belonged.

CHAPTER 10

The gym offered a weekly Pilates class that Ivy decided was probably a better fit for both her physical and mental health than hitting the treadmill. Regular exercise was an important part of managing her diabetes, but she wasn't exactly sitting idle all day long at the store, and intense workouts could wreak havoc on her blood sugar levels—and watching Brett lift weights wreaked havoc on her heart. According to *Crushed: A Ten-Step Program to Accepting Rejection and Putting Your Life Back Together*, a scheduled class with her close friend, conveniently located nowhere near the main cardio and weight room so that she wouldn't be tempted by that cocky grin or confident swagger, was just the thing she needed to focus on herself... and not on those deep-set brown eyes and the rumble of that laugh.

"Did you start your new position yet?" she asked Kara as they settled onto their mats. A week had passed since Kara had announced her promotion, and nothing more had been said on the matter since.

Kara nodded. "This morning."

"How was it?" Ivy asked when Kara didn't elaborate.

Kara pulled her long dark hair into a ponytail and shrugged. "Oh. Fine, fine."

Didn't sound very fine, but Ivy decided not to press the topic. The instructor had taken her place at the front of the room, and Ivy had a feeling she was going to need all the help she could get to keep up with Kara, who had trained as a dancer under her mother's instruction and then went on to do regular yoga and Pilates in recent years.

At the end of the session, Kara turned to her, cheeks flushed, and grinning. "Fun, huh?"

"It was." Ivy rolled up her mat and followed her friend to the door. Her plan was to dart into the women's locker room and take the back exit home, but Kara stopped in the hall, tipping her head in the opposite direction.

"Let's go to the juice bar."

Ivy wrestled with her decision. After working out for forty-five minutes, a smoothie sounded delicious, not to mention good for her, but the chances of seeing Brett were high—she stopped herself right there. This was her town, too, and unless she wanted to live her life in hiding, she was going to have to start getting used to seeing him around. The more she did it, the less of an impact it would have on her. Hopefully.

Forcing back her trepidation, she said, "Sure."

The juice bar was busy, even at nearly nine in the evening, but there was no sign of Brett. Ivy started to relax as she collected her drink and took a seat in the corner of the room.

"I have to admit, when they first opened this place, I was hoping it would be a chance to meet some guys." Kara pursed her lips. "But instead, it's just the usual crowd."

Ivy looked around. Kara was right. She recognized every

single person in the room, even if she didn't personally know them. "Maybe someone new will move to town," she offered, even though she doubted that very much. Briar Creek wasn't exactly a destination point, unless you were a tourist look-ing for a country weekend getaway. The ski resorts were close, and she'd met a few guys there in the past, like the ski instructor she'd thought had long-term potential but who turned out to be casually dating half the other ski instructors and some of his adult students to boot.

"The only new face around here is Brett's," Kara said, and Ivy's heart began to beat a little faster. She took a sip of her drink to distract herself. "Still, I'm happy I joined. It gives me something to do, and it takes the pressure off join-ing one of those adult dance classes my mom is now offer-ing." She rolled her eyes and chuckled under her breath.

Jane had told Ivy all about the adult classes and the book club group in their neon leg warmers, squabbling over the music selection. It had been Henry's idea to start those classes back when enrollment at the studio hit a rough patch, and now that things had picked up again, Jane was never going to let Henry forget it. Deep down, Ivy knew that Jane was pleased, though. She loved teaching dance, just like Ivy loved making beautiful bouquets. It worked out well for both of them, too. Now that Ivy was feeling better, she didn't need as much help around the shop, and Jane had enough hours between the dance studio and the bookstore café to keep her busy.

She wondered, as she often did these days when she spent time with Kara, what her friend might really enjoy doing.

"I take it that working at the dance studio doesn't appeal to you."

Kara's mouth dropped. "Are you kidding me? I can think

of nothing worse! My mother had me in every show until I was old enough to put my foot down and refuse. I still break into a cold sweat when I see blue eye shadow and frosted pink lipstick."

"Gotta love the eighties," Ivy mused, though she had never had the opportunity to take a dance class. She'd envied the other little girls in their sparkly tutus and makeup, and she'd made doll clothes for her sole doll with any bits of shiny fabric she could find, hoping to re-create the event she was missing. Dance lessons were expensive, and besides, there was no one to drive her. Her mother was usually at the bars by seven, if she even came home from the various jobs she had at all. Dinner was cereal; bedtime was of their own choosing. Somehow they'd figured it out. Gotten to school on time every day with a packed lunch, even if it was a little lacking.

Ivy took another small sip of her drink. It was cool and sweet and creamy. And rare. She'd make sure to enjoy it.

Kara, on the other hand, took a long, casual sip of her smoothie as if it were nothing more special than ice water. "My days at that studio are behind me." She played with her straw. "It's not where my interest lies."

"You'd rather be working at the restaurant," Ivy hedged.

Kara glanced around the room. "I'd rather be in the kitchen of the restaurant, actually."

Ivy perked up. "Then why don't you?"

"Because I'm not a chef," Kara said, her shoulders visibly sagging. "Once Anna joined up with Mark and opened Rosemary and Thyme, they hired a whole team of sous chefs. The menu is much more complicated, too. I'm not qualified for that sort of thing."

She had a point, Ivy supposed, but it still made her sad to hear it. "Grace said your cookies were better than Anna's.

They were really delicious." They were—not that she'd be eating one again. "Has Anna tried them? You should get her opinion."

"I gave her a box of my cookies as a thank-you gift... for the promotion. And she never said a word. If she thought they were any good, she would have said something." She shook her head. "I guess I was just kidding myself thinking that..."

"Thinking what?"

"Never mind. It doesn't matter now. I have a promotion. I'm helping Anna and Mark. How can I not be happy about that?" Kara's smile was grim.

"Don't give up on your dreams," Ivy encouraged as they finished their drinks and tossed their plastic cups.

Kara looked her square in the eye. "Face it, Ivy. Some things aren't meant to be, no matter how much we wish they were."

The girls walked outside a little quieter than when they'd come in. It had grown dark in the time that had lapsed, and Main Street was empty. Most people were home, enjoying a summer night with their family, Ivy supposed.

Kara's words echoed in her mind. Maybe that type of life just wasn't in the cards for her.

A burst of fury bubbled within her. Since when was she giving up or standing by and watching Kara do the same? She'd been a fighter all her life—she'd had no other choice. She and Henry had been born hustling and scrambling. It was their only chance. And the only reason she had Petals on Main was because she fought to make it happen. And she still fought for it every day.

"I have an idea for your cookies," she said firmly.

She expected Kara to match her enthusiasm, but instead

she just groaned and lazily turned to face her. "There's no point, Ivy. They're nothing special."

"But they *are* special," Ivy insisted.

Kara thought about it as they crossed the street. "Okay, I'm curious. What's your idea?"

"Forest Ridge Hospital's annual fundraiser is coming up. I'm doing the flowers this year, and Brett is helping out, too." Just saying his name! She checked herself, focused on her friend. "Why not make some cookies for the silent auction, or even see if they'll work for the dessert buffet?"

"Cookies? At a black-tie event?" Kara didn't look convinced.

"Hey, you have to start somewhere, and this kind of exposure doesn't present itself all the time."

Kara took a deep breath. "I guess it wouldn't hurt to ask." She bit her lip, fighting a smile. "Okay, ask him for me."

Ivy felt her blood go cold. "Ask him for you?"

"Brett. Could you ask him for me?"

"But you're his cousin!" Ivy cried.

"So? Mark is his brother! My boss! I don't even know how to bring it up! But maybe if you mentioned you'd had my cookies, and they were really good…" She stopped walking. "Oh, please, Ivy. He likes you."

No, actually, he didn't like her. Not in the way she'd once wanted him to, at least.

Ivy stared into the pleading eyes of her friend, kicking herself for even bringing it up. She shouldn't have said anything. Should have let Kara figure it out for herself.

But she wasn't that kind of friend.

"Oh. Fine." She sighed, feeling it roll through her shoulders.

"Great, let's call him now."

Her eyes sprang open. She'd been planning to mention it next time she talked to him about the flowers, in a real meeting, of a professional nature. But to call him...Her heart began to race and despite the cool evening air, she felt hot and clammy.

Kara moved to a bench under the glow of a lamppost. "I have his number—"

"I have his number," Ivy said. Gritting her teeth, she reached into her bag and pulled out the phone. Sure enough, there in her contacts list was Brett's name.

Kara rubbed her hands together nervously as, with a pounding heart, Ivy tapped Brett's number and put the phone to her ear. Her stomach churned with dread as the first ring went through. She didn't know what she would do if he answered.

Her breath was heavy, and she moved the receiver slightly lest he catch her panting on the other end when he answered. Instead, the call went to voicemail. So, perhaps there was a God after all.

"Hey, Brett, it's Ivy. Um, Ivy Birch." She cleared her throat, her mind going blank. In front of her, Kara was clenching two fists to her mouth, her big blue eyes watching her. "I'm here with Kara and we had an idea for the dessert buffet at the fundraiser. So um..." Blank. It was all blank. What next?

Suddenly it came to her: She should tell him to call Kara.

But before she could say just that, Kara whispered frantically, "Tell him to call you back."

"So call me back."

Oh crap, what had she done? She'd just told the man who was hell-bent on telling her that he wasn't interested in her to call her back. It's just what he wanted. Just what he expected, she was sure. To find some lame excuse to have the guy who rejected you still interact with you.

Ivy disconnected the call with a shaking hand.

Now she had the pleasure of waiting for Brett to call her back. And no doubt he'd be assuming that she'd found a reason to call him just to hear his voice.

Brett walked into the break room and pulled open the fridge, grinning to himself at the carefully labeled items that lined its shelves. Forest Ridge Hospital might be a far cry from what he was used to in Baltimore, but some things were consistent, like triple-labeled yogurt containers and notices of the wrath that might happen if he accidentally took one. Instead, he reached for his own not so carefully labeled jug of orange juice and took a long sip, straight from the bottle.

It had been a busier shift than he'd expected, and he was happy for it, even if his heart was beating a little faster than usual. In the week since he'd been back, he'd already adjusted to the slower pace, already forgotten the jolt that came with thinking quick, reacting on instinct and years of training. With each case he successfully handled, he was that much closer to getting back to normal—and that much closer to a position in a bigger and busier emergency room.

With the orange juice container in hand, he pulled a plastic chair out from an empty table and dropped into it. He was used to being on his feet for hours, and most of the time he didn't have time to even think about it until he was finally able to relax for a few minutes.

He glanced up at the TV in the corner, where the local news was relaying the week's weather forecast, and pulled out his phone. He skimmed through his emails, frowning at the one from his old coworker asking how he was settling in, and moved on to missed calls. Predictably, one from his mother and one from Mark. Less predictably, one from a number he didn't recognize. For a minute, his heart skipped a beat, betraying that little fact he'd come to accept: His dad was long gone, wasn't looking for him, and Brett would never hear from him again. He'd come to that conclusion years before, but he couldn't deny the ping of disappointment when he realized it was a local area code. Briar Creek. Definitely not his father. Connecting to voicemail, he wedged the phone in his ear and took another sip from his drink.

His pulse flickered with interest as Ivy's hesitant, sweet voice flowed into his ear. The connection was bad—there was wind in the background, no doubt an early hint of the storm that blew in an hour ago—but her final words were clear as crystal.

He disconnected the call with a smile. So Ivy Birch wanted him to call her, did she?

He was looking forward to it more than he probably should. Looking forward to hearing the soft melody of her laugh, hearing that soft, feminine sound filling his senses.

He ran a hand over his jaw, recalling the way she looked that other night at the bar. There were moments of flirtation in there. A few glimpses of the woman who had caught his eye and showed him a certain level of interest that he'd then acted on. But only a few. By the end of the conversation, those electric eyes were positively blazing with indignation, and she'd all but left him coolly in her wake, just like she had every other time he saw her since he'd moved back.

A beeping alerted him at the same time Jackie, one of the night nurses, appeared in the door frame, out of breath and paler than usual. "There you are. We've been looking for you. Ambulance just pulled in."

Brett was on his feet, already meeting her in the hallway. "What do we have?"

"Single car accident into a phone pole. Driver is a forty-five-year-old male, unconscious with a severe head laceration, considered critical."

"Blood alcohol?"

"Zero. It appears to be on account of the storm."

"Any other passengers in the car?"

"Two. Also critical. Forty-two-year-old woman in the passenger seat, also unconscious. The child is being taken straight to surgery."

Brett marched into a triage room as the patient was being wheeled in and began scrubbing in frantically. He should have been here, strolling the ER, waiting to see what was rolling through the doors next, instead of sitting in the break room, thinking of Ivy. Or his dad.

Snapping on his gloves, he crossed the room to the patient as the residents and nurses were checking his BP and pulse ox. He opened the patient's eyes, looking for any sign of reaction from the pupils, and with a glance at the chart said, "Mr. Bauer, this is Dr. Hastings. You're at Forest Ridge Hospital. You were in a car accident. Your wife and son are here, too. We're doing everything we can for them."

His mind went on autopilot as he began calling out orders, managing the bleeding from the deep gash on the man's forehead and prepping for surgery. By the time the patient left the room, he was stable and maybe even had a fighting chance at a full recovery.

Brett tossed his bloody rubber gloves in the trash and pushed out into the hallway, his heart beating out of his chest, his mind whirring at everything that had just happened.

That had been close. Too close. And it couldn't happen again.

CHAPTER
11

The oven timer buzzed just when Kara had finally managed to calm herself down for the first time since Ivy had called that morning and asked her to bake a dozen of her very best cookies to present to Brett.

She hurried into the kitchen, snatched her trusty pink oven mitt from the counter, and flung open the oven door, releasing smells of warm sugar and chocolate and vanilla. She knew from practice that they had baked for just the right amount of time, and since they passed her vision test, too, she carefully pulled the tray from the oven and set it on the stovetop.

She studied the twelve evenly shaped cookies with a critical eye, looking for any hint of a burned edge, and decided that they would do. They'd *have* to do, she thought, noticing the time. She'd made two batches, just in case, but she was too nervous to taste test one. It was too late to bake another batch now, and really, she had perfected this recipe, having made it enough times to know exactly what it tasted like. Of all the cookies she made, this was her staple. Classic milk chocolate chip. With a secret twist.

Her heart began to race as she slid off her oven mitt and

reached for the spatula. *Steady,* she told herself as she transferred each golden cookie to the cooling rack. She glanced at the clock and then turned, leaning back against the pristine counter and looking around the equally clean kitchen. She always did that—cleaned up her mess once the treats went into the oven. Anna had taught her that trick back when she'd first started working at the café, and the habit had stuck. Anna had taught her other things, too, like the best way to prebake a piecrust or how to ensure a perfectly flaky croissant each time—cold butter. Anna had taught her many things, but the cookies... The cookies were Kara's creation.

She turned, unable to resist, and checked them again, feeling that same surge of relief when she confirmed they had come out just right. Honestly, she didn't know what she was getting so nervous about. This was Brett—her cousin! But also Mark's brother. There was no overlooking that part. She just hoped that too much didn't get back to Mark and Anna. It wasn't that she wanted to undermine them, but more that, as Ivy had said, this really had nothing to do with them. When the time came for her to finally open her cookie business, she needed to be the one to break the news. She checked the clock again, and her heart dropped straight to her stomach. Ivy would be here in less than five minutes, and then... then the real waiting would begin. She didn't know the first thing about starting, much less running, her own business, and when Ivy had pointed out that this fundraiser was a rare opportunity that wouldn't come around again for another year, she knew she had no choice but to check her fears at the door, stop second-guessing herself, and take a chance. If she didn't now, then when?

She thought about the cookies she'd given to Anna, wondering what had been said, if anything...

Don't start thinking that way, she told herself. She had a chance now. And maybe it wouldn't pan out. She wouldn't know if she didn't try. And if didn't work out...

She pulled in a breath. She didn't even want to think about that right now.

There was a knock at the front door, and Kara called out, "Come in!" as she reached for a pastry box and began transferring the cookies, still slightly warm to the touch but not too warm to fall apart—imagine that!

The nerves were dancing around in her stomach again, fluttering in her chest, as Ivy came into the kitchen, grinning broadly. "It smells so good in here! I could drink the air."

It was just the boost Kara needed. "Here," she said, proffering a platter of her first batch. "Have one."

Ivy's smile slipped a bit as she eyed the cookies. She reached out a hand and took one from the top. "I just had a big meal, so I think I'll save it for later, when I can enjoy it."

Kara plucked a plastic bag from the top drawer and handed it to Ivy. "So what time are you meeting Brett?"

"In twenty minutes. Are you sure you won't come with me?"

It was at least the fourth time Ivy had asked this question, and Kara was starting to feel like she was putting her friend out. She added a few more cookies to the plastic bag and then just emptied the entire contents of the platter into it.

"I'm worried that if I go, Brett will have a hard time saying no. I don't want him doing me a favor just because I'm his cousin."

"So you don't want me to tell him you made these until after he's made his decision?" Ivy clarified.

Kara hesitated, but only for a moment. She didn't need charity, not if she was going to try to make something of this...hobby. "Only once he's decided."

"If you say so." Ivy put the bag of cookies into her tote and, more carefully, accepted the pastry box of the last batch. "You know, if he says yes, you'll need to come up with a logo for these boxes."

Kara's pulse quickened. She'd thought of that herself, but she didn't want to admit it. No sense in getting ahead of herself.

"Okay, then. I'm off." Ivy turned but stopped when she reached the front door. "Wish me luck," she said, her tone laced with trepidation.

But Kara knew she was really the one who needed the luck. That and something to get her through the next few hours while she waited for her fate to be sealed. She wrung her hands, wondering what to do with herself. She could only hope and pray that if her cookies didn't speak for themselves, that Ivy might be able to sweet-talk Brett.

The plan was simple. Brett would swing by the shop, she'd hand him the cookies, and off he'd go. And then...out of sight, out of mind. At least, that was the plan. As for the out of mind part, she was still working on that.

Saturday mornings were always busy. No doubt her regulars would be there. Mrs. Griffin would probably be mulling over her weekend arrangement, allowing Ivy to maintain a professional distance with Brett that she so desperately needed to maintain. After all, they were working together for the hospital fundraiser, and that's all this little meet-up was. Business.

Ivy pulled her car into the alley spot she paid for monthly but couldn't do without for her deliveries and let herself in the shop through the back door. She set the pastry box on her worktable and then went into the back room to deposit the bag of cookies Kara had so generously given her on the counter. She was having dinner with Henry and Jane tonight. Now she wouldn't need to worry about what to bring.

Her green and white ticking-striped apron was hanging on its usual hook on the back of the storeroom door, and Ivy bit her lip, wondering if she should put it on now or wait until after Brett had stopped by instead. Nonsense. What did it matter how she looked? She could be wearing a strapless, form-fitting cocktail dress and he probably still wouldn't care or notice. He wasn't interested, and no amount of fretting over her appearance would change that sad fact.

She tied the strings tightly in the hope of making her waist look just a little slimmer, telling herself it was for her own confidence, because after all, she deserved to feel good about herself in the company of a man who had rejected her, and marched over to the front door to turn the sign. She had hoped Brett would have been available to stop by in the middle of the day when for sure there would be a steady flow of traffic to keep things breezy and quick, but he'd said he had a late-night shift at the hospital, and she hadn't dared offer to drop them off at his house, even if she planned to do it when he wasn't home. No doubt he'd see that as her being eager, looking for an excuse to see his bed or something, and really, she couldn't care less what his bed looked like.

Or what he looked like in it.

Ivy tapped her lips together, just to make sure some of the gloss was still there, and then went to the sink to fill her galvanized watering can. The mornings were usually her favorite part of the day. She loved the way the sun filtered through the big floor-to-ceiling windows at the front of the shop, and the eaves of the big maple tree dipped into view, casting long shadows and filling the top corner of the glass with bursts of green or, in the autumn, vibrant orange and fiery red. She loved the way Main Street was just coming alive when she came downstairs each morning, the way she was greeted each day by a room that popped with colors and soft fragrances. It was soothing and peaceful and so very different from the way her mornings used to start, back when she and Henry were still living with their mom in that drab old farmhouse desperately in need of a fresh coat of paint and a wreath on the front door.

From an early age, she had brought the outside world in. Even if it was just a buttercup or a dandelion or—before she knew better—an armful of tulips from the neighbor's flower bed, it was a reminder that there was a life beyond those four walls. And a hope for something happier.

When she'd finished inspecting her flower supply and making sure each bloom had enough water, she checked her messages for any orders and jotted down a list for her next twice weekly trip to the wholesale market. June was wedding month, and she had her fill of orders between showers and receptions, but she'd need to get started on the decorations for the annual Fourth of July festival, which was only two weeks away. The garland and swag would be easy—she could just recycle the same ones from previous years—but she wanted to add something fresh to the mix, too, just to keep people on their toes. After all, as Kara had pointed out, very little changed in Briar Creek year after year. Well, except for this summer's arrival of Brett Hastings.

The door jingled as she was halfway through her to-do list, and her heart skipped a beat when she saw Brett standing in the doorway, his broad shoulders filling the frame, his smile slightly hesitant. His eyes looked a bit lost as they took in their surroundings.

Not quite the entrance she'd dreamed about, but it would just have to do.

"Hello there," she said, tensing at the way her voice practically echoed in the empty space. Normally Mrs. Griffin or Rosemary Hastings popped in first thing, sometimes waiting outside before she'd even turned the sign, tapping their feet and watch simultaneously, claiming she was a minute or two late and that they needed to get a start to their day. But this morning, there was no sign of them, and from a swift sweep of Main Street through the big windows, no one else was on their way in any time soon, either.

It was just her and Brett. Alone.

She could think of nothing worse, even if, up until recently, it was all she had hoped for.

Brett studied the room with a furrowed brow as he took his time approaching the workbench. She stood firmly behind it, grateful for the two and a half feet of solid wood that would separate her body from his, hoping it would be enough to keep the warm musk from filling her senses and making her go all light-headed and start thinking things she shouldn't.

"This is a pretty nice shop you have here." He stopped at the wrought iron baker's rack where she stored the colorful selection of artisan soaps and candles.

"You sound surprised," she pointed out. She wasn't surprised by his reaction, though. It *was* a nice shop. She'd made sure of that. She had a vision, one she clung to and refined over the years, but one that never lost focus. She'd carefully selected this location, just down from the town square, with the big windows, exposed brick walls, and wide floor planks. Every single item in this room, from each stem to each pot, was carefully weighed against other options. Even her business cards were hand-stamped from a hand-carved stamp, and she only ever addressed each greeting card with the shade of ink that best matched the bouquet in question.

Let Brett be surprised. Let him even be impressed.

He slid his eyes to her, his mouth pulled into a lopsided smile that made her stomach roll over. "I think I underestimated you."

Yep. He had. She thrust the pastry box at him. "Here. These are the cookies I mentioned. Kara and I had some the other day at the bookstore and they're delicious. Grace said that several customers complimented them."

Brett made a face that told her this wasn't going to be as easy as she had hoped. "Do you really think cookies are a good idea for this kind of thing? It's a black-tie event and . . . I really can't afford to screw this up."

"Want to impress the new boss, huh?"

His lips thinned. "Something like that."

"Well, I wouldn't have suggested them if I hadn't thought they'd be a hit. But if you think they're too casual for the dessert buffet, then maybe they'd be better as a party favor. The guests can take them home to their kids. But really, I've never met an adult who doesn't like cookies."

Brett grinned. "Point made." He popped the lid and took a cookie from the stack. Without bothering to really look at it, he crammed it into his mouth. Ivy resisted the urge to roll her eyes by gritting her teeth instead. How many times had she seen men do the same thing when they stopped into the shop? Just take a handful of whatever was closest, instead of stopping to pay attention to the details and aesthetics.

It suddenly occurred to her that Brett might need a little more help with this fundraiser than he thought.

She stopped herself right there. She might oversee the decorations for the town's three annual festivals, as well as the Valentine's Day dance, but unless Brett asked for her help directly, she wasn't offering up her services. Something had shifted between them since his return—the same easy conversation they'd once had was gone, replaced by an unspoken tension.

Brett swallowed the cookie and reached for another one. "These might just be the best damn cookies I've ever had."

Ivy felt her shoulders relax. "Really?"

"Really." His dark eyes glimmered. "Did you make these? Is that what all this is about?"

Immediately, Ivy felt her smile droop. She stared at him and that cocky grin that curled his full lips as his eyebrow lifted. "I told you, I tried them at the bookstore—"

He tipped his head, giving her a knowing smile.

"If you must know, your cousin made them." Ivy set her hands on her hips with a sigh of exasperation. She hadn't intended to tell him that part until after he had officially agreed to let them be some part of the fundraiser, just as Kara had asked her, but he liked them, and she didn't see any harm in being up front now.

"My cousin? Which one?" He tipped his head, curious.

"Kara." Did he honestly think Luke was a possibility? And everyone knew Molly was still in Boston.

He looked thrown for a moment and stared down at the box with newfound interest. "Kara made these?"

Ivy felt suddenly defensive of her friend. "She has quite a talent."

"I thought she was a hostess at Rosemary and Thyme," Brett said, squinting at her.

Ivy licked her bottom lip. "Yes, well, she actually works

in the office now, but she worked for Anna at the Fireside Café before it burned down, and she learned a lot. I think she has a real chance of making something out of this. She just needs an opportunity to get things off the ground."

"And you think the fundraiser will help?"

Ivy grinned. "I was hoping so."

Brett studied another cookie, then took a bite. "Why didn't she just ask me herself?"

"I think she wanted to be judged on merit, not on her relation to you."

"I get that." He finished the cookie and closed the box.

"You?" Ivy managed not to snort. "But you're Brett Hastings. You were valedictorian of our class, you had near perfect SAT scores, and you got a full ride to an Ivy League school. You won every science fair, you were captain of the lacrosse team, and—" And she'd just gone completely fangirl on him.

Her cheeks flamed with heat as she caught the devilish glint in his eye. His smile was wide, revealing that elusive dimple that used to make her heart swell at the slightest glimpse, and Ivy pinched her lips. She'd said enough for one day. She'd said enough for a lifetime.

"Let's just say that I know all about being judged," she finished.

His expression folded, and she hated the look of compassion she saw in his eyes. Hated that it felt good. Hated that it made him seem so approachable, so...nice. She didn't want to think of him as nice. Nice was the guy she held a candle for all those years. Nice wasn't the guy who inflated with every perceived compliment thrown his way.

"Believe it or not, I dealt with my share of rumors, too,"

he said. "When your dad's restaurant fails and then he disappears with one of his coworkers, people talk."

"I'm sorry," Ivy said.

"Don't be." Brett shrugged. "You get it. Few do."

Now, why'd he have to go and do that? She didn't need him coming in here, pointing out things they had in common, bonding over crappy things in their youth. It didn't matter if they had a connection in the past. What mattered was that they had no chance of a future.

He wasn't interested in one. She barely was, either.

"So should I give Kara the good news, or do you want to?"

"I'll stop by her place on my way to your brother's. They live out that way, right?"

Ivy eyed him carefully. This couldn't be happening. It couldn't. "Jane and Henry live out near the lake, yes. When are you going out there?"

"Tonight. They invited me for dinner."

"Tonight," Ivy repeated. The very same night she was having dinner with Jane and Henry. "I'll be there, too."

His smile faltered enough to make her wonder what exactly was spinning through that egotistical mind. He probably thought it was a setup, even though Jane would never do that. Henry either. She opened her mouth to set him straight, just so there wasn't any misunderstanding, but the door opened and a voice trilled, "Oh, Ivy! Hellooooo!"

Ivy did her best to mask her impatience. Mrs. Griffin. About ten minutes too late.

"I should go attend to my customer," she said, scooting out from behind the workstation. She reached for the cookie box at the same time Brett did and laughed nervously at the misstep, but when she looked up into Brett's piercing gaze, she noticed he wasn't laughing at all. The ease of the conversation had faded, and in its place was a heat and intensity she'd be best to avoid.

And she would. Tomorrow. But first she had to get through dinner tonight.

CHAPTER
12

Mark was in the kitchen, whisking a white sauce that Brett knew from his childhood to be a classic béchamel, when Brett stopped by the restaurant later that day. Normally his older brother put him in a good mood and made him focus on the lighter things in life, but he couldn't shake the burden on his shoulders, the knowledge that he'd sent the résumé, updated to reflect his temporary position at Forest Ridge and his participation in the hospital's fundraiser, and that now all he could do was wait and see what happened.

Every time he thought of it, his stomach rolled over. He knew rationally that there were other hospitals in other cities that would eventually have a position open, but that fact did little to reassure him. There was a strong chance he wouldn't get the position in DC, maybe not even be brought in for an interview, and he had to brace himself for the worst-case scenario. The problem was, there were only so many setbacks he could pull himself back from, and his confidence wasn't what it used to be. A new position in a department he was excited about might be just the fresh start he needed to get over this dark spot in his career for good.

And hopefully, his time in Briar Creek would help erase the ghosts from his past once and for all.

"You look tired," was the first thing out of his brother's mouth.

"Thanks for the compliment," Brett shot back. "It was busy last night. Car accident."

"Everyone okay?" Mark frowned.

Brett shrugged. "They were okay when I handed them off to surgery."

"But now?" Mark tossed a rag over his shoulder, giving him his full attention.

"Don't know. I was already on to the next patient," Brett replied, ignoring the pinch of his brother's brow. He looked around the busy kitchen, eager to change the subject. "I thought the restaurant didn't open for another hour," Brett commented, even though he knew as well as his brother what restaurant hours entailed. Their father was barely home when they were kids, and when he was, he was too tired— or stressed—to do much of anything, except fight with their mother. Brett couldn't remember a time they weren't fighting—the good times must have been before he'd been born or could form clear memories. Brett tried not to dwell on the disappointment he'd felt growing up, when the other kids had fathers helping out at scout meetings or volunteering to coach the after-school baseball team, and he and Mark only had each other or, technically, their mom. But he didn't want his mom coming to the scout meetings, even when she offered. He saw that hurt that passed through her eyes when he turned her down, and he felt bad about it, too, but it didn't change the cold hard fact that she was his mother and other kids...they had fathers. Fathers who didn't spend 365 days a year running a business. Fathers who didn't skip out on holidays and birthdays. Fathers who didn't run out of town and never return or be heard from again.

He'd told himself he was different, that he loved his family, thought of them often, that he was just doing his job. But the sorry truth was he'd stayed away, put his career before all else. Before his mother.

And she'd always put him first.

He wouldn't be letting another woman down like that. Not if he could help it.

"You and I know a restaurant is always open. Unofficially speaking." Mark gave a few instructions to another chef at the station and nudged his head toward the door leading to the dining room. "You have time for a drink?"

"I was hoping to see Kara, actually," Brett said, not wanting to lose sight of his reason for stopping by. He'd hoped to tell her in person how much he loved her cookies and see how she felt about Ivy's suggestion to use them as a take-home gift. From everything he'd seen with Kara off and on over the years, she was always waffling between jobs that didn't seem to rely on any specific set of experience. But then, his visits had become less frequent, especially when he was finishing up his residency, so perhaps he'd misjudged her.

"She doesn't work weekends anymore," Mark explained. "Anna promoted her to help out in the office, so she's coming in during the day shift."

Brett wondered if he should mention the cookies and decided against it. He wanted to tell Kara the good news first. She deserved to hear it before anyone else.

"That drink sounds good then." And it did. He hadn't expected to be having dinner with Ivy again tonight...not that he wasn't looking forward to a meal with a pretty girl. But there was something between them, something that was evolving, that made him wary. He liked being around her, even though he couldn't be so sure she felt the same. But he needed to leave it as friends, keep the attraction at bay.

Mark poured them each a beer from the tap and came around the bar to sit on a stool. "I'm whipped."

"Working tonight then?"

Mark took a sip of his drink. "I was supposed to have it off, but one of my sous chefs called in, so here I am." He shrugged. "It's not so bad, though. We're closed on Mondays, and Anna and I usually take another night off each week now that we have a good team in place. Besides, I can hardly complain about long hours when I'm talking to you."

"True." Brett sighed heavily, looking around the room, trying to remember the way it was before, back when it was their dad's place. He hadn't stopped to do that the last time he came in. Maybe because he wasn't ready. Maybe because it all looked so different. Or maybe because it had been so many years he didn't give a damn anymore.

He swallowed back the bitter taste that filled his mouth. That was a lie and he knew it. He did care. He'd always care.

He eyed his brother over the rim of his glass. "Can I ask you a question?"

Mark nodded. "Shoot."

"Does it ever bother you that you followed in Dad's footsteps?" Brett watched as Mark's jaw squared in defense. "I mean, this restaurant, this location...It used to be Tavern on Main."

"That was years ago," Mark said tensely. "It switched hands many times over the years before Anna and I decided to open Rosemary and Thyme. But to answer your question, I think about it sometimes. It bothered me at first, but now...

Now I see it as a chance to rewrite history. I'm not Dad. I never will be."

Brett wondered if he could say the same for himself.

He'd hated that his dad was a workaholic, that he'd put his business before his family, before his kids. But now . . . Brett rubbed a hand over his jaw and reached for his beer. Now he couldn't help wondering if he was doing the same thing. Putting career before all else.

Patients before all else. He shook the cobwebs from his mind. It wasn't the same. His dad wasn't saving lives. People weren't depending on him the way they were with Brett. The only people depending on his dad were his family. And he'd failed them.

But Brett had, too.

"I had planned to leave town, you know," Mark continued.

Brett slanted a glance at his brother. "I didn't know. When was this?"

"About a year ago. I was stuck at Hastings, hating it, and a fresh start sounded nice."

Brett understood. "What made you change your mind?"

"Anna," Mark said with a wink. "And Mom. All that time I thought I was running that diner to help her out. It turned out she was letting me run it because she thought it made me happy."

"She always did like that place. I didn't realize it at first. I always thought it was sad when she started working there, doing everything she could to keep a roof over our heads." Brett swallowed hard, hating the thought of those nights he'd wake up to use the bathroom or get a drink of water and see the glow of a lamplight from the base of the stairs, and the sinking feeling he had knowing his mother was probably sitting at the dining room table, with a pile of bills spread out in front of her, trying to figure her way out of the mess their father had left when he'd skipped town.

"She loved it, though. She liked being out. Seeing people. Friends. Neighbors. She was like Dad in that way."

Brett had been eight when his dad left. He really couldn't say whether this was true or not.

"It's not a bad joint," Mark added. "I didn't mind taking it over when she relapsed."

Brett's pulse flickered, and he brought the glass to his lips. He didn't want to talk about this. Didn't want to think about any of it. He'd been in college when the cancer had come back. And he'd stayed there while Mark came home and held down the fort.

He knew it was what his mother told him to do. He was headed for med school; he had that scholarship to Yale, after all. But was it what he should have done?

The answer had kept him awake too many nights and driven him to work harder than ever, to be the best damn doctor he could be. To make the most of his decision to stay in school, pursue his degree. Even if he couldn't save his mother, he could save someone else. The sacrifice wouldn't be for nothing. He'd promised himself that. And even though she didn't know it, he'd promised his mother that, too.

"Mom's really happy you're home," Mark admitted, and Brett pulled in a long breath. Guilt landed square in chest, needling and prickly, reminding him of the résumé that had been sent that morning and the hurt she would feel when he took off again.

He wanted to spare her that hurt. But sticking around Briar Creek couldn't change the past. It would only ever remind him of it.

He drained his beer. He had come back to town for a

temporary stay, hoping to make the most of it, to better his mindset, prepare for the next phase in his career. There was nothing more to it than that.

The sun was beating down on the pavement when Brett finally left the restaurant after catching the tail end of a ball game on the television they had in the bar area, wishing that he'd been on call or could have made up a polite excuse not to have dinner with Henry tonight. The last thing he wanted to do right now was sit in that cozy little house and start feeling things he shouldn't when he caught a glimpse of Ivy's smile.

He supposed he should bring a hostess gift. Henry didn't drink—and neither did Ivy—but Jane would appreciate the gesture, and unlike his brother, he was worthless in a kitchen, leaving any offering to be of the store-bought variety. He walked down Main Street, toward the grocery store at the far end, watching in growing curiosity as the revving of a dying car engine filled the otherwise quiet evening and a woman climbed out of a bright orange vehicle and started beating the hood.

A woman who looked a lot like Ivy.

His heart sped up with interest as he increased his pace, until he could make out the little wrinkle on her forehead as she set her hands on her hips and glared daggers at the station wagon. He knew that look, he thought wryly. He'd been on the receiving end of it more than once since returning to town. The girl was fiery, with a spark he found undeniably attractive. Most of the girls he'd casually dated would say or do anything they thought would please him. He couldn't have a relationship with someone like that. But Ivy spoke her mind, stayed true to herself. She was the kind of girl who could share things, enlighten him, and keep things interesting for a long time.

If he were looking for that type of thing, of course.

He paused a few feet from the car and watched in stunned silence as she set down her bulging handbag and hit the hood of her car with all her might.

"What are you doing?" he asked, laughing under his breath.

She looked momentarily startled to see him. Her blue-green eyes flashed on him, sparking with awareness that she was being watched, but she just pinched her lips and shrugged. "It just needs a good pounding," she explained, giving it another hard slap.

He struggled to compose himself. "A good *pounding*?"

"Yep." She smacked it again, wincing as she pressed her red palm to the other hand.

She smacked it again, and this time he winced with her. That had to have hurt.

"Here," he said, stepping off the curb. He pulled back his hand and brought it down to the metal hood. All at once a searing pain burned right through his skin, shooting sparks up his arm. "Jesus! Ow." He gritted his teeth and shook his arm in the air.

Her smile was wicked. "I'm tougher than you think." She hit it again and then jiggled her keys. "I think that should do it."

He stepped back and watched as she slid into the driver's seat, her pretty features pinched in concentration as she turned the key. Sure enough, the engine sputtered and then started, and from behind the windshield he caught her triumphant grin.

"I hope those hands are insured," she said, poking her head out the window.

They weren't, but he didn't tell her that. Still, she had a point, and he'd be more careful next time.

If there was a next time. And there wouldn't be. Because he needed to keep his distance from this girl and the way she made him want to fall deep and hard. And because she shouldn't be driving this car around anymore.

He walked over to her open window and leaned inside. He was so close he could smell the vanilla-scented perfume wafting off her skin and hair and that creamy blue dress that hugged her in all the right places.

"You really ought to see a mechanic."

"Why?" she quipped. "The car's working fine now. It just needed a—"

"A good pounding. I know." His mouth twitched. He closed his eyes briefly and thought about the worst case he'd ever handled back in Baltimore—motorcycle crash on a highway, no helmet, no padding. "A car shouldn't need a good—" He swallowed hard. "You shouldn't need to beat your car into submission."

"Well, I don't exactly have money for a new carburetor right now."

"Ah, so you did see a mechanic." Brett grinned.

"I did, and I didn't like what he had to tell me. I could pay up, or I could suffer through a few little inconveniences."

"Or you could end up stranded in the dead of winter on an empty country road. In the dark. Probably without any cellular reception."

"Well, aren't you just the angel of death? I intend to get it fixed, once I have the money for it. It hasn't broken down on me yet, I'll have you know. Sometimes it works just fine, and sometimes it's just slow to warm up, but after—"

He held up his hand. He couldn't hear it one more time.

He stood back, inspected the car. He hadn't seen wood paneling since the eighties. The thing probably didn't even have air bags. "You might drive this car all over the state seven days a week, but tonight, you're not driving it."

She blinked at him. "Excuse me?"

He reached through the window and, before she had a chance to react, turned the key and removed it.

"What did you do that for? It could take another half an hour for me to get it running again!"

He lifted an eyebrow. "Then you've proved my point. We're headed in the same direction. I'll drive you."

"I'm not getting in a car with you," she exclaimed, seeming horrified at the mere thought of it.

That stung, but he didn't show it. Instead, he held the car door open and waited patiently for Ivy to climb out. Her keys were tight in his grip, and there was no way he was relinquishing them tonight. Not when he'd feel responsible if she broke down on the side of the road or the engine cut out while she was driving.

She glared at him and then, with a huff, pushed herself out of the car and strode past him, chin high, shoulders squared, leaving him with a slack jaw in the trail of her soft, sweet scent.

He slammed her car door closed and then, when he heard the rattle, wished that he had been a little more gentle.

"I was just running into the grocery store for a bottle of wine." He shoved his hands into his pocket, locking Ivy's blazing gaze. Even though she said she was fine with it, it still felt awkward to bring up alcohol around her. He supposed it was the same way people felt mentioning the c-word around him. And he'd rather they not dance around the subject. It only made him feel less normal, made him remember things he'd rather forget. He decided to loosen up and have the same approach with Ivy. "Do you think I should bring white or red?"

"White," Ivy replied simply. "It's hot as heck out here, and something chilled would be nice."

If he had any last trepidations about broaching the subject, they were now gone. He pushed the door to the store open and motioned for Ivy to pass through. Her long hesitation told him she wasn't going to be charmed so easily, but just the same, he felt a little lighter in his step as they walked to the back of the store and she slipped him a smile as he selected the bottle. He couldn't say he'd ever been grocery shopping with a woman before. A friend, maybe. His mother, of course. His cousins didn't count. But a girl like Ivy, a girl he was attracted to? Never. It made him think of how it could be to live life with someone else, to share the small duties that married couples did.

He didn't need to think about things that would never be.

CHAPTER 13

Ivy didn't know how she got through the fifteen-minute car ride to Jane and Henry's house. Sheer willpower alone had kept her from glancing over at the perfect slope of Brett's chin, the curve of his lips, the memory of them pressed against hers, grazing down her neck. Once, she had dared to slide her gaze over to his denim-covered thigh, but the quiver that had ripped down her spine and straight to the space between her legs put a quick stop to that.

She stared out the windshield, gritting her teeth and counting down the minutes as she told Brett where to turn. If he hadn't snatched her keys, and if Henry wasn't counting on her showing up tonight, she never would have agreed to ride in his car. Even if it was a very nice car, compared to her own—not that she would admit she missed air-conditioning, especially in late June, when the muggy heat sometimes made her worry the flowers would wilt before they got to her destination—and even if the man driving it was ridiculously attractive. Being here like this with him stirred up all those childish fantasies she'd played over and over all through her adolescence and, sadly, beyond. But it was nothing like in her dreams. It was instead just a hint of what could have been, had Brett been a different man than he'd turned out to be.

She thought of the way he'd snuck his hand through her window and turned off the ignition before she even realized what he was doing. She'd been so damn lost in those dark eyes that she'd been disarmed. She couldn't help but smile at the effort. She might just call it chivalrous, if she wasn't so furious. She supposed it was...nice.

But no. No. Brett couldn't be nice. He *was* nice, as a kid, but not anymore. Brett the nice guy was the Brett she had crushed on for way too long. Brett the egotistical jerk was the guy she could see as attractive and nothing else.

It was probably some part of his doctor's oath. He probably felt he had some civic duty not to let her drive her car, even if it was perfectly safe, even on these empty back roads.

Ivy unhooked her seat belt as they pulled into Jane and Henry's driveway, eager for a quick getaway. Jane was standing behind the screen door with Sophie as Ivy scrambled from the car, looking surprised but pleased when she saw Brett step out of the driver's seat and much more calmly close his door.

If this had been a dinner at, say, Rosemary Hastings's house, Ivy would have been suspicious, but Jane and Henry had no motives when it came to her nonexistent love life. All they cared about was her health. And they cared entirely too much about it, if anyone asked her. Which of course, no one ever did.

"I have a loose tooth!" Sophie announced proudly, bringing her finger up to her mouth to demonstrate.

Jane pushed her hand back. "Let Mother Nature run its course."

"I have two wiggly ones," Sophie continued, ignoring her mother. "See?"

Ivy watched as the child moved the two front teeth with her tongue and tried not to laugh. "Impressive!"

"Do you have any wiggly teeth?" the little girl asked as Ivy stepped into the hall.

Ivy laughed. "I hope not, or I'm in real trouble."

"Thank you for having me," Brett said, coming up to stand behind her in the too-small entranceway. Had it always been so cramped? Ivy hadn't noticed before, but now she felt like the walls were closing in on her, and there were entirely too many people stuffed into such a tight space. She could feel the warmth of Brett's chest behind her, feel the heat radiating off his body and onto hers in a way that was much too intimate and altogether too tempting, as if they were a couple, arriving for a routine weekend dinner.

She tried to inch forward, but at the same time Brett extended his arm, brushing against her bare arm and sending every hair on end. She rubbed her skin with her hand, cursing herself for not having worn a jean jacket or something to protect against the inevitable drop in temperature once the sun went down. If Brett noticed their touch, he didn't show it, other than to drop his gaze to hers for a hint of a second before grinning back at Jane.

"You shouldn't have!" Jane exclaimed, taking the gift. "But thank you."

"It's not every day I get a hot meal. Cafeteria food gets old, and I'm not much of a cook."

Ivy frowned, wondering if this hermit lifestyle he was describing meant there weren't many restaurant meals, either. The thought of him eating his dinners alone, at work or in his bachelor pad, perked her up a bit. So maybe he wasn't going out on dates, wooing other women.

Stop right there, Ivy. Just because he wasn't wooing other women didn't mean he was wooing her.

"Well, Anna is the cook in our family," Jane said, "so I guess between the two of us, we don't stand much of a chance."

"Here," Ivy said, reaching into her bag to retrieve the cookies Kara had given her that morning. "I brought dessert."

"Cookies! Are these the ones Kara made?" Jane asked.

Ivy frowned in confusion. "Yes. How did you know?"

"There was a school bake sale last week I completely forgot about. I stopped by the restaurant to see if Anna had anything I could purchase, and she said she had a box of cookies from Kara on hand."

Ivy considered this information and tucked it away to relay to Kara later. "They're the very same," she said, then turned to Brett, grinning. "In fact, Brett is going to be giving them away at the hospital fundraiser."

His gaze dropped to hers, his smile slow and secret. It set a tingle down her spine, as if they were in on something together.

"Well, I'm glad you brought them," Jane said. "They were gone before I could have a bite last time, and I've been dying to try them."

"That makes two of us," Henry said, coming over to greet them. Ivy couldn't help but notice the nervous flick of his eyes from her to the cookies and back again. She brushed away the twinge of annoyance she felt, despite how valid his concern may have once been. He was just being overly cautious, but she'd put his worries to rest as soon as they had a private moment.

Of all people, he knew when to back off and just let her have a good time.

And she intended to have a good time tonight.

She slid a glance at Brett, and her heart did a little jumping jack. Well, not *too* good of a time.

"Cookies! I love cookies!" Sophie was already reaching for the bag excitedly.

"Not until after you've eaten your dinner," Jane said.

"Awww." Sophie folded her arms across her chest in a huff and pushed out her lips.

All the adults in the room burst out laughing, which, by the low growl Sophie then released, was not the reaction she had been hoping for.

Still, it broke the ice, and therefore it was just what Ivy had been hoping for.

"Come on," Jane said brightly. "Let's go back into the kitchen. I set out some appetizers."

The appetizers consisted of carrot and celery sticks surrounding a bowl of what Ivy knew to be yogurt-based dip. In other words: rabbit food. Jane and Henry did their best to support her diet, even if sometimes their effort went a little overboard.

"I had a patient the other day who could learn a thing or two from you, Jane," Brett said, helping himself to a few carrots. "His wife was hysterical, convinced he was having a heart attack. Turns out he'd engaged in an afternoon eating contest with one of his other retired buddies. Spent the entire day wolfing cheeseburgers, onion rings, mozzarella sticks, nachos with extra jalapeños, and beer."

Ivy laughed. "Sounds delicious, actually." Sighing, she reached for a carrot stick herself. "How's work at the hospital?"

See, she could do this. Simple chitchat. Just like she

would do with anyone else. She'd show him she didn't care. She'd show herself, too.

"Eh." He shrugged.

"Not as exciting as an inner-city emergency room, I gather," Henry said, hoisting Sophie so she could reach the tray.

"You could say that." Brett's expression seemed to darken. "But we still get some serious cases coming through the door. Just not as frequently," he added.

Jane shuddered. "I don't know how you do it. All those people. Hurt."

Brett gave a modest shrug. "I like to help them."

Ivy thought of the way he looked that day she'd come in for the fundraiser meeting, like some doctor straight off a medical drama. Even though she knew he was a doctor, somehow seeing him in scrubs, in his element, made the fact that he actually had the ability to spring into action, call out orders, and potentially save a life...terribly attractive.

And that is just plain terrible, Ivy.

"How 'bout a beer?" Henry asked, opening the fridge. He took out a bottle and held it up to Brett, opting for a soda for himself. Ivy watched as the two men went onto the deck to start the grill, Henry carrying a plate of shrimp Jane had pressed into his hands.

Unlike herself, Henry had a very different reason for never drinking, and it saddened her to think that to this day, he was still haunted by their childhood. She knew he shielded her from the worst of it as much as he could. He was more in tune with the warning signs and triggers, more capable of suggesting they leave the house or that she spend the night at Grace's house. She let him have that role, even when she was finally able to see what was going on, too. It made him feel better to have the sense that he was doing something, when so much was out of their control.

It was why he was so protective of her again now, she supposed. Henry had left town after college, and it was Ivy who had taken over the role of dealing with their mother. She didn't mind—she hadn't had the chance before, and she saw it as a way of making it up to her brother. It felt good to be needed for a change, to be able to care for him in her own silent way the way he had done up to that point. But she knew that Henry felt guilty about not coming back sooner.

"I don't plan to eat those cookies, you know," she whispered to Jane. She'd always played a big-sister role with Jane, but in recent years Jane had felt like more of an adult than she was. After all, Jane had a house, a kid…What did Ivy have?

Petals on Main, she reminded herself. Her pride and joy.

Jane leaned across the breakfast bar. "You know we don't mind skipping dessert when you're here."

"But you shouldn't have to! All my life I've watched people eat everything I couldn't. It never bothers me." She met Jane's knowing look. "Well, not much."

"I just know how I felt when I was trying to lose that baby weight after I had Sophie. I'll never forget the time Anna showed up to our mother's house with the most decadent brownies I had ever seen and then proceeded to polish off six in front of me, not even thinking of the fact that I was practically whimpering inside."

Ivy laughed softly. "I've gotten used to it. But you have to tell Henry to stop worrying so much."

"Yes, but you're his sister. He's always going to be protective of you. Would you rather he wasn't?"

Ivy sighed. "Of course not."

"It's one of the things I always loved about him," Jane

admitted with a secret smile. "He's always looking out for the people he cares about. Even when I didn't want to hear what he had to say sometimes... about Adam... I knew he had my best interest at heart."

Henry had loved Jane all his life, and he stood by and watched as she married his best friend—and the most undeserving man alive, if anyone had asked Ivy. "I'm really happy you guys ended up together."

"Me too." Jane bit into the end of a carrot. "Now what about you? Any knights in shining armor hanging around the flower shop lately?"

"You've been there this week," Ivy said, even though Jane's hours had been cut back a bit.

"I seem to recall you mentioning at some point that you're looking for someone tall, dark, handsome. Stable. Settled. Family oriented." She tipped her chin to the sliding glass doors that divided the kitchen from the deck. "What about Brett?"

Ivy felt her cheeks warm. "Oh, I don't think so."

"Why not? He's cute. Smart, too."

And completely unavailable. But she couldn't exactly tell Jane that without offering up how she knew this information.

"Well, he seems like a catch to me," Jane said. "And I bet a lot of other girls feel the same way."

Jane was right about that part, Ivy thought. But as for Brett being a catch... once she might have thought so. Now she knew better.

It was nearly eight by the time they finished their meals, having languished over the grilled shrimp and salad Jane had prepared. The conversation was light, mostly centered around everything Brett had missed around town, and they'd all shared a good laugh about Rosemary's near miss with renting out the dance studio to a local art center in need of space.

"When I think of the look on her face when she realized paint was involved!" Jane burst out laughing. Fondly, she patted Henry on the arm. "It's all because of Henry that things turned around for the studio."

"Oh, not entirely," Henry said with a modest shrug. "All I did was suggest a few ways to improve the place."

"Well, the write-up you did on Briar Creek didn't hurt much either," Ivy pointed out. It was the last article Henry had written for the travel magazine before taking over the town newspaper and officially ending his wandering days.

"I'd like to see that article," Brett mused.

"You should," Jane said, standing up to fetch him a copy from the stack she kept on hand on the lower shelf of the hall console. She tapped the picture on the cover. "Your brother's restaurant is front and center, and even Hastings is mentioned."

"Really?" Brett flipped through the magazine, until he came to the centerfold of Main Street covered in a blanket of snow. "It looks so picturesque." He seemed baffled by the idea of it.

"What about dessert?" Sophie cut in. "I want those cookies!"

Ivy caught Henry's eye. "I'm stuffed. You guys go on."

Brett laid the magazine to the side and turned to her. "You're not going to have any of Kara's cookies?"

She shook her head and said to Henry, "She made some for the Annex, and the customers were raving about them."

Jane took a bite of one as she set the plate on the center of the table. "Wow, you weren't lying. These are amazing. Henry, try one. Brett?"

Ivy wondered if Brett found it odd that neither her brother nor Jane pressed Ivy to try the dessert, but if he did, he said nothing and happily sipped his coffee and helped the rest of them finish off the cookies.

"I feel guilty," Jane whispered in Ivy's ear as they walked to the front hall, full and tired.

Ivy looked at her quizzically. "Why? Don't." She gave her friend a reassuring hug. "Don't think twice about it. And thanks for dinner."

"That was nice," Brett said as they pulled out of the driveway. It was dark and quiet, and Ivy wished she could flick the radio on for distraction, but it wasn't her car, and that felt like taking liberties.

She kept the focus of conversation neutral as they wound their way through the empty streets and back into town, keeping things light, chattering about the fundraiser and everything planned for it.

Finally, they were back at Petals on Main. The night was over, and that deflated her more than it should. It had been a nice night, pleasant, just as she'd hoped. Full of good friends, family, and laughter. It was a shame it wouldn't be repeated.

"Well, thanks for the ride," she said, managing a smile.

He nodded, his expression unreadable, his features half shadowed in the dark.

She waited, wondering if he was going to say something, if she should hold out for a second before sliding out of the car. Instead, he reached over, his body leaning over the armrest that divided their bodies, his face coming to within inches of her own.

Sweet mother. He was going to kiss her. Her heart sped up as time slowed down and she watched as, for the second time, Brett's face inched closer to hers, and that beautiful mouth was so close to her lips that her body could only tighten and sizzle at the anticipation of his kiss.

Her mind was racing. Should she let him kiss her?

She was still frantically wrestling with this as his arm reached out, and she held her breath, panic now officially setting in.

She watched, in sobering realization, as he pulled the door latch. Cool summer-night air took the heat from her cheeks, all at once clearing her head.

"Well, good night," she said through a tight smile, suddenly more eager to be on her way and out of this car than ever before. She needed space. She needed to be in her world. In her tiny apartment with all her favorite things and no reminders of Brett or his ridiculously handsome face. She wanted to forget the way her body reacted whenever he was near. The way she could lust for something she knew she couldn't have and shouldn't want.

"Wait." His voice as soft as the hand on her leg. She looked down to see it sitting there, just above her knee, gentle and strong, warm on her skin. If he moved so much as a centimeter, she wasn't sure she would be able to control herself. Already, her nerves were on high alert, and a ripple of pleasure was stirring between her thighs.

She clenched her teeth. *He is not going to kiss you. So just stop thinking about it.*

"Yes?" Damn, her voice was weak. She was barely controlling the strain of her body and the easy way it gave in to the slightest graze of his touch.

"Your car." He cocked an eyebrow, and in the shadows of the darkness, his deep-set eyes looked devilish and inviting, like he was suggesting she do something she knew she shouldn't.

"My car." She nodded, as if she followed, but all she could think about was that hand on her leg and how badly she wanted him to shift his thumb a little higher.

"Why don't I take a look at it tomorrow?" He pulled his hand back and leaned on the armrest.

Ivy frowned, trying to understand what he was saying. But one thing was glaringly clear. He was suggesting they see each other tomorrow. And as much as her body wanted to scream, *Yes, yes, yes,* her mind was saying, *No, no, no.*

"Tomorrow's my day off—"

"Perfect."

Quickly, she said, "And I usually go to the flower market to get my inventory for the first half of the week."

"What time do you go to the market?" His eyes seemed to dance in the glow of the lamppost.

Damn him. He wasn't making this easy on her.

She hesitated, and then thought, *To hell with it.* "Midnight."

His chin dipped. "Midnight?"

She nodded miserably and chewed on her thumbnail. His roar of laughter filled the car, and no doubt half the quiet street through the half-open door.

"Then I sure as hell don't want you breaking down or being stuck unable to start the thing at midnight." He shook his head. "How does noon sound?"

It sounded like a far cry from a dinner invitation, but Ivy refused to show her disappointment.

"That should work." She started to slide out of the car and then stopped herself. "Thanks. I didn't know you knew anything about cars."

He flashed her a wicked smile and set his hand on the gearshift. "I'm full of surprises."

Ivy smiled weakly and closed the door behind her, wishing

that Brett hadn't been so nice and that he wasn't sitting there, waiting for her to find her key and let herself into the building.

It would be so much easier if he could just stay the jerk she knew him to do be. Some of the time...

She struggled with the old lock that led to the dark, narrow staircase to her second-floor apartment, feeling his eyes on her back the entire time. When she finally heard it click, she turned and gave him one last wave, expecting him to use that opportunity to just peel off. It wasn't until she walked into her empty apartment and crossed to the swing-arm lamp near the big bay window that she realized he was still sitting there, waiting for her to flick on a light.

She did, and then watched as his car slowly pulled out of the parking space and made its way down Main Street, until it was so hidden by the eaves of the giant maple trees that she could no longer make out its taillights but only the soft purr of its engine.

Brett was right about thing. He certainly was full of surprises.

CHAPTER 14

Kara hung up the phone and squealed. She didn't even care that her windows were cracked open and that the neighbors could most certainly hear her over the soft morning drizzle that collected in her flower boxes. She did a happy dance around her apartment in beat with the pitter-patter of the rain she loved so much, knowing a big sloppy grin was plastered on her face and that there was very little that could wipe it off now. Her heart soared, and somehow, even the thought of going into that dreary little windowless office off the kitchen at Rosemary and Thyme seemed a little more palatable now that she had something to look forward to on her time off.

Gone were the days of baking just for fun or pleasure or to give her something to do on yet another dateless Friday night. She had a real goal now. Some might even call it a gig. Her cookies were going to be used as the party favors for the Forest Ridge Hospital fundraiser and she was...officially freaking out.

She tripped over her bright pink rain boots that she'd propped in her small entranceway and jerked herself upright.

There was so much to do, so much to think about, so much to plan. She wasn't prepared, not for this. Brett said on their call that she should plan on making enough cookies for five hundred people. That made... She was so overwhelmed that she couldn't even do the math in her head. She grabbed a pen from the top drawer in her kitchen and did the division on a sheet of paper towel.

Her hand froze at the sum. Roughly forty-two dozen cookies. In her simple gas oven, with only two racks.

She glanced at her freezer. She supposed she could make them ahead and freeze them, but that wasn't exactly putting her best foot forward, and it certainly wasn't something Anna would ever do. No, she'd have to make them fresh. The night before the event. And if they baked for fifteen minutes each, that would be—she picked up the pen again—ten and a half hours.

So she just wouldn't sleep. Or she'd get up early.

Oh, who was she kidding? There was no way she was going to get a wink of sleep with this kind of anticipation.

Brett had raved about the cookies he'd sampled, so much so that she started wondering if Ivy had let on that they were hers all along. Brett was kind like that. But then he got off track, started talking about how the success of this event was so important, not just to the hospital but to him. She didn't really connect why, other than because he was always conscientious, always a perfectionist, really, because by then her mind was spinning and her heart was thumping, and she was trying to imagine her cookies, wrapped up all pretty, in a big basket...

The packaging would have to impress, she decided. She knew that her sister-in-law Grace always tsked when Kara reached for the prettiest cover on the display table at Main

Street Books, but presentation was crucial. The only trouble was, what should her presentation be? A simple cookie wrapped in a cellophane bag and tied with twine was forgettable at best and did nothing for developing her brand.

Her brand. Was she really going to move forward with this? After all these months of experimenting in her kitchen, licking the bowls and taste-testing her creations, was she really ready to turn her hobby into something bigger? Something legitimate?

She thought of her days sitting at that little desk at the restaurant, while the sounds and smells of the kitchen wafted through the space under the door, and decided with certainty that yes, she most certainly was.

It was exciting. But it was also scary.

She picked up her tote and swung it over her shoulder. She was ten minutes late for coffee with the girls. Somehow, some way, she'd have to hold this information in for herself. But maybe, afterward, she'd get a few minutes to pick Ivy's brilliant brain.

The skip in Kara's step faded the moment she saw her mother's distinct figure through the paned glass window of Main Street Books. Kara hid under the shield of her umbrella, even though the morning rain had faded to a few random drops. She'd studiously dodged her mother for a week—a record, truly—and now she'd no doubt be peppered with questions about where she'd been, and what she'd been up to, and who had been keeping her so busy.

The dread that was forming a tight knot in her stomach only increased when she pushed open the door to the shop and spotted three of her mother's book club cohorts huddled around a table.

Kara propped her umbrella in the stand with the others and wiped her boots on the mat before venturing into the store. One of the girls Grace had hired to help cover a few shifts each week was standing behind the counter, deep in discussion about trends in children's literature as she rang up a few items. Soft classical music played in the background, fading in and out over the din from the adjacent café, and Kara closed her eyes for exactly three seconds to steady her nerves.

It's your mother, she chastised herself firmly. *The woman who raised you.* The way she was acting, she was about to come face-to-face with her worst enemy. Really, she was building up the entire thing to be so much more than it was.

"Kara?"

Kara's eyes popped open. Managing a smile she no longer quite felt, she ducked her head around a stack of books and came face-to-face with four middle-aged women, who were staring at her with far too much interest.

"I thought that was you. Who else in town wears those hot pink rain boots?" Rosemary pinched her lips.

Kara glanced down at the knee-high Wellies. She wasn't sure whether to take the remark as an insult or a simple observation.

You like the boots, Kara. That's all that matters.

"How are you this morning, Mom?" She leaned over to give her mother a peck on the cheek. In return, Rosemary air kissed her, lest, Kara knew, her lipstick get smudged. Already the ceramic mug bearing the bookstore's logo was branded with her telltale color: Crazy for Crimson. The same shade she'd worn since Kara was old enough to pluck it from her handbag and try it out for herself. She'd used the entire

tube on her face, her dolls' faces, her sister Molly's face...
Luckily for her mother, Rosemary kept several gleaming sil-
ver tubes on hand. She was never, ever without Crazy for
Crimson.

Once, Kara had asked what would happen if they discon-
tinued the color, and that very day, Rosemary had made a pit
stop on the way back from ballet class to buy the department
store's entire inventory of her beloved color.

Kara felt her heart begin to soften. Honestly, she was
being silly avoiding her mother like this.

"Your mother was just telling us how worried she was
about you!" remarked Mrs. Nealon, Kara's old music
teacher who, now retired, played live piano for the dance
studio's advanced ballet classes, as well as every recital and
performance.

Kara frowned at her mother. "Worried?"

"Well, I hadn't heard from you in at least a week. Maybe
more like eight days. I started wondering if you may have
gotten sick, but then someone mentioned they saw you at the
gym, so there went that theory."

"I—"

"I know, I know. You're twenty-eight years old and a
grown woman. Whatever—or perhaps *whom*ever—has you
so busy that you can't even call your own mother is your own
private business." Her eyebrows waggled as a slow smile
formed at the corners of her ruby-red stained lips.

Kara felt her eyelids droop. *Yes, Mother, I didn't call you
because I was having hot, passionate, mind-blowing sex
and this is the first time I've been out of bed in a week.*

She fought the urge to say just that, to quiet her mother
once and for all, but instead shrugged and said, "I've been
busy. I'm sorry."

"Too busy for your *mother*?" The women exchanged disappointed looks.

Why was she always apologizing? She couldn't stop, no matter how much she tried. And really, while she hadn't called her mother in eight days, her mother hadn't picked up the phone either, so how was this all her fault?

"Well, maybe we can have coffee this week," she suggested.

Her mother patted her hand. Her lips gave a little curl of satisfaction. "I'd like that."

Kara looked to the back of the room, happy to spot Anna's unmistakable blond ponytail, and inched away. "Good. I'm looking forward to it," she said. Even though she wasn't sure she was doing any such thing.

Brett sidled up to the counter and turned over his mug, grinning at the Hastings logo stamped on its side. He had been coming here since he was a kid, before his mom took over, before she'd even started putting in shifts under the original ownership to cover the stack of bills their dad had left behind.

"What will it be?" his mother asked.

"Coffee," he said, watching as she filled the mug to the rim. He took it black, always did, and his mother always used the best beans. Smooth and rich. He took a long smell of the brew before taking his first sip.

On the days he worked, he stayed away from the stuff. Didn't need his hands shaking, even if it helped his mind stay sharp.

The best way to keep his mind clear was to stay present, in the moment, on the crisis at hand. Not one in the background, out of his control.

He eyed his mother. She was looking healthy. But still,

the anxiety wouldn't go away. He'd already lost one parent. He couldn't lose two.

Mark came up from behind and thumped him on the shoulder before sliding onto the stool next to his. He turned over his mug and grinned at their mother.

"He doesn't even need to ask." Sharon grinned. "What a sight. My two boys. Sitting here together, having breakfast. It doesn't happen often enough."

Brett swallowed hard, but his pulse began to race. "Hey, Mark's the one pulling crazy hours at the restaurant." But it was no use. Mark had stuck around, stayed in Briar Creek, been there for breakfasts and dinners and...the hard times. He knew it. They knew it. Even if they'd chosen not to make him feel bad about it, he did. "Why don't you join us?" Brett suggested, but their mother shook her head.

"Sunday mornings are the busiest time of the week. Now, let me guess. A Denver omelet for Mark and..." She paused slightly, and Brett shifted on his chair. It was subtle, and maybe he was reading too much into it, but her hesitation served as a reminder of how much he'd been away, how little his mother knew his present-day self.

"Chocolate chip pancakes for Brett." She beamed, and Brett felt something in his chest crack open. Chocolate chip pancakes had been his favorite—once. But he was thirty years old now and his breakfasts usually consisted of some scrambled eggs on rye toast with a cup of coffee.

He picked up his mug and stared into the contents. She got the coffee right. As for the pancakes...He just couldn't correct her.

"Chocolate chip pancakes sound perfect, Mom." He smiled against the knot in his stomach and she slid the order ticket under the service window.

"So, to what do I owe the invitation?" Mark asked, leaning into his elbows.

Brett bristled. "What, I can't invite my brother for breakfast?"

Mark looked at him like he was half crazy. "Relax, will you? It was a joke."

"Sorry." Brett rubbed a hand against his jaw and took another sip of his coffee. Good thing he wasn't on call today. "I'm just...on edge."

"Forest Ridge's ER is keeping you that busy?" Mark cocked an eyebrow in disbelief.

"Some days," Brett said. But not enough days. He wasn't used to having most weekends off for starters. Two days with nothing to do was two days too many. "But I do have a favor to ask you."

"Ha-ha! I knew it." Mark grinned triumphantly.

"They've put me on the planning committee for the hospital fundraiser," Brett started to explain, but Mark's guffaw silenced him.

"Wait," Mark said when his laughter had died down. He covered his mouth, his eyes wide in wonder. "You're actually serious. I thought you were some hotshot doctor, not a party planner." He began to laugh again.

"Very funny." Brett scowled. "They like to have a physician head the event, make the introductions, talk about the silent auction and where this year's proceeds are going."

"Sounds like an honor," Mark admitted.

Brett hadn't thought of it quite that way. Burden, yes. Pain in the ass, certainly. One more thing in his life he didn't need? Absolutely. "I suppose it is an honor," he said.

"Where's the money going this year?" Mark asked.

Brett tensed. He knew his brother was just being

conversational, but he didn't want to get into the specifics of the event or the reasons behind his participation in it. He just wanted to ask Mark to cater. Scratch that item off the list.

"It's going to the new cancer research wing," he said casually.

Silence stretched as both men reached for their mugs. It was a sore subject, one he knew Mark wrestled with just as much as he did, and as close as they were, they never talked about that time in their life directly. Some things were just too painful. Some things didn't need to be explained. But for Brett it ran deeper. He owed his brother. A lot. For being there when he couldn't. For postponing culinary school and putting off his plans of opening his own restaurant. All so Brett could pursue his dreams.

It hadn't been for nothing, he told himself. Not entirely.

"Well, I can see why you'd want to roll up your sleeves," Mark said, and Brett thought he detected an edge of bitterness in his tone. Though he'd never come out and said it, Brett couldn't help wondering if his brother resented staying back in town, sitting by their mother's side and taking over Hastings for so many years.

"How about a refill?" Their mother's smile was warm and generous as she finished up with another customer, and Brett felt the uneasy stir of guilt resurfacing.

You're here now, he told himself. But for how long?

He couldn't think about it. Not when he didn't even know if he'd get the position in DC. Or anywhere else. For all he knew, his career was finished, over. His days as a trauma surgeon were gone; the path he'd so meticulously carved had reached its end. He'd spend the rest of his days treating sprained wrists and his weekends drinking coffee at the diner.

Was it really such a bad thought?

It was when he considered everything he'd given up to pursue something else.

"Did you hear that Brett's heading up the hospital fundraiser?" Mark offered, and Sharon's face immediately perked up.

"I was actually wondering if Rosemary and Thyme might cater the event."

"Absolutely," Mark agreed. "Shoot me the details and Anna and I will put together the menu."

"I knew I could count on you," Brett said. He always could. "I secured a table, so be sure to tell Rosemary," he said to his mother. Even though they were technically linked by the now departed Hastings brothers, the two women were as close as biological sisters, and as difficult as his aunt Rosemary could be at times, Brett would never overlook the generosity she'd showed his mother when they needed family the most.

"How about you?" Mark elbowed him. "Bringing a date?"

It was easy for Mark, now that he had Anna, but his brother sure hadn't liked the attention he received back when he was still single, when every woman in town over a certain age was inquiring about the state of his love life.

"I'm working the event. Remember?"

Mark just shrugged. "So? I am, too, now that I'm catering."

"Yes, but you work with your date. It's a little different."

"I'm sure there are plenty of women down at the hospital who would love to be invited," their mother said.

And plenty of women who'd be looking for a second date. And a third. And maybe a proposal, and a white wedding, and two point five kids with a picket fence. He wasn't having any of it.

"I'd rather not mix business with pleasure," he said simply.

"Fair enough," his mother commented, but he heard Mark snort. Brett slid his brother a glance. It was different for Mark. He and Anna wanted the same things. But no woman would want what he did. And no woman should have to settle for what he was offering.

"You should talk to Rosemary about donating some private dance lessons for the auction," their mother suggested.

"Good idea." Dr. Kessler had already secured the majority of the auction items, and tickets had been selling steadily long before he arrived back in Vermont. Now that the food and flowers were arranged, hopefully all he had to do was rent a tux and show up. And give a speech.

He dreaded that part. Public speaking had never been his strength. He preferred science and math and burying himself in a good book. Sure, he was happy to throw a ball, and he had been, as Ivy had mentioned, captain of the lacrosse team his senior year, but being on a team was different than taking the spotlight. It was one of the reasons he'd chosen emergency medicine. There was a sense of camaraderie there you didn't find in other specialties. It was all hands on deck, sleeves rolled, everyone ready for action. No one was going it alone.

But that didn't mean one person alone couldn't be responsible for what happened.

The pancakes were up and his mother set them in front of him. She met his eye for a brief second, and he wrestled with the emotions that stirred inside him at their warmth and familiarity. It had been a long time since he'd looked someone square in the eye, dared to look deep. Most days, especially recently, he couldn't even meet his own gaze in the mirror.

He realized she was waiting for him to take a bite, and he obliged. Sugary sweetness coated his mouth as he chewed, stirring up memories of sitting around the breakfast table, arguing with Mark over who got the comics section of the newspaper, the smell of coffee percolating, and his mother wearing her peach terrycloth bathrobe.

It felt like so long ago. But in so many ways, it felt like yesterday.

When was the last day they had gathered like that, first as a family of four and later as a family of three, not knowing that it was the last time? That the next week their mother would be given a devastating diagnosis and their world would be turned upside down? That their weekends would be spent in the hospital, not lounging around the old table in the kitchen overlooking the tree-filled backyard. That Brett would go off to college and that by the time he returned, Mark would have finally gone, too, and then…Then they were suddenly grown. Life had moved forward. And the casual comfort of their established routine was replaced with responsibility and ambition and a yearning for something different, something that didn't involve lazy pancake breakfasts.

Was it worth it?

He thought of his training, the years of studying, the hours he'd spent on his feet in residency, soaking up everything he could, learning on the job. The desperate gleam in a loved one's eyes as he rushed a patient into triage.

He forced another bite of pancakes into his mouth, even though his tongue felt dry and he'd lost his appetite.

Maybe it wasn't worth it. But it would have to be.

CHAPTER 15

Ivy tapped her shoes together and grinned with satisfaction. The polka-dot kitten-heel sandals hadn't seen the light of day in two years, and their discovery at the far back corner of her closet had been met with a grin of delight followed by a chain of sneezes. After she'd wiped away the dust, they were good as new, and judging from the blister that was starting to form on her big toe, they nearly were.

She slowed her pace so as not to hobble and began heading back to Petals on Main, where, after a bit of thumping and banging and spewing of a few choice curse words, she'd managed to move her beloved station wagon at six o'clock that morning, before most of Main Street had awoken.

A flutter of nerves rumbled through her stomach as she inched away from the bookstore. Brunch with her friends this morning had been her test—if they commented on her clothes in the wrong way, she'd have time to run home and change. Or, rather, limp home and change. But instead they'd simply commented on the cute tank top and skirt, leaving Ivy pleased to know that she was not overdressed for her... whatever it was... with Brett, but rather, simply appropriately attired for what promised to be a sunny Sunday afternoon.

The clock tower of the old church at the end of Second Avenue began to chime, and with a lurch, Ivy realized that there was a good chance Brett would make it to the shop before she did. She decided that was a good thing. Less time to flit around and get nervous. She ran her tongue over her teeth, happy that she'd opted for an herbal tea instead of coffee so she didn't risk coffee breath.

She stopped walking. Why? Why did it matter if she had coffee breath or not? In case he tried to kiss her?

He's not going to kiss you again, Ivy. So just get over it and stop wishing he would.

Because she realized, after last night in the car, that a part of her did still yearn for the touch of his lips. For the excitement she'd felt all through those cold winter months, imagining what it would be like when she saw him again.

But now she knew. Now she knew exactly how it would be. And it would be anything but the grand romance she'd envisioned.

Petals on Main was just up ahead. Normally, Ivy cheered up at the sight of its awning, in a crisp grass green, and the cast iron planters bursting with colorful blooms that flanked the paned front door. Since she wasn't open today, the racks of galvanized pots she usually propped outside the front windows were instead tucked in the storage room, and she spent the rest of the walk back to the shop thinking of what she'd look for at the wholesale market that night... and whether or not she spotted Brett anywhere in her periphery.

She was so busy darting her eyes that she didn't even notice the figure parked on the bench outside the storefront until she was too close to hide her surprise.

"Brett!"

He looked at her quizzically. "You seem surprised to see me. Wasn't this the time we agreed to meet?"

He was dressed casually, in jeans and a tight T-shirt that showed off the ripples of his chest and clung to the curves of his thick biceps. A day of stubble graced his square jaw, framing that slightly cocky grin, and his deep-set eyes danced with invitation, as if daring her to fall for him. And she wanted to. So badly.

She lifted her chin. "No, this was the time. Sorry, I just... I was in my own world," she finished hurriedly, keeping her body a healthy four feet from the park bench, even though she could almost imagine what it would feel like to scoot next to him, relax in the shade of the oak tree that swayed in the breeze overhead, feel the heat of his body radiating next to her own.

Crazy talk.

"The car's around the back," she offered, allowing her eyes to lift as he stood.

"You mean to tell me you actually got that thing to move?" His eyebrow arched in such an overly friendly way that she had to look away.

"I told you," she said as she led the way to the small alley behind the building. "It does drive. I use it every day."

He laughed under his breath, shaking his head as they approached the car. "Let's put it to the test then."

Ivy tightened her grip on the leather straps of her handbag. "No."

Merriment twinkled in his eyes, and in the afternoon sunlight, flecks of copper sparked through the rich brown color. "I'm here to help. There's only one way to know if this thing can run."

He reached out for her handbag, and Ivy tensed, thinking of what she had in the bag. Her blood glucose monitor. Her insulin shots. The juice boxes and fruit snacks. Everything she didn't want him to see.

She turned slowly as she slid her hand into the bag, feeling for the metal keys and the familiar rubber key chain in the shape of a tulip. She fumbled deeper, sensing Brett's eyes from her periphery and noticing the amusement in his grin, the mock impatience he showed by rolling back on his heels, refusing to busy himself with something else, determined instead to make this difficult for her.

Finally, once her face was starting to burn with humiliation, her fingers touched something metal and cold.

"Here," she said, triumphantly pulling the keys from her bag.

"Took you long enough," he commented, turning out his palm. "What do you have in there anyway?"

"Girl stuff." She glanced at his hand, so masculine and inviting, and dropped the keys into it before she did something stupid, like set her own in it.

Brett glanced down at the key chain, his brow furrowing a bit. "You don't have an automatic lock, I see."

"Well, it's too old."

"So no air bags, either." He tsked under his breath as he manually unlocked the door and slid inside. Frowning in concentration, he tried the ignition. Ivy bit her lip, knowing what would happen. The engine revved and surged but never quite clicked. He tried again. And again.

Finally, he stepped out of the car. He set his hands on his hips as he towered above her, but Ivy refused to bristle. She was used to this kind of treatment from her brother; she could take it. But somehow, coming from Brett, it had a whole different meaning. A sort of warm and tingly meaning. A good meaning. Maybe even a sexy meaning.

She suddenly realized what Jane meant when she said she liked Henry's protective side.

"Am I in trouble?" she asked, her voice just above a whisper.

His dark eyes gave her the once-over before locking her gaze. She held her breath, wishing he didn't have to look so good in that tight T-shirt. "You're in trouble, all right," he said, his voice hoarse and scratchy. He cleared his throat and broke her stare. Stepping around to the front of the car, he popped the hood. "Have you considered trading up for a newer model?" He reached inside and started inspecting whatever was in there...machinery, she supposed.

Of course she had, but unlike him, she wasn't earning a doctor's salary. "I like my car. Besides, I'd rather put my money toward other things."

He looked up. "So safety isn't your top priority."

She stepped back, hurt at the accusation, but he just laughed again and turned his attention to the car. Anger surged, stirring up the feelings she'd tried to suppress, the guilt that crept up every now and again when she thought of how recklessly she had behaved and how much she'd caused people who cared about her to worry.

"I do care about my safety," she ground out.

Brett looked up in surprise. "Okay," he finally said. "Then let's figure this out."

She hated how much it thrilled her that he had somehow made her problem something they would solve together. It made them feel almost like a couple.

She suddenly realized that Brett was watching her from under the hood of the car. His dark eyes were intense and unwavering, and she shifted on her heels, feeling the intensity of his scrutiny.

"I don't bite," he said, giving her a slow grin. Ivy felt her heart lurch on his words. They both knew he did bite—certain body parts in the heat of the moment. Maybe he just didn't remember that part. Unfortunately, she couldn't forget.

She reached up and touched her neck, recalling the tender graze of his teeth, and then just as quickly dropped her arm.

"You're not going to learn anything from all the way over there." He rested on his elbows, watching her. God help her, a smudge of grease stained the underside of his forearm, and his fingers were already coated. She swallowed hard. If he looked as rugged and capable working on a patient as he did on a car, it was no wonder the nurses at the hospital could barely control themselves.

"You mean...you want me to help?" A solid five feet of space was a safe distance. Far enough that she could quell any sudden urges she had to reach out and stroke him. Far enough that she didn't have to sense his body, just stare at it. Admire it, the way one might admire an actor on the stage.

Blowing out a breath, she slowly came closer, and this time it had nothing to do with her impractical shoes. Brett was back at work, elbows-deep under the hood, by the time she reached him. She tried to stand at the edge of the front bumper, but it seemed like such a halfhearted effort given how dirty he was getting with the work that she decided to move a little closer, until they were standing side by side. His eyes were trained on the car parts, but hers were trained on his man parts. And oh, they were lovely. His broad back pressed and strained against the thin cotton of his shirt, and she stared at it longingly, remembering how good it felt to press up against his torso, to feel the manly weight of it, so different from her own slender frame. She watched as his arms flexed and pulled, the cords of his muscles flexing as he tugged at something under the hood. Whatever it was, it wasn't nearly as interesting as the way the soft waves of his hair caressed the back of his neck...

"Reach into my pocket and grab my wrench," she thought she heard him say.

She blinked. "Ex—excuse me?"

"My wrench." He turned and looked at her over his shoulder, one eyebrow cocked the same way it had the night of Grace's wedding, when he'd suggested they get some air. And she'd known by the simple slip of his smile what he meant by *air*. "You do know what a wrench is, don't you?"

"Of course I know what a wrench is!" She pinched her lips, but her heart was doing jumping jacks as she lowered her gaze to his backside, where sure enough, a metal wrench was poking out, along with a screwdriver and what was probably his phone.

Was she seriously about to touch the man's butt? Not that she hadn't possibly already done so. That part of her memory was still a bit foggy. But she seemed to recall that as he lifted her leg and pushed his hand down her thigh that she had in fact reached down and given him a good hard squeeze...

Reddening, she stared at the wrench, glinting in the sun. It seemed to wink at her, as if mocking this moment and her totally unacceptable feelings for a man she could not have but wanted nevertheless!

It was no different than being asked to pass the scalpel, she told herself. Brett was probably used to barking out orders like this. *Just pretend you're a nurse. That car is a patient, desperately in need of medical attention. Do not look at his perfect backside. Do not touch anything but the wrench.*

With shaking fingers she used her thumb and pointer finger to grip the top of the tool and then precariously dislodge it from his rather tight pocket. She exhaled in relief. She hadn't even realized she'd been holding her breath.

"Here you go," she said, smiling as she handed it over.

Brett accepted it as if nothing out of the ordinary had just happened. As if he hadn't just more or less insisted she caress one of his personal areas.

Then she noticed his hands again. Of course. They were coated in grease and—she couldn't resist another glance—those jeans looked sort of expensive.

Heart sinking, she decided to make herself useful. "I'll go get you a rag," she offered.

Happy to be away from him for a bit, she let herself into the back door of the store and leaned against the wall, waiting for her heart to stop pounding. The storeroom was dark, but she didn't bother turning on a light. Instead, she grabbed a towel from the stack she kept on hand to clean up dirt and water spills and pulled her blood glucose monitor out of her bag. She had made a habit of checking it throughout the day, regardless of how she was feeling. Every time she did it, she eased the guilt, reconfirmed that she was on the right path, taking care of herself, being responsible.

The meter registered 110. Smiling to herself, Ivy tucked the monitor into her bag.

Brett was bent at the waist over her hood when she came back outside.

"How's it looking?" she asked, hoping he had some good news for her. She knew the car was old—it was old when she'd bought it six years ago—but she was hoping to get a few more years out of it, at least. The thought of coming up with a down payment, much less securing financing, for something new made her stomach clench with anxiety. She'd find the money, but it just meant paying back Henry would be further delayed.

Her plan was to write a check in full as a wedding gift. Then he couldn't refuse it.

And if he tried... then she'd just start a college savings fund for Sophie. She had it all planned out. That is, if other things didn't derail her effort.

Brett tossed her the keys. "Give it a try and we'll find out."

Ivy walked over to the car and slid into the driver's seat. She clicked the key into place and, saying a silent prayer, turned it. The engine revved and then settled to a gentle purr.

Grinning, she turned it off and climbed out of the car. "You did it!" she exclaimed, running over to the front where Brett stood grinning.

Normally, she'd probably hug a friend for this kind of thing, but Brett wasn't exactly a friend, and the last thing she needed was for him to go thinking she was trying to hit on him or something.

Brett wiped his hands on the towel until they were almost clean. "You still want to see the mechanic about this, but it should work for a while at least. When's the last time you changed your oil?"

Ivy felt herself blanch. She'd been so preoccupied with everything these past few months that she hadn't even thought about things like car maintenance.

"I guess I... forgot."

Brett slammed the hood shut and shrugged his shoulders good-naturedly. "You might want to do that. Soon." He winked.

Aw, now why'd he have to do that? A wink and a smile? Damn him.

"You can clean up inside if you'd like," she suggested. "I have a wash sink in the back room. And there's water in the fridge."

"Great." Brett grabbed the dirty towel and headed for the back door, returning moments later with two bottles of water, his bronzed arms now clean. "I grabbed you a water, but it seems like you might prefer juice."

She took the cold plastic bottle from his hand. "Oh, those are for Sophie," she said, waving a hand through the air. "Jane works a few shifts a week for me, and Sophie comes with her sometimes." It wasn't exactly a lie, per se. Once, she had offered Sophie a juice box when the little girl had stopped in with Jane to pick up an arrangement for the dance studio.

Still, she was eager to change the course of this conversation.

"So, where'd you learn so much about cars?" she asked.

"My dad collected old cars," Brett said, hopping onto the hood of the car. He squinted into the sunlight, his gaze somewhere faraway.

Ivy joined him, landing within an inch of his thighs. She stopped herself from scooting over, deciding there was no reason to flinch every time she thought she was sending the wrong signal. The guy had just fixed her car—clearly, she hadn't scared him off—and the more time they were spending together, the easier it was to just enjoy his company and accept the fact that, sad as it may be, they weren't looking for the same things.

"He liked to work on them in his spare time," Brett continued, pausing to take a sip of the water. "And I liked watching. Some of my fondest memories are those of watching him work on an engine."

"That's sweet," Ivy said. "I never knew my dad."

"I barely knew my dad, either," Brett said, his jaw tensing. "He spent all his time in that restaurant, working, and when he was home... Well, we just got the leftovers, no pun intended." His smile was grim. "He didn't have much time for us."

"My mom didn't either," Ivy said. She hesitated—she didn't talk about her mother much, not even with Henry. It felt like a distant part of her past now, and one she didn't want to relive.

Her mother's condition was known around town. No one could overlook the way she behaved at public events, the way she got loud and sometimes disorderly, the way neighbors would have to step in and gently urge her to go home and have a rest. Few people said anything directly, but they whispered, and the pitying looks they gave to Ivy and Henry confirmed it.

She'd hated that kind of attention, almost as much as Henry did. She'd vowed not to let it define her. And she'd almost gone and done just that last summer by letting her diabetes get out of control.

"I always thought that if my mom really cared, like if she genuinely, truly loved us, she would have stopped drinking." Her voice broke a little on the end, and she took a sip of her water. It was the most emotional she'd gotten on the subject with anyone in a while, but she oddly wasn't embarrassed. Brett was easy to talk to. Always had been.

"It's not that easy," Brett said simply. "Addiction is a powerful thing."

She liked his matter-of-fact approach almost as much as she liked how unfazed he was by her admission.

"My dad didn't have any excuse. He was just selfish."

The bitterness in his tone stung, and Ivy frowned at the hurt in his voice. She wanted to reach out, hold his hand. Instead, she slid it under her thigh and put some weight on it. Now wasn't the time to be doing anything crazy.

"Maybe he just didn't know how to balance his life," she offered. "Running your own business can be daunting, and I know from Anna that the restaurant business is particularly high pressure."

Brett looked at her flatly. "He was running a restaurant, not saving lives." He shook his head. "I didn't mean it like that. I just...I just think that you have to pick and choose what it is most important, and if you can't find a way to balance everything, then you don't try to have everything. It's simple."

She eyed him thoughtfully. "You sound a lot like my brother. He found a way to balance everything, though." She thought of how happy he was, working a steady job, still pursuing what he loved, and coming home to the family he'd always wanted but never knew how to have.

"Well, he's an exception to the rule," Brett remarked. He popped the top back on his water bottle and hopped off the car. With one hand on his lower back, he stretched, pulling the cotton T-shirt taut across his broad chest and revealing an inch of smooth skin just above his belt loops. "And he ultimately sacrificed something."

If Brett was implying that Henry had given up his lonely travel writing days, then yes, technically he had sacrificed that job, but Ivy knew he was happier with his decision. It didn't seem like there was any sense trying to convince Brett of this, though.

"You going to the Fourth of July festival?" she asked

as she hopped off the hood. She was standing close to him, close enough to feel the heat from his body, warmer than the summer breeze.

Brett shrugged and gave her another one of those stomach-turning slow smiles. "I was sort of hoping to skip it, but I don't really see how I can."

Ivy looked at him quizzically. "But it's fun."

"So you'll be there?"

"Wouldn't miss it," Ivy said.

Brett shoved his hands in his pockets thoughtfully. His eyes were steady on hers, betraying nothing, even though she felt like there was something he was eager to say. Finally, he just said, "Well, maybe I'll see you there then."

Hope deflated as quickly as a popped balloon. *Maybe* he would see her there? He couldn't have been less committed in his word choice if he'd tried, and she had an inkling he had some practice in stringing together sentences like that. And she'd had her share of practice hearing those types of lines.

"Yeah, maybe," she replied, taking a step back from his tall form, those wide shoulders, and that grin that made her stop thinking clearly. It didn't matter that they'd shared a moment or even that he'd stopped by to help. Whatever his motives were, only one thing was clear, and that was that Brett wasn't looking for a girlfriend.

And she wasn't looking for a fling.

CHAPTER 16

Briar Creek's annual Fourth of July festival was a time-honored tradition and one Ivy was especially thrilled to be a part of for the fourth consecutive year. With the exception of the diner and the pub, shops along Main Street closed down for the day, and everyone in town gathered on the square. It was Ivy's chance to showcase what she did best—not just with the oversized floral arrangements she used to anchor various stations, but to really transform what was otherwise a blank canvas.

"The decorations look even better this year than last," Grace admired as she stared up at the gazebo Ivy had trimmed in patriotic swag.

"That's what I was hoping for," Ivy said, feeling a twinge of pride. She brushed a strand of hair from her forehead and swept her eyes over the green, where people were gathered at round tables covered in red, white, and blue cloths, eating corn on the cob and eagerly waiting for the pie-eating contest to commence. This year, she'd tried to convince Henry to join, but he just shook his head. He may have embraced their small town again, but he had to draw the line somewhere.

"It's a hot one today," Grace said, fanning herself. Even the shade of the giant maple did little to offset the humidity that seemed to cling to their skin and made Ivy's twenty minutes with the hair straightener feel like an official waste of time.

She'd been up since five and hard at work since six, and even though the volunteer committee did the majority of the heavy lifting, Ivy had climbed on a ladder more times than she'd wished to, in a sundress no less.

At the edge of the lawn, Luke called over to Grace, and she blushed a little at the sound of her name. "It never gets old," she said, and Ivy felt her heart sink a little. It didn't go unnoticed that a lot had changed over the course of these events...for some. More and more, everyone was part of a pair, and Ivy was still on her own, still the third wheel, still waiting for her chance to belong to someone special.

At least she had work to keep her busy, she thought as a little boy began jumping up to tug at the flags she had trimmed the gazebo with. Heaving a sigh, Ivy turned to Grace. "I'll be back in a minute. Duty calls."

By the time she had finished repairing the swag and giving the young man in question a no-nonsense glance that sent him running to his mother, Grace was back on the picnic blanket with Luke and her sisters...and their significant others. And Brett was still nowhere to be seen.

She should be relieved, not disappointed. After all, there was nothing healthy about the little tingle she felt when he was around. That tingle represented hope, and she was done holding out any for that man.

"Where is everybody?"

Ivy jumped, and even before she turned, she knew Brett had come up behind her. His voice was deep and low and just close enough to her ear to stir up all those wrong feelings she had tried to deny.

She forced a casual grin as she turned to face him, but her traitorous heart pinged on impact with those deep-set eyes.

"Oh. Hey. You mean Mark and Luke? They're over there, under the tree." She relished the opportunity to look across the square, to focus on something other than Brett.

He was wearing a green shirt, she couldn't help but notice. Not exactly getting into the spirit of things.

By contrast, she wore a red cotton sundress. Standing next to each other, they looked like they were ready for Christmas, not the Fourth of July.

Ill-suited, she reminded herself. Definitely ill-suited.

"Oh." Brett seemed satisfied with her answer but, contrary to what she expected, he made no motion to walk over to join his brother and cousin. Instead, he turned his attention on her, his gaze roaming her face just long enough for her to shift under the intensity. "So, how's the car running?"

She grinned. "Better than ever," she said. She didn't bother to mention that every time she slid into the driver's seat and turned the ignition she thought of him.

"Good. You get that oil changed?"

It had been a busy two weeks with three showers and the Fourth of July festival, in addition to the usual anniversaries and birthdays to accommodate, not to mention all the work she had for the hospital benefit, but she nodded with certainty. "Sure did."

"Good." He nodded slowly, as if appraising her, his eyes lazily drifting over her face until they lingered on her mouth.

She pulled in a sharp breath. The afternoon sun was really beating down and Ivy would kill for a soft breeze right about now, or a cold glass of punch. She set a hand to her head, feeling the onset of fatigue and a twinge of dizziness she knew better than to dismiss.

When was the last time she had eaten anything? She'd told herself she would stop for lunch once she had done the rounds and made sure everything was in order, but then Henry and Jane had arrived, and Sophie had bounded up, begging for a ride on the pony she insisted was named Marshmallow, and well, how could she miss that?

"Do you know the time?" she asked Brett. She ran a mental checklist of what she'd seen to eat. Usually she planned her day around these types of things, either by scoping out possible options or bringing something with her instead. But somehow, between the setup, hanging out with Henry and Sophie, and, shamefully, keeping an eye out for Brett, she'd been completely distracted.

"Just about four," he replied.

Ivy's eyes sprang open. "Four?" She'd missed her second insulin dose. She'd been religious about it, ever since last summer, when she'd attempted to self-medicate by diet alone until she got on a better insurance plan that made the cost of her medication more affordable. Instead, she'd landed in the hospital with medical bills far higher than monthly supplies. And then she'd had no choice but to take help from Henry.

She wouldn't be doing that again.

"I need to..." A wave of nausea stirred in her gut as she greedily eyed a porta-potty. Then she noticed the line for it, and her heart began to beat a little faster.

She'd make up an excuse. Go back to the shop.

Her hands were shaking now and she felt herself sway slightly to the side.

Brett's hand was on her arm immediately. He squinted at her in concern. "Are you okay?"

"I'm just…It's the heat." She waved her hand through the air and gave a little laugh. It sounded hollow and distant, as if it were coming from somewhere else and not her own body. She was shaking and sweating. She suddenly felt clammy and cold despite the temperature.

"Here. Sit down. You need some shade."

"I need…" Food. Juice. Where was her bag? She didn't even remember where she'd left it.

Under the chair for the cake judging contest. Where she had so brilliantly thought it would be tucked away and safe. Now that stand was a football field's length away from her. She wasn't going to make it.

"I need my bag," she whispered to Brett. "It's…" But the words weren't coming out, even as she tried to form them, fighting the numbness of her lips and tongue, and her vision became blurry. She bent over at the waist as her body temperature climbed with heat far hotter than the sun's rays.

Brett's voice was in her ear, urgent and firm. "Where's your bag?"

"The cake…" She managed to gesture to the table across the lawn.

Tears sprang to her eyes as she thought of her mother, all the times she'd embarrassed them with her public scenes at these events. It was like the music came to a halt, and there was Debbie, staggering around, talking loud, making a scene. The fantasy would be over. The fun gone. And Henry would take her hand, hold it tight, and silently walk her across the square to their mother. They'd make their way home and sit in that dark, depressing house, knowing that the other kids were still licking ice cream cones and playing

ring-toss games and that their parents were probably gathered in small circles, talking in hushed tones about the day's
dramatic turn.

Ivy didn't want to be the one they talked about. And she
didn't want the fun to end.

She wanted to sit on the picnic blanket with Grace
and Anna and Jane. She wanted to kick off her shoes and
enjoy the day and not have to worry. Or make anyone else
worry.

"I'll be right back." She felt Brett stand, heard him say,
"Stay here with her," and heard Sharon Hastings's voice in
her ear as she stroked her head.

"Heat stroke, poor thing. Good thing my son's a doctor.
He'll help you."

Only it wasn't heat stroke, and Brett must have known it.
Heat stroke was treated with shade and water. And he wasn't
going for those things. He was going for her bag.

She heard the rustling of fabric, vaguely smelled the
sweet, familiar musk, and heard the opening of her bag.
Sharon was talking, somewhere in the distance, mentioning
water, that she'd be right back, and then there was the sound
of a plastic straw being ripped from a juice box, and it was
pushed to her face, into her mouth. She took a long sip, Brett
patiently talking her through it.

She blinked, looking up into his eyes. She'd never seen
them so sharp. So alert.

He handed her a bag of fruit snacks, already opened, fed
a few into her mouth. She chewed and swallowed, and shiv-
ered as the world around her became clear again, and Sharon
reappeared with a large plastic cup of water.

"Poor thing," she said, leaning down to hand it to Ivy.
Ivy took it with shaking hands. "It's too hot out today. Every

July, I say the same thing. You go take a rest, honey. Brett, get her in the shade."

"I've got a better idea," Brett said. He was still resting on his heels, crouched eye to eye, and the smile that broke his face turned her heart over. "What do you say you and me have an early dinner?"

Brett's heart was still pounding when he pushed open the door of Hastings a few minutes later and waited for Ivy to pass. The diner was empty and cool, and he led them to a booth in the corner, where they'd be uninterrupted if things picked up. Brett pulled two menus from their stack behind the metal napkin dispenser and slid one to Ivy.

"Thanks," she said. Her voice was small, her gaze fleeting, and her cheeks still far too pale for his liking.

Brett struggled to control his breath against the pounding in his chest. That had been scary, and unexpected. As a physician, he was prepared to act when the need arose. When he'd first started his residency, he'd idly considered the possibility every time he boarded an airplane or even walked into a restaurant, but it was different to treat a stranger than to see someone you knew struggling.

He'd experienced that scenario enough for one lifetime.

Ivy waited until they had placed their orders to say, "So, how'd you know?"

He raised an eyebrow and studied her across the Formica table. She seemed more resigned than usual, and less spirited. The fire in her eyes was gone. He found himself missing it.

"I'm a doctor. It's sort of my business to put symptoms together and come up with a diagnosis." Usually he got it right. But not always...

He took a sip of his water and set it back on the table, realizing she was still waiting for a better answer. "I noticed you passed up the cookies at Jane's house that night. I found it odd, given how much you'd praised them, but then I just figured you were like most girls and were watching your weight." He caught the spark in her eyes and grinned. "Not that you need to worry about that. You're just right."

"Just right, eh?" She gave a small smile.

His gaze dropped to the delicate space between her clavicle and lower to the hint of cleavage that skimmed the rim of her dress. "Just right." He swallowed hard and tore his eyes away.

Focusing on what he did best, he cleared his throat, determined to keep this professional and to keep his head where it belonged.

"Then at your shop, I noticed you had a fridge full of juice boxes. Your comment about Sophie didn't seem to add up, especially when Jane mentioned she only works for you a few hours a week now. While Sophie's in school. Then today . . . It's hot out there, but not hot enough for heat stroke." He'd known immediately what was happening, seen the warning signs flash across his mind, alerting him to everything that could go wrong if action wasn't taken.

He reached for his water, forcing it back.

"Good thing not everyone shares your knowledge," Ivy commented ruefully. She took a long sip of water through a straw, her brows pinching pensively. "I suppose I was lucky you came along."

"No one else knows then?" Brett frowned. Diabetes wasn't his specialty, but he'd dealt with his share of cases in the emergency room, and he knew the signs of both hypoglycemia and hyperglycemia . . . and the consequences.

"Henry." Ivy sighed. She poked her ice cubes with her straw. "And Jane."

"And?"

"My mother knew, of course. A few teachers at the school who have since retired."

"What about Grace?" She was her best friend, after all. They were inseparable growing up; everyone knew that.

Ivy shook her head. "Nope. Not Grace. Or Anna. Or their mother. The only reason Jane knows is because..." She trailed off, refusing to look him in the eye.

He rolled over his palms. "Because?"

She hesitated. "I...had a similar situation last fall. At Grace's bridal shower. Jane called Henry and he told her what to tell the paramedics."

"Jesus." Brett blinked hard. If he was understanding her correctly, that meant she could have rolled into his emergency room at some point. The thought of it made his blood run cold.

It was one thing when a patient on the table was a stranger. It was another when it was someone he cared about. Thoughts of his mother lying in that bed, frail and weak, without a hint of color in her cheeks, made his chest tighten until he struggled for breath. He took a long sip of water, trying to banish the image.

"It was a rough time. I wasn't managing my diet properly or my medication. It's one of the reasons Henry came back to town."

"I don't have to lecture you on how serious this is," Brett said. He cursed to himself, knowing damn well the risks associated with the disease. Nerve damage, kidney damage, eye damage. He gritted his teeth, hating the thought of Ivy in that position.

"It was a brief time in my life and I'm not proud of it. I learned my lesson. The hard way, of course." Her steely gaze held his.

"Fair enough. I'm not your doctor. I'm just your friend."

Her mouth quirked. "Friends, are we?"

He raked his gaze over her pretty mouth, the flush that was returning to her cheeks, and the cool, clear blue of her eyes. She was pretty, but she was also sweet. And from the jumping jacks that were still playing in his chest over that episode on the lawn, he had a feeling that *friend* was the furthest thing from the truth. But *friend* was safe. *Friend* he could do.

Their food was up—a burger for him and chicken salad for her—and he doused his fries with ketchup, considering everything she'd said. "When were you diagnosed? If you don't mind me asking."

"No. It's okay." She picked up her fork and glanced at him. "First grade."

Type 1, then. "And why doesn't anyone else know?"

"Why should they?" Her tone was sharp, and her mouth pinched as she stabbed at her food before bringing it to her mouth. "Sorry," Ivy said. "I didn't mean to sound so sharp. Growing up in this town as a Birch will do that to you." Her smile was grim, but the apology in her eyes tore at him.

"It was embarrassing, at best," she continued. "Anywhere I went, I felt like everyone was watching me, knowing my story, that I was the girl with no dad and a drunk mom. I hated feeling that way. All I wanted was to fit in."

"That's all any kid wants," he said softly. He could feel her pain. He knew it himself. Wouldn't he have loved to have been like the other boys, going to baseball games with their dads, tossing the ball around in the backyard?

He punched some fries into the ketchup. He would have

loved that a lot. Instead, he'd had to stand on the outskirts and watch and be reminded of what might have been.

"The diabetes just felt like one more thing that made me different. So I didn't offer it up."

"Fair enough," he said, but it still made him sad to think of her not having a support system in place. She was feisty, and fiery, and fiercely independent. He'd come to admire those traits in her. But the reason behind them was hard to think about. "But we're all adults now. No one associates you with that time in your life, from what I can tell. I certainly don't. And as for your disease, I'm sure your friends would want to help."

"See, that's just the problem," Ivy insisted. "Ever since Jane found out, she treats me differently. She watches what I eat. She limits what she eats in front of me for fear of hurting my feelings or something." Ivy shook her head. "I feel bad. You're missing the festival because of me."

He grinned. "I didn't really want to go to that thing anyway, so in a way, you did me a favor."

"I guess we're even now," she said. "I should have repaid you something for your help with my car."

"Oh, well, I didn't say we were even…" He rubbed his jaw, happy to have a reason to lighten the subject. He didn't want to think of Ivy as sick or struggling. He didn't want to worry about another person, especially not her. She didn't deserve it. But then, who did? "Those decorations at the festival. You really did all that?"

She nodded.

"I never really thought of decorations for the fundraiser, but I'm guessing most people like that sort of thing." When he caught the tilt of her head, he said, "Hey, right brain, left brain."

"Man brain," Ivy replied, but she grinned.

Brett's laugh felt a little hollow. She saw him as a flirt, a cad, no doubt, someone who picked up women and then walked away.

And he couldn't argue with that assessment, much as he hated the thought of his image through her eyes. He'd told himself that he was playing fair, that they were grown women and he wasn't the one getting their hopes up, but maybe he had it all wrong. And maybe Ivy had it all right. Maybe he was a jerk.

He thought of his father, the way he'd treated Brett's mother. He respected women more than his old man had. Respected them enough not to get emotionally involved with them if he was only going to let them down in the end.

And he respected Ivy more than any other woman he'd met in a long time. Respected the way she ran a business, the way she stood up for herself, the way she held her head high and didn't let rough times define her, the way he possibly had.

He swallowed hard. He hadn't felt this way about a woman in a long time—if ever. Which was why he never should have kissed her. And why, now more than ever, he could never do it again.

He took a bite of his burger, tasting nothing, and washed it down with his water, eying Ivy over the rim of his glass. She was pretty, beautiful, really, and far too good for him. She deserved a good man, a strong man, someone who would be there when the times got rough. That couldn't be him. Much as it saddened him, he knew it just couldn't.

CHAPTER 17

Petals on Main looked quiet, and the store windows gave no hint of life behind the black-painted panes. Brett felt his heart skip a beat as he crossed Main Street. It was past noon—he'd waited this long on purpose, knowing that many shops in Briar Creek got a late start on Sundays.

The petal-shaped sign on the door neatly read CLOSED, and panic shot through him until he noticed the schedule of hours at the bottom corner. Of course. She was closed on Sunday. Just as she had been when he'd come to help with the car.

All at once, concern was replaced with something worse: disappointment. He pushed it back, telling himself it had no right to be there, that seeing her should be no different than seeing one of the Madisons. Nice girls, girls he'd grown up with, gone to school with, socialized with in groups. Nothing more than that. Except that he hadn't kissed any of the Madisons. And he'd never felt that spark for any of them, either.

Never felt that spark with anyone, he realized.

He pushed his hands into the pockets of his jeans and

turned on his heel, away from the shop and all reminders of Ivy. Sweeping his eyes down Main Street, he considered his options. A coffee at Hastings or the bookstore. An afternoon drink at the pub. A long, lonely afternoon in front of the television back at the carriage house.

None of it appealed to him. In Baltimore, he never felt stir-crazy like this. He was working more, and on his days off, he enjoyed his downtime, with friends and the casual date. But there would be no casual dating in Briar Creek. Or with any of the women who worked at the hospital—he wasn't that stupid.

And for once the thought of a casual date, company for the sake of company, with no substance, left him cold.

He turned back to take another glance in the window of the flower shop. The sign was handmade and hung from a green ribbon that matched the awning over the shop. The doormat bore the age-old saying "Bloom where you are planted."

Brett felt his lips thin. So much for that.

When he was in Baltimore, he could focus on work. He was distracted from the reminder of everything he'd left behind and the sacrifices he'd made—most of the time. He still struggled to look his mother in the eye, despite the time he was spending with her, hoping it would make up for the past, and his gut churned each time she mentioned this or that friend who had been so good to her when she was going through treatment.

It should have been him. Not some neighbor. Not even Aunt Rosemary. He was her son. And he'd turned his back on her... for his career.

He wouldn't do that to another woman.

He turned to go. Ivy was fine, he told himself. She'd been

fine when he walked her back here last night—fresh faced, full of energy—making it easy for him to overlook what had happened, how badly she'd scared him, how she'd touched upon that fear he'd tried to stamp out over the years. She was probably upstairs, enjoying her day. Or off with friends. Possibly, she was even on a date.

He frowned at the thought of it.

He'd go to the gym, he decided. It was the one true release this town offered him.

He started retracing his steps back to the corner when the sound of a window sliding open caught his attention, following promptly by the sound of his name.

He turned to follow the voice and saw Ivy poking her head out of the window above the shop. Her auburn hair cascaded down, drawing shadows on her face and shielding the better part of it from view. He yearned to reach up, brush it behind her ear, just for a full glimpse of that smile.

"I saw you standing down there. We're closed on Sundays, but I can make an exception for the man who hates flowers."

He grinned. "You're never going to let me forget that, are you?"

"Nope. What's the occasion? Your mom's birthday is January eighth. Is there another special lady in your life?"

Was there? He looked up at Ivy, feeling his pulse begin to race. "How'd you remember my mom's birthday?"

"I told you. I'm in the business of knowing these things."

He couldn't think of more than three or four people who knew his birthday, and he was ashamed to realize that he would have had to pause and think about his mother's for a little longer than it took Ivy to rattle it off. It was one of the differences between their businesses, he supposed, but he couldn't fight a twinge of guilt that stirred within him at the thought.

"I actually came by to see how you're feeling," he called up.

Ivy hesitated for a moment and then tipped her head. "Let me buzz you in."

Brett hesitated, but he did as she suggested and went over to the door between her shop window and the next storefront. Seconds later, the door buzzed, and he pulled it open to climb the stairs and venture one step closer into Ivy's world.

He bit back a smile as he hurried to the landing at the top, telling himself over and over that this was a professional visit and that it couldn't be anything more.

Ivy frantically gathered the pile of unfolded laundry from her bed and shoved it into the closet. She then tossed the duvet cover onto her bed, grabbed the pillows from the floor, and set them side by side.

Ridiculous! It wasn't like he was here for *that*—and even if he was, she wasn't up for it. Well...she wasn't up for the disappointment that would inevitably follow.

She closed the bedroom door firmly, and then, on second thought, left it open a crack. The living room was passable, save the chenille throw wedged in the corner of the sofa. She rolled it into a ball and then, realizing that looked even worse, tossed it over the back of her secondhand armchair.

The knock came as she was frantically loading the breakfast dishes into the dishwasher.

"One second!" she called, dashing into the bathroom. She smoothed her hair and took a deep breath before flicking off the light. Her apartment hadn't looked this tidy in a while, and all it had taken was fifteen seconds. For the first time, she was grateful for its minuscule size.

She flung open the door, not sure if her heart was pounding from nerves or the mad sprint around the three tiny rooms that constituted her home, but the sight of Brett in her door frame confirmed it was the former. Her pulse skipped a beat as his chocolate-brown eyes met hers and his lips curved into that slow, sexy smile. She opened her mouth to speak, but no words came out, so she simply took a step back and grinned as he crossed the threshold.

He looked big and out of place in the living room, drawing attention to its small scale and lack of male visitors. Henry was the only constant man in her life, and she usually saw him at his house, not here.

When her girlfriends popped by, they usually sat together on the sofa or one took the chair, but they were shorter than Brett and smaller boned. Instead, Brett seemed to tower, filling the narrow space between the television and the coffee table, and Ivy ushered him to sit.

He arranged himself on the edge of the sofa, as if suggesting she share it with him.

She eyed the armchair. It would be the sensible thing to do.

"How about some coffee?" She waited, wondering what he would say, if the purpose of his visit was purely professional, if he would start berating her about her diet, question her setback yesterday. She couldn't bear it. Even if he wasn't interested in her romantically, and even if they were just friends, she didn't need another reminder in her life of how different she was. She didn't want the white-glove treatment. If anything, she wouldn't mind Brett getting a bit rough with her.

Oh, Ivy.

"Coffee sounds good," Brett said, plucking a throw pillow out from behind his back. He set it to the side and hooked his ankle on the opposite knee, watching her expectantly.

"Great. So . . . I'll be right back." She calmly walked into her kitchen, but she struggled to push back the small thrill that Brett was in her apartment, sitting on her couch.

How many nights had she lain in bed, dreaming of this type of scenario? Only in her fantasies, she would wake to his fingers stroking her bare back, his smooth, sleepy voice whispering in her ear, and after a round of morning pleasure, she'd lazily climb from the tangled sheets, slip on one of his shirts (because there would be shirts, and they would be his, because maybe he lived with her by then . . . she'd never thought out those details), and pad into the kitchen, humming a little song under her breath while she prepared a breakfast tray, complete with a vase and flower (she'd always envisioned a red tulip) for the man who was waiting for her in bed, propped up on an elbow, chest bare, smile positively wicked.

She sighed now and then stared at the flickering blue flames on the gas range, not knowing how long had passed. Quickly, she filled the kettle, set it to boil, and began filling the French press's carafe with coffee grounds.

"Milk or sugar?" she asked, poking her head around the corner. He was standing now, inspecting some of her paintings.

"Neither," he replied.

She smiled briefly and pulled back into the kitchen, her pulse racing. She decided to busy herself by preparing a tray while she waited for the water to boil—anything to avoid going in there and talking to him until she had officially gathered her wits.

So he was wearing a mossy green T-shirt that brought out some flecks around his irises. So his hair looked adorably disheveled. So his shoulders looked even broader than ever, giving her a little thrill followed by a horrible sinking feeling when she recalled how good it felt to push up against his chest.

The kettle whistled—a high, unforgiving pitch—and with a shaking hand, Ivy flicked the knob and filled the glass carafe. Brett was back in place on the sofa when she entered the room.

"Here you go, sir," she said, setting down the tray and handing him a mug.

"Thanks." He took a sip and leaned back casually. After a beat, his brow pinched. "Aren't you going to sit?"

"Oh." Ivy wrung her hands, her eyes darting from the sofa to the chair. It was a really small sofa. So small that when Henry came back to town last summer, he had refused to sleep on it, even though he wanted to hover about and watch her every move.

But to sit on the armchair across the room might be formal and...unwelcoming.

She slid onto the sofa next to him, sinking deep into the old cushions, as casually as she would with an old friend, though certainly not such a handsome one.

"How are you feeling?" His tone was conversational, but she winced all the same. This was what she was afraid of, what she avoided with anyone she could.

"Fine." She blew on her coffee and took a sip. "Thanks again for yesterday."

He shrugged. "That's what friends are for."

There was that word again. She wasn't so sure how she felt about it yet. "Is that what we are? Friends?" Growing up, they'd been classmates. They'd gotten along well, hung out in the same social circles, and attended the same parties, even partnered together on some school projects.

"We could give it a try," Brett said. "I'm willing if you are."

Ivy held his gaze, hating the part of her that wanted to cry out that no, she didn't want to be friends. Not just friends. How could she be friends with someone who had kissed her so intensely and just as easily walked away? He'd rejected her. And it stung. But he was also being nice to her. Showing her that sweeter, tender side that had made her fall for him in the first place, all those years ago.

She smiled sadly. Briar Creek was a small town. Too small for enemies. And after yesterday, Brett knew her better than most in this town. In some ways, he was now closer to her than Grace or Kara. She wasn't so sure how she felt about that. Could she trust him with her secret?

She held out her hand and gritted her teeth against the spasm of lust that shot through her when he took it in his palm, warm from the heat of his mug. "Friends."

His grin widened, exposing that quirk in his cheek. "I wasn't sure you'd agree to it after…"

She frowned. Was he…blushing? His cheeks were definitely a bit pinker than usual. Brett the ninth grader, who seemed so sweet and accessible and yet so untouchable all the same, had blushed—when he was forced to do a presentation in English class, when he'd won first place in the science fair. But Brett the bachelor who had all the girls at Forest Ridge Hospital swooning? That Brett didn't blush.

Yet somehow he just had.

She fought off a smile. "Aw, you're not all that bad. Believe me, I've known worse."

He seemed to not know whether to laugh or frown, so she decided to make it easy for him. "Let's see, there was the guy who turned out to be engaged. The one who ended up having a criminal record. Petty theft, but still." She shrugged, amused.

Brett choked on his coffee. "You can't be serious."

"Oh, but I can." Ivy shrugged. "So, really, Brett, I'm flattered that you're so concerned about my welfare, but I'm a big girl, you're a big boy, and it was just a kiss."

"Just a kiss." His eyes locked with hers and she glanced away.

"So," she said, huffing out a breath. "I've told you all my dirty secrets. Now it's your turn."

His eyes flashed for a second and a muscle in his jaw flinched. "Not much to tell, I'm afraid."

"Never been dumped, I take it." Of course not.

He shook his head softly. "Always been the dumper, I'm afraid."

Figured. Ivy pursed her lips and set her coffee down. It wasn't personal. It was just who he was. But the part that hurt was that she'd never stood a chance.

"Well, some advice from one friend to another," she forced out. "Don't go breaking any hearts around here. If you do, Rosemary and her book club will be beating down your door, planning an intervention."

His laugh was low and throaty, like rich gravel. She could get used to that sound.

"What do you have planned for the rest of the day?" she asked. See, this was nice. A week ago a question like that would make her worried she sounded suggestive or eager, but now that they were friends, it was totally normal. Yep, totally and completely normal. About as normal as gazing into your friend's eyes and wishing he would just lunge across the couch and slide his hands between your thighs.

"I might hit the gym. How about you?"

"I have to go to the flower market tonight, so I'll probably catch a nap beforehand."

"At midnight." Damn. He looked so cute when he cocked that eyebrow.

"Yep. Midnight."

He leaned back into a cushion. "I'm curious about this market. It must be pretty special to drag yourself there at that hour."

"I'd invite you along, but seeing as you hate flowers so much—"

"Maybe this market will change my mind." He grinned.

She blinked. He wasn't...He couldn't be suggesting he join her? "You did hear me say midnight, right?"

"Honey, I'm an ER doctor. I'm used to operating at that hour." He leaned over and set his mug on the tray. "Besides, I should probably tag along, give some input for the fund-raiser. It's fast approaching."

Ivy felt a little flicker of panic when she considered all the work she needed to do. "True."

His lips curved into an easy smile that made her stomach roll over. "It's a date then."

Ivy swallowed and pushed the swell of her heart back where it belonged. "It's a date."

CHAPTER 18

Brett was downstairs waiting at half past eleven when Ivy slipped out the front door, holding two thermoses of coffee and wearing a grin that made him stand a little straighter.

"We're taking the wagon," she informed him, jingling her car keys. Before he could protest, she added, "It's the only way to transport the flowers."

"Just how many are you planning on buying?" he asked.

She grinned knowingly. "You'll see."

"Something tells me I'm going to regret tagging along," he joked.

Ivy stopped walking, her face serious in the glow of the sensor light behind the alley when she turned to him. "You don't need to come if you changed your mind."

Like hell. Now that he was here, with her again, that familiar twinge was back. He didn't want to go. The few hours that had passed since he'd left her apartment had been long, and even a few hours in the gym with Mark and a homemade dinner with his mother had done little to dull the emotion that was building in his chest. It was one he recognized but one he seldom experienced outside of the hospital when he was waiting for an ambulance to arrive. Anticipation.

He jammed his hands into his pockets. "No, I think I should go. For the benefit and all..."

She didn't question the excuse, and he waited outside the passenger door while she slipped into the car and popped his lock. The engine started without much trouble, and he felt a flicker of pride, wondering if his dad would feel the same, if his dad would have even cared.

He didn't think of him when he was in Baltimore or when he was working. It was one of the perks of being away from here. There weren't any reminders. He could compartmentalize his life into nice, neat boxes. Most of the time. Here in Briar Creek...everything overlapped. There were too many ties. Too much history. It was messy. And he didn't like messy.

Which was exactly why he shouldn't be going for a midnight road trip with a girl he was wildly attracted to. A girl with health problems. A girl who could end up being an official patient one day if she didn't take proper care of herself.

His gut tightened at the thought.

"So," Ivy said, once they were on the road that took them straight out of town, "you aren't going to cause a scene or anything, are you? Because I can promise you that everyone who is at the market will love flowers about as much as I do. You need a florist license to get in."

"I promise I'll behave," he said when she met his eye for a moment before skirting it back to the road. Only he wasn't so sure he wanted to behave when he trailed his gaze down over the curve of her breasts to linger on her endlessly long legs.

"So, let me get this straight. You don't like flowers because you see them around the hospital too much."

"It's more complicated than that," he said, shifting in the seat. It was hard and uncomfortable, and he doubted he'd ever get the hint of rose scent out of his clothing.

"I've got time," Ivy said, flicking her turn signal, even though there wasn't another car in sight in any direction.

He hesitated. "I was in high school when my mom was diagnosed with cancer." He didn't know why he was bothering with this, why he couldn't have just made up an excuse—he was good at that. But something about being here with Ivy in this dark car, the radio turned off, the road open, gave him a sense of peace and connection he hadn't felt in a long time.

"I remember," Ivy said, and he could detect a hint of regret in her tone. Normally, that type of thing would make him slam on the brakes, but her gentle encouragement was different than overt pressing, and so he decided to go on.

"My dad had been gone for years by then, and it was just me and Mark. He stayed back from going to culinary school initially to help." He shook his head, squinting at the unfairness of it. The horrible position they had all been put in—boys forced to grow up too quickly, his mother left with no one else to depend on. "I just remember wishing, more than anything, that there was something I could do to make it stop. To make her better. And wishing there was another adult, since my dad wasn't around to step in and take control of the situation."

"And instead they sent flowers," Ivy finished.

"Yep. Flowers and balloons, and more flowers. And every time the nurse knocked on the door holding a new bouquet, it was a fresh reminder that there was nothing anyone could do to help. Not the way we needed to be helped."

"They did what they could to show they cared. That they were thinking of you."

Brett narrowed his eyes at the road. "Deep down I knew that, but I felt so helpless at the time. I swore I would never feel that helpless again."

"Is that why you became a doctor?"

"I hated hospitals. Never wanted to step foot in one again. But I never wanted to feel that way again, either."

Ivy turned onto the highway and stepped on the accelerator. The engine revved and clanked, and Brett eyed her for a reaction, but from the casual way she merged into the empty lane, he could only surmise she was used to it.

He chuckled under his breath. She was a scrapper. Got by on what she had. Made the most of her situation. He admired that about her. Understood it all too well.

"So, can I ask why you didn't choose to become an oncologist then?"

It was an obvious question, and one Mark, his aunt Rosemary, and his cousins had voiced at some point, too. Only his mother had never questioned his decision, most likely refusing to think his career path should be about her and what she'd been through. He'd always been good at science; medicine was a natural choice.

But it was more than that, and deep down, everyone knew it.

"I like the pace of emergency medicine," he said. "Not just the sense of urgency but the fact that most people are in and out, moved into surgery or transferred to a department, then another case rolls through."

"But you don't have a chance to connect with a patient, then," Ivy observed.

Exactly, he thought. "You don't need to connect with a patient to know how to treat them."

He glanced over at her, noticing the way her profile

creased at this. "Yes, but most people want a doctor who cares. Who's vested." She caught his eye. "Are you trying to tell me you don't have any bedside manner? I find that hard to believe."

He'd been accused of it, more than once, but it had been overlooked by the precision of his skill, his ability to quickly assess a situation, make a plan of action, and implement it. No one could fault him for a job well done.

But they could fault him for messing up.

"People die in the emergency room, especially in a big hospital like I came from. It's better not to let emotions interfere," he said simply.

"Yes, but you're a doctor. You obviously care what happens to the patient."

"Of course," he said tersely. "In the ER, it's all action; no one is lingering. There's no time. It suits me better, that's all. I want to go to work, help where I can, and leave it at that."

Only sometimes that was easier said than done, wasn't it?

Brett leaned against a table and watched Ivy carefully study a bucket of pink flowers. They had a name, one she had pronounced with great enthusiasm, but it was lost on him, lost on the way his heart felt a little lighter at the glimpse of her smile and the way he didn't want to peel his eyes from her as she eagerly sought out the best of the bunch.

She looked up, catching him watching her, and blushed a little. "I get a little swept away when it comes to peonies."

He couldn't hide his amusement. "So I've noticed."

"They're my favorite," she said, glancing down to admire the bouquet in her hand.

"Now that doesn't seem very professional," he joked. "Shouldn't you be a little less biased?"

"Not when it comes to these," she said. "But of course, I do love all flowers, and sometimes it is hard to choose... Except, I don't really like daisies." She leaned into him as they turned into the next aisle. "But don't tell anyone. That stays between us."

He winked down at her. "Your secret is safe with me."

He caught a flicker in her gaze, something that reminded him of another secret he was holding, another inner part of Ivy she kept closed off from the rest of the world, even if there was nothing to hide. Still, he understood her reasons for keeping things to herself, and the knowledge he harbored both frightened him and connected him to her. She could take care of herself—hell, she'd been doing it for a long time already—but she'd trusted him enough to tell him something private. He couldn't take that lightly.

Ivy stopped and held up some large white flowers he recalled seeing before. "What do you think of these for the fundraiser?"

He stared at her blankly, almost forgetting that he had suggested tagging along under the guise of giving some input on flowers of all things. Her blue-green eyes were wide and questioning as she waited for him to respond, but it was her lips he was focused on. So pink, so full...

"Brett?" She slipped him a little smile. "Remember, you promised not to let on about your true feelings about these things, so... be nice."

Be nice. He wanted to be nice with Ivy... maybe even a little naughty. And the last thing he wanted to discuss was flowers. "Those will do."

She shook her head and gave him a long look. "I'm going to give you some options," she warned. "And I'm eager for your input."

"Trust me that much, do you?" He cocked an eyebrow, his pulse kicking.

"Well. When it comes to flowers, I am the expert, so while I will take your opinion into consideration, I will only be giving you a handful of options to consider."

He laughed. "Good. I've never been good at making choices."

She looked at him doubtfully. "I would think just the opposite. You're an ER physician. You think on your feet."

"True, but rarely are there varying courses of action."

"So you're talking about your personal life then," she surmised. Her eyes raked over him and then held his gaze long enough to make his gut tighten. He rolled back on his heels, suddenly feeling like she could see straight through to the heart of him.

"I guess you could say that."

"Interesting," she murmured. "What makes it so difficult?"

He shrugged. "The fear of making the wrong choice, I suppose. The fear of letting someone down."

Her eyes went sharply to his and then drifted back to a bunch of flowers as she set them on her cart. Brett stepped forward, surprised at the amount she was buying, and said, "Here. Let me."

Her expression seemed pleased as she pulled back, her hip skimming his thigh as they switched places. Heat shot straight to his groin and he gripped the handle of the cart tight, pushing it along as Ivy added more.

Finally, they reached the counter. Brett had expected the transaction to be straightforward, for the flowers to be tallied and paid for, but it seemed that Ivy had other ideas.

"These here aren't worth what you're asking," she said, motioning to some red flowers.

The graying man behind the counter gave her a long look. "You don't need to take them."

"Well, no one will for this price. I'll give you seventy percent of asking," she said steadily.

Brett felt his mouth begin to twitch as she held her ground, and his heart sped up when the man nodded. "Fine."

Before he could reach for her credit card, Ivy quickly added, "Same goes for the irises."

Brett stared at her, but she didn't meet his eye. She stood tall, patiently waiting for the man's response, unwavering in her stance.

"Fine," the man eventually said.

She didn't show any reaction until they were out the door, and only then did her mouth curve into a slow smile. "I think that trip was a success."

Brett grinned down at her, felt his desire mix with something a little deeper, a little closer to admiration, and swallowed hard. He hadn't known what would come of the night. What he even wanted to come of it, other than a few more minutes of her company. "I couldn't agree more," he said.

Ivy finished loading the last of the flowers into the back of the station wagon, grinning at her loot. The wholesale flower market never got old, and she knew that a few times Brett had caught her looking around like a kid in a toy store. The colors, the textures of the petals, the shapes and sizes of each variety were still exciting and always reminded her why she was doing this and why she was willing to do anything to keep her shop going.

Unable to resist, she climbed in the car and said to Brett, "Now wasn't that wonderful?"

She was teasing him, sure, but she was surprised when he begrudgingly said, "Maybe a little."

"Excuse me? I don't think I quite heard you." She leaned forward, close enough to catch a hint of his musk over the fresh smell of flowers that filled every pocket of the station wagon. "What was that you said? I could have sworn you said it was wonderful."

"It was better than I expected."

Ivy pulled back, grinning in satisfaction as she started the car and pulled it out of the still-packed parking lot. Florists from all over came to this market—it was the best in the state, and she'd tried them all—but by daybreak it would be cleared out, the best flowers gone.

"So what do we do now, then?"

"Well, I drop these off in the shop, and then I try to catch a few hours of sleep. The store doesn't open until ten, so I try to be down there by eight to get everything ready for the week. It's not so bad now that I close the store on Sundays. It helps to have a day off."

She hadn't admitted that to anyone before. She must be more tired than she thought.

A good night's sleep would help her to think straight again. But something told her that after spending so much time with Brett, sleep wouldn't come easily. If at all.

Still, she'd have to try. It was part of staying healthy.

She'd just have to count sheep and pray that Brett's image would stay out of her mind for a few hours at least.

"Did anyone ever tell you that you're working too many hours?"

"And you're not?" she shot back, bristling.

"Hey, I'm not the one with—"

She flashed him a look and he stopped talking. She blinked at the road. She didn't want this. Didn't need this. They'd been having such a nice time; she hadn't even remembered that he knew about her condition. So much for living in bliss.

"My brother tells me I'm working too many hours. He worries about me too much, though."

"That's what family is for," Brett said.

"I suppose." Ivy sighed. Her mother hadn't worried about anything other than what time the pub opened and closed and whether or not there was enough wine in the house to get her through the night. "But if we're going to be friends, you can't treat me like a patient. Even if you are a doctor."

Brett seemed to consider this. "Fair enough. But can you do me one favor?"

Dread pooled in her gut. She knew the sound of this. It was the same way Jane worriedly asked if she needed a snack or if she needed to sit down because she looked pale.

"Can you check your levels at the next light?"

She had half a mind to stop the car right there and tell him to find his own way back to Briar Creek. And good luck with that, because cabs weren't common in these parts. But then she thought of what Jane had said about Henry. How much it meant to her that he cared enough to make her business his own business, and she felt a little part of her stubbornness begin to chip away.

For a moment, she even dared to wonder if he cared as more than a friend. Until she remembered that he was a doctor, a doctor who had helped her in a time of need, and that he was probably just covering his bases.

"Fine," she ground out, but only because she knew she should check the monitor. It was late, her routine was always off on market nights, and she always checked before she went to sleep anyway. It had absolutely nothing to do with the fact that he'd asked. In fact, she'd have loved nothing more than to have had the satisfaction of informing him that she'd already checked and everything was fine.

At the next four-way intersection, with no cars around for seemingly miles in any direction, she flicked on the interior light and pulled her monitor from her bag. It read eighty—not great but not a problem, either. Yet.

"I'll eat a snack," she sighed, reaching into her bag for some crackers. She wasn't even hungry.

They fell into silence for most of the ride, and soon they were turning onto Main Street.

Brett met Ivy at the back of the car. She hated the tug in her chest, the disappointment that this evening had come to an end. It was dark in the alley, and quiet, making her more aware than ever that they were completely alone.

She glanced up at him, surprised to see him looking down at her. The light from the moon shone down, casting shadows over his face and drawing attention to the strong line of his jaw. Her heart began to beat a little faster as their gazes locked, and her breath caught as his eyes roamed her face. A chill ran down her arms as crickets chirped somewhere in the distance, the only sound she could hear above the pounding of her heart.

She stepped back, laughing under her breath to release the tension. "Thanks again for coming along. This is the first time I've had an escort."

His mouth curved, but his gaze remained steady and intense. Her breath felt shallow.

"I find it hard to believe a beautiful girl struggles that much with men." He cocked an eyebrow, his mouth turning mischievous.

Ivy set a hand on her stomach, trying to calm the flutter. "Perhaps my standards are just too high."

"Keep 'em that way," Brett said firmly, and Ivy narrowed her gaze, wondering where he fit into that.

She glanced at the back of the station wagon, unable to make out any of the flowers through the window in the moonlight. It was time to steer this conversation back to more neutral ground. "Well, I'm glad I have your seal of approval on the arrangements for the fundraiser."

"I would have been fine with whatever you'd chosen, actually," he replied, his voice low and smooth.

"I figured as much." She grinned.

"About that, though." He chewed on his lip, studied her as he rolled back on his heels, letting his eyes drift all the way down to her toes and then back up to her eyes.

Damn it if her heart didn't skip a beat. "Yes?"

"Would you mind extending your services to decorating the place? I don't know a thing about that, and I wouldn't know who else to call."

"Well, since you asked so nicely..." She gave him a rueful look.

He set a hand on her bare shoulder. It felt warm and sturdy and entirely too comfortable. "I didn't mean it like that. You're talented, Ivy. The way you transformed the town square for the festival was really amazing, and I'm not just saying that. I don't know anything about making things pretty, and I don't want this event to be ruined on account of that."

She held back a smile just long enough to make him sweat a bit, long enough to see if he'd drop his arm. But he didn't. Instead, he kept it there, cupping her shoulder, his thumb grazing the curve, tracing the edge of her collarbone. "Of course I'll help. Why don't I check out the venue next week? That way I'll have plenty of time to brainstorm some ideas for you."

"I'll go with you," he said instead, dropping his arm and shoving his hands in his pockets. "Next Sunday. Neither of us work, right?"

Her mouth went dry, and she nodded dumbly. "Sunday. That should work."

His smile broadened into something way too sexy for this time of night. Quickly, she pulled open the trunk door and filled her arms with irises. "Well, good night then."

He frowned at her and reached into the car for a bucket. "You didn't think I was going to leave you here to do this on your own, did you? It's the middle of the night."

Like that wasn't painfully obvious. Everyone in town had been asleep for hours...everyone but her and Brett. "Well, I…"

"I'm not that kind of guy." He grabbed another bucket—twice what she could have carried in one trip—and began heading to the back door to the store, his muscles straining against his tight T-shirt, conjuring up all sorts of images she shouldn't be thinking about, until he dipped into the shadow, out of sight.

Just what kind of guy are you? But she didn't know if she was ready for the answer. Because everything in her head was telling her he was a smooth talker, a charmer with good looks who knew how to get what he wanted with a simple flash of those perfect white teeth. But everything in her heart said otherwise.

And she wasn't sure which one to listen to anymore.

CHAPTER 19

The oven timer dinged just as Kara was finishing dusting her coffee table and bookshelves. She tossed the rag over her shoulder and ran into the kitchen to turn off the heat before sliding on an oven mitt.

A sweet aroma filled the air as she gingerly placed each cookie on the cooling rack. She checked the clock on the oven—just a few minutes to spare before her guest arrived, and knowing her mother, she was never late.

She set the rag in the laundry basket in the hall closet and went into the bathroom to clean herself up a bit, resenting every brush stroke of her hair. Finally, deciding the heat of the apartment outweighed any potential criticism, she pulled it back into a ponytail. Her eyes were bright, her makeup light, and she was just deciding whether or not to give in and put on some lipstick or take a stand and refuse when the knock at the door came.

She knew it was wrong to feel angry at a knock. After all, she had invited her mother over, hadn't she? Because she was guilted into it.

A dozen potential arguments and hypothetical comebacks

raced through her mind as she flicked off the bathroom light and made her way to the front door. Her mother was smiling, her hair pulled back in a headband, her earrings jingling as she pulled Kara in for a hug.

"This is so nice. We don't do this often enough!" She smiled again. Warmly. And Kara felt like the biggest jerk on earth.

This was her mother! Her mother! Sure, she had her quirks, but there was no reason to be avoiding her like this. It was all in her head. She had built it all up to be so much more than it was.

"Come on in," Kara said, deciding then and there that this was nice and that she'd make a regular habit of it from now on. Once a week. At least.

"When did you get home from work?" her mother inquired as she slipped off her shoes.

"Oh, about an hour and a half ago," Kara said. She'd had just enough time to race home to bake the cookies and make sure her apartment would pass inspection. Because there was always an inspection.

She pushed that thought back and focused on how happy her mother looked in that moment and vowed to be a better daughter going forward.

"Did you go to work dressed like that?" Her mother's expression betrayed nothing as she tipped her head and waited for the response.

Kara felt her back teeth graze together. She looked down at her outfit. Navy tank top, pink cotton A-line skirt. "Yes."

"Hmm." Rosemary pinched her lips together.

Don't lose your temper, Kara. Don't even feed into it. Just pretend she didn't say anything and move on.

"Well, I guess you're not at the front of house anymore, so it doesn't matter."

Before Kara could close her mouth, which seemed to be permanently slack around Rosemary, her mother just patted her arm and smiled eagerly. "I'm just so excited for you about this promotion! I told all the gals in book club. They were certainly impressed."

"Oh…" Kara managed a shaky laugh. "Well, why don't we sit in the living room? You go make yourself comfortable and I'll bring in some tea."

From her pocket, Rosemary pulled out a plastic bag. "I brought my own."

Of course she did, Kara thought. Because apparently her own tea wasn't good enough.

With a smile she didn't feel, she reached out and took the tea bag and then slipped into the kitchen, cursing silently.

Now, stop it, Kara. She is your mother. And she's well intentioned. Just make the most of it, and in an hour, she'll be on her way, and you can pour yourself a nice tall glass of wine.

With that promise made, Kara boiled the water for the tea while she plated the cookies and set everything on a tray, the way she'd seen Ivy do the times she went over to her friend's place. Her stomach fluttered with nerves when she anticipated her mother's reaction to her part in the hospital fundraiser, and she almost spilled the water in her excitement to share the news. It wasn't often that something big happened in her world, and certainly something like this would get her mother's mind off finding Kara a husband. After all, Rosemary was a businesswoman herself, and a successful one, too. She'd made a solid living for herself when Kara's father had died. Maybe she'd have a few pointers to give Kara, one entrepreneur to another. Kara was eager to hear them.

"Here we—" She stopped in the entrance to the living room, the tray rattling in her hands as she watched her mother swipe a finger over the mantel, glance at it, and grimace.

She had forgotten the mantel.

One. Two. Three. Deep breaths. Maybe she'd have two glasses of wine. Yes, definitely.

"Here we go!" She cheerfully set the tray on the coffee table and settled onto the sofa next to her mother.

"Oh. This couch. I forgot how you just... sink into it."

Kara smiled through gritted teeth as she reached for her mug. She'd brought out the best she had. The matching pair. Not the funny ones she liked to collect with various catch-phrases or slogans or souvenirs of places she'd visited. But there was no credit for that.

"I like the way you sink into it. It's comfy." She kept her tone deliberately light.

"Hmm." Rosemary widened her bright blue eyes. "Well, let's just hope I can get out of it."

Silence fell for a moment, and Kara eyed the plate of cookies. The mood was dead, but maybe this would turn things around.

"Would you like a cookie?"

Rosemary waved a hand through the air. "You know I don't eat sweets."

Of course. A dancer's figure... Kara tried again. "I made them, actually."

"Oh?" Rosemary looked at them with new interest and slid one onto her plate. "Well, in that case."

Kara's heart began to pound as she eyed the cookie, wondering what her mother would say and questioning her sanity for subjecting herself to potentially crushing criticism. She already knew that Grace and Ivy and Brett liked them. And Jane had mentioned something, too. And then there were the customers at the bookstore who had apparently complimented them. What more did she need?

It should be enough, but somehow it wasn't. All her life it seemed that her mother looked at her like some kind of failure, and maybe she was. After all, she didn't have a successful career like Grace or Luke. She didn't own her own restaurant like Anna. She wasn't engaged. She'd never been married. Even Jane had found love twice, and Kara was yet to find it once.

She had so little to show for herself, it seemed. But the cookies...this might just be her chance.

"Jane taught today," Rosemary commented after she took a long sip of her tea.

Kara eyed the cookie. "Oh?"

"She's planning her wedding. It sounds so pretty. So much pink. My favorite, you know. I kept thinking, wouldn't it be wonderful to be able to plan a wedding?" Her gaze was steady and unnaturally long. "I know that Luke and Grace did just get married, but it was Luke's second wedding, and as with the first, it's really the bride's day. A special experience for the bride and her mother to plan together."

For the love of God. Kara thought they were past this speech. She'd heard it all through Luke's engagement, when Grace was so indecisive about colors and flowers. It had taken everything in Rosemary not to just step in and take over. But she hadn't. And instead she'd put it on Kara. How when it was Kara's turn...Molly, being the youngest, didn't have to bear that burden. And Luke, being a guy, was given a free pass. So it all fell to Kara.

"I'm very happy for Jane," Kara said diplomatically.

"After everything she's been through the past few years, she deserves a happy ending."

Her mother looked successfully disarmed. "Yes. Of course. Henry is such a catch. She just snatched him right up!"

If her mother was implying that Henry might have had any interest in her, Kara knew better. The man had loved Jane since he first met her. "Well, it will be a beautiful wedding. I'm looking forward to it."

"Did you RSVP yet?"

"Yep."

"Oh." Kara could see it. The wheels turning. The pregnant pause. Here it came... "With a guest?"

"Nope. Just me."

The disappointment that crossed Rosemary's face was palpable.

Kara picked up her mug of tea. So maybe getting together with her mother once a week was pushing it. Maybe once a month would be more manageable.

She picked up a cookie and bit into it, hoping it would trigger her mother to do the same. Instead, Rosemary just said, "Is that skirt new? What size is it?"

Kara set the cookie down and turned to her mother, determined to take control of the conversation, and—though she'd promised herself this before—her life. "So, how are things going for the summer ballet gala?"

"Wonderful!" Rosemary crooned. She launched into a variety of stories from the studio, dancers who had potential, dancers who did not but thought they did, mothers who thought their daughters had more potential than they ever would, some costume ordering drama, and the fact that she was toying with getting a new piano.

"Forest Ridge Hospital's annual benefit is in a few weeks. The proceeds are going to the oncology department this year, and so the studio is donating some lessons for the private auction."

Kara took a breath. This was her chance. Finally her moment to show her mother that she, too, was involved in the event. That she was doing something...exciting. Something people respected and were proud of her for.

She licked her lips, considering how she'd phrase it.

"Brett mentioned it," she began.

"Oh Brett." Rosemary tutted. "There's another one in our family who needs to settle down."

Ignoring the implication that she and Brett were somehow lumped together in the family disappointment pile, Kara said, "Well, Brett's a doctor. He's focusing on his career right now. I don't see anything wrong with that."

Rosemary huffed out a sigh. "That's just what's wrong with your generation. You all think you have all the time in the world."

"I'm only twenty-eight."

"I had three children by the time I was twenty-eight," Rosemary replied.

Kara could feel the heat rising up her neck and spreading over her cheeks. She clenched her teeth and willed her heart to stop racing so fast it felt like it could burst. She had heard all this, many, many times before. Why did it still upset her so much?

She turned to the subject of the book club and asked what they were reading, hoping that it wouldn't be a love story of some kind that would launch another wave of comments about all the ways Kara was letting her mother down. Fortunately, it was an autobiography of a former First Lady.

Careful to keep the topic safe, they chatted pleasantly for the next hour until Rosemary announced she had to go. Kara eyed the uneaten cookie, feeling her spirit sink a little. She knew that if she just told her mother how much it meant, came flat out and asked her mother to please take a bite and tell her what she thought, that of course her mother would. But somehow, having to do that depressed her, and so she stayed quiet.

"Thank you so much for a lovely evening," Rosemary said after she slipped her shoes back on.

Kara saw the warmth in her eyes and realized just how much it must have meant to her mom to have come over tonight. Maybe she'd been overly sensitive. Her mother loved her. She could see it in her eyes.

She reached in to give her mother another hug, feeling that familiar surge of guilt as she always did when the negative thoughts started mixing their way in, but the smile fell from her face when Rosemary tugged her ponytail.

"You have such pretty hair, Kara. When you let it down."

Kara closed the door behind her mother and closed her eyes. She counted to ten before she marched into the kitchen, plucked a bottle of wine from the fridge, and pulled the cork from the top.

She could practically hear Rosemary's tsk of disapproval when she took her first sip.

Brett watched his mother as she moved around the kitchen, stopping to lift the lid on a pot or lower the heat on the burner for another.

"What can I do to help?" he asked.

"Nothing," she insisted yet again as she reached for one of the colanders she stored over the fridge.

Nothing. Was there anything more he hated than sitting idle?

Pushing his chair back, he stood and crossed the kitchen to retrieve the colander his mother had been straining to grasp.

"Thanks," she said ruefully. "Now go sit and relax. You've been on your feet all day at the hospital."

"I'm used to it," he replied, staying put. "Besides, how many hours did you put in at the diner today?"

"Maybe five or six. I didn't count." She brushed past him to the sink and began rinsing vegetables.

Five or six was more like eight or nine. She was gone when he'd left for work, and she didn't return until after his shift. He didn't like it. But try telling her that.

"You should be taking it easy."

Sharon groaned but kept her back to him. "I told you not to worry about me. I'm fine. You saw the test results."

True, all true, but it didn't mean he could stop worrying. She'd relapsed within five years of remission. They were coming up on another five-year mark. As a doctor, he knew the significance of this. As a survivor, she did, too.

"Besides, sitting around, watching television, reading, knitting, whatever you're suggesting... That won't change anything. If it's going to come back, it's going to come back, and I'm not going to put my life on hold waiting to see if that happens."

He squared his jaw. "I can't argue with that." Much as he wished he could. He didn't like thinking of cells doing what they would, of having no control over what would happen and what wouldn't.

He itched to be in the hospital suddenly. To keep busy. To put his skills to use. To take measures into his own hands.

"Besides, it's not like you've given me any grandchildren to keep me busy."

Brett was almost happy for the shift in conversation. "You've got Mark for that."

His mother wrinkled her nose. "Oh, I'm not so sure. Those two are too busy at the restaurant to even set a wedding date, much less start a family. You boys and your careers. Just like your father."

"Not just like our father. Not at all like our father," Brett struggled.

His mother turned to him in surprise, but her expression softened when she saw the steel in his eyes. "I meant that your father was passionate about his work, that's all."

Passionate enough to put work above all else. To put a career ahead of loved ones, ahead of family. He knew what she meant, and the truth hurt. The anger wasn't for her; it wasn't even for his deadbeat dad. It was for himself.

Pushing back the guilt that threatened to ruin the evening, he began setting the table. Mark was at the restaurant tonight, so it would be just the two of them. As much as he valued the time with his mother, he found himself wishing his brother could join them, just to breathe some life into the evening. Mark had a way of keeping things light. Whereas Brett... Well, he'd always been the serious one.

"So how do you like the job now that you've settled in?" Sharon asked as she joined him at the table.

Brett loaded his plate and wondered how to tactfully answer that question without lying. "It's slower paced than I'm used to," he finally said. Today he'd removed a raisin from a four-year-old boy's nose. He'd handled bigger cases as a first-year resident.

"Well, they're lucky to have you. And so am I."

Brett managed to swallow the piece of roasted chicken, even though his throat had started to close up. She'd never asked him to stay, never pushed for him to be in Briar Creek even when he was needed the most, and now, now she was changing her mind it seemed. Panic flickered when he considered the reasons why. Did she know something she wasn't sharing? About her health? Or had she wanted him back all this time but never dared to say it before? That thought was almost too much to bear. He'd convinced himself all these years that she'd wanted him to go, pursue his path. It was the only way he managed to sleep at night.

The doorbell rang, and before Sharon could even stand to answer it, his aunt Rosemary's voice called down the hall, "Yoo-hoo! Shar-on?"

"In here!" Sharon and Brett exchanged a knowing glance before Rosemary swept into the room. "Have you eaten? I'll fix you a plate."

"Oh, don't mind me. I was just on my way back from Kara's and thought I'd stop in."

"How's she doing these days?" Sharon asked as she opened the cupboard and brought out another plate. "Mark gave her a promotion, I hear."

"Hmm, yes." Rosemary didn't look pleased at this. Instead, she turned to Brett, giving him her full attention. "Brett, tell me, are there any single men at the hospital?"

Brett almost choked on his beer. "I haven't really paid attention to that."

Rosemary's shoulders slumped. "That girl is never going to find a husband at this rate."

"Is that such a bad thing?" Brett asked, genuinely curious.

"It wouldn't be if she had any other direction in her life.

I worry." She shook her head and frowned down at her plate. "I really do."

"What is it with me and worrywarts?" Sharon laughed, but her eyes crinkled when she met Brett's gaze across the table. "Brett worries about me too much," she explained to Rosemary.

"Well, he's a doctor. And your son. And we all worry about you, Sharon." Rosemary's look was pointed.

Sharon sighed. "What will be, will be, isn't that right?"

"Wrong," Brett replied, setting down his fork. It wasn't his mentality—or his business—to let nature take its course. It was his job to fight it, to do whatever it took to intervene. Anger pulsed in his jaw when he considered his mother's attitude. She'd always been a fighter. Where was this coming from?

"I'm just saying, Brett, that there are some things in life we can't control. That's just a sad fact." Her eyes held his a second longer until she blinked and looked away.

Brett stared at his plate, knowing she was right but still not wanting to accept it, either.

It's what his boss had told him that night, after the patient died. Nothing more could have been done. But he couldn't believe it. Didn't want to believe it.

His phone beeped in his pocket, and he pulled it out, forgetting for a moment that he wasn't back in Baltimore, and he wasn't even on call. He went to turn the device off, eager to tune out and unwind, when he saw the sender's email and the subject line pop up at the top of his screen.

It was from the hospital in DC.

His heart pounded as his finger hovered over the button. One click and he would know.

"Go ahead and take it if it's important," his mother said. "Don't mind me."

He looked up at her. At the unsuspecting ease to her smile as she fell back into conversation with Rosemary, and felt his stomach ball into a tight knot.

"It's not important," he said, turning off the phone and sliding it back into his pocket. Not important at all.

CHAPTER
20

The hospital benefit was held each year at an old winery nestled at the top of a large hill with sweeping views of the valley. Ivy had helped with at least a dozen weddings here over the years and knew the venue well. The building was a renovated barn with huge, beamed ceilings and a wall of French doors that led out onto a stone veranda, where guests could enjoy the view. Lanterns hung from the pergola overhead, and white-painted wood furniture was clustered in small groups.

"This is a good place to serve drinks before dinner," she said, motioning to the large space at the end, where a bar could be set up. "It's casual, and the sun sets right over those hills there." She pointed out to the horizon, and Brett came to stand next to her and follow her gaze.

"I suggest a few small arrangements on these end tables, and then on the bar tables if you choose to have any."

Brett looked at her in alarm, and she couldn't help but laugh at his bewildered expression. "You want the bar tables. Five should do."

He grinned. "Thanks."

They walked back through the doors and into the main room. The smell of wood was sharp, warm, and inviting, cozy enough to make Ivy imagine what it would be like to host her own wedding in this space. She'd thought of it every time she'd been to an event here. And she'd imagined Brett by her side.

Ridiculous.

She crossed the room, pretending to assess the space, even though she already knew how to best fill it. A few plants in the corners, with some strings of lights for ambience. A centerpiece for each table, two for the bar, and tea lights scattered on all the surfaces. The hospital was on a budget, and she knew that whatever money wasn't spent on decorations could be put to better use. She'd make things pretty, but she wouldn't go overboard. Seasonal flowers like white hydrangeas should work just fine, especially with the rustic environment. She'd talk to the supplier tonight at the market, see if he'd cut her a deal.

"The tables and chairs they use here will be fine. As will the linens. I suggest white and green for the color scheme. Elegant but simple."

"You're the expert," Brett said.

Ivy frowned at him. She'd arranged to meet him here, telling herself it was the sensible, safe choice, but he'd seemed distant since she'd first climbed out of the car. "Is everything okay?"

His dark gaze traveled back to her. "Fine."

She never knew *fine* to mean anything close to it, but she decided not to press the issue. He wasn't her boyfriend; he wasn't her brother or cousin.

But he was her friend, right? She looked out onto the hills, thinking about it. She might have agreed to be his friend, but she still wasn't so sure how she felt about it. A week had passed since the last time she'd seen him, not that she had been opposed to running into him around town. She'd even tried the treadmill at the gym one night, but he never appeared, and the sense of disappointment she carried with her on the walk home only confirmed the fact that she still wasn't over her crush. No matter how much she wished she could be.

She looked up at him, at the way the sun caught the chestnut highlights in his dark hair and how his hawklike gaze was set on the distance, and felt that little pang. Yep. Still there.

"Well, I should be getting back to the shop..."

"I thought you were closed on Sundays," Brett said, turning to give her his full attention.

"Oh." Ivy gulped. Couldn't she have thought of a better excuse? But she could barely think at all, not when Brett was staring at her like that, all moody and sexy and silent. "I'm closed to customers, but I have to catch up on some paperwork before the week hits. And of course, there's lots to do for this event."

"The heat's let up a bit. Let's walk around," Brett suggested.

She hesitated, and then, because for some reason she still couldn't quite resist him, she began following him down the gravel path that she knew led out to private gazebo near the edge of the property. Most brides came down here for the formal photos. She especially loved seeing it in the fall, when the leaves had just turned and the splash of color contrasted brightly with the white wood and dresses.

Today, though, despite the drop in temperature from last weekend, the sun beat down, and by the time the neared the end of the hill, Ivy was regretting the jeans she'd worn.

"Do you have anything to drink in your bag?" Brett asked as he leaned back against a post.

"Of course." She reached inside and retrieved a bottle of water, but he just held up a hand.

"Drink it. It's hot."

Ivy narrowed her gaze on him. "I can take care of myself."

"Oh, I have no doubt about that. In fact, it's one of the things I admire most about you."

Her hand froze on the water bottle cap. "Oh really? Go on," she teased, grinning.

"I mean it. You've faced a lot of adversity in your life. Some people would let that kind of thing hold them back, define them. But you pressed on. You're a strong woman, Ivy."

"I'm just a little sensitive when it comes to suggestions on how I should be taking care of myself."

"I was just trying to be chivalrous," he said, his brown eyes twinkling. "And I'm a doctor. It's hard to check that kind of thing at the door. Concern follows me wherever I go."

She told herself not to feed into that even as a pleased smile teased her mouth. "I thought you didn't like to get emotionally involved with your patients."

He shrugged. "Doesn't mean it doesn't happen."

His frown deepened and Ivy stepped forward, worried she'd misspoken in her effort to defuse an awkward moment. "I'm sure you're an excellent doctor, Brett."

"I could be better." He scowled, looking down at his feet for a moment. "I messed up. In Baltimore. That's why I'm here." His gaze was sharp when it caught hers, as if waiting for her to question him or judge him, the way he so clearly judged himself.

"Everyone messes up," she said, feeling the familiar knot return when she thought of all the ways she'd let people down. Let herself down.

He shook his head. "I don't mess up. Every time I walk out of that ER, I know I did all I could. Whatever the outcome, I did everything, my best, and that's enough for me, even if some cases are rough. But this one night…" She waited, sensing the weight he carried. "I didn't do my best. I was distracted. Tired. God, I was so tired." He paused, eyes on her as he hesitated. "No one knows this, but a few months ago my mom had a health scare. She thought…she thought she was sick again."

"But she's not?" Ivy felt a flicker of alarm. Sharon Hastings had already been through so much. She was a good woman. Kind and friendly. Not the kind of person to let circumstances knock her down.

"No, no, it turned out to be nothing. But when she called and told me…asked for my opinion on some things…it was all I could think about. I offered to fly back, but she said to wait until they'd done more tests. I listened. For the second time in my life, I listened when she told me to put my career first and her second." He gave a low, bitter laugh. "What kind of son does that make me?"

Ivy set her hand on his forearm, feeling the fine hair under her fingertips. His skin was warm and soft, and he didn't push her away, even though he seemed to be fighting something. "She wanted you to carry on with your life. Then. Now. She knew how much potential you had. She didn't want to hold you back. You're a brilliant surgeon, Brett. Everyone knows that."

He turned to her sharply. The intensity in his gaze silenced her. "A patient died on my watch. Because I was distracted.

Because I was only half present. It's my fault. Mine alone. It will settle, of course, but that doesn't change the cold, hard fact that I am responsible for a man losing his life."

She wasn't sure she wanted to know the details, and she couldn't even believe what he was telling her. He was too hard on himself. "I'm sure you did everything you could," she tried, but she knew her words weren't enough to ease the pain she saw in his eyes.

"No. I was tired. I wasn't focused. My shift was almost over, and I just wanted to finish up and go home. I wasn't thinking about anything but my mother, my personal problems, not the professional ones I was there to deal with." He dropped down onto the steps, and after a beat, she joined him.

"It was a young man. Forty years old. Triage said the chief complaint was fever and cough. He was sweaty, but it was attributed to the other symptoms. I had another case in the next room—a boy with a distal femur fracture. A broken leg," he explained wryly. "Normally, I'd reduce the fracture and have a nurse set the cast, but I was almost grateful for the task—doing something with my hands, something simple and routine. It cleared my mind, took my worry off my mom for a bit. I sent the kid home, went in to check on the other patient and…It was too late. Pulmonary embolism. Blood clot."

"Oh, Brett." Ivy grimaced. "But…how could you have known?"

"Because I'm a doctor," he ground out, clenching a fist on his thigh. "That's how I should have known. Because I'm trained to spot these things. To stop them. To…help."

"But certainly other people were involved."

"The triage nurse, yeah. But he was my patient. Mine." He swore under his breath. "I've gone over it and over it. If

I'd just been more thorough, taken more time. Been less distracted. Prioritized the right patient." He cursed.

"You did the best you could at the time," Ivy insisted.

"And the worst of it... The wife was pregnant. And now she's alone. And that baby will never know its father."

Ivy moved her hand to his and gave it a squeeze, but she stiffened when he gripped it tight and held it close in his. His palm was warm, and she could feel the steady beat of his pulse against her skin.

"I've held this in for so long."

Ivy nodded, wishing she could ease the weight. He said he didn't care, that he didn't connect with patients, but it wasn't true. The hurt in his eyes confirmed it. The softness in his voice, the way he struggled to forgive himself. He cared. About his mother. His family. His patients.

About her.

His face was close, his eyes searching hers as he leaned in. Ivy gasped as his mouth met hers. So gentle. So familiar. She opened her mouth as every nerve ending in her body zipped with awareness, wanting so much to recapture the sensation, but her mind began to spin with warning.

He didn't want a relationship. He didn't want anything from her. He'd said it. After their first amazing kiss. And chances were, he'd be saying it again after this one.

She pulled back and freed her hand from his. "I... I should really go."

She stood, leaving him sitting on the steps of the gazebo, and ran all the way up the path to where her station wagon was parked next to Brett's sleek black sedan.

Brett didn't want what she wanted. Not the quiet, small-town life. Not the simple pleasures. Not a human connection.

And most of all, he didn't want her.

• • •

Henry was in his office when Ivy finally left the shop that night, hoping some fresh air would clear her muddled thoughts and the image of Brett sitting on those stairs, his expression unreadable as she broke their kiss.

The office of the *Briar Creek Gazette* was tucked in an old brick building just off Main at the other edge of town, so she and Henry rarely crossed paths during the day unless they arranged to meet. The door was locked, but when she tapped on the window, Henry looked up from his laptop screen and smiled in surprise.

"How'd you know I'd be here?" he asked after letting her in.

"I'm your twin," she replied, dropping into a rickety wooden chair near his desk. "I can sense these things."

"So can I." Henry closed the laptop and gave her his full attention. "Which is why I know something is wrong."

"Nothing's wrong!" But she knew it was no use. Like it or not, Henry knew her. Inside and out. She wouldn't have it any other way.

She smiled at him, her heart filling with gratitude that he was here, that she could stop by his office like this, connect with someone who'd known and loved her all her life, pop over for a family dinner whenever she wanted. He'd been out of her life for too long, and she'd never said a word, because she'd loved him and wanted him to be happy, even if that was far from Briar Creek. She'd never make him feel guilty for those years he was gone, but oh, it really was amazing to have him back again. For good.

Henry gave her a long look. "You can't hide from me, Ivy. I know you. What's up?"

Where did she even begin? She longed to tell Henry

everything that happened, but it bordered on girl talk, and besides, Henry and Brett were sort of friends. And what was there to even say? If Henry found out that Brett had tried to kiss her again just to...comfort himself? Distract himself? Have a little fun? Well, it certainly wouldn't go over well at all. Henry was protective of her, and she didn't need him punching anyone on her behalf. The thought of it almost made her giggle.

"What's so funny?" Henry asked, a small smile curving his mouth.

She brushed away the question. "It's nothing. I just...I was imagining you coming to my defense."

He arched a brow. "Do your defenses need protecting?"

"No." She patted his arm. "But it's nice to know you have my back if I do."

"Always," he confirmed.

She leaned back, the warm, fuzzy feeling suddenly replaced with a twinge of dread. Still, the conversation had to happen. "I wanted to talk to you about the money you lent me," she said.

Henry leaned back in his chair and groaned. He raked his hands down his face and glanced at her through parted fingers. "You're not still hung up on this, are you? I told you, Ivy. It wasn't a loan; it was a gift."

"But I want to pay you back," she protested. "I told you that all along."

"I don't need the money, Ivy—"

And she knew that. And he knew that she knew it. "But I don't feel comfortable taking that kind of help." She took a deep breath. Here went nothing. "Now, I know how you feel about my schedule—"

As expected, Henry opened his mouth to voice his

opinion on the matter, but Ivy held a hand up firmly. "I'm doing well, Henry. I really am. I wanted you to hear this straight from me. I've decided to start offering those monthly flower arranging classes."

"Ivy—"

"I know you worry about how hard I'm working, but nothing you can say will change my mind. I'm healthy, I'm taking care of myself, and I know my limits. Now, I'm not asking for your permission. I'm simply informing you."

Now it was his turn to raise an eyebrow. "And I'm not going to try to stop you."

She blinked. "You're not?"

"No. Like you said, you're in a better place now. If you say you're taking your medication and following the diet plan the doctor gave you, then I believe you."

Ivy chewed on her lip, recalling the incident at the Fourth of July festival. She forced herself not to indulge in it. It was one time, and she was human. A human with a condition that took management and care. She was doing her best. Unlike a year ago. That counted for something.

"I'm glad we had this talk." She smiled.

Henry grinned. "Me too. Now, want me to run an ad for the class in tomorrow's paper? Free of charge."

No matter what, Henry would always be the one man she could count on. Perhaps the only one.

CHAPTER
21

For her first class, Ivy decided to dress for the occasion, in a floral-printed sundress. Eight people were registered, albeit most of them her friends, and she figured a few more walk-ins would make an appearance, too.

Ivy looked around the shop with a critical eye and went over her list one more time. She'd pushed most of the display stands to the front of the room to allow for a large folding table where everyone would gather. Tonight's project would be simple, and small glass vases were stacked on her workspace at the back of the room, ready to be handed out along with the mix of stems she'd selected.

Jane had offered to help out, but Ivy was using this class for extra money to pay Henry back, not that she would tell Jane that, and with the wedding fast approaching, she knew Jane could use some extra time to focus on last-minute details.

Grace was the first to arrive, with Anna following just behind.

"I've always wanted to learn how to do this," Anna admitted. "Every time I buy flowers at the market, they end up looking all wrong when I put them in a vase."

"Same here." Grace winced.

It was true that the most basic principles of proportion and ratio could make even the most beautiful flowers look sad or stark when placed in the wrong-sized vase. Just hearing her friends' words confirmed her decision to offer the class, and she felt another bubble of excitement as she eyed the door, anxious for things to begin.

More people filtered through the open door, and soon the shop was filled with the sound of voices, all talking over one another, often interspersed with a peal of laughter. Ivy felt a warm tingle rush through her. This is what she loved about this town. This is why she did what she did. Even if she wasn't going to get rich running this shop, her life was completely full.

And she knew the same could be said for most of the people in this room.

Kara poked her head in, calling out a cheerful hello, but her smile seemed to slip a bit when she noticed her mother already positioned near the head of the table.

"Come on in!" Ivy called. Three walk-ins had already joined, but it was time to get things started. She motioned to the opposite end of the table from where Rosemary sat. "Why don't you sit here, next to Anna?"

Kara seemed to smile a little easier. "Perfect."

Ivy watched as her friend gave her mother a warm but brief greeting and took her seat. She knew Rosemary could be difficult at times, but she still craved the connection Kara had with her mother, no matter the occasional strain. What she would have given to have a mother to take her shopping once in a while or meet for lunch. She and her mother had never had that type of bond—and now it was too late.

Henry couldn't understand why she'd stuck around, why

she hadn't run when she could. It wasn't just for this town, though. It was also for her mother. She'd never given up hope that their relationship could be something it wasn't.

She shook her head. Denial was a powerful thing.

And one she should put in check, she thought, as Brett's image floated back to the surface.

Except…Oh, no. No. This couldn't be happening. Brett was here. In the doorway. Standing sheepishly, with his hands in his pockets, that boyish grin making her heart flip over.

"Room for one more?" he asked, and Ivy was aware that her jaw had slacked.

She set the glass vase she was holding down on the table before she broke it and managed a casual "Of course." Because of course it made sense that Brett, the man who hated flowers, would want to take this class. Because of course it didn't matter that the last time they had seen each other, she'd been running away from him. Because of course it was just fine that he was here, in her shop, pretending like none of that had even happened.

And because of course it was fine that as he slipped into a seat next to Rosemary, he—God help her—winked.

Brett tore off a piece of cellophane tape and extended it over the rim of the vase, imitating the crisscross pattern Ivy so expertly—and neatly, he marveled—demonstrated for the group. He watched her out of the corner of his eye, waiting to see if she would look up, catch his stare, but she seemed determined to avoid him as she went through her instructions in that flustered little way of hers, her cheeks flushing every time she reached a new point on her list.

God, she was cute. Her auburn hair was swept off her face in a low ponytail, revealing her long, graceful neck and highlighting her delicate jawbone. But it wasn't just her sexy appearance that caught his interest. Ivy was in her element, and he loved seeing the way her eyes shone as she walked the group through the steps.

A knock at the closed door jarred his attention, and he glanced over his shoulder to see a tall, well-dressed man standing behind the paned glass door, grimacing in apology as he hesitantly waved. Turning back to Ivy, Brett watched with a growing frown as her face broke out in an ear-to-ear grin and she stood to cross the room just as the man entered.

"I'm not too late, am I?" he asked.

"Never!" she exclaimed, and, to Brett's horror, flung her arms around the man's neck.

Brett glowered at his glass vase and the stubby strips of tape that zigzagged over the opening. It had been a stupid idea to come here. When he'd seen the ad at the gym, he'd seen more than a flower arranging class, which, obviously, he had no interest in. What did interest him was the woman running it. She interested him a lot. More than she should, judging from her reaction to the preppy guy who was cozily pulling a chair over near hers.

He listened with a growing heaviness in his chest as she talked about greenery versus flowers and something called fillers, which was when he stopped listening and started focusing on the man across from him. The man who had no trouble casually setting his hands on Ivy's wrist when he had a question and whose endless stream of whispered comments sent a peal of Ivy's laughter sailing across the room.

He gritted his teeth and shoved some leaves into one of the square spaces between his tape strips.

Yep, a big, big mistake. He should have stayed at the hospital, asked for another shift, or joined Mark for that beer he suggested. Instead he was here, with half the women in Briar Creek, watching the woman he had just kissed flirt shamelessly with another man.

Maybe she was trying to tell him something. As if running off the other day hadn't said everything. He'd crossed a line. Told her things he hadn't dared to admit to anyone. But that wasn't the worst of it.

No, the worst of it was that he didn't want it to stop there. He wanted to keep going. To kiss her. Tell her everything. To get…close.

She'd given him an out. If he was thinking clearly, he would have taken it.

But he wasn't thinking clearly. He was in a flower arranging class discussing the merits of baby's breath, for God's sake.

"Making that for your mother?" his aunt Rosemary crooned.

"What?" He scowled as Ivy's special friend cracked a joke that sent the entire table into a roar of laughter. He was so angry, so mad at himself, so…jealous, he realized with a start, that he hadn't even heard what was said.

"I asked if you were making the bouquet for your mother. I told her to join me tonight, but she had to work at the diner."

Brett frowned. It bothered him that his mother was choosing to stand on her feet rather than sitting here chatting with friends and…that preppy guy with the perfectly straight teeth and fresh haircut. He knew it wasn't for money. She'd bounced back years ago from the strain his father had left her in, even with all the medical bills. He told himself that if she was happy at Hastings, then she should do it, but he still wished she would cut back.

"Yes," he said decisively, "these are for my mother."

Because really, who else should they be for? A week ago he might have said Ivy, but that was crazy talk.

About as crazy as the unopened email from the hospital in DC.

Ivy smiled with encouragement at the finished arrangements scattered around the table, resisting the urge to fix half of them. It was a fine first effort, she told herself, and really, it justified why people paid her to do what she did. Anna's had turned out nicely, which didn't come as a surprise given her creative eye and touch of perfectionism. Rosemary, Grace, and Kara all followed instructions well, and Mrs. Griffin took things to a bigger scale, resulting in quite a dramatic piece.

And then there was the rather sad, lopsided, and half-dead-looking thing that belonged all to Brett.

And damn it if that didn't endear him to her even more.

"Nice effort," she said, almost managing to look him in the eye. Hoping to keep the tone light, she motioned to a broken tulip head and said with a grin, "I hope you're a little more precise with your scalpel, Doctor."

He grunted something of a response as he shifted into his coat, and Ivy opened her mouth, compelled to say something, but her mind went blank. What was there to say? To bring up the kiss would be awkward at best, and chances were he was probably just here to make sure she hadn't yet again taken any notions from it.

Instead, she turned to Darren, who, though he'd arrived late, had succeeded in making the most exquisite arrangement of the group.

She eyed the perfect symmetry of the flowers and joked, "I hope you don't have any plans to open a flower shop anytime soon, or I'll be out of business."

He swatted her arm playfully. "Nonsense. No one can compete with you, darling."

From across the table, Ivy thought she caught Brett scowl.

"Well, I'm just glad you could join us," she continued to Darren, trying to focus on her friend and not on her sort-of friend who was looking less than happy at the moment. "Hopefully Robby can make it next week."

"Let's just hope this arrangement makes up for me ditching him to come here." Darren gave a conspiratorial grin. "He's the only person I know who manages to catch a summer cold every year, and tonight of all nights. I said, honey, I'm sorry you're sick, but here's a stack of tabloids and a bowl of chicken soup. I have important business to attend to!"

Ivy laughed and caught Brett's gaze as he stood a few feet away, seeming very interested in her conversation. For lack of anything better to say in the moment, Ivy was grateful to have an opportunity to play hostess.

"Oh, I don't think you've met. Darren, this is Brett Hastings. Dr. Brett Hastings," she corrected herself. "This is Darren. He and his partner moved to town last year. He sold my mother's house."

Darren held out a card and pressed it into Brett's palm. "Have you found a place yet?"

Brett stared at the card and then glanced at Ivy. "I'm in temporary housing for the moment."

"Perfect." Darren tapped his card. "I'm the best Realtor in town. Well"—he slid Ivy a glance—"the only Realtor in town. When you're ready for something more permanent, call me." With that, Darren gave Ivy a fleeting peck on the cheek and, clutching his arrangement, caught up with Rosemary at the door. He paused only briefly to turn back and mouth "Cute!" before pushing out into the summer night.

Ivy managed not to roll her eyes. Did everyone have to point out the obvious? Of course Brett was cute. She wasn't blind! He was too cute. And that was just the problem.

She felt his eyes still on hers. There was a glint to them and a grin she might go so far as to call mischievous. "What?" she asked warily.

"I just thought..." He shrugged, barely able to suppress his grin, and that's when it hit her. He'd thought that Darren was flirting with her. And she with him. Maybe even that there was something between them.

"Oh, you thought...Darren. We're just friends." She laughed in realization, happy to find a release for the nerves that were bubbling inside her, but her amusement was cut short by an emotion far more powerful.

It was something in his grin, in the steady depth of his gaze, and the way he lingered in the shop long after everyone else had already said their goodbyes and gone home for the night. The laugh, while genuine, wasn't one of amusement as it had been with her. No, it was, if she dared say so, almost one of...relief.

And if she didn't know better, she just might think that Brett had been...jealous.

If she didn't know better.

CHAPTER 22

It was late, not that Brett minded—he was used to strange hours. The sun had long since faded behind the Green Mountains and the lampposts glowed in the dark, illuminating the quiet street. Brett glanced to the left, knowing he should say goodbye, get in the car, and go back to the carriage house, but right now, the thought of sitting in that empty place, with only the television to keep him company, seemed about as unappealing as fishing another piece of food from a curious child's nose. Here, with Ivy... this is where he wanted to be. Even though everything in him was telling him he shouldn't be here at all.

"I'll help you clean up," he offered, seizing a legitimate excuse. The folding table was still in the middle of the room, covered with leaves and stems and the occasional broken flower, which he guiltily realized had been his doing.

Ivy slid him a knowing smile. "I knew you didn't like flowers, but did you really need to punish them?"

Brett barked out a laugh. It felt good. About as good as it felt to be in this quiet shop, alone with Ivy. He raked his gaze over her as she began brushing the clippings into a bin, feeling his body tighten and tense as he took in the curve of her waist, the cute little set to her lips as she concentrated on her task, and the hint of cleavage that made him long to do something he shouldn't.

She'd run away from the kiss. Broken it off. Torn away in that beat-up car. She wasn't interested.

But oh, he was...

"Why did you come to the class anyway, if you don't mind me asking?"

He watched as she carried the bin around to the back of her worktable and then returned to the center of the room to pick up a folding chair. He took it from her instead, and after a brief flash in her big blue-green eyes, she relinquished it.

He'd folded two chairs before he answered her question. "I came in to see you."

A flush of pink worked its way up her cheeks as she stared at him. "Oh?"

He set another chair against the stack and shrugged. "I didn't like how we ended things the other day. I didn't mean to upset you."

Ivy nailed him with a hard look as she reached for another folding chair. "I told you, Brett, you don't have to worry about me. I'm not hung up on you. But maybe you should stop trying to kiss me if you're so determined to keep telling me there's nothing between us."

His expression didn't waver. "What if I said maybe I wanted there to be something between us?"

She froze mid-task and then quickly recovered. The metal chair clanked loudly as it hit the others. "I'd tell you to get your head checked, because last I heard, you were hell-bent on telling me every chance you had that you did not want to pursue something with me."

"And do you feel the same?" he asked, holding her stare. Her gaze was steely, defiant almost, but the little lift of her chin gave her away.

"I thought you wanted to be friends," she said, but her pulse skipped with sudden possibility.

"You didn't answer my question."

"I thought you wanted to be friends. Then you try to kiss me. I don't kiss friends."

"Neither do I," he said.

She seemed to consider this for a moment. "You had no problems kissing me at Grace's wedding," she pointed out.

"Yes, but we weren't close friends. We just grew up together. It's not the same. Now...we've shared things, Ivy. Things we haven't shared with other people."

She let out a sigh of exasperation and set her hands on her hips. "Then why did you kiss me that night?"

"Because..." He shook his head. Because he couldn't resist her. Because, for the first time, something other than the pace of the ER was making him feel alive and excited. Because he'd thought it would be for one night. "Because I wanted to."

She raised an eyebrow. "And do you always get what you want?"

His breath was heavy as he took her in. The curve of her nose, the slight parting of her lips, the light in her eyes. Her expression was still poised in question, or maybe, he thought with a jolt, expectation. His chest was pounding as he considered his options, but no amount of thinking through this was going to sway him one way or another. He wanted to kiss her. Taste her. Feel her mouth, hot in his. Run his hands over those hips and explore her soft, sweet skin.

He took a step forward, matching her expression. "You tell me."

A small gasp escaped from her but was quickly silenced by the firm press of Brett's mouth on hers. Unlike their last kiss, which had felt so tender, this time Brett was leaving no room for confusion about his intentions. She stiffened against his touch, trying to resist him, but pleasure pooled warm in her stomach and the space between her legs began to ache as he wrapped two arms around her waist and pulled her to his chest.

Oh, God. She wanted to fight this. The feeling he was stirring within her. The need for more. She opened her mouth to him, letting him in. He kissed her deeply, not giving her a chance to break away, and she wasn't so sure she could, even if she wanted to. Her hands, which had been pushed off her hips by the strength of his arms, hung loosely at her sides, as if determined to stay out of this drama she was creating for herself, but, like her mouth, they lost the fight. She slid her hands up onto Brett's arms, taking in every curve of his hard muscles, and up onto his shoulders as she leaned into him. His breath was heavy as he kissed her harder, and she parted her legs to let his slide between and press against the tightness that was building within her.

"What are we doing?" she asked when they finally came apart. She blinked up at him and resisted the urge to flatten his disheveled locks. *I did that*, she realized with a flutter.

"I don't really know." Brett's voice was low and coarse. "But I like it."

She firmed her mouth and smoothed her dress. Not good enough.

Turning to stare at the folding table, she felt her spirits begin to sag. She'd let him in again. Let him take her to places she'd wanted, to dream dreams that should have stayed in her unconscious. And nothing had changed. *Men don't change, Ivy.* That's what her mother had always said. When would she learn?

"Well, it can't happen again," she insisted.

"Oh no?"

She glanced back to see that slow, sexy smile. "No." But even as she said it, her body was saying yes.

She reached under the table and starting fiddling with the legs, suddenly desperate to get the thing closed. To have the shop cleaned up and ready for tomorrow. To have Brett gone. Out of sight and, hopefully, out of mind. Only it was harder now, after that kiss, after knowing that he shared her secret, that he was somehow closer to her than most.

She reached lower, fumbling, and then stood back up. A rush of dizziness hit her and she set a hand on the surface to collect herself for a moment.

Brett was quick to notice. "What is it?"

She resented his sharp tone. He sounded like Henry. Overly concerned at the slightest little thing.

Then she thought of the reason why Henry always sounded that way. It was because he cared.

Was it possible that Brett did, too?

"I'm fine." She brushed him away and went to reach down for a table leg again, but the blood rushed in her ears, and she knew it was no use.

It was late. It had been a busy night. And her blood sugar was low. She didn't need to prick her finger to know it.

Neither did Brett.

"Sit down," he ordered, grabbing a folding chair from the stack and tenting its legs. He strode to the back of the shop, returning with a juice box and her handbag.

"I don't..." She sighed. The truth was she did need, well, help. Help from Henry. Help from Brett. "Thank you."

He nodded brusquely and watched her take a sip from the straw. Then, as she finished the juice box, he disassembled the folding table and carried it and the chairs to the storage room. She was just starting to slide one of the display tables back into place when he came back through the doorway.

"Don't even think about it," his voice boomed.

"But I know where it goes," she protested. There was a very precise angle to these tables to allow for optimal visual presentation when a customer first entered the shop. She'd gone so far as counting the floorboards to know where the corner of each one went. "If they don't get put back right, the room will be too cluttered and customers won't be able to move around, and it won't have the same impact."

Brett was listening to this with forced patience, which she gathered by the slight flare of his nostrils. His hands were set firmly on his hips as he tipped his chin, staring her down. "Anyone ever told you that you need to let people in more?"

She gave him a long look. "You should talk."

He shrugged and, grabbing her waist, gently pushed her away from the table.

She hated the thrill that simple gesture gave her.

Her body still warm from his touch, she stood back and verbally guided him to the floorboard where the left front table leg needed to be. "An inch to the left should do it."

His brown eyes widened. "An inch?"

She nodded primly. "An inch."

Muttering something under his breath, he did as he was told, and eventually, all the tables were put back in their usual places. Just to be sure, Ivy did a lap of the room.

"Okay, you really need to chill out," he said, but she noticed the amusement that flashed through his dark pupils.

"And would *chill out* include casually kissing, or friends with benefits, or whatever else you have planned?"

His jaw twitched, and his eyes fell flat. "I don't have anything planned, Ivy. But that doesn't mean I don't want something."

Her mouth went dry as she stared at him across the room, and suddenly her cozy little shop felt very small. Too small. Like the walls were caving in and she didn't know which way to turn. Or what to believe. Or if what he was offering was good enough.

"You should get some rest," he said, reaching for his coat and the sad arrangement of flowers. "Good night, Ivy."

She stood still, watching as he slipped out the door and disappeared into the darkness.

So he was proving to be a nice guy after all. The guy with all the qualities she'd first noticed in him. That didn't mean he was capable of giving her what she needed.

She'd have to reread *Running from the Ring: Men Who Simply Can't Commit* again tonight. Lord knew she wouldn't be getting any sleep.

The flower arrangement looked out of place sitting on the coffee table in the carriage house. He'd have given them to his mother if they'd turned out any better, but the sad state of things would only call into question who made them, and there was no disguising the fact that he had. No doubt his brother would tease him for months over taking this class, if Rosemary hadn't already let everyone in town know about it. There'd be no explaining it, not unless he wanted to profess his feelings for Ivy.

Feelings. He'd made it his point not to have any. For women. For patients. Sometimes, even for his own family. And he'd failed on every account.

His gut stirred as it always did when he thought of that woman out there somewhere, with a baby by now. A baby who would grow up without a father. Just as Brett had.

He clenched a fist, trying to hold back the building emotions, but it was no use. Nothing could change the fact that a man was dead. Nothing Brett did could bring him back.

Just like nothing could have changed the fact that his mother developed cancer that he couldn't wish away.

That Ivy had diabetes.

He'd promised himself a long time ago not to get close, not to care so much, to distance himself from that type of hurt and pain and potential loss that came with illnesses and diseases that could only be managed but not cured. He'd vowed never to cry himself to sleep the way he had so many nights when he was young, alone in the house with Mark, their mother still in the hospital hooked up to machines.

Headlights illuminated the backyard, and Brett stood, walking to the windows to see Mark's car pulling to a stop in front of the garage below. Grinning, he unlocked the door and cracked it, then walked to the fridge and took out two beers.

"Saw your light on," Mark said. "Do you mind?"

"Not at all." He was grateful for the company. He handed his brother a beer and nodded toward the leather couch.

Boxes were still stacked along the far wall and Mark gestured to one. "Still moving in or moving out?"

Brett took a long pull on his beer. "I can't stay here forever."

Mark frowned. "The carriage house or Briar Creek?"

Brett shifted against the couch and considered his options. Mark understood him better than anyone. "Honestly, I'm not sure."

He took another sip of his beer, unsettled. As much as he hated to admit it, now that he was back, a part of him would be sad to leave.

"What about the job?"

"It's temporary," Brett reminded his brother. "Through the end of the year. It's not exactly what I set out to do, either."

"Does Mom know that?"

He gave his brother a knowing look, and Mark whistled under his breath. "She's not going to be happy."

"I know." Brett frowned.

"Neither am I," Mark admitted. "But I get it. Briar Creek's a pretty small place for so much history."

Too much history, Brett considered. And now, after getting close to Ivy, there would be even more. He didn't want Ivy to be a girl he looked back on or who triggered additional bad feelings and guilt about his hometown. He wanted… more than he could have with her, he supposed.

Her life was here. And his wasn't.

"It won't be easy to leave again." If anything, it would be harder than ever. Last time he'd come to town was before his mother's scare, before her cancer was foremost in his mind again. Before he started thinking of Ivy, caring about her.

Mark just shrugged. "You've done it before. I would have thought you'd be a pro by now."

Brett narrowed his eyes. He and Mark had always gotten along, but he still wondered, and worried, what his brother really thought of him. Now his worst fear was being voiced. "Do you really think I'm that cold?"

Mark held his stare evenly. "I'm just saying that you've had no problem staying away for long periods of time in the past. Hell, we've barely seen you for more than a few days at a time in over a decade. I don't see what's changed now."

"It wasn't all by choice," Brett said, feeling his defenses rise. His hours were unforgiving, always had been.

"I know. But it doesn't change the facts."

Nope, it didn't. Brett shook his head and drained his beer. His brother had a point, one he didn't want to hear, but it was the last part of his statement that hit him the hardest.

Something had changed. And that made him uncomfortable.

He glanced at the flowers, still on the coffee table, and wondered if Mark had noticed them yet. Instead his brother shifted topics to the restaurant and his wedding plans. When he stood to leave, Brett stopped him.

"Do me a favor and don't say anything to Mom just yet about my plans. Nothing's decided yet."

Mark held his stare for a long time and finally nodded. "Hey, it's your life. Only you know what's best."

Only he didn't. Once he thought he knew, but not anymore.

He closed the door behind his brother and eyed the blinking light on his phone. The email from the hospital in DC, still unopened. His finger hovered over the button, so close it wouldn't take much to press down, learn his fate once and for all and adjust accordingly. He'd always let opportunity be his guide—how could he justify ever passing it up? But emotions were starting to cloud his judgment, make him doubt himself. Make him rethink his past and his future.

He set the phone on the kitchen counter. Only a few weeks ago, the thought of checking that message would have filled him with hope and relief. But now...now it just filled him with dread.

CHAPTER
23

As Ivy had hoped, the sun came out just in time for Jane's bridal shower on Sunday, filling the Madisons' childhood home with light. Ivy shifted a vase to a better angle and stepped back from the dining table that had been set up as a buffet. She hadn't been back in this house since the fall, and that visit was one she was trying not to remember.

Sophie skipped up to her, grabbed a cookie from a tray, and flashed her a big smile. Immediately Ivy noticed the grown-up tooth that was already starting to fill the gap where her front teeth used to be and realized the little girl was waiting for her reaction.

"My, my, is that a big-girl tooth I see?" She couldn't help but smile as Sophie nodded proudly.

"Yep! Hopefully this one won't fall out any time soon or my mom will start crying again..."

Ivy laughed. "Hopefully that tooth never falls out. I like your dress, by the way."

Smiling, Sophie smoothed the skirt of her dress. "Henry bought it for me. Is he your brother?"

Even though this had been established, the concept was

still a lot for Sophie to take in. "Yes, he is my brother. The best brother a girl could have."

"I have a brother," Sophie said quietly. Though it wasn't talked about much, Jane's ex and his new wife had welcomed a baby boy in the spring. "Mommy said maybe after she and Henry get married, I'll have another one."

Ivy's heart swelled for her brother. Just seeing how he was with Sophie, she knew he would make a wonderful father. "How do you feel about that?"

Sophie scrunched up her nose. "I told Mommy that sounded all right, but only if it's a girl this time. Boys aren't fancy."

With that she took another cookie and darted into the living room, where the rest of the women were gathered. Ivy watched the little girl go, her pink dress trailing behind her, and eyed the buffet. Cookies. Cakes. It had been Sophie's idea to make the shower a tea party, and Jane being Jane went along with it.

Of course that meant there was next to nothing that Ivy would be able to eat, unless she wanted to increase her insulin and spend the majority of the party monitoring her sugar levels. She'd reassured Jane over and over that she didn't care, that it was her party, after all, and Ivy could eat a cucumber sandwich or something...but she hated cucumber, and the truth was, she did care. Even now, all grown up, she still felt singled out and different. Like an outsider, instead of one of the group.

She looked around at the beautiful house she'd spent so much time in as a child, always finding comfort and happiness here and always feeling the abrupt sting of reality when it was time to go home. To her real home. With Henry, and her mother, and the unknown...

"There you are." Kathleen Madison's smile could be heard in the warmth of her voice, and Ivy felt her eyes tingle a little as Jane's mother set an arm around her shoulder. "The flowers look lovely. Thank you for being such a good friend to my girls."

"Sisters now," Ivy marveled. It still hit her every once in a while that her brother was marrying her best friend's little sister and that somehow, in a roundabout way, she was almost a part of the family now, too. An official part.

"Come on in and join the others. Did you try Anna's cake?"

"Oh. I saw it. It's beautiful." And it was, white and pink with such pretty piping and sugar flowers that it was nearly too pretty to eat. But as she followed Kathleen into the living room, she saw that its aesthetics hadn't stopped the others, who were happily scooping silky frosting onto their spoons and bringing it to their mouths.

Anna noticed Ivy's empty hands and looked startled. "Didn't you get a piece? There's more." She stood and cut a perfect wedge for Ivy.

Ivy picked up a fork weakly and eyed the three perfect layers of the cake.

Anna was watching her expectantly, as was Kathleen, and for lack of anything else to do in the moment, Ivy winced and lowered her voice. "I'm actually having some stomach problems today..."

Anna's blue eyes popped. "Oh. Oh, you poor thing. Here," she said, taking the plate, "I'll wrap it up for you for later."

"Thanks." Ivy smiled in relief. The party was going to be a success—not overshadowed by her drama, like Grace's had been.

But as she looked around the room at all the women, she started to feel the walls pull away from her. Most of them were married or engaged, several already had children, and the closest thing she had to a love life was a guy who couldn't figure out what he wanted and seemed hell-bent on leading her on and letting her down.

It had been a week since the night of the flower arranging class. A week since Brett's kiss. A week with no phone call, no sight of him, nothing.

Just like before…

Ivy spotted Kara across the room and quickly made her way over to her. "Is it just me or does it seem like we're the only two single girls here?"

"Tell me about it," Kara sighed. "I'm on my third piece of cake. If my mother notices, I'll never hear the end of it." She shoveled the last bit into her mouth and chewed woefully.

"She means well," Ivy said.

"That's easy for you to say. She's not your mother." Kara set a hand on Ivy's arm when she winced. "I'm sorry. I didn't mean to be so insensitive. It's just…"

"I understand," Ivy said, and she did. Rosemary had a big personality, and Kara wasn't as self-assured as her mother. It couldn't be easy living in that shadow.

Ivy should know.

"No, I shouldn't make comments like that."

"I'm your friend. You don't need to treat me with kid gloves," Ivy reassured her, or maybe *pleaded* was a better word. All her life, she'd been treated differently because of her mother, and she didn't need that following her into adulthood. "Is she still trying to set you up?"

"Oh, probably." Kara pursed her lips. "I'm just tired of feeling like nothing I do is ever right."

"What about your cookies?" Ivy brightened. Come to think of it, she hadn't seen them on the buffet table. The ones Sophie kept snatching were from Anna—she'd come to recognize them over the years. "You should have brought some today."

"No," Kara said quickly. "This is Jane's day, and Anna's her sister. I didn't want to overstep."

"About the cookies," Ivy suddenly remembered. "Jane told me Anna gave her your box for Sophie's school bake sale."

Kara looked at her with interest. "The box I gave her as a gift?"

Ivy nodded. "Apparently Jane forgot about the event and went to Anna to see if there was anything on hand."

"So she might not have commented because she still hasn't tried them..." Kara beamed.

Ivy surveyed the room. The conversations were winding down, and they'd be opening gifts soon. While they were discussing Kara's cookies, she decided to indulge in a topic she had promised herself all the way here she would avoid, because, well, she couldn't resist.

"So, um, have you...talked to Brett lately? About the cookies and the fundraiser and all that?" *Smooth, Ivy. Real smooth.*

Luckily, Kara was too busy scraping what remained of the frosting on her plate to notice the eagerness Ivy felt. "Oh, not recently. I think he went back to Baltimore for a few days."

This news came as a surprise. A ping of hope surged through her. Maybe that was why he hadn't called.

"Knowing him, he's probably already making plans to go back," Kara added, and walked into the kitchen to deposit her plate.

"Ivy! Come sit here!" Sophie was calling across the room, grinning ear to ear. "My mommy just told me that when she marries Henry, I get another aunt . . . and it's you!"

Ivy blinked away the tears that had now formed in her eyes and crossed to give the little girl a hug. Only she wasn't so sure what was hitting her harder: the fact that she was finding that perfect little cozy family she'd always dreamed of or the fact that yet again, it felt a little secondhand.

The first place Brett stopped when he got back to Briar Creek was Hastings. It had been a long drive from DC, and he was still wound up from the interview. As surprised as he was to admit it, only one thing could ease his agitation right now, and his mother would be pretty pleased to hear it.

"Chocolate chip pancakes," he said, sliding onto a stool.

She poured him a cup of coffee, even though it was late afternoon. "How was the drive?"

"Long," he said. Too long and too quiet. He'd been up since light broke, and he had a solid nine hours to replay the interview, oscillating between worrying he would get the job and worrying he wouldn't. It was a first-class hospital, one of the best emergency departments in the Mid-Atlantic and a place he'd be proud to put on his résumé. But it would also be much like the position he'd come from. High stakes, high pressure. High stress.

But it was also the kind of job he'd set out to have. The kind he'd stayed on the path for. Sacrificed for. How could he turn it down?

He eyed his mother as she took another order, laughing at something one of the regulars said. The old man had been coming here since Brett was a kid. Brett had left town, gone on to build an entire life somewhere else, and all this time,

Mr. Adams was sitting here, sipping his coffee and reading the paper.

For a moment, it was hard not to envy the guy.

The same thought took over every time he considered the path he'd not chosen. What his life might have looked like if he'd stayed. He'd eased the guilt by telling himself the outcome would have been the same. His mother would have gotten well, and then she would have relapsed. Being here couldn't have changed that.

He was hoping one day he'd finally accept it.

"Heard you went to that flower arranging class last week," his mother said with a gleam in her eyes.

Brett set his forearms down on the table and sighed. "Who told you?"

"More like, who didn't?" Mark's voice boomed behind him. Sliding onto the stool beside him, he slapped Brett on the back and grinned. "Heard you broke more than a dozen flower stems. Are you causing Ivy trouble?"

Brett stilled, then, after he realized what his brother meant, tried to relax. His laugh felt strained as he reached for his mug again, only to find it empty.

Causing Ivy trouble was the last thing he wanted, but he had a bad suspicion that was exactly what he was doing. There was no point in getting involved with her now—not when he could be leaving town as early as next month.

"What were you doing in that class anyway?" Mark asked, walking around the counter to help himself to a carafe of fresh brew. "I told you all the girls were going—" He stopped, his eyes lighting up like they used to when they were little, when he discovered Brett had kept that snapping turtle in a box behind the garage instead of marching it back to the lake per their father's instructions.

Setting the pot back on the burner, he folded his arms over his chest and asked, "Who is it?"

"It's no one." Brett scowled. There was no getting out of this one. Mark wasn't dumb. Not dumb enough to think Brett would ever take a flower arranging class for the sheer hell of it. "It was just... research."

Mark lifted an eyebrow. "Research?"

"For the fundraiser. I was thinking of asking Ivy to auction off a series of classes. I wanted to see what they were like." He considered the idea. He'd bring it up next time he saw her.

Mark held his stare, unwavering, for a length of time— an old intimidation tactic they used to use to see if the other was bluffing—and finally, almost convinced, shrugged and sat back down.

"So you're still overseeing the event then," Mark said quietly. He was the only person Brett had told about his interview in DC. But it stopped there. The reasons behind it all were still something Brett wasn't ready to share with anyone... other than Ivy.

It had been a moment of weakness, he'd rationalized. A bad day that he couldn't shake. But it had felt good to open up to Ivy, to voice his demons, to feel her soft skin on his hands as she listened.

"Of course I'm still overseeing it," he said.

"Still doing what?" Sharon asked, coming out of the kitchen with his order.

Guilt heated his blood. "Organizing some silent auction items for the fundraiser."

Sharon patted his arm, smiling warmly. "I'm just so impressed with your efforts. When I think of where the proceeds will go... It's high time they spruced up that wing.

I'm sure it's not what you've been used to in those fancy city hospitals."

God, he wished she would stop talking like this.

"There are merits to bigger hospitals," he said tightly.

"There's no denying that Forest Ridge Hospital needs some improvements. It's not the same as Burlington, but for a lot of people on the outskirts, that's their best option, and some can't even manage that."

Brett frowned. "What do you mean?"

"Oh, just some stuff I've heard about cost of care these days." She shook her head. "If I'd been sick any sooner, I never would have gotten out from under those medical bills. Not with the debt your father had left us in. I suppose I have this place to thank for getting us through." She opened her arms to the diner.

Brett wasn't finished with the conversation just yet. "The cost of care has gone up for some."

"It affects more people than you doctors realize," Sharon scolded.

Brett tightened his grip on his fork, thinking of what Ivy had said about her setback last summer and then her comments about doing the fundraiser to help her business.

That cemented it. He'd stop by, talk to her about the silent auction, and make damn sure that this benefit helped her cause. In every possible way.

CHAPTER 24

Even though Ivy was technically off work, that didn't mean she always followed her own rules. People still had birthdays on Sundays, after all, and she couldn't control when a baby would be born. By the time she made it back to the shop after the shower, weary and tired, she had five bouquets to make and deliver.

She decided to start with the simplest: a dozen apricot roses, no frills. Working with her hands always eased her mind and gave her a sense of purpose. It was hard to let your mind trail to its troubles when you were focused on a task. And the outcome of her hard work, always beautiful, colorful, and original, brought a smile to her face each time and a feeling of satisfaction that could only come from within.

At least she loved her job, she always thought, and today she needed to remind herself of that more than ever. She hadn't mentioned it at the party, but it was the anniversary of her mother's death, and while she'd made peace with it and, perhaps, sadly, even had a touch of relief from it, there would always be a sense of regret that their relationship had never evolved into the one she had longed for. She'd never given up hope, and now that hope was lost.

Henry didn't want to talk about their mother, and Ivy respected that. He'd dealt with the brunt of it by trying to fill an absent father figure's role, trying to be the man of the house, trying to grow up faster than he needed to.

Sort of like Brett had, she supposed, and then shook her head. There was no use thinking about him like this, not when Kara had made such a valid point. Brett hadn't made Briar Creek his home since he left for college. Why start now? The only reason her brother had stayed was because he'd fallen in love with Jane. Judging from the way things were going with Brett, she didn't think she'd be so lucky.

She stopped for a snack, even though she wasn't hungry, and checked her levels just to be sure. Satisfied, she spent the next hour finishing the arrangements and then fetched her delivery list. Four she would drive, and the last was just at the edge of Main, about a quarter of a mile down Orchard. She'd take that one on foot. The fresh air would do her good.

She was just coming back from her last delivery when the skies opened up with a crackle of thunder that made her jump, and a steady downpour splashed down. Ivy cursed under her breath and began jogging back up Main Street to the shop as best she could in her rubber flip-flops, wishing she hadn't been so lax with her gym membership these past few weeks. But there were only so many hours in a day, and between her regular business and the hospital fundraiser quickly approaching, she needed every spare minute she had.

Head bowed to keep the rain from blurring her vision, she watched her feet splash and dodge puddles as she slowed to what she knew Rosemary referred to as a power walk. While the temptation to march her arms as she had seen the woman do was tempting, she resisted, instead feeling the burn in her calves as she counted down the blocks. She was halfway up Main when two feet darted from her left and blocked her path. All at once the rain stopped, and she looked up to see Brett grinning down on her under the shield of an umbrella.

He looked relaxed and happy and terribly sexy. And she probably looked like a half-drowned rat.

"What are you doing out in this?"

"It wasn't raining when I started." Ivy gave a helpless shrug, but her heart skipped a beat when she met Brett's gaze—dark, mysterious, and entirely too sexy given he hadn't reached out to her in a week.

"You headed back to the shop?" The question was rhetorical as he turned on his heel to stand at her side. "I'll walk you."

Part of her wanted to tell him not to, that she was already sopping to the bone and that it didn't matter now, that she really needed space from him if nothing was ever going to happen between them other than an occasional—and knee-bending—kiss. But then she felt the warm, smooth graze of his arm against hers, and her heart began to beat a little faster. His stride was quick and purposeful, and she had to take almost two steps for each of his, but she didn't complain. She was too busy enjoying the scent of musk that had filled the humid air they shared under the large golf umbrella.

"Do you always come so prepared?" she asked, breaking the silence.

"I was at the diner and I saw you coming up the street. I grabbed this umbrella from the back office."

Her heart beat a little faster at the gesture. "Well, thank you, then. I suppose that makes you my hero."

"I'm just doing what any other decent guy would do." He elbowed her playfully and she laughed.

Decent. He was a decent guy, she knew it deep down. He was still that same sweet, studious boy she'd crushed on all through high school...and beyond. Somehow it was easier to see him in this light than in the womanizing role she'd cast him in. It made it harder to not care—about him or a potential letdown.

"Besides, the last thing you need is to catch pneumonia."

The words hit her sharper than he'd probably intended, bringing up every reason she'd had to keep her health issues to herself. "Because I'm a diabetic, you mean."

"People with diabetes are considered to be at higher risk for developing pneumonia," Brett said simply. Catching her frown, he nudged her again. This time she didn't laugh. "Hey." He stopped walking and stared at her until she looked up. "I'm only saying it because I care."

"As a doctor or a friend?"

"Maybe as something more," he said quietly.

Her heart was pounding out of her chest now, but somehow she managed to keep from jumping up and down or whooping out loud. Instead, she slid him a smile and nudged him back. "In that case, I guess it's all right." And it was, she realized. It felt good to let someone in, to take a risk, to share a part of herself she didn't usually open up about. But it was scary, too. It made her feel connected to him in a way she wasn't sure she should.

They crossed the street to Petals on Main, and Ivy reached in her handbag for her keys. Hoping to prolong the moment, she fished around for several moments after her fingers had grazed the cool metal.

"Well, thanks again," she said with a smile, giving him one last long glance. His forearms were wet with rain, but it was the occasional splatter on his T-shirt that brought her gaze to his broad shoulders and the hard plane of his abs.

"Don't I at least get a cup of tea for the effort?" he replied, tossing her a lopsided grin.

Ivy blinked, barely managing to pull her attention from the cords of his muscles. "I think that can be arranged," she said, pushing into the stairwell of her apartment. She smiled with each of the thirteen steps until she realized with a horrified jolt that she hadn't been expecting any visitors, and that she'd been in a real rush to get to Jane's shower on time, and that dirty breakfast dishes were still in the sink, that the bed had most definitely not been made, and that she had tried on close to ten outfits before settling on this one and the rejects were tossed randomly about.

She stared at her hand as she slid the key into the lock. How to get out of this one...

With a deep breath, she turned to him, her heart doing a little dance when she caught the curl of those full, smooth lips. Oh, those lips.

"I should warn you," she said. Her chest was rising and falling with dread. "I had a busy morning, and I wasn't expecting anyone."

Brett's brow grew to a point. It wasn't lost on her that he was standing close. Very close. So close that she could feel his heat, see the hint of a bump on his otherwise perfect nose, sense the pull of his lips, which she wouldn't mind exploring again. "And?"

She wrung her hands helplessly. "And, well…" She leaned back, eager to get away from that mouth, soft and pink and oh so close, and those eyes, so intense and penetrating and unrelenting, and felt the door push open under her weight.

"And, well..." But she didn't need to say anything more. It was all there, worse than she'd remembered, for him to see. Her dirty laundry, literally.

"Oh my." Brett's eyes widened as he stepped into the small vestibule that separated the three rooms of the apartment, his gaze darting this way and that, to the dirty dishes that were not in the sink but actually on the counter, to the five or six dresses flung on the sofa, to the glimpse of a rumpled duvet through the partially open bedroom door. The self-help books were strewn about, their covers unforgiving, especially the one of the grown man in a silly green cap, under the glaring title *I Won't Grow Up! How to Detect Early Warning Signs of Peter Pan Syndrome*.

Brett slid his eyes to her, his mouth tugging into a wicked grin that made her feel like she was being silently scolded. "Just who are you, Ivy Birch?"

"I. Well." She darted past him into the kitchen and all but shoved the plates and mugs into the sink with a loud clank. Brett was already in the living room, studying the dresses and—God help her—the assortment of corresponding bras that littered every surface. She'd forgotten those.

"I told you I was in a rush this morning." She felt her face heat.

Brett just laughed good-naturedly and carefully moved the dresses from the sofa to the armchair. "Or perhaps I should have flung them across the room instead?" Noting the horror in her expression, he laughed loudly. "I'm joking. Come sit." He dropped onto the sofa and patted the seat beside him. "Do you honestly think I care if your apartment is a mess?"

Ivy roved her eyes over the living room, landing on the heap of clothing that now covered the chair. Cringing, she said, "I'm not sure."

"I'm fascinated," Brett declared. His eyes twinkled, and Ivy felt her color return to normal.

"It's not an everyday thing," she explained hastily. Not every day. Maybe just…five or six days a week. At least once a week Grace or Kara stopped by…

Not that Kara cared. The only time Kara properly cleaned was when her mother was dropping by.

"Here I thought I had you all figured out, and then." He opened his palm and, like a game show host, swept it over the room.

"You don't know me that well," she said tersely. Maybe he knew her mouth, and the shape of her body, and the fact that she had diabetes, and that her mother had drunk herself to death…Okay, maybe he did know her pretty well. She wasn't so sure how she felt about that.

She suddenly felt at a disadvantage. Most of what she knew of Brett was the little he had told her, and he was a man of few words. He was guarded; he preferred to keep things to his chest. But there was a lot in there. He'd revealed some of it. To her. Just to her.

"I guess I know you, too," she observed, coming to sit down next to him. "You don't like to get close."

The laughter in his eyes disappeared, and for a moment Ivy wished she hadn't steered the conversation in this direction, but then she thought of the last time they'd seen each other, and that kiss, and she settled against a toss pillow, waiting for his answer.

"You're right. I don't." Other than a blink, his expression was blank.

"So that's it then. That simple?"

He shrugged. "If you don't get close, you don't get hurt."

Ivy considered his words, knowing the source of his feelings. "True. But what an empty way to live."

"There are some things in life that change you," Brett said. "My dad leaving was the first. My mom getting sick was the second."

"It doesn't feel good to stand back and know there is nothing you can do to change things." Ivy nodded, thinking of her mother. How many times had they hidden the bottles, tried to distract her, and when they were older, downright begged her to stop drinking? Henry had even paid for her to go to some expensive rehab clinic in California, and after two days she'd checked herself out. She knew Henry had never forgiven himself for not finding a way to make her go back, but he was too hard on himself. Just like Brett.

"Everything was going wrong back then. First my dad left, then there were money troubles, then, just when it felt like everything was getting better… it only got worse."

"But it's all worked out," Ivy pointed out. "Your mom is healthy and happy."

"But for how long?" He gave her a long look.

"We can't control those things," Ivy said gently.

"See, I don't like to believe that," Brett said, his jaw pulsing. He shifted his body until he was a bit closer to her and propped his head in his hand, looking her square in the eye. "I told myself I would never feel that out of control again. Never sit back, in a position to do nothing, knowing nothing, while someone I cared about suffered."

"But even doctors can't save everyone," Ivy said. She knew. They hadn't saved her mother, after all.

Brett pulled back, the look in his eyes suddenly distant. "No. They can't."

She touched his arm. It felt warm, soft. He didn't move away. "I didn't mean it like that."

"I know," he said softly. Brett was quiet for a few minutes. "You said you were in the hospital last year. What happened?"

Ivy stiffened. "It's what I told you. I ... wasn't taking care of myself properly. I'm not proud." Ashamed. Humiliated. Not proud. "I got behind on my medication. Thought I could get by with less than I was supposed to be taking. At first it was to cut back on spending, and then it became something more. It's like I could almost convince myself that I was normal."

He looked at her sharply. "What do you mean, cut back on spending?"

"Well, the shop doesn't pay for itself, and I don't have a partner. Between overhead and my rent here, the medical bills could be steep. Cutting back on my dosage helped. I knew it was a risk, but I guess I thought I might be able to get away with it."

"That's terrible." Brett shook his head, his expression pained.

She shrugged. "I'm not alone. I delivered flowers one time to a woman who said her son's asthma medication is almost as much as their monthly mortgage."

Brett reached over and slipped a strand of hair behind her ear. "I hate hearing this."

Ivy swallowed as his fingers slowly trailed the skin behind her ear and down the length of her neck. "What can you do?" she said casually.

"Consider alternatives, I suppose. If there are any. Or

listen. I've sort of made it a point to keep things brisk," he admitted.

"Part of that whole not getting close to anyone thing, huh?"

"Except you." Brett's voice was husky and low and Ivy held her breath, knowing he was about to kiss her again. There was no doubt this time. She held his gaze, waiting for the contact, for the touch she had once enjoyed, her lips parting as his eyes dropped to her mouth and he leaned closer, until his lips were on hers. His lips were soft as they brushed hers, but his kiss was deep and long and left no room for doubt that he wanted this moment just as much as she did. He explored her mouth as his arms wrapped around her hips, his grip firm and solid, leaving her no chance to break away even if she'd wanted. And she didn't. His mouth still on hers, he closed the distance between them, lowering her back onto the couch until the plane of his chest was level with her pounding heart, the weight of him spread over her body. She slid her hands onto his hips, up, under his shirt, to his warm, taut skin. Her skin was cool from the rain, but the heat of his body quickly warmed her, spreading over her as he kissed her mouth, his tongue lacing with hers as his hands slid over her body, reaching down to caress the length of her thigh, teasing her as it reached higher until she gasped with pleasure.

"Maybe we should go into the bedroom," he whispered, so low into her ear that she squirmed from the tickle of his breath and then relaxed into the tingle of warmth that spread deep into her belly from the nearness of his heat. She hesitated, but only for a moment, feeling a shift between them, a change from hope to something deeper.

He kissed her neck, sliding her wet hair free so his mouth could trail her skin. She closed her eyes, luxuriating in the moment, not wanting it to end. Slowly, he unbuttoned her blouse, peeling it from her still-damp skin, and brought his mouth back to hers, his kiss deeper as he wrapped his arms around her waist and pulled her tight against his chest. She could feel the beating of his heart, the heat of his body, the smell that was so familiar by now. She trailed her hands up his chest and around the back of his neck, where his hair met his skin, weaving the silky tendrils through her fingers.

Breaking their kiss, Brett inched her closer to the mattress, his hands never leaving her body, his eyes locked with her own. Her heart began to speed up as anticipation grew, and she sat down on the edge of the bed, her hands on his waist, pulling him near her, not wanting to lose this contact or this moment. Brett ran a hand down over her collarbone, his touch so light it sent a shiver down her spine, and edged toward her as his hand trailed lower, to cup her breast. Quickly, Ivy brushed the self-help books to the side before he could notice. They landed with a thud.

She turned to him, and his eyes flashed on hers. "I saw those, you know." His mouth quirked, and she kissed his smile away, laughing with him as they fell back against the unmade bed.

CHAPTER 25

The alarm clock went off much too early, and Ivy reached over to silence it, eager to make the most of the next five minutes before it chimed again, pulling her from the warm down cover and the soft heat of Brett's skin next to hers.

Groaning, Brett rolled over and wrapped an arm around her waist, nuzzling against the nape of her neck. Ivy curled into him, smiling into her pillow, almost wanting to pinch herself that three nights this week had been spent in Brett's company, three mornings spent waking up to that smooth voice and that touch...

"What time is it?" he asked, teasing her earlobe with his teeth.

"Almost time for your shift, Doctor," she whispered. "Do you have time for breakfast?"

His hand moved from her waist to her breast as he pressed himself closer to her. "I can think of a better use of time than breakfast." He smiled mischievously as she rolled onto her back to look at him.

"Care to enlighten me?" she asked, grinning.

He lowered his mouth to hers, and the intensity of his

kiss was all the explanation she needed. She arched her back as his arms reached behind her, pulling her tight as his hands slid lower, sending a shot of fire deep within her.

The alarm buzzed again, and this time it was Ivy who groaned.

Brett kissed her neck, once, twice, and then lifted his head, giving her a reluctant smile. "Rain check?"

She reached up and mussed his hair, sighing. "Tonight?"

"It's a date," he said.

She rolled over, covering herself with a sheet while he walked into the bathroom, allowing herself a moment to appreciate his perfect naked form. She listened as the taps turned on and the water started to rush and decided, begrudgingly, that it was time to start her day, too. It just would have been so much nicer to spend it in bed, the way they had for the better part of yesterday.

She was already dressed and pouring coffee when Brett appeared in the living room, scrubbing his hair with a towel, his shirt unbuttoned to reveal the cords of the muscles that rippled over his taut stomach.

"If you keep having coffee with me in the mornings, your mother might start to get a little suspicious," she joked, handing him a mug.

He took a sip. "No doubt she has her suspicions, but she's keeping them to herself."

Ivy peeled a banana thoughtfully. They hadn't established what was happening between them, and Ivy was enjoying it far too much to ask. She didn't want to rush things, didn't want to get carried away. And she didn't need the input of half the town, which is what would happen once they knew about this.

"Would you like some jam on your toast?" she asked, motioning to the sugar-free variety she had in her fridge.

Brett set his mug on the table and cocked an eyebrow. "I can think of something sweeter."

"But you just showered! And you have to go to work..."

"So?" Brett set his hands on her hips and ran them lower.

Ivy giggled and playfully pushed at his chest. "Stop. We can't do this. You'll be late for work."

"I don't care," he whispered, lowering his mouth to hers.

Ivy wasn't about to argue with that, not when his hands were sending shivers over her skin, heating her in places that longed for his touch, and his mouth was persistent, warm, and eager. She ran her hands over the smooth skin of his chest and kissed him fully, her tongue moving in motion with his in the way that was quickly becoming very comfortable.

Just as she began to feel his body responding to hers, she pulled back, knowing that if she didn't they'd get carried away, and both of them would be late for work.

"You should get to work," she said, taking his hands. "Because I know you. And you do care."

His expression turned rueful. "You're right. I do." He buttoned his shirt and tucked it into his slacks, then drained his coffee. It was too late for the toast by now, and it had probably gone cold anyway.

"Tonight?" He turned to give her one last kiss at the door.

"Can't wait," Ivy said, leaning against the doorjamb as he jogged down the stairs.

But she would. She'd waited years for this, after all. What was a few more hours?

Ivy listened patiently as a bride went through her wish list in exact detail, even though she sometimes found this part of her job tedious.

She glanced at the clock on the bottom right corner of her computer as she typed in the order. Brett would be getting off his shift in an hour, and then... Her stomach flipped, as it had every day for the past week since he'd first slept over. She knew it was just a week—such a short, routine span of time that usually went by in a rush—but already she'd adjusted to a new routine and a new person in her life. Brett had spent the night whenever he wasn't on call or working a late shift, and already in the mornings when she woke up to find his side of the bed empty and cold, she missed him.

She finished with the bride and checked her phone, smiling at the text he'd sent her when he arrived at the hospital, already making good on his promise for tonight.

Tucking the device back into her pocket, she found her pitcher under the sink, filled it, and walked around the shop, testing soil in her potted plants and offering a drink where needed. Outside, the stall of colorful blooms brightened the sidewalk. The sun had been beating down all day, and she doused them liberally, deciding to leave them out until just before closing.

At the sound of her name being called, Ivy looked up and shielded her eyes from the glare of the sun as she saw Kara waving at her from across the street.

Ivy grinned. "Hey! Come on over!" she called.

She was bursting to tell Kara her good news, but she knew it would be better to hold off. Brett was her cousin, after all, and if Kara slipped and said something to her mother, there would be no end of it.

Ivy considered the recent interaction between mother and daughter and realized there would probably be little threat of that, though. Things were tense with Kara and Rosemary, and the situation didn't seem to be resolving itself.

"Are you closing up now?" Kara's cheeks were flushed by the time she reached the store.

Ivy nodded. "I'm closing on time for once tonight."

"Hot date?" Kara asked, and Ivy felt herself pale until she realized that Kara was joking. It was just assumed, of course, that she didn't have a hot date, or that if she did, she would have mentioned it to her friend.

"If you call spreadsheets and a pile of bills a good time, then yes." It wasn't a lie per se. She did have a mound of bills to go through. She'd stuffed them aside for the past week, preferring instead to bask in her good fortune, but reality couldn't be avoided forever, and the last thing she needed was a bill collector getting involved or the pressure of a late payment fee.

Kara craned her neck to see through the glass windows and then turned back to Ivy. "Can I ask you your opinion on some things?"

"Sure." Ivy drained the last of the water into a potted hydrangea and opened the door.

Kara followed her up to the workbench, her blue eyes wide. "I'm getting really nervous about this fundraiser. I'm worried I've overstepped. Anna's been so good to me. And she and Mark are catering the event."

"Anna's one of your best friends. Why don't you just tell her?"

She bit her lip in thought. "I will. But I don't want to make things awkward or look like I'm competing with her or anything."

"I think she'll be happy for you," Ivy said, but she could understand Kara's concern. Anna was a hard worker, and she took her culinary skills seriously. She'd also trained and coached Kara for the past couple of years. "What about the new position at the restaurant? How's that going?"

Kara made a face. "I hate it, Ivy. I mean, it's terrible. I'm so bored, so lonely, and just so...uninspired."

"Are you planning on leaving?" The smart thing to do would be to stay until something better came along. But Kara didn't always operate that way.

"I've been thinking I need to do something more...me. You know, something that makes me feel excited again."

Ivy nodded with growing dread. She'd heard all this before. No job seemed to keep Kara's interest. The only job she'd really enjoyed had been helping Anna out at the bakery, before she'd opened the restaurant with Mark.

"I look around at what you have, even what my mom has...what Anna and Mark have...I want that." Her expression was so earnest that Ivy felt her heart tug. It was true that she was fortunate; she had built a business that she loved, and not a day went by that she didn't feel like pinching herself. But it didn't come for free. Or without a lot of hard work and sacrifice. "I guess I just wish I could do something with my cookies...like a cookie business...or something. Something more than a few sales here and there." Kara faded off, her cheeks reddening as she studied her nails.

"A cookie business is a great idea!" Ivy exclaimed.

Kara was grinning now. "You sound so confident."

"And you should, too," Ivy said firmly. "Look, it's scary to start your own business. You never know what will come of it. But I think you have something here, Kara. Would you open a shop?"

"I'm still thinking about everything," Kara mused. "I have my inheritance from my dad...I just don't know what my mom would say about me spending it on something like this." A line appeared between her brows as she fell silent.

Ivy sighed. "I know you and your mom don't always get along, but she loves you, Kara. I'm sure she'd be supportive."

"Loving someone and being supportive of their choices don't always go hand in hand," Kara replied. "My mother has strong opinions on how she thinks I should be living my life. So far, it seems I've done nothing but disappoint her."

"She wants the best for you. But what she thinks is the best and what you think is the best may not be the same thing. This is your life, Kara. Follow your heart. She just wants you to be happy."

Kara eyed her. "You really think so?"

"I'm sure of it." After all, wasn't it what any family member wanted for their loved ones? She could still remember being around Sophie's age, picking wildflowers for her mother in a hope to cheer her up, because even then, when she was so young, she couldn't stop thinking that if her mother was just happy, things might be different.

Kara reached over and gave her a quick hug. "You're the best, Ivy. I think I will do what you suggested and talk to Anna. And if you don't mind, I might have a few other ideas to bounce off you, too. Like, some logos for the labels?"

"I'd love that!" Ivy grinned as her friend walked out of the shop with a bounce in her step Ivy hadn't noticed in a long time. Things were looking up in Briar Creek.

Brett pulled the rubber gloves from his fingers with a snap and tossed them in the bin. It had been a long day, and he was ready for it to be over.

"Dr. Hastings?" A nurse appeared in the doorway, her expression turning coy as he nailed her with a hard stare.

Here we go again, he thought. Some men would be

flattered. Others would take advantage. "Yes?" He kept his tone as professional as possible.

"A patient was just brought in by ambulance. Do you have time?"

Technically, his shift ended in five minutes, which meant he couldn't turn away. He gritted his teeth, wondering how long this would set him back, and then shook that thought away immediately. He was due to meet Ivy, but someone needed his help. And he was the doctor on shift. Letting his thoughts wander to his personal life right now was exactly what he had promised himself he wouldn't do. Couldn't do.

"Absolutely." He followed her out the door just in time to see the paramedics wheeling in a young woman on a gurney.

"We have a thirty-year-old woman in hypoglycemic shock," the first paramedic said, and everything after became a blur. Brett quickened his pace to a run, his eyes searching the half-covered body that was being lifted onto a table.

He blinked down at the face, immediately noticing the dark hair and the pale skin. It wasn't Ivy. It wasn't Ivy. He said it over and over to reassure himself.

It wasn't Ivy. But it could have been.

Relief was quickly replaced by action as he gathered her vitals and assessed her condition. Her pupils were dilated and she was unresponsive. The situation was critical.

"Start a line of dextrose," he ordered as the nurse hurried with the IV.

"You're going to be all right," he said to the patient as much as to himself. "Everything is going to be all right."

Petals on Main was closed by the time Brett pulled up to the front of the building. Bypassing the shop, he walked through the open door to the stairs that led to Ivy's apartment. He could hear the rustling of her feet behind the door before he knocked, no doubt in some last-minute effort to tidy the place up. He grinned, but he still felt unsettled.

That woman in his ER today could have been Ivy. Hell, it *had* been Ivy a year ago.

She'd let things get that far before. How could she be so sure it wouldn't happen again?

His gut was twisting by the time his knuckles fell against the wood. The locks turned and the door swung open and the air rushed out of him at the sight of that face, that smile...

"Hey." He stepped inside and slid his hands onto her slender waist, wanting to pull her in and hold her tight, know that she was safe and well, watering her flowers and probably shoving clothes under the bed, not being revived by paramedics.

He dropped his mouth to hers, felt her sweet taste in his mouth, the tenderness of her touch he craved just as much as the hungrier side of her, the one that made him stir with need, making it impossible to think straight. Because that was just the problem. He wasn't thinking straight.

Ivy was sweet and caring and funny and smart. And he was a doctor who couldn't balance his life and let everyone in his world down eventually, even if they didn't admit it, and even if there was always some excuse for it. He didn't want to do that to Ivy. He just wanted to protect her. But he wasn't so sure he could.

"I don't know about you, but I'm famished." She grinned up at him after she'd pulled away, her hands lightly tracing a pattern on his arms as she looked deep into his eyes.

Brett felt a flicker of panic. She wasn't supposed to let herself get to this point. If she was hungry, her blood sugar could be low, and then it could crash, and...He stiffened.

Ivy frowned. "Is something wrong?"

"No. Yes." He rubbed his forehead. "It was a rough day at work. A bad day." They were nothing new. Back in Baltimore, a day like today would have been light. He would have left feeling relaxed, maybe even gone out for a few drinks before heading home. But now he felt weary, run-down and tired, and depressed as hell.

"Do you want to talk about it?"

Brett studied her. Talking about his work wasn't something he often did. He'd trained himself to leave work behind him when the shift ended, to not spend his free time dwelling on the outcome of a patient he'd sent off to surgery. He'd purposefully avoided anything requiring long-term care. But all he could think about was that young woman. And he didn't want to think about her. That was hospital life, and this... here with Ivy... this was personal life.

Except they were colliding all over again.

"You taking all your doses?"

"Yes." She narrowed her gaze. "Where is this coming from?"

"I just meant that if it was a problem again, I could help you out—"

"Stop right there," Ivy said, holding up a hand. She looked so sad all of a sudden that he felt like the biggest jerk on the planet. He'd offended her, when all he was trying to do was help her. And help himself, he supposed.

Like it or not, he'd developed feelings for this woman. And he knew the complications of her condition.

"I'm not your patient. I have this under control."

But did she? He wasn't so sure. He hadn't forgotten the day of the Fourth of July festival or the times she'd let her sugar levels drop too low before taking action. She was being too reactive for his comfort zone. But if she said she had it under control, he probably had to accept that. She wasn't his patient. And that was almost worse. It meant there was nothing he could do but sit back and watch and hope for the best. Just like he was forced to do with his mother.

And he'd promised himself a long time ago not to get in that position again, especially with someone he cared about.

"I had a patient today," he said, looking her square in the eye. "With diabetes."

"And it made you think of me?" She pursed her lips in disappointment. "See, this is why I don't like people knowing about my personal life."

"Even me?" Brett raised an eyebrow. "I've shared things with you, too."

"Yes, but you don't see me telling you how to do your job. Please don't tell me how to take care of myself."

He tossed up his hands. "What can I say? I'm a doctor."

"Not when you're here, you're not," Ivy said, sliding him a suggestive smile. She slid her hands onto his hips and lifted her face until her mouth found his. "Can't we just have a nice night?"

He was overreacting. Getting sensitive. Brett stroked her hair, forcing back the anxiety that was forming a hard knot deep in his gut, but it didn't want to go away. "Let's order the food," he said quickly.

Ivy was touchy about her condition. And fiercely independent. It reminded him of someone else he knew and cared about. And it made him uneasy. How many times had his mother casually remarked that he shouldn't worry, that she was taking care of herself, that she was fine?

Before he could go down that dark path, he pulled out his cell phone and made a call to the local pizza joint, where he ordered most of his meals that weren't spent with his mother or brother, at the diner, or now, with Ivy.

Ivy went into the kitchen to get them some beverages while he placed the order, and he could hear the soft hum of her voice as he waited on hold. The day began to wash away from him as he settled onto the couch in her tiny living room, and by the time he'd disconnected, he was feeling almost at peace.

And then he saw it: a missed call. Washington, DC, area code. The call.

Ivy came back into the room, carrying two glasses of iced tea, or sun tea, as she called it—she brewed it on her back deck while she worked. He shoved the phone into his pocket and took a sip, already knowing its aftertaste, already finding it familiar, and tried to push back the pounding of his heart as she set her glass down and leaned against his chest, running her fingers up and down his arm.

He could stay here forever like this if he wanted to. But now, thinking of that hospital in DC, he wasn't so sure that he did. Or if it was even an option.

CHAPTER 26

It was a particularly hot day, even for August, and of course, that meant that Ivy's air conditioner would choose today of all days to burn out. She stared at the window unit she'd purchased secondhand three years ago, cranked a couple of knobs, even tried another plug, and still nothing but silence.

She sighed. It wasn't the end of the world, she knew, but buying a replacement was just another expense on top of an already mounting pile. She'd spent most of her morning going through orders and invoices and trying not to worry about how she would ever come up with the money to pay her brother back.

Luckily the benefit was just around the corner. Between the decorations and the silent auction item she was listing for a year's worth of monthly flower arranging classes, she should have an uptick in clients that would put her far into the black and maybe even give her the fresh start she was hoping for.

Unlike Kara, she hadn't had an inheritance to get Petals on Main off the ground or keep it going. Instead, she'd done it the old-fashioned way, by taking out a loan and paying it back, bit by bit. She'd sunk so much into supplies and inventory, with only a wish and a prayer that it would pay off, and by the first anniversary of the shop, she was officially turning a profit. Not a big one, but enough to add a few new luxuries here and there. Not enough to keep up with the medical bills, though.

She'd pinned every hope on the sale of her mother's house. Even though Henry had invested in some upgrades, the sale price ultimately covered only what he'd sunk into it. Other than getting on a better health plan, she was almost no better off than she'd been when Henry first came back to town. Worse, because now she owed not just the bank, but him, too. And no matter what he said, she took both loans equally seriously.

Most of her clients were centered in Briar Creek, but the Forest Ridge Hospital benefit could expand her pool of business, and not just for immediate needs, but possibly going forward.

She bit her lip as she began to let her mind wander with possibilities. No time to feed into temptation like that now. If she kept daydreaming, she wouldn't be focused, and none of those dreams would have a chance of ever coming true. There were a few more details to go over for the event to make sure she made the most of it.

She picked up the phone to call Brett, and then, with a glance at the clock, grabbed her car keys instead and turned the sign on the door before locking it. She rarely took a proper lunch break, but it was a slow day and she knew she wouldn't be gone too long. Even though Sharon Hastings didn't know that she and Brett were spending time together, Ivy decided to take a chance and drop by the carriage house. If Sharon noticed her pulling into the driveway, she'd just explain she was there on official business matters, which she was, sort of. Brett's car was outside the garage as she pulled to a stop behind it. There was never any denying where she was in town; the ancient station wagon was noticeable from a fair distance. Brett opened the door before she even had a chance to knock.

"This is a pleasant surprise," he said, but something in his smile didn't quite meet his eyes. When they kissed, he didn't pull her in long and deep the way he usually did.

Ivy pulled back, searching his eyes. Exhaustion, she decided. The man was an ER doctor. She couldn't even begin to know how draining that could be.

Still, that little voice she'd tried to ignore flickered to the surface, the one that had enough experience with rejection to sense when something was amiss.

"I had a few questions about the event, if you don't mind." She felt nervous as she remembered her notes. "The venue manager told me that instead of end tables on the patio, they're having coffee tables. I think we should add a small centerpiece for each."

"Sure, whatever," Brett said, brushing past her.

She tried not to read into his lack of interest. After all, planning this event was not high on his priority list or his area of expertise.

"Is there room in the budget?" she asked, knowing this was his main task in the process, along with hosting the event and, along with the chief, thanking the donors.

He shrugged, unconcerned. "If there isn't, I'll just write a check."

Ivy couldn't argue with that. She started to say something, but his generosity was overshadowed by the restless way he prowled his living room and the distance in his eyes.

Something was up. She'd seen this look before. Felt the distance. The shift in tone.

"Something's up, Brett." She swallowed hard. If she hadn't come over today, then what? Another day of innocent bliss? Another day of thinking they were starting something?

He held her stare for a long time, his jaw tense, his eyes flat. He didn't need to say anything more.

"I should have known," she said bitterly. He wasn't a relationship kind of guy, and now, once he'd gotten her, he was over it. "The chase is over, right?"

"That's not what happened," he said firmly.

She folded her arms. "Oh no?"

"I'm leaving, Ivy. I'm leaving Briar Creek."

Kara's words flashed to the surface, and Ivy heard herself bark out a laugh. It felt hollow. "Of course you are. You never stick around here for long. Are you going back to Baltimore?"

"Washington, DC. I'm lucky they'll take me, given everything."

"Well, they're lucky to have you," Ivy said, her voice thick. She told herself to be strong, to not take this personally; it was a career decision, after all, but something about it felt like anything but that. "How long have you known?"

"I've been thinking about it for a while now."

A while. All this time she'd been thinking they were building a future, he'd had one foot out the door. She blinked back the tears that stung her eyes. "I'm sure everyone here will be sorry to see you go."

"It's an opportunity I wasn't sure I'd have again. It's a prestigious hospital. They get the majority of the big cases in the city. I'd be doing something important." He stared at her, as if seeking her approval. Well, she didn't intend to give it.

"You could be doing something important here, too." She peered at him. He really didn't get it. "Every patient is important, Brett. If you take the time to notice."

"What's that supposed to mean?"

"I mean, all you care about is advancing your career. But you went into medicine to help people. I know you did."

"Damn straight I did, and the hospital in DC could benefit from my skill set more than Forest Ridge Hospital."

"I'll remember that next time I'm rushed there by ambulance," Ivy said flatly. "I'll remember you're too good of a doctor to stoop to that level of care."

"Stop it, Ivy. That's not what I meant."

She folded her arms tightly across her chest. "No? Because from where I stand, you think you're too good for this place."

He took a step toward her, his expression pleading. "I worked hard, Ivy. I went to the best schools. I was top of my class. I earned my slot at the best hospitals. That's where I should be."

"Well, I'm glad you think you'll be making a difference."

"You wouldn't understand." He shook his head, looking away.

Anger rose within her. "No, I suppose I wouldn't understand how it feels to make a difference in someone's life. I suppose that when I stop by a sick or grieving person's house and deliver the bouquet I put extra care into creating, the smile on their face, however brief, doesn't matter. At least not to you. But it matters to them, Brett, and it matters to me. I might not be saving lives, but at least I care about people, and even if the help I offer is fleeting, even if I can't change the circumstances, for a second at least, I've made someone's day a little better, and that's what I understand. And *you* wouldn't understand *that*."

Brett blinked, and the room fell completely silent.

"You never should have gotten involved with me if you were planning on leaving town," she said, gripping her handbag straps tightly.

"I never should have gotten involved with you at all," Brett replied.

She froze. "What's that supposed to mean?"

"You need more than I can give you, Ivy." His jaw was tense, his eyes steely.

Ivy stared at him, searching for a hint of the man she knew was in there, but it was gone again, overshadowed by the jerk he'd become. "Hey, I never asked for anything other than a straight answer. But it seemed like you weren't ever able to offer one of those."

"You want a straight answer? Here's a straight answer. I'm a doctor because I watched my mother fight for her life while I sat there knowing there was nothing I could do to help her. I'd already lost one person I loved, and I was scared as hell of losing another. I swore to myself I would never be in that position again. Ever. And then I met you."

"And?" Ivy frowned, but the words began to take shape in her head and she stared at him in disbelief. "Wait. You don't want to be with me because I'm a diabetic?"

"Your condition is more serious than you think," he replied.

She narrowed her eyes on him, took one step closer, and pulled herself up to full height. "I know all about the complications of my condition, Brett, and I have it under control. And *shame* on you for using that against me." She turned and walked to the door, her body trembling with anger. She put her hand on the knob, knowing she should go, that everything that had been said was said, that no good could come from dragging this out, and that nothing could change what he'd decided. Or who he was.

She turned slowly, taking one last look into the dark depths of his eyes, but the light had gone out. "Life is a lot more enjoyable if you start letting people in instead of shutting them out."

"You're just as guilty of that as I am," he countered.

"Goodbye, Brett," she replied, and pushed out the door. She was crying by the time she got to the car, not sure what she was more stung by. That whatever they'd started to build was over or that what he had said was true.

But how was she supposed to let anyone in when the one person she'd let get close had only let her down in the end?

Brett stared at the closed door until Ivy's footsteps had faded and the door at the ground level had slammed. He felt the thin walls of the carriage house shake, and he closed his eyes, making two fists at his sides to hold back the mounting emotions.

Ivy was perfect, in so many ways, and that's what made the situation impossible. She'd been too good, too sweet, and she'd made him want things...things he couldn't have. Things that couldn't last.

He'd done what he had to do, ended it swiftly. But it had gotten more personal than he'd wanted it to be. It was supposed to be about him moving, clean-cut and simple. Long-distance relationships rarely worked, and Ivy was a businesswoman; she should have understood. But she'd hit a nerve, exposing that raw part of himself he tried so hard to keep covered, the one that nagged and needled, the one that told him he wasn't a good doctor, not really, or that he could be better. *Should* be better.

A better doctor. A better son. A better person.

His jaw twitched, and he rubbed the spot where it was starting to ache from grinding his teeth. He'd done what he had to do. Ended it now, before he got in deeper. Before he let her down even more.

Before he let himself down even more.

He shook his head. He needed to get out, distract himself, put some distance between himself and this moment. He grabbed his keys and went to the window. The space below where Ivy's car had been parked was now empty, and his stomach tightened at the realization that she was gone. Gone from his house. Gone from his life. It was what he'd been hoping for—confirmation that it was over and that the worst was behind him, that she wasn't going to fight for him, wasn't going to try to make him change his mind—but now, staring into the backyard of his childhood home, he felt a loss so deep he thought it would break him.

He'd given this house up. His home. And now Ivy.

And once again he was back to the place he'd tried to avoid, wondering if he'd made the right choice, and if it was worth it.

Or if at the risk of protecting his heart and hers, he'd just made the biggest mistake of his life.

One of the perks of running your own business was being able to take a day off whenever you wanted. One of the downsides, however, was having no backup, and that meant that no matter how much Ivy wanted to crawl under the covers and have a good cry, she had no choice but to fulfill the remaining few orders of the day or risk not only losing customers but also letting people down.

And unlike someone she knew, she didn't like letting people down.

Ivy read the order on the computer screen through blurred vision. A fifty-year anniversary bouquet from a loving husband. Would it ever be possible for anyone to love her that long? Through all the ups and downs and turns in life's road?

Right now, it didn't seem possible. She'd dated over the years, but none of the men she'd seen had ever known about her diabetes. She'd been too worried how they would react, how it might affect their future, if she wouldn't be in a healthy enough position to have their children...

Any doubt she'd had that she was better off keeping things to herself had been confirmed today. Brett could have offered a long-distance relationship, but instead, he'd cut it off, hitting her where she was most vulnerable, reminding her that she was different and that at the end of the day, he was a doctor and she was...a liability.

Somehow, she managed to make the bouquet, resisting the urge to reach for the dark, broody stems and instead forcing herself to do what the person had asked for: something light, feminine, and, above all, romantic. She opted for shades of cream, pink, and lavender, using up the last of her Sahara roses. When it was ready, she wiped her eyes and went back into the alley to the car, hoping the drive would clear her head.

But by the time she arrived at the small Colonial with the pretty perennial garden tucked behind a picket fence, she was feeling deeply sorry for herself. The bastard had dumped her. Kissed her, messed with her head, and now, the pièce de résistance, he had ended things.

Fool, fool, fool, fool. He'd played her harder than any guy had before.

Worse, because she knew Brett. Knew the quiet, shy, studious boy he was. Knew the tender side of the man he now was. Worse because she thought she knew him, saw through to that sweetness. Worse because she'd let him in. And worse because she'd cared.

And she'd dared to think he'd cared, too. But judging from today, that wasn't possible.

He'd taken something about her, something she never revealed to anyone, and he'd used it against her. And that was unforgiveable.

With a sigh, Ivy shifted the arrangement in her arms, took the cobblestone path to the front door, and knocked. There was a shuffling of feet and finally a turning of the locks. Ivy was expecting to see a woman dressed for a celebratory dinner in town or maybe, given the occasion, at the country club over in Forest Ridge. Instead, she was surprised to see a pale face and eyes red from crying.

Ivy frowned and glanced at the brass numbers nailed to the door frame, wondering for a moment if she had the wrong address. "I'm sorry, there might be some confusion. Are you Linda—"

"Yes, that's me." The woman glanced at the flowers, confusion knitting her brow.

"Well, then, these are for you," Ivy managed to smile and handed the vase over. "Happy anniversary."

Normally the response was a thank you, a gasp, and a smile. But the woman just blinked back tears that still started to fall as she carefully searched for the card. "I don't know who these are from..."

Ivy had written it herself, so she already knew what it said. Still, it wasn't her place to say. The card, she'd found over the years, could mean just as much as the flowers themselves. "Here," she said, plucking it from its holder and handing it to her.

"To my darling Linda," the woman whispered. "The day I met you, my life was forever changed. Every day after, it was made more complete. We've had our beginning, and our middle, but some things don't have an end. I love you."

Ivy wondered if she should stay or leave. It was unclear if Linda was speaking to her or to herself.

"Very sweet," she said tightly. She backed up, but the woman was crying harder now, and so she hesitated.

"He always planned ahead, my Dennis. Always thought of me. Always sent me flowers, every year." The woman's hands trembled as she inspected the flowers. When she glanced at Ivy, her eyes were bright, but there was a shine in them where the sadness had been just a few minutes ago. "Dennis died three months ago," she explained, and this time, Ivy was the one to gasp. "I thought this would be the first year I wouldn't receive them. Now I know it's my last, but somehow, that's okay now."

She shook her head, not knowing what to say. She hadn't even checked the original order date, just the delivery. Now she seemed to recall the flowers she'd made in honor of a man...a war veteran. A father of four. She glanced into the hallway. The house was pretty, the walls lined with photos showcasing a happy life and one that had reached its end. The curtains were drawn, just a bit of summer light shining through, no sound coming from a television, a radio, or anyone.

She steadied herself on the rail and set a hand on the woman's wrist. "I'm so sorry."

The woman looked up at her, tears still shining in her eyes but a smile where her frown had once been. "Don't be. I thought today was going to be one of the loneliest I'd had in a while," Linda continued. "But thanks to you, I'm not alone.

A little piece of Dennis came back to me. These are the last words he'll ever say to me. I thought I'd already heard all he had to say." She reached out and squeezed Ivy's hand. "These flowers mean more to me than you'll ever know. Thank you, young lady. Thank you."

Ivy swallowed the lump that had wedged in her throat, unable to do anything other than mumble a response.

She sat in her car for a long time, staring at the house from the edge of the road, imagining the woman inside, thinking of how quickly and easily her day had been turned around. How lucky she was to have been able to share in that moment, wondering, with bittersweet hope, if she'd be lucky enough to have what that woman had once had, and still, in some way, did.

And then she thought of Brett...and just how much he was missing.

CHAPTER 27

By the next day, Brett had expected to wake up feeling energized, refreshed, and as close to normal as he could anymore. He was used to setbacks. Used to dealing with the tough days and then moving on. Except moving on was becoming more of a struggle lately, and today it was proving impossible.

The look in Ivy's eyes still felt like a punch to the gut, and every time he managed to close his eyes to her image, her words echoed in his ears. In time they would fade, just like most things did, but for now, they were sharp and, worse, they were true.

He sighed and opened the back door to his mother's house. She was in the kitchen, preparing breakfast, and she smiled in surprise when she saw him.

"How'd you know it was my morning off?" She grinned and pulled another mug from the cabinet.

"Lucky guess," Brett managed. Only there was nothing lucky about it. One way or another, he was going to have to tell his mother his plans today, before she heard it from someone else. His stomach burned.

"You look tired," she said as she studied his face. She frowned and tsked under her breath. "Working too hard!"

"I had a night shift," Brett explained. He knew some doctors could crash after that, but he never could, and certainly not today. He was agitated, too wound up, and the knowledge he was harboring was almost worse than the thought of letting it out.

He'd say it. It would be over. He'd deal with the fallout.

This was just reality. No different than delivering a bad diagnosis.

Only this time the person he was addressing wasn't a stranger. It was his mother. And she was the last person in the world he ever wanted to see hurt. Again.

"I was just going to make some eggs. Fried or scrambled?"

He couldn't think about food right now, but he said, "Scrambled." Taking the mug from her hand, he poured himself a coffee from the pot she'd already brewed. Even now, though she lived alone, she always made a full pot and kept it on low heat until she had to go. He supposed people in town stopped by, and she wanted to be ready, but a twinge of guilt made him wonder if it was something else, something subconscious. If deep down she wasn't lonely in this big old house, if she was still waiting, just in case Brett came back or his father.

He waited until their eggs were ready and they were seated at the table to tell her about the job. She'd be proud of him, he knew, but there would be no denying the hurt she would be selflessly hiding. And that was almost the worst of it.

"Mom, there's something I have to tell you," he began.

"There's something I've wanted to tell you, too," she said. "Do you mind if I go first? I feel bad that I haven't had the chance before this—you've been so busy at the hospital."

His mouth felt dry. She certainly wasn't making this any easier on him.

"It occurred to me that you moved back to town because of me."

Brett opened his mouth, but she held up a hand. "Please. I need to say this. Now, I told you about my concerns in the spring because you're a doctor but also because you're my son. I've seen the way you hover around since you've been back, and I want to make it clear once and for all that you don't need to worry. I'm healthy, for now at least, and I have a team of excellent doctors if things take a turn. I'm not your patient, Brett. Don't make me one."

"Mom." He stared at her. "I'm a doctor. How can I not have an extra layer of worry?"

"Just answer me this: Was the reason you came back to town because of me?"

Her eyes were clear and determined, and Brett knew there was no use glossing over the truth to spare her feelings. "Yes and no." He sighed. There was a time in his life when he used to tell her everything. Every cut and scrape, every disappointment about anything less than a near-perfect grade. The good and the bad, it was all open, all shared. When did he start pulling back from her? When did he shut her out?

When she got sick. When he had to stop being the kid and start being a man. Start putting her needs first. Stop giving her another thing to worry about.

If he told her the truth...it would break her heart. She'd blame herself. They had that in common, he supposed.

"I left Baltimore because I was asked to take a leave of absence," he said carefully, and there was an audible gasp across the table. He pressed his hands flat on the table and stared at his eggs, which had now gone cold. "I lost a patient. It happens. It went to review. I wasn't held accountable."

Sharon shook her head and closed her eyes for a moment before blinking up at him. "I'm confused. If you weren't held responsible, why did they ask you to leave?"

"Because I was distracted. Upset. I couldn't get past what I'd done. How I could have avoided it."

"Oh, honey. You always were too hard on yourself. You're a wonderful doctor, Brett."

"I'm not so sure about that anymore," he said.

She frowned. "What's that supposed to mean?"

"I mean that maybe, if I'd taken the time to invest in the patient, things might have gone differently."

Her smile was wan. "Don't ER doctors usually move from one patient to the next as quickly as possible?"

"Yes, but some balance things better than I think I have. Some . . . care."

"You care, Brett." She looked at him like he was crazy.

He shook his head, struggling to meet her eye. "I've tried not to. If you let yourself care . . ." He pulled in a long breath. "The job becomes harder."

Sharon nodded slowly. "I think I understand."

"I've been offered another job, Mom." There it was out. "In Washington, DC. It's one of the top hospitals on the East Coast. It's a trauma center. It's a good job. The kind where I can be useful."

"Are you going to take it?"

He struggled to confirm it but forced himself to nod. "I'd be doing something important."

"What you're doing now is important."

She sounded like Ivy. He didn't need the reminder. "Yes, but there my skills would be put to use. Those patients need me."

Sharon lowered her eyes. "I see. Well, I won't try to stop

you. Only you know what's best. But do one thing for me, Brett. Make sure you're taking the job for the right reasons."

"What would the right reason be?" he asked, hoping she would tell him, because he wasn't sure anymore. "You sacrificed so much, Mom. And Mark, too. I went off to college, then med school. Some of the best schools in the country. I wanted to make you proud."

"I am proud!" she insisted.

"Then why do I feel like all I ever did was let you down?"

Her eyes softened. "Oh, honey. Did I ever make you feel that way?"

"No, but I still felt it. Felt like I should have been here. Shouldn't have gone to Yale." She'd already had one man bail on her in life. And he'd gone and made it two.

"You wanted to be a doctor," his mother said, and Brett nodded. He had. He wouldn't take that back. "And you had this amazing opportunity. If you hadn't taken it, it would have been me feeling like I'd let you down. Do you see that?"

Brett considered this for a moment. "I do. I just wish circumstances had been different."

"All my life, I tried to protect you boys. I put you first. You'll understand one day when you have a child of your own." She wiggled her eyebrows at him, then turned more serious again. "Remember when you were little, how I offered to come with you to those scout meetings?"

He frowned. "And I didn't want you there. Because the other kids had a dad with them, and I didn't." He remembered the hurt that had flashed through her eyes. At the time, he'd felt bad, assuming she was stung by his refusal. But now…

"It broke my heart to see you miss out. What I would have done to give you that opportunity."

"Aw, Mom. You did the best you could."

"And you did, too," she said, smiling through tears. "We all make choices in life. And now you have another one. Don't feel bad about leaving me when you did. You went on to make your mark on the world. And now it's up to you how to make the next one."

Brett picked up his mug and took a sip, tasting nothing. She hadn't tried to stop him, just as he knew she wouldn't, but she hadn't encouraged him, either. She'd challenged him instead.

It had been a few weeks since Ivy had last been to the gym, and she was feeling the burn in the Wednesday night yoga class, unlike Kara, who breezed through it without so much as breaking a sweat.

"If you come every week, it gets easier," she said as the girls rolled their mats.

"It's not always easy to break away from the store," Ivy said, not to mention other distractions that had kept her mind on things other than her health these past few weeks.

"I understand. I'll probably skip next Wednesday's class to get ready for the fundraiser."

At the mention of the event, Ivy's stomach dropped, and she pressed a hand to it to ease the queasiness. Given the turn of events, she wanted nothing more than to just drop out or ask Jane to go in her place, only Jane would question that, and besides, Jane was Henry's guest—he was covering the event for the paper. A front-page photo, no doubt featuring one of her bouquets somewhere in the background, was fantastic publicity, as was the exposure to new clients. But the thought of seeing Brett again, even for that one night, knowing it was probably the last until he deigned to come back for a holiday down the road, was hard to take.

But she would muster the courage. Because that's what she did. What she'd always done, really.

And besides, if she didn't go, if she didn't fulfill her part in the event, then she never stood a chance of paying that loan back to Henry, at least not anytime soon.

"Did you decide on the flavors?" Ivy asked.

Kara nodded. "I think I'll do three different flavors, so people can choose. I'm meeting the Madisons at the bookstore after this. Want to come?"

She grinned. "I'd love to." She'd been hunkered down in her tiny apartment for days, but it felt good to be out again, and out with friends. She was right where she'd been before Brett came back to town. Well, almost. A secret part of her had considered that she might bump into him tonight. She'd been highly selective with her outfit, just in case. She'd even taken the front doors, done a casual, albeit heart-pounding, lap around the cardio room, sure to linger at the water fountain, just in case he happened to stroll by, notice how good she looked, how badly he had messed up.

She supposed she'd have her chance at the fundraiser, but that was different. It was an event she'd been looking forward to, and now it was overshadowed. Worse was that everyone would be there, and she'd be forced to pretend nothing had ever happened between them—good or bad—just like when he'd first come back.

The Madisons were already gathered around a center table in the bookstore's café when Ivy and Kara arrived a few minutes later, still wearing yoga pants and tank tops. It was a warm night, sticky and muggy, and lightning bugs dotted the dark sky. Ivy settled onto a chair between Grace and Jane, trying to stay in the moment and trying not to think that a week ago she'd been buzzing with excitement for a future, and now it all felt more uncertain than ever.

The girls chatted about Jane's wedding, Anna's inability to set a wedding date, and Sophie's part in a camp play. Across the table, Ivy could tell Kara was waiting with bated breath for an opportunity to mention the cookies, and when the topic of the fundraiser came up and what everyone would be wearing, Ivy gave her a little grin of encouragement across the table.

"I'm actually contributing something, too," Kara began, her eyes darting to Anna and away again. "I didn't know how to tell you this, Anna, but do you remember those cookies I made the day the pastry chef was out?" When Anna frowned in confusion, Kara glanced at Ivy, who nodded. "Well, Grace was telling me how much everyone loved them. I... I've been working really hard on perfecting the recipe, and, well, Brett decided to offer them as a party favor."

"I didn't know that part, Kara!" Grace exclaimed. "Those are seriously the best cookies I've ever had. Other than yours, Anna," she added quickly, but the casual wink she threw her sister proved there were no hard feelings. "That's great! Isn't it?"

"Of course!" Anna looked at Kara in wonder. "I had no idea. Why didn't you tell me?"

"Well, I know you're catering the event. I guess I was worried you would be . . . mad."

"Mad?" Anna repeated. "I'm thrilled for you, Kara! I always knew you had a gift when it came to baking."

Kara looked like she could almost cry with relief. "Really?"

"Really. I just didn't know if that's what you were interested in."

"Oh, it is!" Kara nodded. "I'm actually thinking that if

people like the cookies, I may...do something with them. Maybe."

"You should! Briar Creek could use a bakery now that I've opened the restaurant," Anna said.

"I've already come up with the name," Kara admitted. "Sugar and Spice. What do you all think?"

"I love it!" Grace cried, and everyone began talking at once, in full agreement.

Ivy watched the scene unfold with unease. Brett's comment had stuck with her, longer than she'd hoped. He was right—she did keep people at arm's length; she didn't trust them the way she should. Now, looking around at her oldest and closest friends and seeing how supportive they were of Kara's decision, she felt a wave of shame for holding in a part of herself, when all they'd ever done was accept her. They hadn't cared that her mom was a drunk and had made a spectacle of herself at every town function. They didn't care that she chose not to talk about that time or that she wanted to forget it. They hadn't even cared when she'd almost ruined her best friend's bridal shower—all they'd cared about was that she was okay.

Shame bit at her. She'd always been a little different. They didn't care.

"I have something to share, too," she said a little hesitantly.

Four sets of eyes swiveled to her, and Ivy sat back in her chair, wondering if she was just caught up in the moment. It wasn't too late to make an excuse. Under the table, she felt Jane's hand give hers a brief squeeze. The youngest of them all but somehow the wisest.

"Grace, do you remember what happened at your bridal shower last fall?" She hated even bringing up the event, how she'd ruined it.

"Remember? How could I forget? We were worried sick about you!"

Ivy cringed. That was the worst of it—the worry she brought on people. It was a reason not to share, not to open up...but it wasn't a good enough excuse anymore.

"I felt bad about that," Ivy started. "Something you all don't know is that I'm a diabetic. My blood sugar wasn't under control that day." She didn't get into details or explain why things had reached that point. What was done was done.

She looked around at the confusion that spread across the table. Grace spoke first. "You have diabetes? Did you find out then, at the hospital?"

Ivy almost laughed at that. "No. I found out in first grade."

"You mean you've kept this from us for all these years?" Grace looked so hurt that instantly Ivy regretted her decision.

"With all the talk about my mom, I never felt like a regular kid. I just wanted to be a regular kid." She swallowed. "Then, when I grew up, I finally had a chance to be my own person. Not Debbie's daughter. It was liberating. I didn't want to do anything to taint it."

"And no one else knows?" Kara blinked rapidly, as if trying to process this.

"Henry and Jane." She glanced guiltily at her future sister-in-law and back to Grace. "I asked her not to say anything."

"I think I understand." Grace smiled sadly. "I just wish it hadn't taken you this long to know we don't care. Well, we care, but it doesn't change the way we think of you."

"Some people would care, though," Ivy said, thinking of Brett. He didn't want to be burdened by her condition. Didn't want to deal with the complications that could arise. Didn't want to get close to someone who came with risks.

"Well, you're the only person I will say this to, then, but Ivy, do not buy one of my cookies. Ever." The women all laughed, and even Ivy joined in. Phrased any differently, that type of remark would have been her worst fears coming true, but in the company of true friends, it was just what she needed to lighten the mood.

Ivy wondered if she should take the opportunity to tell them about Brett and decided against it. Some things were worth sharing. Some were better forgotten.

The emergency room was quiet, but Brett roamed its halls just the same, trying to push back the urge that wouldn't go away. Finally, in the break room, he couldn't hold back anymore.

One of the nurses was eating a microwaved dinner, one eye on the evening news, one eye, he noticed with chagrin, on him. She'd been here the night they'd brought in the woman. The woman he'd thought for a fleeting moment had been Ivy.

He never asked. Never in all his time working, but this hit too close to home, as did Ivy's words.

"You know that woman that came in last week? Hypoglycemia?"

The nurse pushed air out of her lips and squinted at the wall, as if trying to recall. "I think so. Thirtyish?" She poked her plastic fork into the dish. "Why?"

"I was just wondering if there was any follow-up on her condition."

"Check the system," the nurse replied, and Brett blinked. He'd never considered it. Never, in all his years learning and practicing medicine. He wondered what that said about him. As a doctor. As a person.

Quickly, he went to the nearest computer and pulled up

the logs from the night she'd been brought in. The cursor hovered over his name, and then he clicked it, scanning the information on the screen as quickly as his eyes would let him. It wasn't until he saw that she'd been discharged with no complications that he was able to let out a breath.

He turned from the screen and took the next clipboard from its rack before pulling back the curtain of an exam room. An older woman sat on the edge of the table, looking at him worriedly.

"Hello, I'm Dr. Hastings." He glanced down at the chart again before setting it on the counter. "Let's see what's going on here." He set his stethoscope against her back and instructed her to take a big breath in. He listened carefully and then reached for the chart, making a note.

"It's these headaches," the woman was saying. "They won't go away."

He nodded, frowning, and began strapping the blood pressure cuff on her thin arm. He already suspected the issue, and the results proved it. "It says in your chart that you take medication to control your blood pressure. It's elevated today, and that could be one of the causes of your headache. It's a serious condition." *And a silent killer,* he thought to himself.

"I wasn't able to refill my pills this month," the woman explained.

He stared at her, his jaw tensing as he considered the situation, thinking of Ivy, of what his mother had said, of how many other people were dealing with this same dilemma. There were plenty of doctors who would write the script, tell the patient what they needed, give them a stern lecture if needed, and then move on to the next patient. But this woman was alone, she was old, and she needed his help.

And somehow, he was going to find a way to give it to her. It was why he'd gone to med school, why he'd left his family behind. Why he'd made every choice he had over the years. To help people the very best way he could, plain and simple.

He gave her a reassuring smile. "Well, I'm glad you came in when you did. Let's see what we can do about this."

After an in-depth examination and sample of pills that should last until her next scheduled appointment, Brett told the nurse he'd be back to check on the patient in an hour and walked to the nearest elevator.

He had an idea. And something told him it might just be the best one he'd ever had.

CHAPTER 28

The hospital fundraiser was off to a good start, Ivy noticed with satisfaction, but it still did little to keep her nerves at bay. She couldn't help it. The thought of talking to Brett—heck, even the thought of seeing him—made her stomach feel all queasy and her heart speed up. It had taken everything in her to come today—at least a dozen times she'd almost turned the car around. But she was too close, and she'd come too far, to let this latest setback get her down.

After all, she was used to dusting herself off, even if she was growing tired of it.

The white hydrangeas were the perfect complement to the small candles that lit every table and created a glow out on the veranda. The sun was starting to set over the hills, and soon dinner would be served. Brett was yet to surface, at least as far as she could tell from the frantic sweeps of her eye around the room, but he'd have to show up for the meal, thank everyone for coming, and explain where the proceeds of the event were going.

And she, well, she would just have to keep her back to him, focus on the pretty centerpieces she'd made and not the ache in her chest.

Kara came up beside her as she was studying the silent auction table, pleased to see that several bids had already been added to her sheet and that her stack of business cards had been cut in half.

"I hope dinner is ready soon, because I feel like I could fall over." Despite her complaint, Kara had never looked happier.

Ivy was happy to have someone to talk to. The worst thing that could happen was for Brett to find her unaware, alone, to want to talk or explain himself again. She'd heard enough. "Don't tell me you've been baking all day," she said, noticing a bit of shadowing under her friend's eyes.

"Try all night." Kara grinned. "Anna let me use the kitchen at the restaurant, but I had to clear out before the staff took over this morning." She leaned in closer. "My mom saw the cookies."

Ivy looked at her, startled. "Didn't she know?"

"I never found a way to tell her. But...she was happy for me. I think she almost seemed...relieved." Kara smiled.

"All she wanted was for you to be happy," Ivy said.

Kara nodded. "We're going to meet for lunch next weekend. She's going to give me some tips on running a business. I was hoping you might share a few, too."

"Me?" Ivy was flattered. "Sure, but I'm not certain what I could add."

"More than you know," Kara said. "Look around, Ivy. You've got your name stamped all over this event. You've made it."

Ivy looked around the room, from the crisp white table-cloths to the tasteful arrangements, neither too big nor too small, and then, realizing she might accidentally catch the eye of a certain someone she didn't want to see, turned back to her friend. Maybe she had made it, without even realizing it. And maybe, like Kara, it would be enough. Enough to fill her heart. Enough to give her purpose.

Not everyone was meant to have the cookie-cutter family life. She'd never had that, and she'd ended up just fine. Somehow.

The girls promised to meet later and hurried to take their seats as the bell was rung for dinner and the waiters began filling the Champagne glasses at each place. Ivy kept her head low, weaving her path to her assigned table, and slid in next to Henry.

"Beautiful event," Henry said, holding up his glass of Champagne. Ivy reached for her water glass, but he grinned. "One sip won't kill you."

She blinked in surprise and reached for her Champagne glass. It was slightly reckless, but not overly so, and it was the gesture that meant more than the drink. She held up her glass and clinked it with Henry's before taking a minuscule sip—one that would last her all night.

Feeling better than she had since Brett had ended things, she turned just in time to see Brett lift the mike. At once, she felt her smile slip, but she lifted her chin, determined to stay strong, to remind herself that it wasn't meant to be, that he wasn't the man for her, even if at one point she might have wished he could be.

She glanced around the room, at so many familiar faces that made up her life. He was just one person who had come and gone through it. But the others...they were permanent fixtures.

Brett tapped the mike, and the room quieted. Pausing, he tucked one hand in the pocket of his black suit pants and welcomed everyone to the event. He paused to thank the staff, the contributors, and, catching her eye, Ivy.

She looked away quickly, hating the flush that worked its way up her cheeks. She reached for her water glass with a shaking hand, and then, on second thought, left it on the table, where it couldn't tip or spill. So he'd thanked her. It was the polite thing to do, and really, she had done quite a bit.

"As most of you know, this year's proceeds are going to support the new oncology wing, scheduled to break ground next spring." He motioned to a rendering of the expansion, and the crowd clapped. "However, we've decided to do something a little different this year, and that is to ask for your support in another endeavor, one that we don't want to put off until next year's fundraiser." He paused to straighten his tie. He looked handsome, standing at the head of the room, the tall, dark-haired doctor, but that's all he was. A good-looking man. And the one who had broken her heart.

"Many of you in the crowd are people who know me. People who know my family. Maybe even the reason why I became a doctor to begin with." He looked at Ivy, and she glanced away. This was the hard part, she knew. Soon, he would take his seat, and that voice, those eyes, would be out of her mind. "Most of us become doctors for one reason: to help people. And I'm happy tonight to announce that in a few short months, Forest Ridge Hospital will be opening a free clinic so that everyone who needs medical care can access it, twenty-four hours a day."

A cheer went up in the crowd, and Ivy scanned the room before returning her attention to Brett. This couldn't mean... But why hadn't he told her?

Dr. Feldman took the microphone. "On behalf of Forest Ridge Hospital and everyone who participated in tonight's event, I'm happy to announce that Dr. Hastings will be overseeing the clinic, as an extension of his emergency department duties. We're lucky to have him."

Ivy felt the color drain from her face as she gaped at Brett. He was staring at her, his eyes dark and penetrating, but she couldn't read his expression, couldn't understand what he wanted her to feel, or if he even cared at all.

She looked over at the table where Sharon Hastings sat with Mark and Anna. No one looked surprised by the news, not even Kara. So they'd known all along. He'd told them, everyone, just not her.

"I think I see an arrangement that needs tending to," she whispered to Henry as she set her napkin on her plate.

A look of alarm flashed over her brother's face, pulling his attention from the front of the room, where Dr. Feldman was explaining the benefits of the clinic, the people it would help, the care they would finally receive, closer to home.

"Is everything okay?" Henry hissed.

"Yes, of course." Ivy managed a tight smile and hurried away from the table, desperate to leave, to get some air, and to get away. She'd thought she was over him. She thought she'd finally put this silly crush to rest once and for all. But then Brett had to go and do something nice…something noble. Something respectable. Something that reinforced all those feelings she didn't want to have, because he didn't hold any of them for her.

"Ivy."

She turned, her heart pounding, and saw Brett standing in the lobby behind her, his jaw tense, his eyes flat. They stood like that for several seconds, until she had the nerve to speak.

"Sticking around town after all, then?" Her tone was bitter, betraying her hurt, and she hated that he had the satisfaction of knowing just how much pain he'd caused her. "Why the about-face?"

He shrugged, a small smile playing on his mouth. "You."

She blinked. He hadn't just said that. It was her imagination, running wild again. "Me." She folded her arms across her chest, not buying it.

"It was what you said . . . about not caring about my patients enough. About not getting invested. Not getting close." He took a step toward her, and she backed up until her heel caught the bottom of the coat rack. She had to steady herself with it to keep from falling over. With nothing to do other than turn and bolt out the doors, she sighed and stayed put. She'd hear him out, and then she'd go. Home. To her apartment. To the bed she'd so recently shared with him. To her little shop that was the corner of her world that would always be sunshine and roses, no matter how rough things got.

"I'm happy to hear I could help." She pursed her lips together, wishing he would just go away.

"You did help. More than you know. You opened my eyes, Ivy. You made me look inside myself. Face my fears. Question what I want for myself. For my life."

Ivy wasn't sure how long it had been since she'd taken a breath, but all at once the smell of warmth and musk washed over her as he stepped closer, then closer still. There was nowhere to run, even if she wanted to, and she wasn't so sure she did anymore. He was walking slowly, closing the distance between them, his eyes so dark and earnest, his smile gentle, his voice kind.

She wanted to believe him. Every word he was saying. Every good deed he'd done. She wanted to believe he was the good, kind, solid man she'd known since he was just a boy, but she still couldn't see past the jerk, the cold heart, the man who had told her he couldn't be involved with her, couldn't deal.

While she…she had no choice but to deal. And that's what she'd always done. Sucked it up. Put one foot in front of the other.

She didn't run. And she wouldn't run now.

"Somewhere along the way, I fell in love with you, Ivy. You made me want to be a better man. You saw me as a man I could have been, and maybe still can. The man I want to be."

She now wasn't sure when she had last blinked. But when she did, a single tear rolled slowly down her cheek. "But those things you said—"

"I was scared." He shook his head, frowning. "Scared of getting close. Scared of losing everything I cared about, really. People. My work. You."

She almost smiled at that. "Guess that made two of us."

"I want to try again, Ivy. What do you say?"

"I…" She was scared. Scared to give in again, to the feelings, to him, to have this exact scenario repeat itself in another few weeks. But then she thought of what he was saying, what he was asking. He'd taken a leap of faith. Could she do it, too?

"I'm not a perfect man, Ivy. I'm not a perfect doctor. I thought I was, but…now I think I can be even better." He reached out and took her hand, holding it between his two warm palms. "I messed up, Ivy. I know I don't deserve a second chance, but I promise you, I never make the same mistake twice."

She looked up at him, noticing the calmness in his face, the peace that hadn't seemed to have been there all summer. The line between his brows was gone, and there was a light in his eyes, which had once been flat. He'd found peace with himself. She'd seen it with her brother, when he finally discovered where he was meant to be.

Here, she realized. In Briar Creek. At the community hospital. With her, if she'd have him.

"Your boutonniere is all crooked," she mumbled, reaching up to adjust the single white rose that was pinned on his lapel. "I'm surprised you even agreed to wear it, given how you feel about flowers."

"Actually, I've had a change of heart about that, too." He grinned, and her heart began to flutter.

"Oh?" She slid the stem to the left, letting her hand rest on his chest. "Any reason in particular?"

Brett sighed. "Well, there's this girl . . ."

"Ah, it always starts with a girl." Ivy grinned.

He lifted an eyebrow. "Yes, but how does the story end, Ivy?"

She held his gaze warily, her chest rising and falling with each breath as the weight of the moment bore down on her. The choice was hers. To run or leap. And she'd never been a quitter. For some reason, life was determined to make her work for the good times, but she'd learned to spot them, reach for them, and fight for them. And this was one of those moments.

There was only one way her story could ever end, she thought, smiling. She reached up and flung her arms around his neck. "Happily," she said before planting a kiss on his lips.

EPILOGUE

There was a decided chill in the air, even though it was only September, and Ivy swore she had seen a tip of red on a few maple leaves this morning. She took a bucket of sunflowers from Chloe, her new full-time assistant, and got to work on an arrangement for Rosemary and Thyme, humming under her breath.

Anna and Mark were having a goodbye party for Kara tonight, now that her bakery was ready to open. It was the first party where she wouldn't have to worry about fake-eating cake, or pretending to sip Champagne, or claim she had more stomach issues. It was freeing, and a weight on her shoulders she hadn't even known was there all these years was now finally lifted.

When the arrangement was finished, Ivy turned to the computer screen and looked over her schedule. She'd expected some uptick in business after the fundraiser, but she hadn't prepared herself for the windfall of orders that hit almost immediately following the event. In addition to Jane and Henry's wedding next weekend, she had ten more to plan for, eight baby showers, six bridal showers, and enough Christmas parties to keep her busy all year round, not to mention a waiting list for her monthly flower arranging classes.

She thought of the check she had filed away and smiled giddily. She couldn't wait to present it to Henry. He'd never expected it, which is why he'd insisted she not worry about it, but deep down he knew how important it was to her to pay him back. And once she did...the sadder part of their past would officially be put to rest. From here on out, only good things, she thought.

The door chimed and Ivy looked for Chloe, but she must have gone into the back room while Ivy was wrapping up the day's orders. Sighing, she checked her watch. She'd hoped to go upstairs and change before the party—she didn't want to be late. Still, a customer was a customer, and she didn't ever want to lose that personal touch, even if her business was expanding almost faster than she could keep up with.

"Can I help you?" She smiled as the confused-looking man wound his way through the display tables.

"You Ivy Birch?" he grunted, glancing suspiciously at the arrangement she'd set to the side of her workbench.

She looked at him quizzically. "Yes."

"Then these are for you." He thrust a white-paper wrapped bouquet into her arms. Mixed in with all the other blooms in her store, she hadn't even noticed them in his hands.

Her heart skipped a beat as she stared down at the bouquet. She held it as gingerly as she might a newborn baby, as if she had never held a flower before in her life. Because even though she handled flowers every day, she was yet to ever hold any that were meant for her.

"Flowers! For me?" She beamed at the man, who just muttered under his breath and shook his head.

"You'd think the girl had never seen a flower before," she heard him grumble as he pushed back through the door.

Ivy pivoted with joy and brought the bouquet to her nose, drinking in the scene. Oh, it was lovely—all her favorites! She peeked through the paper, careful not to bruise the petals, in search of a card. Finally, she found it, small and white, and while admittedly the cardstock was far below the quality she used, it was perfect.

She opened it slowly, preparing herself for potential disappointment. Maybe it was from a client, offering their thanks. And if so, she would be grateful. It wouldn't be what she had dreamed of all these years, but it would be a kind, thoughtful gesture, and she must force herself to remember this.

But as she slid the card from its envelope, she felt her apprehension melt away. The words were typed, and the message was clear. Still, she had to read them five times to make sure her mind wasn't playing tricks. But no, no, it was there. A simple question. With the most obvious answer.

She looked up through the blur of her tears and saw Brett standing in her shop, surrounded by bursts of petals and stems, his hands pushed bashfully into his pockets, his eyes deep, his grin hesitant as he stepped forward, got down on one knee, and pulled out a ring box. And in that moment, the journey to this day seemed to fade behind her, replaced by a bright, wide-open future, and all she could think of was that she had better consider hiring a second assistant because she now had another wedding to add to her list.

It's Christmastime in Briar Creek and
the annual Holiday House decorating
competition is in full swing. Determined
to promote her new bakery, Sugar and
Spice, and put her own spin on the
contest, Kara Hastings is creating a
gingerbread house for the win—until
the competition really heats up. The
exasperating Nate Griffin is the one
person who stands in the way of her
dreams…and maybe the only one who
can make her dreams come true.

A preview of

Christmas Comes to Main Street

follows.

CHAPTER 1

The wind whipped down Main Street, stirring up gusts of snow that swirled and danced in the glow of the lamplights and landed on the fresh spruce wreaths secured to each post by a red velvet ribbon. Inside Sugar and Spice, the air was warm and fragrant, the music low but festive, and the mood positively cheerful.

Well, mostly cheerful.

Each morning, when Kara Hastings tied on her crisp cotton apron and started her first batch of cookies for the day, she felt energized and excited, but by the time dusk fell, she struggled to remember what she had been thinking, starting her own bakery, right before the holiday rush.

Nonsense. This is what she had wanted! A cookie business all her own. Days spent in the kitchen, creating new flavors and taste-testing samples. But hours upon hours on her feet were taking a toll, and oh, how she longed to snuggle under her warm duvet, pop in a Christmas movie, maybe pour a little eggnog, and—

Nope. No time for that. Not when she planned to get a head start on her gingerbread house kits tonight. Her sister-in-law Grace had offered to sell some at Main Street Books, and Briar Creek's first annual Holiday Bazaar was just days away. Kara had envisioned dozens of gingerbread kits, all wrapped and ready for sale, tied with a big satin bow, and trays upon trays of cookies in every shape and flavor. After weeks of very little sleep plagued by nightmares of spilling flour canisters and mixing up the sugar with the salt, she had decided to give herself a break and set the bar a little lower. But only a little, because the first year of a new business was critical, after all, and 'twas the season to make it or...close it.

It was just what they all assumed would happen, Kara thought as she turned the sign on the door to CLOSED and marched back to the kitchen, just in time for the oven buzzer to alert her that the latest batch of gingerbread was ready. Sliding on her red ticking-striped oven mitts, she pulled the tray from the oven and began carefully transferring each piece of gingerbread to the cooling rack, her mouth set with determination.

One down...four to go, she calculated as she popped the next sheet into the oven and set the timer. Even with the multiple ovens, she'd be here for another couple of hours. She made a mug of peppermint hot chocolate and took a seat at one of the small tables in the storefront to work on the decoration part of her kits: clear plastic tubes filled with colorful sprinkles, packets of glistening gumdrops and other candies, and an instruction sheet she'd designed herself, complete with stamps of little gingerbread men dancing their way down the paper.

A knock on the door startled her and caused her to spill some candies on the floor. It wasn't the first time she'd had to shoo away a last-minute customer, hoping to pick up a quick item for a holiday party or school event. Flustered, she looked up to see her sister Molly waving through the glass, her hand covered in a thick red mitten that was nearly the same color as her nose. Kara hurried to unlock the door and let her in.

"I didn't think you were coming back until tomorrow!" Kara said excitedly. She could still feel the chill on her sister's wool coat when they hugged.

"I decided to come back a day early." Molly grinned at her as she pulled back. Her blue eyes lit up as she looked around the room. "Wow, you've done a lot with this place since the last time I saw it."

It was true. In the three months since she'd signed the lease, Kara had gradually added to the shop, slowly bringing it to life. For the holiday season, she'd decorated with a candy cane theme, focusing on glittering red and pink ornaments that went nicely with her pink and white logo. Most customers picked up cookies to take home, but a few liked to stay and enjoy them. This made her nervous at first, but she was yet to hear a complaint, and now she looked forward to the company.

Someday she'd like to hire an assistant, someone to manage the storefront while she did the baking in the kitchen. But for now, until she could afford it, she was on her own.

In every possible way, she thought a bit sadly. One by one her friends and family members were pairing off, getting married, and she . . . well, she was still waiting for Mr. Right, even if she'd long ago stopped looking.

She shook away the thought. She was getting sentimental. The holidays were good for doing that. It was too easy to notice all the couples cozily holding hands as they walked down Main Street or shared a cookie in her shop, arguing over which one to try. Too easy to then notice how quiet her apartment was, night after night.

She supposed she should be grateful she was so busy. She was almost too busy to notice enough to care. Almost.

"I guess that's what I get for not coming home for Thanksgiving." Molly flashed a rueful smile and brushed past Kara to the glass display case, which was mostly cleared out by this hour. Snow still rested on her red knit hat as she shook her head and bent down to admire one of Kara's newest Christmas offerings. "These gingerbread houses are too cute. Such detail!"

Kara grinned. She took special care in making sure each one was unique. It kept things interesting and also helped her to challenge herself. She was learning as she went, experimenting really, and she had a long road in front of her. Hopefully.

"Will you make me one?" Molly asked, turning to give her a hope-filled smile, and Kara burst out laughing. The youngest of the three siblings, Molly had never been shy to ask for what she wanted. But this was one time Kara was putting her foot down. Time was getting away from her, and the holiday demands were more stressful than she'd prepared herself for. Even if some of it, like the gingerbread houses, was of her own doing.

"If I have any left over after Christmas, then yes, you can have one." The chances of it weren't likely, though. She'd originally made this one for her counter, just for decoration, but the reaction she'd had from the customers had opened up a new possibility, and a whole lot of work to boot. She was now selling at least a few a day, in addition to her kits and cookies sales.

"Maybe you can set one aside for me," Molly suggested.

Again, Kara laughed, though this time, less amused. "Nice try. Come on back to the kitchen. You can help me roll out dough."

"Okay, but I can't stay for long. Mom is expecting me in time for dinner."

"So you told her you were coming in a day early and not me?" Kara stopped at the marble counter and stared at her sister, who stood in the doorway to the kitchen, still wrapped up in her scarf.

"I tried calling you." Molly plucked a cookie from a tray but hesitated as she brought it to her mouth. "Can I?"

Kara waved her hand through the air. The shop was closed now, no use letting things go to waste, and that one was a little burned around the edges, which was why it hadn't gone out with the rest. "Yes, go ahead." She pulled a plastic-wrapped ball of dough from the fridge and brought it over to the center island, sighing when she thought of the work ahead.

"Didn't you get my messages?" Molly asked, licking the crumbs from her fingers.

Kara coated the counter surface with flour and did the same with her rolling pin. "I saw you called, but no, I'm sorry, I didn't have time to listen to the messages." She hadn't even had time to eat lunch, unless you counted nine cookies around three o'clock to be a square meal.

"Well, can you take off early to come to dinner? Luke and Grace will be there, too," Molly said, referring to their brother and his wife.

Kara sighed. She hated letting the people in her family down, but lately, she didn't seem to have much choice. "Can I take a rain check?"

Molly's face fell, and for a moment Kara saw a flash of

that five-year-old girl who had a way of getting the last piece of cake, even though it was left over from Kara's birthday. She quickly did the math, estimating the number of hours she had left tonight. She supposed she could slip out to dinner, then come back, work until about two-thirty, then get a few hours of sleep before being back at six tomorrow...She blinked. What was she thinking?

"I'm sorry, Molly, but I didn't know you were coming back early, and I have about four more hours of work here before I'm done for the night."

"Can't it wait?" Molly pressed. "I just got home!"

Kara felt her shoulders sag. She only saw her sister a few times a year, and she would love nothing more than to lock up and reconnect over a glass of wine. "I'm sorry, but no."

"Oh, fine."

From the corner of her eye, Kara could see Molly's exaggerated pout. *Don't give in. If you give in, you'll be here all night.* Besides, even if she did slip out for a bit, she'd hardly be able to enjoy herself worrying about all the work she still had to do.

"I just couldn't wait to see everyone and share my news," Molly said casually, playing with the fringe on her scarf.

Kara stopped rolling the dough. It was another well-practiced tactic of her sister's, and this time, it worked.

"What's the news?" she asked, wiping a loose strand of hair from her forehead with the back of her hand.

Molly's smile turned sly as her blue eyes began to gleam. "I'm engaged!" she squealed, jumping up and down. Stepping toward Kara, she plucked her other mitten free and fluttered her fingers in front of Kara's face, showing off a huge diamond ring.

Kara stared in stunned silence, trying to take in the overwhelming amount of information coming at her all at once.

She knew her sister was looking for a reaction, for Kara to be jumping up and down with her, squealing right along, but her mind was spinning, and the ring was flashing, catching the bright overhead lights, and all she could manage was, "To *who*?"

Molly's eyes widened. "To my boyfriend, of course." She took a step back, her shoulders slumping. "Todd."

"Todd." Kara nodded slowly. "I thought you two broke up last year."

Molly dismissed this statement with a wave of her hand. "Oh, I wouldn't say we broke up. We were just taking a break."

Given the tear-filled midnight phone calls, the chocolate that Kara had sent via overnight post when Molly insisted it would make her feel better, the trip Kara had taken to Boston to wallow with her pale sister in a bed that hadn't been made in weeks, Kara would stand to disagree with Molly's hindsight view of that time in her life, but she said nothing, because what could she say?

"Congratulations," she said, shaking away her confusion. She smiled a little wider. "Congratulations, honey!"

"Hopefully the rest of the family is more excited for me than you are," Molly said, quickly shoving her hands back into her mittens.

Kara took a step toward her sister and set her hand on her shoulder. "You caught me by surprise, that's all. I had no idea you two were even back together. But I'm happy for you, Molly. Honestly I am."

Molly smiled. "I knew I could count on you. And that's why I want you to be my maid of honor."

"Me?" It was the obvious choice, given that they were sisters, but Kara was still trying to process the fact that her sister was getting married at all. Her younger sister. Married. Deep down she'd always thought she'd be next in line, even though she hadn't dated in…forever. Who was there to date in Briar Creek? Childhood friends? That didn't sit right somehow. And the handful of dating experiences she'd had over the years with men from neighboring towns hadn't lasted more than a matter of months, and none had made her heart soar the way she thought it should.

"I'm thinking winter. Valentine's Day. Won't that be romantic?"

That was two months away. "So soon?"

"Why wait?" Molly looked at her quizzically. "Anyway, we'll have lots to go over while I'm in town. Guest lists. Wedding dress shopping. Flowers…I'm depending on you, Kara. Please say you'll help me!"

"Considering you write for a bridal magazine, I doubt I can be much help," Kara began.

"But it wouldn't be any fun without you," Molly replied, wiggling her eyebrows playfully.

Kara looked into her sister's pleading gaze and tried to ignore the knot of panic that had formed deep in her gut and the sirens that were going off in her head, reminding her of everything she had to do and how little time she had to do it.

The oven. That wasn't a siren. That sound was the buzzer going off.

Kara hurried to grab her oven mitts, but by the time she had flung open the door, she could see she was just a minute too late. The edges of the gingerbread were dark, and nothing could be done to salvage them. She'd have to redo the batch.

Kara dropped the tray onto the counter and willed herself not to cry. It was just exhaustion taking over, making her emotional. Making her think about throwing in not just the towel but the oven mitts, too.

Beside her, Molly was still waiting for a response, her eyes wide and earnest, her smile so bright that Kara felt ashamed of herself for even feeding into her own problems. Her sister was getting married. Her only sister. If the roles were reversed, wouldn't she be shouting it from the rooftops, wanting Molly to match her enthusiasm?

"I can't think of a better way to spend the holidays," Kara said through a desperate smile, and she was immediately rewarded with a whoop of delight and a long, hard hug.

"Thank you, thank you!" Molly cried. She pulled her hat back on her head, talking quickly. "I'll call you tomorrow. Or stop by. Or maybe I'll stop by tonight. If I'm not too tired. Oh, this is going to be so much fun!" She clapped her hands, the sound muted through the thick wool, and then shook two clenched fists in front of her to underscore her joy before turning and disappearing through the kitchen door, leaving Kara alone once more.

Kara stared at the ball of gingerbread dough, still waiting to be rolled out, and sighed. Christmas had just become a little crazier.

It was past ten by the time Nate Griffin pulled to a stop in front of the white mansion across from a snow-covered town square. He sat in his car, tense from the drive, and took a few minutes to decompress before he dared to knock on those front doors. Or did one just let themselves into a B&B? Not one to patronize small-town inns, he wasn't sure of proper etiquette. He'd knock, he decided, though no doubt his aunt was already staring out the window, tapping her foot, wondering what was taking him so long.

No good deed, he thought, dragging out a sigh. He'd thought he was off the hook for the holidays this year. And yet here he was. In Briar Creek. For the next two weeks.

And Briar Creek loved Christmas. At least, that's what his aunt had told him when he announced his visit. The poor woman probably thought she was selling him on something, when all she was doing was making him wonder again why he'd sent his parents on that Mediterranean cruise, so carefully planned, booked specifically for the season as a Christmas gift—to both his parents and himself. It was the perfect coup, until his father had to go and suggest he spend the holiday with Aunt Maggie, because they couldn't bear the thought of either of them being alone...

He'd tried to point out that Maggie never spent Christmas with them anyway. Christmases were spent as just the three of them, year after year after year. But then his mother had pointed out that this year they had intended to spend it at her inn in Briar Creek, and oh, she'd be so disappointed. And she had that hernia after all. And she really was looking forward to it. And oh, Briar Creek was such a charming town...

Charming indeed. Dead was more like it. On his drive through town—if you could even call it that—the lights were out in every storefront he passed, even the few restaurants. Only one light glowed in the otherwise empty stretch—from a bakery.

He had half a mind to stop in, bring his aunt a gift. Then he remembered how picky she was about her food and decided against it.

No good deed, he thought again.

He roved his gaze over to the town square, illuminated by the twinkling white lights wrapped around the center gazebo. Fresh snow glistened, conjuring up every travel-book image he'd formed of Briar Creek at Christmas-time, and he felt his spirits lift a bit.

He was just grouchy and tired from the drive from Boston. It had been a long week. Hell, it had been a long year. The break would do him good. Or so he kept telling himself every time his phone pinged with another email, always seemingly urgent, from the office.

Nate killed the ignition, and there was an almost immediate hint of chill in the car. Grabbing his duffel bag from the passenger seat and deciding to come back for the rest tomorrow, he pushed out of the car and walked up the salt-sprinkled cobblestone path to the inn. Two identical wreaths made from red berries hung on the black-painted double doors, and from the windows that framed them, he saw a shadow cut through the golden light. Before he could even reach for the door handle, the door swung open, and there stood his aunt Maggie, looking even more festive than the Christmas tree in his office lobby.

"Ho, ho, ho!" she sang, grinning so wide, Nate felt an immediate pang of guilt for the less-than-generous thoughts that had plagued him for the duration of his two-hundred-mile drive.

"Aunt Maggie." He smiled warmly, taking in the familiar lines of her face, which had grown deeper since the last time he'd seen her. He was suddenly aware of how much time he'd let pass, and seeing how much his visit meant to her, he felt a wave of shame he couldn't put in check.

"Come here and give your old aunt a hug," she ordered, and pulled him in. One of her dangling, glittery, reindeer-shaped earrings caught his scarf, and Nate wrestled with Rudolph's flashing nose as Maggie giggled, her head bent as she waited to be freed.

"I see you have a matching sweater," he said once he had untangled himself.

Maggie patted the reindeer on her stomach and adjusted her flashing earrings. "Women like to accessorize. You'd have known that already if you'd settle down and find a nice girl."

And so it began...

"I made you dinner," his aunt said as she ushered him into the sitting area of a lobby. Sure enough, there was a steaming pot pie on a plate and a glass of milk. His favorite meal as a kid. He was touched that she remembered, even though he'd kill for a beer.

He didn't bother to mention that he'd already eaten after work. She'd gone to great effort, and he was never one to turn down a home-cooked meal. They didn't come often. Though perhaps if he visited his parents a little more often, they might.

Guilt churned in his gut, but there wasn't any time to dwell on it, not when his aunt was looking at him so pertly, her hands folded patiently in front of her, her green eyes wide, waiting for a reaction.

"This looks delicious," he said honestly. "Thank you."

He shrugged out of his coat, eager to relax and settle in, even if he still felt a little uneasy about being here at all. The flames flickered in the hearth and the lobby was quiet. He didn't know what he'd been expecting. More guests perhaps? A bar? But then this was an inn, not a hotel, and above all, it was his aunt's home.

Maggie brushed the snow from the shoulders of the thick wool before hanging it on a rack near the front vestibule. Nate took the time to look around. He had only visited the inn a few times, and he was too young then to form a clear image. Now he was impressed with what he saw. The lobby was tastefully furnished in a traditional but lived-in style, impeccably clean and modestly decorated for the holidays. Fresh garland was wrapped around the banister of the winding stairs, and an arrangement of red, white, and green flowers was set on the polished cherrywood check-in desk. It was clear that his aunt took pride in the place, and no doubt people paid a pretty penny to stay the weekend. The ski resorts weren't far, he knew, though he'd only picked up skiing in recent years and didn't get to the mountains much. But people liked country getaways. Some people.

"You're looking a bit thin," Maggie said as she came to sit across from him near the crackling fire. "Tell me. What do you normally cook?"

He was hardly thin, but Maggie liked to fret, and he decided to humor her. She eyed the fork, and so he picked it up, happy he'd done so when he brought the bite of pie to his mouth. Rich, buttery, and creamy. Just like he remembered.

"I don't cook, Aunt Maggie," he said, grinning. He didn't need to meet her eye to sense the disapproving pinch of her lips. "That's what microwaves are for."

"Microwaves!" She tossed her hands in the air and shook her head. "Well, good thing I've got you for a couple weeks. You'll be fattened up by the New Year."

Nate paused as he brought another forkful of pot pie to his mouth, recalling the six o'clock trip to the gym he'd put in that morning. There was no telling how much butter and cream had gone into this thing—enough to undo forty-five minutes on the treadmill, that much was for sure.

He opened his mouth, savoring every bite. This was a vacation—sort of—and people were supposed to indulge a bit on vacations. He eyed the milk, wondering if he could ask for a glass of wine at least.

"Drink up," Maggie said, noticing.

Nate grimaced. "I think I'll pass," he said.

"I understand." His aunt winked. "It's late. You don't want any accidents."

Nate choked on the last bite of his pie. "What? Aunt Maggie, I'm thirty-two years old."

But she just gave an innocent shrug. "So? Why don't I show you to your room? I'd love nothing more than to sit and chat with you all night, but it's late and I have to be up at four to start breakfast."

Nate frowned as he pushed himself off the couch. His aunt was in her early seventies, older than his parents by a handful of years. She'd never had any children, and her husband—his father's brother—had died years back, leaving her alone with this inn to run. He thought of what his parents had told him, the concerns they'd had for Maggie's health, and hesitated.

"Why don't I make breakfast tomorrow and give you a chance to sleep in?"

She stared at him blankly before bursting into a roar of laughter. "My dear boy, I appreciate the gesture, but it's the one meal I offer here, and, if I do say, I'm known for my breakfasts for miles around. I wouldn't want to let my guests down..." She patted his arm and gave a little smile.

Nate opened his mouth to protest but then decided to drop it. He'd already admitted he couldn't cook, at least not from scratch, and the last thing he wanted to do was cause trouble for his aunt by upsetting the guests...and something told him they wouldn't appreciate his scrambled eggs with buttered toast, which was about as far as things went with his culinary skills.

"But I'd like to help while I'm here," he pressed.

A look of interest passed over her face. "I'll remember that," she said mysteriously.

Nate picked up his duffel bag and flung it over his shoulder. From the gleam in his aunt's eye, he had the unnerving suspicion she had plans for him while he was in town, and he couldn't begin to imagine what they entailed.

Fall in Love with Forever Romance

NACHO FIGUERAS PRESENTS: RIDE FREE

World-renowned polo player and global face of Ralph Lauren, Nacho Figueras dives into the world of scandal and seduction with this third book in The Polo Season. Antonia Black has always known her place in the Del Campo family—a bastard daughter. And it will take a lot more than her skill with horses to truly belong within the wealthy polo dynasty. She's been shuttled around so much in her life, she doesn't even know what "home" means. Until one man shows her exactly how it feels to be safe, to be free, to be loved.

Fall in Love with Forever Romance

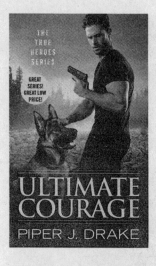

ULTIMATE COURAGE
By Piper J. Drake

Retired Navy SEAL Alex Rojas is putting his life back together, one piece at a time. Being a single dad to his young daughter and working at Hope's Crossing Kennels to help rehab a former guard dog, he struggles every day to control his PTSD. But when Elisa Hall shows up, on the run and way too cautious, she unleashes his every protective instinct.

WAKING UP
WITH A BILLIONAIRE
By Katie Lane

Famed artist Grayson is the most elusive of the billionaire Beaumont brothers. He has a reputation of being able to seduce any woman with only a look, word, or sensual stroke of his brush. But now Grayson has lost all his desire to paint...unless he can find a muse to unlock his creative—and erotic—imagination...Fans of Jennifer Probst will love the newest novel from *USA Today* bestselling author Katie Lane.

Fall in Love with Forever Romance

LOVE BLOOMS
ON MAIN STREET
by Olivia Miles

Brett Hastings has one plan for Briar Creek—to get out as quickly as possible. But when he's asked to oversee the hospital fundraiser with Ivy Birch, a beautiful woman from his past, will he find a reason to stay? Fans of Jill Shalvis, Susan Mallery, and RaeAnne Thayne will love the next in Olivia Miles's Briar Creek series!

A DUKE TO REMEMBER
By Kelly Bowen

Elise deVries is not what she seems. By night, the actress captivates London theatergoers with her chameleon-like ability to slip inside her characters. By day, she uses her mastery of disguise to work undercover for Chegarre & Associates, an elite agency known for its discreet handling of indelicate scandals. But when Elise is tasked to find the missing Duke of Ashbury, she finds herself center stage in a real-life romance as tumultuous as any drama.

VISIT US ONLINE AT

WWW.HACHETTEBOOKGROUP.COM

FEATURES:

**OPENBOOK BROWSE AND
SEARCH EXCERPTS**
•
AUDIOBOOK EXCERPTS AND PODCASTS
•
AUTHOR ARTICLES AND INTERVIEWS
•
**BESTSELLER AND PUBLISHING
GROUP NEWS**
•
SIGN UP FOR E-NEWSLETTERS
•
**AUTHOR APPEARANCES AND TOUR
INFORMATION**
•
SOCIAL MEDIA FEEDS AND WIDGETS
•
DOWNLOAD FREE APPS

BOOKMARK HACHETTE BOOK GROUP
@ WWW.HACHETTEBOOKGROUP.COM